# NOVA RANGER ACADEMY

Published by Clockwork Dragon Books
www.clockworkdragon.net

First printing, July 2018

*Nova Ranger Academy* is a work of fiction. People, places, and incidents are either products of the authors' minds or used fictitiously. No endorsement of any kind should be inferred by existing locations or organizations within it.

No dogs, teenagers, Brazilians, military personnel, superheroes, or supervillains were harmed in the making of this book. We make no claims regarding the disposition of Nazis.

Copyright © 2018 by Lee French & Jeffrey Cook
All Rights Reserved

ISBN: 978-1-944334-27-7

The Clockwork Dragon sprocket-C logo is a trademark of Clockwork Dragon LLC and may not be reproduced without permission.

Without limiting the rights reserved under copyright above, no part of the this publication may be reproduced, stored, or entered into a retrieval system, or transmitted in any form or by any means (electronic, mechanical, photocopying, or otherwise) without the prior written permission of the copyright owner.

The scanning, uploading, and distribution of this book via the internet or any other means without the permission of the copyright owner is illegal. Please purchase only authorized electronic editions, and do not participate in or encourage piracy of copyrighted materials. Your support of the authors' rights is appreciated.

# NOVA RANGER ACADEMY

## LEE FRENCH
## JEFFREY COOK

This book is dedicated to Ira Cook. Grandfather, farmer, soldier, survivor of the Bataan Death March. Though we never met, he remains a reminder of service with distinction, and of the ideals our nation fought for in WWII.

Special thanks to Jonathan Brazee and Colin Lampson for lending their military expertise.

# CHAPTER 1

## CAPTAIN KINETIC / BENJAMIN TSUKUDA

November 17, 2007
16:12

Balmy November air thick with jet fuel and salt clung to Ben's black tactical bodysuit as he crossed the tarmac in Ceiba, Puerto Rico. He led his team to a C-17 cargo plane waiting under lazy afternoon sunshine. Carrying a pack full of gear, an oxygen mask, and a parachute gave him an easy way to avoid behaving unprofessionally toward his wife.

While working, he knew her as Springfire. She walked a few steps behind, chatting with Omen too low to overhear. Crash flanked Ben to the right. Maverick and DPS brought up the rear. Everyone wore the same kind of unmarked suit and carried similar gear. Except Maverick, who didn't need half the crap everyone else did.

As Ben and his team approached the plane, the lieutenant waiting at the end of the cargo ramp saluted. Ben supported his gear with his telekinesis so he could return the salute.

"Lieutenant Ramirez," he said with a nod. The man had his name and rank insignia on his Air Force uniform, of course, but Ben remembered him. Ramirez had supervised ten of their insertions to date. "Why aren't you flying the plane yet?"

"I guess I'm just a slacker, sir." Ramirez gestured for the team to enter the plane. "Captain Rogers is handling the flight today."

They climbed the cargo ramp. Their combat boots clunked on the metal deck as they passed the small boat their extraction team would use later. Ahead, four Navy men sat in the forward jump seats on the left. They'd pilot that boat for the post-mission extraction.

"Pass on for me that I was glad to hear his wife made it through that surgery."

"Yes, sir." Ramirez pointed to the forward jump seat on the right. "Make yourself at home. Flight time should be three hours and twenty-seven minutes. Captain'll flash the red light when it's time to put on your masks."

"How's the certification going?" Ben asked. He and his team had done this many times before. They all knew the drill. No one needed orders or instructions.

Ramirez beamed. "I'm almost through the testing phase. They'll let me into the cockpit soon."

"If I don't see you before then, good luck." Instead of clicking his harness into place by hand, Ben manipulated the pieces with his mind until they latched and held him snug against the wall.

"Thank you, sir. I'll let the Captain know we're ready to go." He hurried to the cockpit.

Crash took the seat beside Ben. She clipped in, found a comfortable position, and closed her eyes. Until they woke her, she'd sleep through everything.

Maverick sat on the end of their six-man line. Her large, feathered wings folded behind her into a poofy mass and prevented her from using the built-in safety system. Instead, she wore her own harness. DPS helped her clip it to the plane, then checked Springfire's and Omen's harnesses before securing his own.

Ben exchanged a nod with the men across the way.

That team, led by Captain Winters, had scooped them out of the water a few times before. Despite that fact, he, Springfire, Omen, and DPS all wore full masks that left only their mouths and chins visible. The Navy guys, like most people, had only ever connected their code names to the lower parts of their faces.

The moment anyone heard Ben's code name, Captain Kinetic, they knew him as the grandson of the legendary Kenzo Tsukuda, Japanese-American hero of World War II. But they didn't know his face, or his father's face. Everyone knew his grandfather, but Ben could still walk down a street with no one recognizing him. He clung to the relative anonymity for his family and his sanity. The other three did the same for similar reasons.

Crash and Maverick didn't bother. No one cared about Crash's identity. Maverick's feathery white wings meant no one paid attention to her face, and even if they did, she had no real way to hide for long.

As Ben secured his gear, he noted DPS retrieving a handheld game system. Maverick leaned toward him to watch. Omen stuffed a wad of bubble gum into her mouth and listened to music with one earbud. Springfire pulled out a book and started to read.

The cargo ramp whirred shut and the engines spun to roaring life. Ben's one earbud and one earplug kept the noise at a tolerable level. The earbud transmitted the team's communications through their subvocal microphones.

He pushed the button on his shoulder to activate his mic. If he needed to, he could press a different button to ping Nova Operation Control so they knew he wanted to speak to them instead of his team. Without the ping, they monitored and recorded, and didn't interrupt. He'd heard that regular special forces teams had more interference from stateside voices than Nova teams. Thank goodness he didn't have to put up with micromanagement.

"Any last requests now that it's too late to grant them?"

"I'm hungry," Springfire said. She unzipped a

watertight pocket on her leg and retrieved a protein bar. Over the course of the flight, she'd eat three or four of them.

Omen blew a bubble and popped it. Along with her short stature and ridiculous black lipstick, the gum made her look like a kid sitting with a bunch of adults. "Me too. Does this flight offer meal service?"

"Can I get a coffee?" DPS asked. He took a stick of gum when Omen offered it.

"I'd like to order a big bowl of Ramirez," Maverick said with her light Southern twang.

Ben grinned. "Ask him when he comes back."

The cavernous plane moved, rumbling and creaking over the tarmac. Acceleration pushed them sideways, toward the rear. The plane's nose tipped upward, and they left the ground. Ben glanced across Crash to see his wife, her nose already in her book and the food gone. She crumpled the wrapper and passed it over Crash to him without looking.

He took the wrapper and stuffed it into a garbage bag hanging on the wall. After spending a few minutes going over the mission plan one more time in his head, he relaxed and used his power to fold and unfold a piece of paper into different shapes. The exercise helped keep his fine control in good shape.

An hour later, he took another wrapper from Springfire and passed her a paper version of her namesake. The red, feathery flower, reminiscent of a bottle brush, bloomed all over the neighborhood where she'd grown up in Guam. Crafting dozens of filaments from a single piece of paper without tearing it took all the precision he could muster. She smiled, and he knew she'd say something later.

For the rest of the flight, Ben wanted to sleep but couldn't. Even on long flights, he could never manage it. He kept an eye on the red light, reviewed maps of the target area, checked his wristwatch too many times, wished he could bring his phone on missions, and handled Springfire's garbage.

Three hours into the flight, the red light flashed.

"Time for oxygen," Ben said. He pressed his breathing mask over his mouth and nose and snapped it onto hooks on his face mask designed for the purpose. Springfire did the same. Maverick used a standard pilot's mask and helmet.

Crash didn't need the oxygen, so he let her sleep.

"I hate this part," Omen grumbled. She held a hand in front of DPS's face and he spat his gum into it. She passed both wads to Springfire, who stuck them inside her final wrapper and passed it to Ben.

Omen and DPS snapped on their breathers.

Maverick laughed. "Let's do it the hard way, Cap."

"I think we'll follow the plan." Ben stuck the last wrapper in the trash bag.

"Bah," Maverick said. "You're no fun."

"We all know that's true," Springfire said. She unscrewed the valve on her mask to let the pure oxygen flow and returned her attention to her book.

"I remember learning in Basic," DPS said as he resumed his game, "that becoming a Captain requires the surgical removal of your sense of humor."

"You're confusing me with military police and drill sergeants." Ben flicked the switch to turn on his mic so it no longer required a button press to function. Others in the line did the same. Across the way, the Navy guys also put on their masks.

Maverick leaned forward to look up the line at him. "Maybe they made a mistake with you, Cap. Put you in the wrong line. What did you miss out on while they took it?"

Ben rolled his eyes. "The ability to ignore how gorgeous my wife is."

Springfire chuckled. Omen snorted. Maverick laughed.

Lieutenant Ramirez emerged from the cockpit and secured the door. He already wore a mask, though his was more a precaution than a necessity. With his reappearance, Ben nudged Crash awake. The team unbuckled their harnesses and stood. Everyone snapped goggles into place and took hold of the safety line bolted to the wall. Ben,

Springfire, and Maverick checked their pistols and holsters. Omen patted the survival knife sheathed on her belt. Crash popped and re-fastened the upper strap holding a machete on her thigh. Ramirez secured his harness. The Navy guys stayed in their seats. DPS kept playing his game.

They waited.

The red light flashed again. Wind flooded the plane as it depressurized. Ramirez unlatched and pulled open the side door. Ben gripped the handle mounted on the wall and stepped to the hole to wait for the signal. Night had fallen and he saw clusters of bright lights on the ground. He activated the night vision mode on his goggles.

The moments between ready and go expanded to fill a lifetime. Ben thought of his son, training to follow in his footsteps, and his daughter, staying with his parents for the mission. In five days, they'd have Thanksgiving as a family. In a month, they'd all visit Guam together for the Christmas holiday. He'd drink beer on the porch with his father-in-law and anyone else who wandered past.

The green bulb next to the red one flashed. Ramirez patted Ben's shoulder with a gloved hand and flashed him a thumbs-up.

Feeling a surge of adrenaline, Ben stepped out of a fully functional plane and into the frigid night air at twenty-seven thousand feet. His team followed. He rolled to watch them in the lights of the plane. Crash dove like she jumped into a swimming pool. Springfire took the step like Ben had, without hesitation or fear. Behind her, a beat passed, then DPS shoved Omen out. Omen fell like she always did, stiff as a board and her eyes screwed shut. DPS tossed his gamepad at Ramirez and jumped. Maverick leaped with the grace of a swan. Her wings snapped open, and she let gravity give her speed.

Ben popped his parachute first, cueing the rest of the team to do the same. Omen matched them despite not looking. Her power of precognition never failed to keep her safe, no matter the circumstances.

Getting his gloved hands on the steering lines, he looked down at the darkness. The large clump of lights northeast of their position marked Belém, a sizable city on the coast of Brazil. They aimed for a dark patch inland from the Tocantins River.

He steered his parachute, trusting Maverick's superior night vision to get them to their planned drop site. Nothing but the mission filled his head. Timing mattered. Their extraction team would jump out of the plane soon with their boat to land in international waters, then navigate into Brazilian waters without permission to do so. Clearance to cross their airspace for a "training mission" didn't translate to anything else.

Maverick veered to the left as they neared the ground. Ben stayed close and slowed his descent as they reached treetop level. Their path took them into a water-filled depression surrounded by trees with gnarled roots on three sides.

According to satellite imaging, their target lay on a rise one mile to the southwest. No homes edged this depression, and it had no roads or driveways within a thousand feet. Ben had been surprised to discover how many people lived in the rural parts of northeast Brazil, and how hard they'd had to search to find a suitable dropzone.

Maverick landed without a sound. Ben splashed into cool water up to his waist. The moment his boots touched the soft bed, he took hold of his parachute with his power and folded it back into its pack. As the rest of the team landed, he did the same for them. His earplug went into a pocket.

Springfire hit the water running and never touched it with more than the soles of her boots. She released her parachute and reached the trees in an eyeblink. Her power moved her body faster than any other creature on Earth. Ben gathered her parachute and stowed it in his own pack.

The team moved out of the water and into the trees. Ben and Maverick drew their pistols. Crash held her machete. Omen needed DPS's help to climb out of the water because it reached her armpits.

Before Ben finished folding DPS's parachute, Springfire said into her mic, "Area clear." She stood beside him again a second later. "We hit dead on," she whispered.

Everyone removed their masks, securing them to their belts. The air smelled of damp earth and rotting plants. Insects buzzed and chirped. Something screeched in the distance.

"DPS," Ben said, "compass."

Without a word, DPS produced an old-fashioned, magnet compass from a pocket and held it where Ben could see the display. Springfire shone a tiny LED flashlight on the face for him.

"One mile that way." Ben pointed with his hand. "Maverick into the air. Let's move."

Springfire sped into the distance, making no more noise than leaves stirring in the wind. Maverick rushed back to the water and leaped, her wings pumping for altitude. The rest of the team picked their way through the twisted tree roots, wide ferns, and broad-leafed shrubs. They moved as a group, making no noise other than the occasional slip of Omen's boot on rotting wood or moss.

"Target in sight," Springfire reported within a minute. "No sign of guards, but I see cameras and lights."

"Arc to the north," Maverick said. "There's a loud-ass party with lots of light in your path. Maybe we should stop and say hi, though. I could use a beer."

Ben ignored Maverick, but did alter their trajectory. "Scout the perimeter and report."

Both women gave an affirmative and went quiet.

They slipped through the trees and darted across streams. The team ducked past the party. Drunk voices shouted to the music in Portuguese. Ben thought he recognized a samba beat from ballroom dance classes he'd once taken with his wife. They'd both preferred the tango.

"Perimeter check complete," Springfire reported as the

loud music faded into the night. "Concrete wall surrounds the compound. Iron gate has two cameras and a code lock. No guards patrolling. Ten other cameras mounted on the building. Six visible gun turrets. No obvious signs of activity. Tire treads at the front gate suggest recent use."

"Good work." Years ago, Ben had found the sweet spot of commending her publicly without appearing to favor her. At that point, he'd stopped worrying about it. "Wait for us at the rendezvous point."

"Already there."

"Cameras, guns, and no guards is an interesting combination," DPS said.

"Means we can blow stuff up without worrying about casualties," Maverick said.

"No one is supposed to know we were here." Ben didn't have to say anything else. They knew what that meant—low body count, avoid destruction, and leave no trace.

"I've got a potential breach point," Maverick said. "Second floor, open window. Check it out, or wait for initial breach?"

Ben glanced back at Omen and saw her shake her head. "Maverick, wait. We need to deal with the cameras."

"Yes, sir. Rendezvous point, or wait over here?"

"Rendezvous point."

The team went silent again. Ben stopped the group when he saw bright light through the trees. Springfire appeared at his side. In the dark, sometimes it seemed like she teleported.

"Any closer and they'll be able to see you," she said.

Ben nodded and held up a hand to keep everyone else in place. He holstered his gun and crawled forward until he saw a camera pointed at his position.

He pushed against the camera with his mind, nudging the lens to shift aside one millimeter per two seconds with a smooth motion. Any faster and a vigilant guard might notice.

# CHAPTER 2

## DPS / MATIAS ROJAS

November 17, 2007
20:47

Matias leaned against a tree and squatted to wait for the all clear. He glanced at Springfire as she tapped her hand against her leg. Staying still always made her jumpy. Crash stood like a rock, her dark hair gathered in a thick braid down her back. Maverick could wait like a champ too, standing in the shadows with her gun ready. Her platinum blonde hair and pearly white wings would give her away in a heartbeat, but she'd learned to deal with that.

Omen chewed on her fingernails, as usual. He saw her tense and stick out a hand to steady herself against the nearest tree. Her power had gone active, warning her about something.

"Cap, wait," Omen said into her mic. "Stay still. When I say, move back into the trees."

Matias shrugged off his backpack and rooted through it. Spare bodysuit, satellite uplink, extra socks, MRE, water, and the thing he wanted. He pulled out his mobile hacking rig. The keyboard folded in half, the small LCD screen had a built-in cover, and the computer separated into three parts. Then he fished a cable from a pocket, connected to a thick battery.

By the time he had everything ready to use, parts sat in different pockets and cables criss-crossed his body. The screen plugged into the keyboard, and the keyboard rested on a custom rig clipped to his belt so he could type with both hands. In his pack, he also had a mini solar array to recharge the battery.

He'd seen little laptops that took up less space than his rig, but he got to use state of the art parts. His frankenstein creation, put together with his little sister's expert hardware help, could process rings around those little pieces of shit. Besides, it was easier to pack for a mission.

Captain Kinetic reappeared from the shadows. He couldn't poof like Springfire could in the dark, but he aced the whole stealth thing. DPS remembered the time Cap and Crash scared the shit out of a Marine sniper and his spotter in Congo by accident.

"There's a window coming," Omen said, holding two fingers to her temple. "I can get DPS to and through the gate."

"What kind of window?" Cap asked.

"Guard needs to use the bathroom."

Cap nodded. "Make it happen."

Matias straightened with a power screwdriver in hand, ready to move. "Just say when, chica."

"When I say, run to the gate. You'll have four minutes."

"He's gonna use the bathroom for four minutes?"

"He has to walk there and back, dumbass."

Maverick grinned at him. "I've got the timer, dumbass."

"Oh baby, whisper dirty time in my ear. Just don't breathe it."

He heard Maverick snort.

"Cut the chatter," Cap said.

Matias smirked at Maverick and stepped forward. Omen told him where to stop and wait. He stopped and waited. Not trusting Omen got people killed. He'd seen it happen.

"Go," Omen said. "Start the time."

One hand securing his keyboard setup, Matias sprinted out of the trees and across the access road. He skidded to a stop in front of the keypad and pried the cover plate open.With a push of a button, flanges popped out of the tip, turning his standard screwdriver into a Phillips. Two screws blocking access to the wires underneath fell to the ground.

"Three minutes," Maverick said. "Someone's been slacking on running, Cap."

"I said cut the chatter."

"Standard setup, no big deal," Matias said as he spent a few precious seconds examining the device. "It's got a—"

"DPS, for fuck's sake," Cap snapped, "shut up and get the job done."

"Yessir." He yanked out wires and jammed in spikes from his rig. With a command on the keyboard, he ran a short program. Instead of producing the code, the program bypassed the security to activate the gate. Creaking gears carried the gate upward.

"Boom, done."

"One minute thirty seconds," Maverick said.

"Move it," Cap said.

While the team minus Maverick rushed under the opening gate, Matias sent a command to stop the gate and shut it. He didn't see Maverick fly over it.

"Thirty seconds."

He ripped his wires free and ducked inside as the gate slid down. The iron clanged against the ground with enough noise to attract anyone within a hundred yards.

Springfire disappeared. Everyone ran across the empty ground between the wall and building. The place reminded Matias of his elementary school in the shittiest part of Seattle. A concrete block with few windows, the building seemed designed to drain the life out of anyone entering. Double doors offered an obvious way inside. As he dashed across the blank buffer zone, Matias noticed a key card entry system on the front doors.

Like most of the team, he flattened himself against the building near the doors. Cap flicked a finger and knocked a camera askew.

The more intense the situation, the more likely Cap used hand gestures to control his power.

"Time's up," Maverick said through the mic.

Matias grinned. "I'm just that good, chica."

Crash glared at him. She didn't need to say anything to shut him up.

"Internal perimeter check complete." Springfire appeared in the shadows beside Cap and Omen, on the other side of the door. "Nothing to report."

"In position on the roof," Maverick reported. "Ready to hit this window."

"Springfire, assist with that window. Breach if you're clear. The rest of us hit the front door. Stay quiet."

Springfire blurred out of sight with a whoosh of wind.

"I can open the door in two seconds," Matias said. "Tell me when."

"You're clear," Omen said. "First door on the left is the guard office."

"Crash, take care of it."

Matias rolled around the corner and sprinted to the front door. For this entry, he used a fake keycard connected to his rig. Easy stuff, no time delay. The rest of the team followed. He swiped and stood aside. Cap threw open the door and Crash rushed in, machete in hand. Cap followed her with his gun ready.

Wood crunched. Something crashed.

Matias glanced at Omen. She nodded. They moved inside together.

Blank white walls and a bare concrete floor greeted them. Banks of fluorescent lights lined the industrial tile ceiling. Half of a wooden door lay on the bare concrete floor. The other half hung from its remaining hinge in a doorway.

Cap filled that space with his tall, lean frame. Beyond the doorway, an intersection offered three options—left, right, and straight.

"Cameras are unmanned," Cap said. He moved away from the door.

"Window entry is not safe to breach," Maverick said. "Returning to your position. Also, I may have revealed our presence. Fuck."

If their cover had been blown at least Matias didn't need to hang back anymore. He hurried to the center of the intersection and spun, checking all three directions. Doors lined all three hallways. Judging by the space between them, he guessed most led to small offices. Or cells.

He kept a hand on his computer rig, thinking about putting it away to avoid damaging it. "Fuck, that's a lot of doors. What's the plan, Cap?"

Springfire appeared beside Matias. Crash stepped through the doorway, blood smeared on her machete.

An alarm bell rang and red lights mounted near the ceiling flashed.

Omen groaned and leaned against the wall. "Fucking fuckity fuck."

"Yeah. Sorry," Maverick said. She landed on the front stoop.

Every door in sight opened.

"We're going to talk about this," Cap said.

Matias saw bright blue tentacles coming from a door to the left. "Uh, Cap? Maybe that should wait until later." From another door, a misshapen, too-large canine snout poked out and sniffed. To the right, a Latina woman's head, covered with tiny, pulsing red spots, stuck through a door as if she had a three-foot-long neck.

More abominations emerged. Matias backed toward Maverick.

"Outside!" Omen screamed. She held her head and groaned again.

Cap picked up Omen and carried her outside while the

rest of the team followed.

Except Crash. She faced the intersection with her machete in hand.

Matias stopped in the middle of the empty space between the building and the outer wall. Springfire stood beside him. Maverick leaped into the air and perched on the roof, watching and readying her weapon.

"Get a grip, Omen." Cap took a position behind Matias and Springfire, keeping Omen by his side. "This isn't the time. Everyone, by the books." By the books, standard operating procedure meant Crash slowed them down, Springfire and Matias picked off what got through, Omen called out warnings, and Cap coordinated, messed with the environment in their favor, and filled in where he had to.

The creatures rushed Crash. DPS had never seen a collection of more hideous things. Some had fur or scales. The rest looked Latinx to him, which sent a shiver down his spine. He didn't always feel his Chilean heritage, but he saw his own skin tone among those monsters. Whatever had happened to them, he wanted to save them and knew he couldn't.

What could anyone short of a god do for someone whose limbs bent the wrong way? Nothing. These people were hideous and piteous.

"Mother of God," Springfire said.

Matias agreed.

Crash did her job. One monster bit through her arm. She ignored it and hacked off its head with her machete. Another swiped claws across her leg. Her follow-through carried the thick blade through that creature's arm, severing its hand. Two knocked her down.

Matias lost sight of Crash. He called the warmth in the air, and it answered. His body dropped several degrees in temperature, and a jet of fire surged from his outstretched hand to engulf the creatures rushing past Crash and her attackers.

Springfire blurred as she ran inside, dodging the fire.

Creatures flew into the walls hard enough to crack the concrete.

The half door on the floor lifted into the air and cracked against two skulls.

"Maverick has incoming," Omen whimpered.

"Fuck," Maverick grumbled.

Matias registered movement on the roof, but saw nothing. Inside the building, more monsters flew aside. Crash leaped to her feet with her wounds healing fast enough to see it happen. She threw her shoulder into a Latino with his head on sideways and his legs sticking in the opposite direction.

Gunshots rang from above.

"Cap, I got a flier up here," Maverick growled.

"Keep him busy," Cap said.

Walking flames stumbled toward Matias. Another torched monster followed it. Matias stopped shooting fire and focused on what already burned. When he concentrated, flames existed to him as a living thing, a mass of writhing, flickering heat he could direct and shape.

At his command, the closer fire stole heat from its surroundings. A thin layer of ice coated the concrete around it. The fire shrank as it turned white. Inside, the creature howled in unearthly agony. Its voice faded as its body turned to ash and collapsed.

Matias maintained the white-hot fire and sent it jumping to the second target. The second monster shrieked and disintegrated. Crash held the rest of the creatures too far away to keep the fire jumping from target to target. Letting the flames dissipate for lack of fuel, Matias checked the situation.

Crash stood at the mouth of the intersection, hacking off limbs and heads, keeping the monsters bottled up at the chokepoint. The fuckers had ruined another tac suit for her with claws, teeth, and spines, but she carried spares. Through the rips, he saw plenty of her Native brown skin and not much blood.

More gunshots cracked in the sky.

"Cap, I can't hit this motherfucker," Maverick growled. "He's too fucking fast."

"Stay ahead of him and line it up. We'll do a slingshot," Cap said. "Crash and Springfire, get out of there. DPS, wall of fire." The half door flew out of the building, missing Matias by a wide margin. "I've got a platform, and I'm ready to collapse the floor. Omen's got the ball."

Calling more heat, Matias made sure he stood outside the building. Springfire stopped behind Crash, wrapped her arms around Crash's waist, and whooshed past Matias with her cargo. Matias filled the hall with fire.

Behind him, Crash grunted. Springfire moved so fast that she almost always broke Crash's neck during that kind of extraction.

"Springfire. Ready."

The fire danced across the floor and up the walls to lick the ceiling. Matias's skin chilled. His body burned. Ice covered every surface near him. He fueled the fire and the fire fueled him. Raising a hand, he took a step toward his inferno. If he got close enough, he could be the fire. Crackling filled his ears. Sulfur filled his nose. Feathers of fire tickled his flesh.

Distant voices murmured in his ear. Matias ignored them and took another step.

Arms flailed through the wall of fire, through him. He grabbed one without touching it and turned the arm to ash.

The floor shook under his feet.

"DPS!" Cap bellowed. "Three steps back!"

Matias blinked and shook his head. He let the fire go and ran outside. The floor buckled and smashed together, crushing the last few monsters. Snapping his head around, he saw Omen, two fingers on her temple, pointing to his left.

What a shitty time to let the fire subsume him. He turned and saw the spot marked for him.

"DPS, on my mark. Five, four, three, two, one, burst."

As Omen said "burst," Matias still saw nothing, but he

knew his part of the slingshot maneuver. He flung an explosive blast of fire at the marked spot on the ground. As he did so, he saw Springfire stop. The explosion hit under the half door she pulled, that Crash rode like a surfboard. Cap had kept it level enough for Crash until she found her balance, then he'd shifted his focus to the floor.

Between the explosive wave and Cap's telekinetic guidance, Crash flew into the air, missing Maverick by a few feet. She plowed into Maverick's tail. Crash and the target hit the outer wall with a heavy thud and loud crack.

Knowing Crash would get up again, like she always did, Matias spun to check on the rest of the party. Something still burned in the ruined hallway, but nothing else moved. He hurried inside to check the flames and corpses.

Once, he'd taken an enemy death for granted. He chose to be thankful that lesson had only earned him one knife scar.

Picking his way over the uneven floor and charred bodies, he nudged everything with a boot. Nothing reacted. Pieces of twisted human broke and shattered on the concrete.

"He's dead," Crash said.

"This crew is all dead too," Matias said.

"We had no capture scenarios here," Cap said. "Everyone inside. Watch for ambushes and runners."

Matias scooped up the fire and let it dance over his fingers. The rest of the team joined him and filled the intersection.

Cap patted him on the arm and gave the fire a meaningful look.

The team knew he could get lost in the fire. When it happened, no one said anything so long as he didn't fuck up the mission. He hadn't fucked up the mission like that in a long time. Not since that time in Australia.

Knowing he had no time to play, he closed his hand over the tiny fire and snuffed it.

# CHAPTER 3

## BEN

November 17, 2007
21:06

Springfire checked the open doors and found the stairs for the team. Crash climbed the stairs first, followed by Ben and Maverick. At the top, they discovered a huge laboratory. Patient slabs with restraints, robotic arms, rolling stools, and trays of medical tools filled the room. Computer equipment ranging in age from the 70s to the present covered one wall. Steel lockers lined another wall.

Omen stopped at the top stair and sank to the floor, hugging herself. Springfire crouched beside her and turned off their mics.

Ben saw no living creatures or people, so he didn't need to cajole either woman into action. The room did have a dead body, but it could wait. "Maverick, where's that window?"

She pointed to a door. "It opens into a small office. I activated a gun turret by sticking my head inside."

"Crash, Maverick, breach the office." Ben checked for DPS and saw him already taking a seat at the computer system's workstation. "DPS, get whatever there is to get."

"On it," DPS said.

Maverick followed Crash with her gun ready. Ben approached the corpse. The dead man wore a suit and lab coat, and he lay on a patient slab without the restraints in place. Through the blue-tinted pallor of death, his skin seemed white. He had light brown hair and seemed thinner than average for an adult man of unknown age. His body had dessicated a small amount, suggesting a relatively recent death, though Ben couldn't tell what had caused it.

Behind him, Ben heard gunshots. Maverick squawked. The gunshots stopped.

"Office is clear," Crash said. "Maverick needs medical."

Ben turned and saw Maverick leaning against the wall, holding her arm. Blood seeped through her fingers.

DPS rolled his stool to her side. "Don't be a baby," he chided as he pried her fingers loose.

Springfire zoomed across the room and dropped her pack. She produced the team medkit and got to work.

"Thanks for the warning," Maverick snapped, the comment clearly meant for Omen.

"Shut it," Ben said. "You know she can't see everything." Convinced Springfire and DPS would handle Maverick, he turned his attention back to the corpse. While he had no formal training for it, he bent to examine the body for a cause of death. The neck and head seemed intact with no obvious bruising.

He hated touching dead bodies, even through his gloves. No one else had better skill with it, though, so he set to the task of removing the lab coat and suit.

"Whoa," DPS said. "That's a serious collection of Nazi shit."

Ben would've turned to look, but he found trackmarks on the man's right arm. Drug use might've explained his death. "DPS, shut up and get the job done." He didn't need to tell Crash what to do.

"Right. Computer. Yessir."

On the dead man's right shoulder, where doctors liked to inject vaccines, Ben noticed a small area covered with reptilian scales. The left shoulder had a cluster of what looked like chicken pox scars.

"Cap," DPS said, "there's a giant pile of encrypted data here. I don't have enough juice in my rig to crack it. This needs NSA nerds."

"Do we need to haul hard drives, or can you transmit?"

"I can transmit it all. So I'll get the uplink going."

Ben nodded and fished a small camera out of a pocket. "What's Maverick's status?" He took pictures of the dead man's face, trackmarks, and both shoulders.

"I'm dying," Maverick said with a melodramatic groan.

Springfire snorted. "She's fine. Through and through in the meat, no artery hit. Should see Doc when we get home to keep the scarring minimal, but she'll live."

Maverick groaned again. "I might need to be carried to the pickup."

"I'll carry you," DPS said. "And by carry, I mean drag. By one arm. Probably the wrong one. You know how my aim can be."

Ben chuckled as he crossed the room to DPS's side. "There're reasons he doesn't carry a gun." He handed the camera to DPS so he could transmit the pictures through the uplink and pinged OpCon.

"OpCon, this is Captain Kinetic. Target is breached and pacified. It's a doozy, considering we got this off an anonymous tip. Incoming encrypted data and photos via uplink."

"Message received and understood, Captain." Ben recognized Colonel Marks's gruff voice. "Standby for uplink confirmation."

While he waited, Ben stepped around Maverick to get a look at the office. DPS was right. The guy had a hard-on for Nazi stuff. Crash sat at a desk festooned with tiny Nazi flags, in front of a display case filled with swastikas and other obvious memorabilia. A portrait of Hitler hung on the wall. Holes in the wall pointed to where the gun turret had been mounted. He assumed Crash had ripped it off the wall and thrown it out the window.

Crash leafed through a journal with tiny, cramped writing. "This is in German. I can read a little. Looks like a lab journal, keeping track of dosages and timing. I think each of these four page sections is for one test subject." She flipped through enough pages to account for at least fifty subjects. Then she pointed to a stack of similar journals.

If each journal represented fifty trials, the lab must've gone through at least four or five hundred tests. Ben stared at them, hoping the guy had started with animal trials.

"We'll take however many journals we can and lock up on our way out." He left Crash and handed the camera to DPS again.

"Uplink confirmed," Colonel Marks said. "Receiving data. How long do you think it's been since the facility was last used?"

"A few days at most, sir. There are fresh tire treads, and the resistance we encountered couldn't have survived long without fresh food and water."

"Any chance of someone returning and not realizing you've been there?"

Maverick giggled. Someone else snorted.

Ben stifled his own bark of laughter. "No, sir."

"Then I agree with your assessment to take what you can, lock up, and get out. The extraction team will be in place in another three hours. Report on arrival."

"Yes, sir." Ben checked the time on his watch. They had a maximum of four hours to reach a beachhead two miles downriver from Carapajó, thirty miles from their current location. If they took any longer, they'd all have to hunker down and wait through the day before they could leave the continent.

Springfire and Maverick would have no trouble meeting that deadline. The rest of the team would have to jog the entire distance, through swamp and stream, and over uneven ground.

"DPS, how much longer on the file transfer?"

"Five minutes, boss."

Ben nodded his approval. "I want to be ready to leave in five minutes, everyone. We've got a long way to go." He saw Springfire duck into the office, and knew the packing would get taken care of. "Maverick, on your feet." Leaving her to struggle on her own, Ben hurried to Omen and offered her a hand.

She took it and stood. "I'm okay. We're not going to make it to the boat in time to leave today."

"What's going to stop us?"

Omen shook her head. "It's just too far for me to run. I'll slow everyone down too much."

"Ah." Ben squeezed her shoulder. Omen could normally keep up, but if she said she wouldn't make it this time, he believed her. "How about if Springfire takes you?"

She touched two fingers to her temple and stared at her knee. After a few seconds, she nodded. "Yes, that'll work. You guys can make it without me."

"Good deal." He straightened and watched his team help each other pack as needed. Springfire's arms blurred as she wedged journals and papers into their bags. Maverick shouldered her stuffed pack with a wince. DPS stowed his rig and the uplink box. Crash took her pack from Springfire and carried Ben's to him.

The team moved out. DPS paused at the front gate to find the screws he'd dropped with a magnet and replace the gate panel properly. Maverick launched into the air. Springfire held Omen around the waist and braced her neck, then streaked into the distance. Crash, Ben, and DPS jogged up the road as far as they could, then plunged into the jungle.

All three of them fell into a rhythm of running and breathing, with Crash in the lead, then DPS, then Ben. The nighttime wildlife quieted at their approach and chattered in their wake. They darted through a dark, quiet village. Their path took them through small farm fields and clear-cut plots. They avoided water as much as possible.

By the time the trio reached the extraction point, the Navy crew had arrived. Springfire, Maverick, and Omen had all settled onboard the small boat. Ben thought he might sleep for a year after running that hard for that long. His lungs burned and his legs ached. Crash was, of course, fine. DPS collapsed with him on the boat deck with five minutes to spare.

Both men passed out in the darkness.

In the pre-dawn twilight, Ben woke because the boat rendezvoused with a Navy frigate cruising off the coast of Brazil. Twenty hours later, they landed at the Groom Lake Nova Ranger Base in southern Nevada, courtesy of an Army pilot flying a small jet. They'd missed an entire day while traveling and arrived at home base in the middle of the night.

No one had bothered to change out of their tactical gear, other than Crash, who'd changed into BDUs on the extraction boat. When Ben opened the plane door, cool, dry air blasted him in the face. He breathed it in and sighed. This beat the Amazon rainforest any day of the week.

Corporal Jackson, a young man who Ben knew had transferred to the base a month ago, met them with a jeep and drove them across the sprawling base. Ben couldn't muster the energy for small talk.

Outside the OpCon briefing room, the team emptied the evidence from their packs into bins and left Ben to deliver his report. Springfire tugged off her mask to reveal her long, dark hair in three twined braids, then she helped him pull off his own mask.

"You need food," she chided. "Don't let him keep you too long."

"I won't." He kissed her cheek and watched her walk away with the rest of the team. He'd meet them again when he finished his report.

The OpCon briefing room had ten chairs, two tables, harsh lighting, and a whiteboard. Colonel Marks, a man ten years Ben's senior, sat in one of the chairs with a laptop and a stack of papers.

As he shambled into the room, Ben rubbed his face and raked both hands through his short, black hair. Despite spending the last twenty hours on various ships and planes, he hadn't slept much. Of the team, only Crash had been able to get as much rest as she wanted.

"Report," Marks said without looking up.

By now, Marks had listened to the recordings five or six times, so he knew the basics. Ben took a seat and filled in the details of the mission, including the kinds of mutant creatures he'd seen. He left out only Omen's endurance issue, which hadn't been discussed on mic and didn't seem important.

"At this point," Ben finished, "it looks like we found a lab where someone was experimenting with a mutagen, trying to induce powers. I'd guess the dead man was in charge, and he injected himself a few days before we arrived. The serum probably killed him. The unidentified flier was probably one of his successes who didn't have anywhere else to go."

Marks harrumphed. "Shame we weren't able to question him. Maverick botched the scouting run. That might have changed the capture options picture."

Ben's eyelids drooped. He fought to stay awake. "She did. Which isn't like her. I'll back any recommendation for further training." That, at least, amused him. She'd take being sent back to training as much worse punishment than official discipline, and maybe it would help her focus. She was too much of a veteran to make those kind of mistakes. "But with limited intel, these things happen."

"I noticed you and Omen shut off your mics for that conversation, and at least a few others."

"For fuck's sake, Kevin, you already know we do that routinely when we don't want to distract anyone."

Finally looking at him, Marks raised an eyebrow. "Didn't sleep on the ride home?"

"Not really." Ben rubbed his eyes again.

Marks nodded. "Is anything wrong with Omen?" The question sounded casual, but Marks hadn't asked that about any of the team members since their rookie years.

"Wrong with her?" Ben glared at him. "I'm too tired for fishing. What's going on?"

Offering a noncommittal shrug, Marks said, "I noticed she was quieter than usual, and she didn't catch Maverick getting shot. Her gift has a history of being problematic, which is why she's classified bravo instead of alpha, but she's never showed those signs before. I just want your team to be one hundred percent."

Though Omen had missed relatively minor injuries like that before, Ben thought about her behavior on the mission. Aside from the one joke about in-flight meal service, she'd been almost silent. Something had made her sit at the top of the stairs.

Springfire had spent a few hours with her at the rendezvous point. She'd know if Omen needed anything. Maybe she felt ill or had something happen with her family.

He didn't like to lie to Marks, but he didn't want to raise a false alarm either. "I didn't notice anything significant, but I'll sleep on it and talk to her. I'll let you know if anything is going on."

"I'll accept that."

"Am I dismissed?"

"The team is working on the encrypted files. Expect to go out again once we've gone through the information."

Ben sighed. "Does it have to be our team? Why don't you have us handling powered-incident intercepts? They haven't stopped popping up. Kitty's team took down a guy calling himself the Blue Avenger last week."

"The new prison in the Keys is holding, so we're only seeing new ones that don't have any experience. The other teams can handle them. Kitty's team doesn't have any Legacies or alphas, and only has one bravo. Besides, they had that fuckup at Ramstein.

"I've got a handful of teams with a single alpha Legacy, and a few more than that with multiple bravos. Unlike your team, which has three alphas and three bravos, and two are Legacies. But get Maverick and Omen in line, okay? I need my best team on their A game to handle this weird shit." Marks flashed him a sympathetic smile. "Your father and grandfather wore big shoes, and you're filling them well."

"Thanks." Ben felt dismissed and stood. He knew how lucky he'd been to get his team and keep it together. "Can we try to let the team have Thanksgiving?"

"You know how it works. You go whenever we get the intel." Marks shooed him. "Dismissed. Stop by for dinner tomorrow. Bring DPS so he can run the barbeque."

Ben chuckled. "I'll do my best to remember when I wake up."

# CHAPTER 4

## SPRINGFIRE / IARIESAH TSUKUDA

November 18, 2007
21:47

The team's preferred canteen never changed. Army in uniform lined the bar and sat scattered among the tables. Bikers pausing along the twisting backroads of southern Nevada camped in the corner, monopolizing the electronic dartboards. Kele had arrived first and claimed a table, and she sat with a bottle of beer and her feet up. She hadn't gotten the channel changed on the TV yet, though. The screen mounted above the bar showed some cheesy horror movie with clowns.

Springfire had shed her work identity with her tac suit. Iariesah walked into the bar wearing jeans and a red sweatshirt over a tank top. She'd been tempted to take a shower and go to bed, but knew everyone else would show. Ritual and routine helped them all process their job.

She stopped at the bar and waved to the man working behind it. He nodded and held up a finger to ask her to wait while he poured a mug of beer. The Army boy on the stool beside her turned, gave her a once-over, and grinned. Iariesah raised her hand, flashing her platinum wedding band and the ruby engagement ring welded to it.

"That's a damned shame," the Army boy said with an exaggerated sigh. "Is he deployed, baby? 'Cause I'm right here."

Iariesah rolled her eyes and ignored him. Reaching behind the bar, she found the remote where they always kept it. While stuffing pretzels in her mouth and searching the channels, she felt a hand on her ass. Her husband sometimes greeted her that way, so she turned to look.

Army boy grinned at her smug enough to peel paint.

Her arm moved faster than the eye could track as she punched him in the face. His head snapped to the side with blood spurting out of his nose. He crumpled into his buddy and fell to the floor. The rest of the Army boys at the bar stared at her.

"Don't fuck with the ladies in this bar," the bartender said. He set a mug of root beer, two full shot glasses, and a sandwich on a plate in front of her. "Good to see you, Risa."

"Thanks, Barry." Risa stopped the TV on a football game and handed Barry the remote. She knocked back one shot, set the glass down, and waited for the momentary rum buzz to pass. By the time she picked up her plate and two glasses, the Army boy had curled into a fetal ball, holding his nose.

"He should probably see a medic," she told his closest buddy as she stepped around him. With that, she ignored the guys in favor of the table. The seat beside Kele offered the best view of the game, so she took it. "Niger against…is that Morocco?"

"Tunisia," Kele spat. She hadn't changed out of her BDUs. She'd probably come straight to the bar after checking in.

"They both suck."

"Yeah, but Tunisia is worse."

Risa watched the Niger forward and striker pass the ball with all the skill of overexcited teenagers. Not that she cared. She would never root for Tunisia.

Matias walked into the bar with Charlie. He laughed at

something she said, and she grinned. Here at their home bar, Charlie didn't bother trying to hide her wings. People knew Charlie came here, and people knew about the base. When they spent time in public on missions, she wore a blanket-backpack creation that made her look like a weird geek instead of an angel.

"Barry!" Matias called out. "Get Charlie some poppers!"

Charlie tossed her leg over the back of a chair and sat while Matias waited at the bar. "Where's Vivian?" She wore a white halter top with jungle camouflage pants. Risa noticed the faint white lines forming a starburst scar on her bicep, where Doc had healed her gunshot wound.

"Waiting for you to ask." Vivian appeared behind Charlie, dressed in black lace and spandex. The roots of her copper-red hair showed under her cheap black dye job.

In Risa's opinion, Vivian wore too much eyeliner and the black lipstick made her look gaunt. But she didn't say so.

"Because I knew you would." The precog slid into the seat beside Risa. Her eyes seemed glassy and she slurred her words a smidge, as usual after a mission.

"Bless your heart, vampire princess." Charlie stuck out her tongue. "But you didn't know I'd get shot."

Vivian grinned. "Maybe I did and let it happen."

"You did not," Risa said. She took the first bite of her sandwich and reveled in the crunch of fresh vegetables mixed with the tang of mustard and pastrami.

Matias brought three bottles of beer from the bar and set one in front of Charlie, Vivian, and the last empty seat. He went back for his own beer and a plate covered in fried food. The plate, he set in front of Charlie, careful not to touch anything on it. His dire allergy to capsaicin meant he didn't dare breathe around the fried food here, let alone eat it.

Risa stood, leaned across the table, and snagged two of Charlie's fried jalapeno slices. She sat and handed one to Kele while shoving the other into her mouth. Her attention slipped to the game, with Niger running the ball toward the goal. Tunisia's closest player slipped and fell. The Niger player passed the ball to his teammate, who drilled it past the goalie.

She and Kele both cheered.

"We're rooting for Niger?" Vivian wrinkled her nose. "Why?"

"They're playing Tunisia," Kele said.

"Fucking Tunisia," Charlie grumbled. "They can shove their fucking beach umbrellas where the sun don't shine."

"The sun always shines in Tunisia," Matias and Vivian chimed together.

Everyone laughed because that horrifying mission had happened years ago.

Risa caught sight of Ben walking into the bar. He'd taken the time to change into his regular uniform, as usual. Aside from the weariness in his shoulders and around his eyes, he presented a picture of crisp decorum. She smiled at him through her latest bite of sandwich.

Ben rounded the table to give her a swift kiss, then slumped in the seat they'd left him, between Matias and Vivian. Only when he was truly tired did he slouch that much. Missions took so much more out of him than he pretended. They weren't twentysomething kids anymore.

"We're on call for a follow-up," he said as he picked up the beer in front of him.

That meant they wouldn't pick up Kay tomorrow. She'd stay in LA until either Marks lifted it or the last minute before Thanksgiving. They'd have to fly her home instead of Ben driving to pick her up, which Kay hated. Unless they decided to grab her anyway, in which case she might fly three or four times in one week.

Risa sighed and finished her sandwich. They couldn't do anything about it except give the kids a good Thanksgiving.

Charlie crunched through a popper and kept her head turned away from Matias. "No rest for—lordy, check that ass."

Vivian and Risa turned to look. An Army boy disappeared into the hallway with the restrooms.

Risa didn't see anything to get excited about. She returned her attention to her food. "I don't know what you see in these white boys."

Ben grinned at her. She returned it.

Charlie sighed and leaned her chin in her hand, still staring at the hallway. "Honey, I don't care if his ass is purple when it looks like that."

"So go fuck him already," Matias said. "You can breathe on him all you like."

"Breathing doesn't even scratch the itch of what I'd like to do to that hunk of meat."

Still watching the game, Kele held up a hand in front of Charlie's face. "Don't care."

Vivian slumped against the table, crumpling like a rag doll. "He's prettier than Aaron."

Risa laid a hand on Vivian's back. Vivian had been quiet on the mission, even for the ride home, and now Risa thought she knew why. "What'd Aaron do now?"

"Nothing," Vivian said. She heaved a melodramatic sigh.

Ben caught Risa's eye and raised an eyebrow. She shrugged. He barely understood the concept of boy trouble when she could use full sentences to explain, let alone trying to tell him with facial expressions and hand gestures.

The Army boy left the bathroom. Charlie watched him with vulture-like intensity.

"Stop drooling and go jump him," Matias said.

Charlie huffed. "Naw, I have a boyfriend. I'm just looking."

Surprised she hadn't noticed, Risa stared at her. "You do? Who is he?"

"Guy on base."

"Don't fuck down the chain," Matias said. He tipped his bottle toward her as if he'd offered profound wisdom.

"Do I have to hear about who Charlie is fucking?" Kele asked. "I'm trying to drink beer."

"Who cares who or what Charlie is fucking!" Vivian whined. She made an exasperated noise at the ceiling.

"Sorry, princess," Charlie said with a roll of her eyes. "Didn't mean to steal all your attention. But you should've seen it coming."

Risa gave Charlie a dirty look and rubbed Vivian's back. "You're just tired and hungry. Let's get you something to eat." She pushed the beer aside, managing to slosh some down the side of the bottle. That could only happen if Vivian hadn't touched it yet.

"She's just sober, you mean," Matias said. "C'mon, Vivian. Relax. Mission went well. Charlie only got shot once."

Charlie stuck out her tongue at him.

Risa ignored them and headed for the bar. The remaining Army boys gave her plenty of space. "Barry, gimme one of those big chocolate chip cookies." Saying it out loud made her hungry. "Make it two."

Barry fetched two cookies, each the size of a bread plate.

She devoured half of her cookie before reaching her chair again and handing the second to Vivian. Niger scored another goal. Risa raised her cookie to them while Kele raised her beer.

Kele shook her head. "Can't decide if they're on fire or Tunisia just sucks that hard."

The channel flipped. Risa, Kele, and Charlie all jumped to their feet and shouted at the Army boy holding the remote. They startled the kid enough to drop it. He scrambled to pick it up and put back the batteries.

"Jesus," he said as he straightened and fumbled to change back the channel. "What the fuck do you people watch soccer for, anyway? It's a stupid game."

Risa glared at him. Charlie crossed her arms. The temperature in the room slipped a few degrees as Matias simmered without letting it show.

Kele thumped her beer on the table, stalked around the team, and stepped into the kid's personal space. "Maybe, someday, when you've seen more than your mommy's lap, you'll realize that everyone else in the entire world watches real football, you fucking moron." She yanked the remote out of his hand, use it to fix the channel, and stowed it behind the bar.

"Fuckwit," Vivian snapped.

The Army boy gulped and blushed.

Ben sipped his beer and flicked his hand with a suggestion for the team to sit down and let it go.

Watching the Army boy slink to his buddies, Risa sat. How many times had they sat in bars like this, watching football, drinking, eating, and talking? Too many to count. In Tunisia, Cambodia, Argentina, Serbia, Oman, Pakistan, Australia, and dozens more countries, they'd always been able to find a bar and unwind with a game. Only in America did people object. They preferred American football, which had nothing to do with feet touching a ball and paled in comparison to rugby. Barbarians. Most importantly, it was something familiar to people who sometimes didn't get a lot of familiar.

She sipped her root beer while Kele and Charlie returned to their seats. This felt like the right time to have their usual toast. Tapping her shot glass with a fingertip, she met Ben's gaze.

He nodded and held up his beer. The rest of the team lifted their beers. Risa raised her shot of rum.

"Here's to nobody getting dead and another mission accomplished."

They clinked. Risa downed her shot. Once again, she felt a momentary buzz, then it faded. She noticed Vivian only pretended to drink, then set down her bottle again.

"You know, Vivian." Risa nudged her shoulder. "You're allowed to have three beers."

"But only three," Matias said.

Kele smirked. Charlie grinned. Ben sipped his beer.

"I dunno," Vivian said, her thumb swishing through a drop of beer on the table. She flashed Risa a sly smirk. "I don't want you to take advantage of me."

"Watch out for those fast women," Risa said with a nod, pleased Vivian could tease despite whatever had happened with her boyfriend.

"Sweep you right off your feet," Charlie said.

"Carry you through the jungle and everything," Matias added.

Everyone laughed, though Ben only chuckled to fit in. He'd never understood the joke. She'd tried to explain it once and gave up. For some things, you had to have been there.

Risa noticed Ben fading. His eyes fluttered shut and his head bobbed as he fought to stay awake. She patted Vivian's shoulder and stood.

Niger had a four goal lead on Tunisia, and the game had five minutes to go. Not even Pele could beat those odds. She wouldn't miss anything by leaving.

"I think it's past my bedtime. Everybody have a good night." She snatched Ben's beer as it tipped to the side and squeezed his shoulder.

He blinked and rubbed his face. "Yeah, get some sleep. No idea when the next call will come." Standing, he took back his beer and laced his fingers with hers.

"My turn for the tab," Kele said. She stayed in her seat. Matias and Vivian each offered their farewells and left. Charlie gave Risa a hug, then stayed with Kele.

Outside, Risa let go of Ben to wrap Vivian in a hug. "Whatever it is, I know you'll be okay."

Vivian clung to her and whispered into her ear, "Thanks."

"You know any of us will punch Aaron in the face for you, anytime," Ben said. "Just say so."

"Not right now," Matias said. "I'm beat."

"I hear that." Ben clinked his bottle against Matias's. "Ask in the morning, Vivian."

Risa let go and draped an arm around Vivian's shoulders to walk with her. Half a mile later, under the bright light of a four-story watchtower, they flashed their IDs to get into the base. Matias and Vivian headed for for their rooms in the Nova barracks. Ben and Risa reached their tiny house and fell asleep without bothering to undress.

# CHAPTER 5

## BEN

November 19, 2007
14:25

Ben stood at a thick window the next afternoon, watching a small commercial jet approach its gate at McCarran International Airport in Las Vegas. Though he didn't have to, he wore his regular uniform. Airport security questioned him less when they saw it. The one time he'd worn his BDUs, they'd gawked over his Airborne and Ranger patches, wasting his time and making him late.

The gangway jerked toward the plane. Ben moved to the door and nodded to the airline employee opening it. He watched down the ramp. As soon as his daughter's head poked around the corner, she saw him. Her face lit up with surprised joy. She jerked free of the flight attendant trying to escort her up the ramp and ran with an excited shriek.

"Daddy!"

They often had to leave on short notice, which meant sending an Army driver to pick her up and drop her off.

Kay showed all the signs of having her mother's super speed, but it hadn't kicked in yet. Most inherited superpowers hit with puberty, like his had.

The seven-year-old girl ran into his arms. He lifted her off the floor and held her close. She hugged him and kissed his cheek.

"Daddy, did you drive the Firebird?"

He grinned as an airline employee pushed a clipboard at him. "Yes, I did."

She squealed with glee. He signed the form and carried her through the airport.

Fishing a bagged peanut butter and jelly sandwich out of his pocket, he asked, "Are you hungry?" Like her mother, she ate everything, all the time, so he knew the answer.

Kay nodded. "The snacks sucked. They had weird bars instead of pretzels and peanuts, but Sobo gave me a banana to take, so it was okay." She snatched the sandwich from him and tore into it.

"I have more food for you in the car." He carried her to the garage, knowing she didn't have luggage.

As soon as he set her down next to his cherry-red '67 Pontiac Firebird and opened the door for her, she scrambled inside. Kay took care not to smear peanut butter on the leather of the passenger seat or the cloth of her racing-stripe booster. Since she had her hands full, he clicked the seat belt for her.

"Daddy," she ordered around a mouthful of sandwich, "make it go!"

Grinning, he shut the door and hurried around the car to slide into the driver's seat. The engine roared into life. The radio blasted AC/DC.

"Vroom, vrooooooom," Kay shouted, mimicking him turning the key. She licked peanut butter off her fingers, then the plastic baggie as he backed out of the parking space and navigated out of the garage. Without his prompting, she found the stash of fruit, juice, and crackers her mother had packed for the ride.

He turned down the radio volume when they reached the freeway. "I need to tell you that Mom and I might have to go again soon."

"Why?"

"The same reason we have to go any other time."

"That's not fair." She stuck out her lower lip and pouted at him. "Make someone else catch the bad guys."

He reached over and tousled her dark hair. "You like spending time with Sobo and Sofu, don't you?"

"Only when you drive me there. Daddy, when I'm older, can I have the car?"

Pretending to consider it, he shrugged. "I don't know. You'll have to get your license, then prove you can handle the responsibility."

She crossed her arms and huffed. "You showed me how to change the oil! And fix the carborate. And the radioliator. And we made a perfect model of it, so I know all the parts already. It has two doors, and four wheels, and a hood. And vents! Lots of vents."

Ben chuckled at her. He imagined handing the keys to a sixteen-year-old version of Kay and cringed at the idea. His father had given him this car when he'd retired. "You have nine years before you can drive. We'll see how things are then." Even if he waited until her twenty-first year like his father had, that still felt too soon to give up his favorite possession.

She reached over and cranked up the radio, signaling she didn't want to talk anymore. As soon as they left the city limits, he dropped the gas pedal. The car flew down the road, blazing through an Air Force base along the way. With an hour to go, he had to stop for an ID check, then follow the speed limits through craggy, barren hills or risk the wrath of roving MPs.

In daylight, they could see the Academy where Jay studied, a stately manor perched on the shore of Groom Lake. The water glimmered in the sunshine. Ben remembered his father telling the story of how, during his childhood, they'd forced open a spring to feed the shallow lake so the base had water year-round. The surrounding desert hadn't improved for it, but at least they had plenty of water.

In another five years, Kay would transition from the regular on-base elementary school to the Academy. That same year, Jay would graduate and shift to tactical training, then field missions. When Ben started, they didn't have an Academy. He'd gone through basic training and officer school, like any other Army officer. They'd thrown him into his father's unit when Dad retired.

The 11th Rangers battalion functioned a lot differently from fifteen years ago. In his grandfather's time, the Allied supers had been a ragtag baker's dozen of men and women from America and Europe. Kenzo had helped build this base, called Area 51 by some people. The funding for it had been authorized in 1951, and the whole project had enough secrecy surrounding it to spawn conspiracy theories.

Two hours and forty minutes after they left the airport, Ben shut off the engine in the garage. Kay scrambled out of the car and dashed inside, screaming for her mother. The shrieks stopped before the garage door closed. Ben found his wife holding his daughter, rubbing their noses together.

Ben smelled chicken and coconut. Along with rice, most of Risa's best dishes included those ingredients.

"Are you hungry?" Risa asked. "Because we're going to a barbeque, but I've got snacks for now."

Kay wriggled for freedom and ran to the dining room. "It smells good!"

He kissed Risa and left them to the food, intending to change out of his uniform, but he wound up standing in front of the mantle in the living room, staring at two plastic models in glass cases.

At the age of three, before Kay had come along, Jay had built the M1 Abrams tank with Ben's help. More accurately, Jay had picked it out for his Christmas present to Daddy and Ben had let him think he put it together. They'd sat at the dining room table, Jay in his lap, with the kit, a sharp knife, and model glue. Every piece Jay had touched, Ben had used his power to position so the model fit together with precision.

And then Kay had turned three. He'd tried to do the same with the red '67 Firebird model she'd picked out, but she'd refused to let him help. One time, she pushed her small hand against his face and shoved until he couldn't see anything. At that point, he'd given up and let her do what she wanted. The result was this crooked model, complete with globs of dried glue and one tiny, askew bumper sticker.

The rest of their models, eight for Jay and three for Kay, lived at his parents' house. These two, he wanted close at hand. He wondered what they'd pick for their models this year and whether Jay would build his by himself or let Ben sit with him through the construction.

He had a teenage son. At Jay's thirteenth birthday this past summer, he'd noticed that uncomfortable fact. It resurfaced in his head from time to time. Worse, he hadn't seen his teenage son in three months, and the boy lived less than two miles away. Last year, Jay's first at the Academy, they'd seen him every weekend with no mission. This year, Jay had asked to spend his weekends there.

"Risa, I want to go see Jay tomorrow."

"So do I!" Kay chirped.

"He's not off for Thanksgiving yet."

He turned away from the models to lean against the door frame and watch his wife and daughter devour more food than he ate in a normal meal. "I don't care."

Kay crossed her arms and lifted her chin. "I don't care either, Mom."

Risa raised her hands in surrender. "Fine, I'll make the call right now. If Lou doesn't like it, she can complain to Marks. Who will then complain to you tonight, making it your problem."

Her math seemed off, but Ben didn't argue. He commanded missions, not the household. "That's settled, then. We should get going to the barbeque."

They walked to Marks's small house. The colonel, his wife, and their youngest daughter lived in the same grid of identical on-base housing, all occupied by married Novas and soldiers. Laughter and cooking meat enticed them to the backyard, where they found Matias manning the grill and a dozen other Novas and officers with their spouses and kids.

Risa took Kay straight to the food laid across a picnic table. Ben picked up a beer and greeted everyone. He wound up sitting with Marks and two other people. Kitty, a fellow Nova, had earned her team's command two years after Ben. Unlike him, she ranked as a charlie, with the ability to manipulate water. The other person was Louisa Kilkenny, the headmaster of Nova Academy. Risa had called her on the way over with no idea they'd see her tonight.

Across the small yard, Kay hovered at DPS's side, watching him handle the grill and peppering him with questions. Risa sat with Mrs. Marks and three other Novas.

"You can't come to the school whenever you want, Ben," Louisa said. "It's disruptive, especially during a short week when the kids are all obnoxious anyway." She sipped her beer and glanced at Marks.

"Don't look at me," Marks said. "I have no authority over the Academy."

"You have authority over him." She pointed to Ben.

Kitty giggled. "Like that ever stops any of us. Go ahead, Ben. I'll cover you with a flood in the showers. Then I can steal away my little girl."

Marks snorted. "You want me to order him not to go over there?" He pointed to the hulking building in the distance.

"Just wait until Thursday!" Lou glared at all three of them.

Ben tried and failed to suppress a grin. "We're on call, Lou. I just want to make sure we get to see him. It would mean a lot to Kay. And Risa. And also me."

"Do you have any idea how many parents want to pull out their kids early right before every damned holiday?" Lou rubbed her eyes. "I didn't even know how many Jewish holy days there were until I took this job."

"He won't take his boy home," Marks said. "He's on call. That would be stupid."

"Ben may be an annoying pain in the ass," Kitty said, "but he's not stupid."

Ben sighed. "You're both so helpful. But no, we weren't hoping to take him home tomorrow. Just see him for an hour or two. Maybe have lunch with him. We're not even sure we'll be around on Thanksgiving." He left the worst-case scenario unspoken.

Lou met his gaze and sighed. Her power of receptive empathy hadn't made her a good fit for field work, but she'd served as part of the battalion support team for two decades. She understood what he didn't say. "You're too much like your father. Jay's year is running the obstacle course tomorrow at ten-thirty. If you come then, you can watch in the control room, then have lunch with him afterward and he won't miss any classes."

"Thanks, Lou." Ben sipped his beer.

"It's Thursday morning for you," Lou said, pointing at Kitty. "And everyone else."

Kitty raised her hands in surrender. "I know, I read the paperwork. Kelly's looking forward to the program on Wednesday night."

DPS, wearing a scorched, grease-stained apron over his jeans and t-shirt, stepped into view with Kay in his arms. "Special delivery, Cap. She conked out while accusing me of killing Bambi to make burgers. Not that I would've denied it."

Marks and Kitty both laughed. Lou chuckled.

Ben stood and took his daughter in his arms. "I guess we should go. We'll see you tomorrow, Lou."

"Wait in the lobby when you get there," Lou said. "I'll come down."

# CHAPTER 6

## IARIESAH

November 20, 2007
9:53am

The next day, they walked together to the Academy in warm, mid-morning sunshine. Ben wore his uniform, as always. Risa hadn't stayed in the military long enough to keep uniforms. She, Vivian, and Matias all served as civilian consultants.

Nova Academy, the training facility for all young people who expressed superpowers, covered two full acres along the shore of Groom Lake. The manor itself covered one-third of that space with dormitories, classrooms, workshops, and training rooms. An obstacle course, a shooting range, and a practice area for destructive powers filled the rest of the grounds.

They approached from the visitors' side, where the grounds along the smooth, fresh-painted access road had been landscaped for the sake of appearances. The academy entertained parents who had never served in any way, and needed to impress them.

Three wide, marble steps flanked by seas of blue, white, and yellow flowers led to the oak double doors carved with the Nova service patch symbol. No one ever wore the patch, to protect their identities, but they all had one. Everyone pulled them out for funerals and strapped them onto their left sleeve with a black band across the middle.

Though the front doors appeared unguarded, Risa knew the academy had vigilant instructors and guards. Monitored cameras watched the approach, and the front doors could lock down as needed. For Risa and Ben, they opened on mechanized hinges.

Every surface in the grand, airy entry gleamed with polished wood or polished marble. Real plants with blue, white, and yellow flowers in ceramic and gold sconces decorated the walls. Twin chandeliers glittered with crystals and light. A huge print of the picture that had inspired the WWII Nova Memorial in Washington, DC hung in a prominent position on the wall.

Hurricane Betty, Lady Foresight, Cowboy, and the rest of the Allied Novas stood in a tight group, hamming for the camera. Betty, an Irish redhead dressed like a pinup girl, hung on Cowboy's shoulder. Like all the other men, he wore his combat uniform, but Cowboy had his signature Stetson with the legendary bullet hole. On her other side, Lieutenant Eagle Eyes flashed a thumbs-up with a cheesy smile. The other woman, a stout Pole named Lady Foresight and dressed in coveralls like Rosie the Riveter, leaned back to back with Haywire.

Ben's grandfather, the original Captain Kinetic, stood in the second rank. They'd relegated him to the background for the crime of having Japanese ancestry, despite the fact his family—on both sides—had crossed the ocean almost eighty years before Pearl Harbor.

An original copy of this photograph hung at Ben's parents' house. Rather than dwell on how Kenzo had been treated, the Tsukudas chose to be proud of the man who'd fought Nazis in Europe, then fought anti-Japanese discrimination at home.

Beyond this entry, the ornate decoration followed a single path, up the sweeping stair to the right and into the headmaster's office. The rest of the building had industrial carpet or tile, student artwork or nothing on the walls, and fluorescent light fixtures. Normal parents never saw any of that.

"Daddy, can I go find Jay?"

"No. We have to wait for an escort so we don't interrupt any lessons."

At that moment, Lou stepped through her door. She hurried down the stairs with a broad smile. A younger man Risa didn't know trailed in his wake. Both wore Army uniforms.

"Welcome, all of you." She shook Risa's hand and tried to shake Kay's, but the girl hid behind Ben. "This is Greg Boone. He's my most capable assistant."

"She's exaggerating," Boone said with a friendly smile.

"Nice to meet you," Ben said. The two men shook hands.

Boone didn't offer to shake with Risa.

"You're just in time," Lou said. "The class is assembling for their run. This way." She and Boone escorted them up the stairs and to her office.

"How is Jay doing?" Risa asked. "Everyone was so forthcoming last year, and this year, we've heard almost nothing. It's like he moved to another country."

Lou nodded and gave her a sympathetic smile. "After they finish one year, most kids feel a drive to succeed that narrows their focus. They forget about little things like calling Mom."

"In particular," Boone said, "Jay is a stellar student. He's ahead in all his classes, courteous, and friendly. That combination, along with his Legacy status has made him well-liked and a favorite among teachers. They give him extra work because they know he can handle it."

"Quite," Lou said. "He'll be an excellent leader for whatever team he's placed with."

"He's only thirteen," Risa said with a frown.

Ben touched her shoulder. "I was like that at his age."

"You weren't training to be a Nova. I just don't want him to get overwhelmed."

"Jay has a good head on his shoulders," Lou said. "And every student has free time, every day. They have a chance to do stupid things, I promise."

"And they use it well," Boone muttered.

Picking up Kay to carry her as they stepped into Lou's office, Ben laughed. "I'm sure."

The spacious room held a desk, several chairs, and a couch facing a wall of screens. Plush, neutral carpet muffled their footsteps. Framed photos and paintings on the walls seemed chosen for their inability to offend anyone. Potted plants and fake flowers brightened the room.

"The outdoor sections of the grounds are all camera monitored so we can record and analyze their actions, which helps us pinpoint their weaknesses and get them the right training. Also, I've found the kids perform better when they know they're being watched but can't see their observers. They sleep better knowing no one is watching them."

"Other teachers watch the same feeds elsewhere," Boone said.

Lou picked up a remote and pointed it at the screens. All twelve flickered to life, showing different sections of the obstacle course. One offered an overhead view of a wall with handholds, another gave a side view of a rope bridge.

"Part of the point is general physical fitness. They'll run this course hundreds of times in different conditions before they graduate. We also give them specific objectives. Sometimes they have to capture a flag, it could be about their course time, one member of a group might be designated to fake an injury, groups could work against each other, and so on. We have a number of scenarios for them to keep it interesting. At their age, many students are shaky with power control, so they aren't allowed to use them on the course. It's too dangerous."

The screen showing the staging area drew Risa's attention. She picked out Jay among a cluster of kids. He had the same look about him as all the Tsukuda men, though his Islander heritage softened the angles. Until Ben fell for a girl from Guam, all the Tsukudas, as far back as anyone could trace, had been one hundred percent Japanese.

All the kids wore gray sweatpants and t-shirts marked with the Nova logo. A black girl with a thick braid down her back stood beside Jay. Risa also noted a boy with the same square jaw and sandy blonde curls as the original Cowboy.

"What's today's scenario?" Ben sat on the couch with Kay, holding her on his lap.

Lou carried a chair to sit beside the couch. "Basic group time trial. Four students per group. We're deliberately pairing students who don't get along well to force them to work together. It's not something we do often, just once in a while."

"Jay's never mentioned issues with other students." Risa sat beside Ben and took Kay's hand.

"They're teenagers," Boone said, standing behind them. "If they all got along with each other, it would be a miracle."

Lou chuckled. "We've never had a major problem, but some kids just don't mesh well. They self-select into cliques, just like regular kids, and we do exercises like this to keep it from getting out of hand."

On the screen, an adult shuffled the kids into quartets. Jay wound up in a group with the Cowboy kid, the black girl, and an Asian-American girl. Risa noted the Cowboy kid complaining to the adult and pointing to another group. She couldn't decide if she wanted to hear him or appreciated not having audio.

Jay and the two girls seemed annoyed by the Cowboy kid, but Jay patted him on the shoulder. The two boys shook hands with a notable lack of enthusiasm.

"Jay is the best." Kay pointed to him. "He's being nice to that jerk."

"Kay," Risa said, "we don't know that boy. You shouldn't call him a jerk."

"Anybody who doesn't like Jay is a jerk."

Ben grinned behind Kay.

Risa narrowed her eyes at him.

Ben coughed. "Kyoko Lily, that's not polite."

Kay loosed a stream of Japanese. Risa knew a smattering of words and phrases from spending time with Ben's family, but she'd never gained fluency. Out of the rapid-fire complaint, Risa caught Jay's given name, Ichiro, and something about a dog.

Sticking with Japanese, Ben answered Kay. They exchanged more words.

Risa watched the screen. If she needed to know about the conversation, Ben would tell her later.

"And here I thought we were set for translators with Chinese and Spanish," Lou said.

On the screen, the adult lined up Jay's group and sent them into the course. Ben pointed and Kay stopped griping. They watched Jay and his group drop to the ground and crawl under ropes in single file.

As soon as they passed that obstacle, the Cowboy kid rushed to the front of the line with a toothy grin for the camera and led the group over the rope bridge. Jay rolled his eyes. The group kept going.

At the climbing wall, the Cowboy kid swarmed up like a squirrel, paused at the top to flash the camera a big smile and a thumbs-up, then jumped off the thirty-foot tower. Jay let the two girls go in front of him, and helped the Asian-American girl when she faltered.

"I take it back, Kay," Ben murmured. "You're right. That boy is a jerk."

Risa shoved her elbow into his side. "Don't encourage her."

Kay beamed and kept watching her big brother.

Lou cleared her throat. "I'll just point out that a lot of growing up can happen in five years. At any rate, they're about done. He knows you're coming. You can wait in the entry if you want. Or here. Either way."

"I wanna see the picture of great-grandfather again." Kay scooted off Ben's lap and ran for the door.

Risa let her speed free and beat her daughter to the door. She took Kay's hand and made her walk to go see the picture hanging on the wall. Ben joined them a few minutes later.

A bell rang. Within seconds, the entry filled with students passing from one side to the other, all chattering and clattering. Jay separated from the crowd, waving to the black girl as she continued without him.

Kay squealed and launched herself at him, knocking them both to the floor. Students paused to watch and laugh.

Ben scooped Kay off the floor with a sigh and hauled her outside.

Risa helped Jay to his feet and hugged him. He had a growth spurt or two yet to hit, because he still stood an inch or two shorter than her.

"I'm fine, Mom. She just took me by surprise."

"I know."

"Are you and Dad going out again tonight or something?"

"We're on call."

He squeezed her. "Then I guess we should have lunch."

She shifted to keep her arm draped over his shoulders and walked outside with him. "You're a lot like your father."

"Everybody says that."

Risa laughed. "They tell him that too."

Ben sat on the front steps in the sunshine with Kay. The girl stood with her head hung enough to shroud her face with her long hair.

"I'm sorry I hit you," Kay mumbled.

"It's okay." Jay let go of Risa to tousle Kay's hair. "Just not so hard next time, yeah?"

Kay threw herself at Jay and hugged him.

"Not so tight," Jay gasped. "I can't breathe."

"You're never around anymore," Kay whined.

"I have stuff on the weekends this year."

"It's not fair!"

Risa wrapped her arms around Kay, forcing her to let go of her brother. "Let's have a nice, happy lunch in case we have to send you back to Sobo and Sofu tonight, okay?"

Kay heaved a melodramatic sigh. Risa dragged her toward Ben's Firebird in the parking area, where they'd left lunch.

She glanced back and saw Ben pull Jay into a hug.

"You should bring your girlfriend home for Thanksgiving if we're here," Ben said.

"I don't have a girlfriend."

"What about that girl you waved to?"

"Ew, Dad, no. She's not my girlfriend."

"No? What do they call it these days?" The pair fell into step behind Risa and Kay.

Jay huffed. "We're not dating. She's just a friend who's a girl. That happens, you know."

Ben chuckled. "Yes, I'm aware that happens."

Risa turned and said, "Bring her anyway if she's not going to see her family. You're allowed to bring home friends who happen to be girls, and she seems nice."

"Sure." Jay shrugged. "Her name's Phyllicia. I'll ask."

# CHAPTER 7

## CRASH / KELE CHOSPOSI

November 20, 2007
08:38

The call came in the middle of Kele's morning sparring session. At the sound of her pager buzzing, her partner, one of the Academy trainers, stopped and backed off. She checked the number and smiled. Another mission had popped up to keep her busy before she succumbed to the tyranny of waiting.

"Thanks for the workout," she said as she shucked her protective gloves. She wore them for his benefit, not hers.

"You too." He picked up a towel and mopped his brow. "I want to practice that takedown again when you get back. I have some kids who'd be a good fit for the technique."

"No problem." Kele shook his hand. She liked sparring with Sergeant Ohler because he came to practice and learn, not to flirt or prove his manhood. "I'm sure you'll hear about it when we get back." She'd show up for training that next morning at oh-eight-hundred, like she always did, and Ohler knew it.

"Good hunting," he said as he collected his bag.

"Good luck with the kiddies." Kele picked up her bag and jogged to OpCon.

As she reached the door to the building, Charlie landed beside her in a flurry of feathers and opened the door. They moved through the building together, following a path they'd taken dozens of times before.

Risa already sat inside the OpCon briefing room with Colonel Marks, frowning and drumming her fingers on the table. She wore neon orange and black, like she'd been out for a run. A file folder lay a few inches from her hands.

Kele and Charlie both stopped at the door to snap salutes at Marks.

"At ease," he said. "Take a seat."

Within half a minute, Matias strolled through the door. He dropped into a chair beside Charlie, looked around, and pulled out his smartphone to tap on the screen. Kele had, so far, resisted the whole cellphone thing. Her pager worked fine, and no one had forced the switch yet. If she smashed it in a fight, the quartermaster could get her a new one in five minutes. A replacement phone could take hours.

Besides, she had no reason to call anyone. Everybody she cared about would be in this room within the next five or ten minutes. If they wanted to talk to her, they knew where to find her. She saw all of them for at least one mission per month anyway.

Kele put her feet on the table to wait. Charlie and Matias put their heads together over the phone, muttering to each other in voices too low to overhear.

Risa bounced her legs. "Are you sure this can't wait until after Thanksgiving? It'd only be a three day delay."

"You know how this works," Marks said. "We delay for weather and intel, not family."

"I might feel sick." Risa gave a fake, hollow cough. "Maybe the team should go without me."

Marks gave her a flat stare. "Very funny."

Risa sighed and blurred to the other side of the room, then returned to her seat. "Ben won't be here until he can convince Kay to get into the jeep without him. She's very upset, and only Daddy can fix it."

"We all make sacrifices for this job," Marks said.

Kele curled her lip. As if any of them had a real choice. What else would she do? Roam the countryside, getting into bar fights? Here, she made a difference. She saved lives and kept her friends safe. Without that, she didn't think she'd stay sane.

Risa didn't answer. Everyone present already knew the rest of that conversation from start to end.

"We can wait," Kele said.

Vivian shambled through the door with dark circles under her eyes. Whatever the woman had going on with her boyfriend, she needed to figure it out and get her head screwed on straight. Slurring like a drunk, she mumbled something incomprehensible and lurched into a chair.

Marks watched Vivian with clear annoyance.

Ben rushed through the door. He stopped one step inside, snapped a salute, and hurried to a chair beside his wife. "Sorry I'm late." He put his hand on the folder and slid it close so he could flip through it. Risa leaned over and they murmured to each other.

"Let's get started," Marks said.

The door shut with no sign Ben had done anything.

"The intel you recovered from Cairari gave us a new target." He tapped on a laptop and a projected image appeared on the whiteboard. The same map they'd used to orient for the prior mission appeared. Small dots marked the towns of Mocajuba, Carapajó, and Cairari, with a larger dot to indicate Belém. Their target had been near the Cairari dot.

"There's another target fifteen miles south of the Cairari site." Marks put a red X on the whiteboard to mark the spot. "This mission is the same as the last one, but I'd like a prisoner this time." He looked at Kele as if to accuse her of killing opponents on purpose.

Kele scowled. She didn't take prisoners when the enemy looked like those things had. One had ripped thick chunks of flesh off her arm, exposing her bones. Another had rammed something through her eye. The rest did the usual—gashes, slashes, and smashes.

As for that flier, she didn't control the slingshot's effect. Vivian did. Had they not hit the wall, she could've subdued the guy.

"The man running the facility appears to have been the name on that certificate you found. The certificate is fake, but we believe the name is real. Wilhelm Otto doesn't match the names of any known Nazis, but he may have been unknown, and there were several Ottos, so he could have used a different first name in official paperwork. His research definitely delved into inducing superpowers. Considering that, he may have been a genuine 1930s German Nazi, but we haven't found any confirmation of his identity yet."

Without the type of research this Otto man did, Kele wouldn't have gained her powers. She wondered if the US had a secret stash of soldiers turned monsters by failed experiments. Maybe the guards put a bullet in their heads and shipped them home for burial in a closed casket. After they'd taken plenty of samples to figure out what went wrong, of course.

"Without the body, we can only guess at the cause of death, but it seems clear he experimented on himself, and had at least one success in that flier. It's in your best interests to assume you'll find more at the second site. And when you do," Marks pointed at Ben, "I don't want any executions unless it's the only option. Even then, think very hard about it."

Kele snorted. As if Ben ever did anything other than think very hard about field executions. He hadn't ordered one in months. Not since Buenos Aires last winter. That guy had deserved the double-tap to the head so hard that Kele had been willing to do it for him, twice over. The woman in Bangladesh had deserved it too, but they'd brought her to the Florida prison because Ben made that call.

Marks ignored her. "Because it appears that a number

of Brazilian citizens were abducted by Otto, I've been advised the Brazilian government will be informed about the Cairari site and asked for collaboration. That information will be passed when our ambassador returns from Brasilia on Wednesday for the Thanksgiving holiday, which means you have, at most, two days to get in and out. Insertion and extraction is already in motion. Your plane takes off at ten hundred. Maps are in the folder. Any questions?"

Vivian raised her hand. She seemed marginally more awake than when she'd walked in. "I don't like this mission."

Kele stared at her. The whole room gave her their attention. When the precog didn't like something, everybody listened.

"What's the problem?" Marks asked.

"I don't know." Vivian pressed her palms against the sides of her head, leaned forward, and groaned. "It's hazy."

That answer reminded Kele of a briefing in Vietnam, not long before the Tet Offensive clusterfuck. Kele hadn't been able to save a platoon because Lady Foresight, Vivian's mother and the second Nova to use the code name, had given her bad intel. Like mother, like daughter.

Out of the corner of her eye, Kele caught Marks throwing Ben a look like this verified something they'd talked about. Marks must've noticed Vivian acting strange in Cairari. Good. Ben knew, so Risa would handle whatever boy shit Vivian needed to work out. The rest of the team just needed to support her.

"In that case," Marks said, "the mission is on. Ten hundred hours, suited up on the tarmac. You have about an hour. Dismissed."

Kele hopped to her feet, the magic word propelling her toward the door. Charlie reached it with her and they didn't stop until they left the building. On the sidewalk, the two women glanced at each other. Until someone started the talk with Vivian, neither would leave. They could change into their tac suits on the plane if necessary.

Matias stepped outside and held the door for Vivian.

Ben and Risa followed them. Charlie blocked Vivian as she tried to stumble home. Kele gestured to Ben and Risa, telling them they had a problem to deal with.

"What the fuck, Charlie?" Vivian rubbed her eyes.

Risa nodded and draped an arm around Vivian's shoulders. "Honey, you seem a little off this morning."

When Vivian didn't shrug off Risa's arm or try to bolt, Kele felt she'd done her job. She checked with Ben.

Ben gave her a crisp nod. She and Charlie moved to his side, facing away from Risa and Vivian. Matias kept walking with his face glued to his phone screen, oblivious to the situation.

"Before you say anything," Ben said, "Risa thinks Aaron broke it off, but she can't get Vivian to talk about it."

"She needs to get her shit together." Charlie rubbed her shoulder.

Kele nodded. "If Risa can't sort it out, you have to bench her. A fucked up precog is worse than no precog."

"So far, she's only missed one bullet, and you were fine, Charlie." Ben crossed his arms and watched his wife. "We handled the alarm, and it turned out okay."

Glancing over her shoulder, Kele saw Risa giving Vivian a hug. "It's your call, Ben."

"I love Vivian," Charlie said, "she's great. I just don't want to eat the next bullet she misses."

Ben rubbed his chin. He gave the single nod of a decision made. "She's coming, but I'm going to talk with Marks to put a notice in her file. If she fucks up anything worse on this mission, she'll get an evaluation. We know she's a weak link, so we're going to compensate for it. She still didn't screw up anything, she just missed a few things. We're partially to blame for getting sloppy and expecting her to wipe our asses for us."

He had a point, Kele thought. Even if he didn't, making tough decisions was his job, not hers. "Yes, sir."

Charlie set a hand on her hip and shrugged. "Feathers fall where they fall."

Ben turned around and headed back inside.

Kele didn't envy him the task. She'd stayed at sergeant all these years for a reason. For many reasons.

# CHAPTER 8

## IARIESAH

November 20, 2007
23:00

The second site covered half as much territory as the first. Instead of a wall surrounding the place, a wide, murky jungle stream encircled the site. Springfire paused at the bank because she saw a large, reptilian head at the waterline. Her run would've carried her over its head. It wouldn't have caught her, but she didn't think it would've appreciated her using it as a stepping stone.

"They're using local fauna as a partial barrier," she said into her mic.

"I just stepped on a cockroach the size of my fist," DPS said. "It wasn't that scary."

"How do you feel about alligators?"

"They burn just like anything else."

Maverick snorted. "Brilliant, DPS. Light a fucking neon sign while you're at it."

"Cut the chatter," Ben said. "Springfire, check for a good path. Whoever's using the site isn't risking an attack every time they come and go."

"I've got a possibility to the north," Maverick said. "Maybe a road, maybe a stream. But I don't see any buildings."

Springfire ran across the river, angling away from the alligator. Beyond the curtain of large-leafed trees and oversized ferns, she found a series of low concrete buildings with bark for roofing. Tall trees scattered among the buildings provided a canopy cover from satellite imaging. No wonder they hadn't found this location without the encrypted data from the first site.

Soft yellow incandescent bulbs hanging naked under the eaves provided dim light for the weed-lined dirt paths between buildings. More lights glowing through thin curtains over glass-free windows and large-wheeled trucks pointed to inhabitants less monstrous than the prisoners of the first site.

She circled the camp, looking for the road. Tire treads led her to a narrow gap in the trees, wide enough for one truck at a time. The river narrowed here, and they had a bridge made of thick tree trunks lashed together.

"Bridge to the site on the northwest side. Follow the river to find it. Evidence of people is here, but I haven't seen people yet."

"Where are you?" Maverick asked. "I don't see a damned thing."

"At the target coordinates. It's little huts among the trees, and they made an effort to shield the lights."

"Damn. They're good."

"Both of you," Ben said, "meet us at the rendezvous point and Springfire will lead us all in."

Springfire raced into the jungle. The suit prevented her from feeling the wind on her skin and through her hair. She'd learned the hard way a long time ago to keep her mouth shut. Her eyes didn't need protection, a fact she'd appreciated since the first time her power became active.

Less than half a minute later, she stopped beside a tree to wait. The rest of the team would take at least five more minutes to reach her. Her speed had its drawbacks.

She sat to wait, wondering if they'd made a mistake

bringing Kay home for such a short time. The elementary school teachers had proved understanding, giving her self-directed work to take to LA as needed, and letting her reschedule tests and quizzes. They'd sorted that whole mess when Jay started first grade.

In three more years, Jay would start driving. Nothing made her feel older than that. Thirty-three years old and she had a teenage son. In another six or seven years, she and Ben would talk about retirement. Ben's father had retired at forty-five. Ten more years before Ben hit that age. Jay would have a few years as an active Nova under his belt by then.

Maverick landed, her wings buffeting leaves and branches. Moments later, Ben stepped through the shadows without making a sound.

No, Cap snuck up like a ninja. If she didn't think of him as Captain Kinetic, she had to work harder to keep from taking his hand or arm. Thirteen years of marriage had made her enjoy his touch more, not less.

Springfire hopped to her feet without a word and led the team at a slow jog to the bridge. Keeping herself to normal human speeds while running took concentration and effort. She could walk without a problem, but the moment she started running, her body ramped up and demanded speed.

At the bridge, DPS and Crash took the lead. The team darted across in pairs, though Springfire left Maverick behind in a blur. Cap stayed with Omen, keeping watch at the rear. They crept through the trees to the first building. Cap and Maverick drew their weapons. Springfire followed their lead. Crash slipped her machete out of its sheath.

Omen seemed more alert and present than she had at base. She stuck close to Ben, keeping two fingers on her temple.

Crash leaned around a corner and waved DPS forward. The pair ducked out of sight.

"I don't think I'm going to be super-helpful here," Maverick said through her mic.

"You still have a gun," Cap said. "Get into the trees."

"Stop," Vivian said.

The entire team froze.

"There's something…not right here. I don't know what."

Springfire glanced back and saw Cap put a hand on Omen's shoulder. "We need more than that."

"I don't have more than that!"

Cap covered Omen's mouth.

An unfamiliar voice called out a question in a foreign language. Springfire thought it sounded like German spoken with a Brazilian accent. She flattened against the wall. Cap dragged Omen next to her. Maverick edged toward a tree with huge leaves.

In the quiet, Springfire heard the wind rustling through the trees and over the roofs. Someone gurgled.

"Target down," Crash said.

Cap frowned. "Take prisoners."

"Just a guard," DPS said. "One more. We'll grab him."

Omen held her head with both hands. Cap had to support her to keep her from collapsing.

Gunfire cracked and echoed off the trees.

"Contact," DPS and Crash reported at the same time.

Cap turned off his mic and crouched beside Omen. He waved for Springfire to go help DPS and Crash.

Maverick's tree swayed while she climbed it.

Springfire surged around the corner to find DPS holding his hands in front of him. Fire writhed in an arc in front of him, deflecting bullets around his body. The shooter focused on him, ignoring a second man who tangled with Crash. The second man took Crash's fist across the jaw like he didn't feel much.

"Supers." Springfire flew around the nearest building, hoping to flank the shooter, and ran into a third man. The high-speed collision knocked her off her feet and through a wall. She dropped her pistol. Chunks of concrete rained on her and dust filled the air.

Someone inside the building scrambled to his feet and ran for a rifle hanging on the wall. Springfire flashed to her feet and knocked the weapon aside. He threw a punch at her. She dodged. His fist hit the wall and crackled with a discharge of electricity. Sparks shot across the wall to hit the ground and light the roof on fire.

"Delta level at best for this one," Springfire said. She swept his leg, knocking him to the ground.

"Crash's dance partner might be a—" DPS grunted. It sounded like someone hit him.

Springfire used her most potent tactic against a single opponent, hitting him with a dozen kicks to the abdomen in the span of one second. She finished with a boot to his face. He slumped, but kept breathing.

"Target subdued," she reported. In a flash, she returned to the hole she'd made in the wall and saw another hole in the next building. Whoever she'd hit probably hadn't gotten up yet. She checked the ground for her gun and found it half-concealed by a block of concrete. Picking it up, she watched the other hole for movement.

"Fuck you," DPS snarled.

A man screamed.

Stepping to the second hole, Springfire noticed movement in the corner of her eye. The bullet her new opponent fired only missed her head because she ducked. She snapped her gun to the side and fired, putting three shots into the man's chest. Someone else jumped her from the hole, knocking them both to the ground.

This time, she kept hold of her gun. The man on top of her punched her in the face. She reeled from the hit with a groan.

"Three targets down," Crash said.

"I've got one bleeding a bit," Maverick said.

"Regroup," Ben said.

"Springfire," Omen screamed, both in her ear and from across the compound, "take your finger off the trigger!"

Springfire obeyed.

"Springfire," Cap said, his voice tinged with concern, "where are you?"

"I've got her," Maverick said. She swooped in, descending to attack Springfire's opponent.

The man grabbed Springfire's wrist and smashed her gun hand to the ground. If her finger had stayed on the trigger, she might've pulled it by accident and hit Maverick.

Maverick snagged two fistfuls of the man's shirt and hauled him to the side. She slammed her knee into his chest and smashed her pistol grip into his face.

He grunted and kicked her shin. Maverick's leg snapped straight. She fell forward with a groan.

"Report! Crash, find them and deal with it!" Distress tainted Cap's voice.

Still lying on the ground, Springfire pointed her gun. "Busy." She squeezed the trigger and fired twice into the man's side.

He winced and grunted. Crash charged from behind the building and plowed into him as Springfire shot him again.

Crash knocked him into a tree. Springfire scrambled to her feet and holstered her gun. It hadn't helped anyway. She touched her mouth and checked her hand. Blood.

The man howled in agony. Springfire looked up to see that Crash had hacked off his arm at the elbow.

"Target down," Crash said. "Unless someone wants to keep him from bleeding to death, that is."

Springfire didn't want to watch him fade. She turned her back on the gory sight. "I'm fine."

"Me too," Maverick said. "Ate some dirt, but I'll live."

"What the fuck happened?" Cap snapped.

Springfire returned to her previous target. "I had a collision on my way to flank for DPS." Cap would hear the unspoken comment. The guy remained unconscious. She took his arm and dragged him at low speed to find Cap and Omen.

"The fuck, Omen?" Maverick said. "Springfire coulda

been killed by that!"

"I didn't see it," Omen said, sounding like she wanted to cry.

Springfire saw Maverick stalk toward Cap and Omen. She followed with her burden.

"That's not fucking good enough!" Maverick screamed.

"Stand down," Cap ordered.

Springfire rounded the corner to see Cap standing between Maverick and Omen with his arms crossed. DPS leaned against the wall, not involving himself.

"This is bullshit," Maverick growled. "She's fucked up! You're cutting her too much slack. Somebody's gonna get killed if you don't fucking bench her."

Cap leaned toward her with a stern glare and pointed two fingers at the ground. "I said. Stand. Down."

Behind him, Omen covered her face and crumpled to the ground. "I'm sorry." She sniffled. "I didn't think it would matter."

Crash dragged another live man into the space. "Didn't think what would matter, Omen?"

Omen looked up, her eyes brimming with tears. "I'm pregnant."

Everything made sense. Springfire dropped her prisoner and rushed to Omen's side. "Oh, honey, why didn't you say so?"

Maverick stared. "Sweet Jesus riding a whiskey barrel."

Crash tossed her prisoner at Cap's feet.

Omen tensed and raised a hand toward Cap. "Look out!"

Cap dove for the ground, hitting Maverick and taking her with him. DPS raised his fire shield again. Crash spun.

Two men with machine guns sprayed bullets at the group.

Springfire grabbed Omen and hauled her around the corner. The air cooled. With DPS shielding them, Cap and Maverick joined Springfire and Omen.

Cap held his gun ready in case any other attackers circled around the other side of the building. Maverick used the momentary respite to launch into the air. DPS stayed close enough to protect them as needed.

"Crash has this," DPS said.

"Help her anyway," Cap said with a wave for DPS to join the fight. "She can't heal everything."

Springfire touched Omen's cheek, brushing away tears. She must've known at the bar, and decided not to drink because of it. "You know my power went a little funny while I was pregnant. Both times."

"This can wait," Cap said. "We need recon for any more targets."

Leaning in, Springfire kissed Omen's forehead. She hoped the other woman could hold on long enough to keep them safe for the rest of this fight. "We're here for you," she reminded Omen, then she dashed to run a circuit of the compound.

This time, she turned wide corners. Before, she should've known better. When she ran at home, she never cut tight corners. She'd learned that lesson before joining the Army. Hitting two roaming chickens had infuriated her whole neighborhood at home.

She passed a tiny hut and heard clomping boots. The door opened. Springfire stopped around the corner and watched.

Men in tactical gear poured out of a building too small to hold them. Eight pairs stomped past her with assault rifles and backup weapons. They wore helmets and moved with military precision, but she saw no insignias, nameplates, or service patches among them.

"Incoming. Sixteen mercenaries."

"Understood," Cap said. "Return and assist."

Springfire saw that the last man hadn't shut the door. Sloppy. She dashed inside on her way back to Cap and saw enough to make sense of the situation.

"Targets down," Crash reported.

"Form up on my position. Maverick, stay in the air."

As he finished the last word, Springfire stopped by Cap's side.

Omen still sat on the ground, covering her face. Her shoulders heaved with sobs she managed to keep quiet. Springfire wanted to hold her and tell her everything would turn out fine. They didn't have that luxury at the moment.

"There's an underground component," Springfire reported. "I found the stairs. It's empty. They're all coming for us."

"Good work." Cap held out a hand and dragged a tree by the branch.

Springfire saw what he intended and raced to the trunk to help him knock it down. Two pushes, combined with his telekinesis, dropped the tree across the ground. Thick branches and fat leaves blocked access to his position from that angle. He twisted the thinnest branches to wrap around the wrists of their two prisoners.

Maverick chuckled. "They heard that, Cap. I see them. They're headed to you."

"In position to intercept," Crash said. She sounded tired. The two machine gunners must've hit her with at least a hundred rounds.

DPS rounded the corner and flashed a thumbs-up while he waited to support Crash.

Springfire paused on her way to DPS to pat Omen on the top of the head. Standing beside DPS, she glanced back at Omen. They'd have to work without her for a while. Cap had made a good point when he said they'd gotten lazy by relying on her.

She saw Cap crouch beside Omen and switch off his radio. He hit the button for Omen's radio too. He murmured to her.

Someone around the corner shouted a hostile question in accented German.

"I don't understand you," Crash said.

Springfire knew Cap spoke German, but he stayed

quiet.

"Ah, American," a man with a heavy accent said. "What you do here, American?"

"Just looking for a place to take a nap."

"Nap?"

German voices chattered to each other.

"Oh, asleeping. No beds for using here. Private land. Get out or we shoot."

Springfire heard the telltale sound of a dozen or more men raising weapons. She braced her foot against the wall, ready to do whatever Cap ordered.

"Omen has the mark." Cap straightened with his gun ready. "Standard rank takedown."

"Springfire. Three," Omen said. "Two. One. Go."

Given the order, Springfire flew into motion, following a routine they'd used a dozen times before. As she rounded the corner, she heard Omen call out Maverick's name and count down. Springfire hit the first pair of men from the side. She whacked their rifles and kept going.

Once, she'd tried running through people with her fist. Not only had she broken her arm, she'd been horrified by the gross level of gore. Rifles didn't resist the same way bodies did, and she'd done this maneuver dozens of times without hurting herself.

Springfire zigzagged through the mercenary squad as the rest of her team followed in her wake on Omen's count. Maverick fired her gun from fifteen feet above them. Crash charged through the two lines. DPS and Cap kept them from fleeing with barricades of fire and wood. When Springfire reached the last two men, she kept going and circled to return to Omen.

One minute after Springfire started her run, sixteen mercenaries lay on the ground. None of the team had faced any danger alone.

"I don't see any live targets," Crash said. "These were all regular people."

"They seemed sloppy to me." Springfire sat beside

Omen and draped an arm around her shoulders. "Military training, but not crisp or professional."

Maverick snorted. "That's mercs for ya. Lazy fuckers."

"No, more than that." Springfire groped for the words to explain and came up short. "I don't know, something just seems off about them."

"Seemed. Past tense," DPS said. "Cap, burn the bodies or leave them?"

"Search and burn." Cap returned to the prisoners. "Springfire, go scout the underground area." He dropped his pack beside the prisoners and rummaged through it.

They needed to interrogate the two men, a practice Springfire found distasteful. They'd stay within the rules, but it still wasn't pleasant duty. Cap never let anyone do anything he wouldn't do, but the process involved demanding answers to questions. Once they became prisoners, Springfire couldn't stop seeing them as human beings. As someone's sons or daughters. Cap knew that about her. The whole team knew that.

"Permission to take Omen?"

Cap looked up from his gear search and flicked his gaze from one woman to the other. "Granted. Maverick, go with them."

"Yes, sir."

Springfire helped Omen stand and walked with her to the tiny building. Maverick landed beside them on the way. They stayed quiet until they reached the stairs. Cap and Crash turned off their mics, as they always did while performing interrogations. DPS said nothing while carrying out his own grisly duty.

At the top of the stairs, Omen stopped the other two women from descending. "I'll go first."

"Like fuck you will," Maverick said. She shouldered past both with her gun out and disappeared into the dim underground.

"Don't be dramatic," Springfire said to both women. "She's not suddenly made of spun glass." Despite her statement, she stepped in front of Omen to descend the stairs. She wanted to ask Omen about Aaron, about how she found out, about a lot of things. Those things were personal, though, and didn't need to be in the official record of this mission.

Springfire considered shutting off their mics to do it. But with Cap and Crash gone radio silent for a while, someone needed to offer team chatter. Everyone participated in the fiction that interrogations didn't happen, and Cap and Crash just had nothing interesting to say for a while.

The stairs led down two flights to a vast underground chamber of rough-hewn stone. Tables and chairs littered the space. Mismatched rugs covered areas of the floor. Electricity powered a section of bare light bulbs screwed into housings along an insulated wire secured to the ceiling with metal spikes. Metal shelves lining the walls held weapons, canned food, plantains and other root crops, cooking gear, and crates.

"I don't get it," Omen said. "What did they do here?"

"Guard that?" Springfire pointed to a large, matte black vault door. It reminded her of the kind banks always had in movies but never had in real life, complete with a sprocket-style handle.

Maverick approached the door. "That Nazi guy had a giant vault and he didn't keep his old experiment journals in it? Leaving them lying in his office seems like it's kinda begging to start a fire. Any decent mad scientist would know that."

DPS snorted into his mic. "He was a Nazi. What makes you think he'd be decent?"

"Never mind that." Springfire approached the vault and laid her palms on the cool metal. The paint seemed fresh. "Any ideas for opening it? The walls are solid stone and the door is probably thick metal. I don't see an access panel or other electronics. There's no obvious way to open it even for the person who owns it."

"Spin that wheel thing as fast as you can?" Maverick

suggested.

Springfire pushed on the wheel, but it only turned a small amount before stopping. "Nope. It doesn't spin freely, and I can't get momentum on something like this."

"Fire probably won't help," DPS said. "I'm done here. Tell me where it is and I'll come take a look."

While Springfire guided him with words to the small hut, she watched Maverick and Omen walk through the room. Maverick clicked on a flashlight and stayed close to Omen as she plunged into the darkness. They moved far enough for Maverick's light to become a small pool in the distance.

Something on the ceiling caught Springfire's attention. She saw it for a split second while Maverick's flashlight played across the stone. Then she and Omen moved on. Springfire stared at the inky black, not sure what she'd seen.

DPS arrived at a jog. "I got this."

"Can I see your compass?" Springfire asked.

He fished it out of a pocket and handed it to her, then set down his pack and ran his gloved hands over the door surface.

Springfire retrieved her flashlight and headed toward the spot she'd seen. The compass showed she walked along the northeast wall of the chamber. The Cairari site was northeast of this site. She played her light across the stone, watching near the ceiling.

"Found the panel," DPS said. "This isn't too hard. I can get through it in ten or fifteen minutes. Twenty if it's more complex than it looks."

A strange deformation of rock near the ceiling made Springfire stop. She focused her light on it and tried to make sense of it among the irregularities of the stone. Stepping to the other side and back a few times helped her see that she'd found a latch. In addition, the corner had a crack down the center—a crack too straight and even for coincidence.

"I think there's a door or hatch here."

"We're coming back to your location," Maverick said.

Springfire slipped off her glove and pressed her hand to the stone. No matter how much effort put into concealing a door, it still had to have a way to open on this side. Not even Cap could telekinese something he couldn't see.

Running her hand across the surface, she closed her eyes and focused on the bumpy, cool, and solid feel of the stone. Her fingertips brushed across a section smoother than the rest. Without looking, she sought and found the edges of a rounded section, close in shape and size to Ben's hand. A man's hand.

She opened her eyes. Knowing where to look, she saw a slight discoloration marking the spot under her hand. "Maverick, cover me."

"On it."

Springfire waited until Maverick stood with her gun out, pointed at the wall. Then she pushed.

The spot under her hand sank into the wall until it clicked. Metal clanked. A section of the ceiling lifted, revealing an empty, dark space. Maverick and Springfire shone their flashlights into the space and discovered a tunnel.

"I'll scout it," Springfire said.

Maverick stepped aside. Springfire crossed the room, then let her speed loose. She ran up the wall and into the tunnel. A few feet into the tunnel, she stopped and pointed her flashlight into the distance. The tunnel sloped downward and she couldn't see an end.

"It looks long." Without waiting for a response, Springfire ran.

She kept going and going, expecting to find the end at any moment. When her light finally showed a solid surface, she thought she'd gone at least ten miles. Near the dead end, the floor sloped up enough to notice. Once she reached the end, she found a metal lever at waist height connected to a large gear assembly overhead.

Pulling the lever made the gears clunk and whir with motion that seemed driven by tension instead of electricity.

This time, the ceiling descended. Springfire climbed up the concrete-backed stone to find the bottom of a stairwell. The door stood open, and through it, she smelled rotting meat.

No, she realized as she peered through the door, she'd gone fifteen miles. "The tunnel connects to the Cairari site."

"It travels underground for fifteen miles?" Maverick asked. "Who digs a tunnel fifteen miles through stone and under rivers and shit?"

Springfire shook her head. She didn't understand either. The effort involved in such an engineering challenge couldn't have matched the benefit of having the tunnel. Anyone wanting to travel from one site to the other could've gone overland. That trip would've taken less time despite being twice as long because they could use vehicles.

"Someone worried about being seen moving people or gear," Cap said. Springfire heard the subtle tension of new nightmares in his voice. The interrogation had ended. Later, she'd listen while he talked around it to excise the poison without distressing her.

"Vault is unlocked," DPS said. "Maverick, back me up while I open it."

Springfire headed up the stairs, wanting to take another look in the lab. Armed with the new information that Otto had a penchant for secret doors, she suspected she'd find another. The body remained on the slab, and nothing had been disturbed since they left.

"What the fuck," Maverick said.

"I don't understand," DPS said. "Not only did he build a fifteen mile tunnel, he put in a decent security vault and then left it empty. I mean, there's a small stack of aluminum sheets and a spool of wire, but I could pick up this shit in any home improvement store. It's not worth much and easy to replace, even out here in the middle of fucking nowhere."

"Check for a hidden door," Springfire suggested. She walked the perimeter of the lab, finding nothing, then stepped into the office. Poking through the Nazi paraphernalia in the cabinet, she noticed a stack of photographs under a swastika paperweight and flipped through them.

She recognized Adolf Hitler in a few of black and white photographs. Halfway through the stack, she realized the photos all contained a particular man in various forms of Nazi regalia. Some featured a woman on his arm, then a baby. She watched the baby age, picture by picture, until he stood with his father in front of a stone castle with Nazi banners.

The last few pictures depicted the family on a ship, then in a small house. At the bottom of the stack, she found a color photograph of two men, neither the same as the previous pictures. Both shared similarities in appearance, including facial structure. The apparent age gap between them suggested a father and son. Their clothing choices told her nothing, as she had no knowledge of Brazilian or German historical fashion trends.

Someone at base would appreciate having these pictures. She stuck them into her pack and took another look through the cabinet, moving everything.

"Reporting in. Taking a second look at Cairari."

"I found a leather briefcase in the back corner," Maverick said. "It kind of blended in with the stone. No hidden doors, though. This thing has some handwritten notes in German, a blueprint that doesn't match either of these sites, and two addresses. One is in Cametá, the other is in Belém."

"We shouldn't go to Belém." Omen sounded firm, which meant they wouldn't go to Belém.

"There's something fishy about these two sites," Springfire said, "but I can't put my finger on it. I think we're missing something." She peeked behind framed pictures and posters, but found nothing.

"These notes are nothing," Cap said. "They don't say anything. It's fake German, or someone using a code. We could have the extraction team takes us across the river from Carapajó to Cametá before we leave."

Springfire left the office and scanned the lab one more time. With no clear reason why, she rolled the four different tool trays together and checked them all at once. She knew little about medical tools, but she could see the differences between the four sets. Two sets had identical tools. The other two sets had a different group of identical tools.

Two different purposes explained this, except they had a lot of similarities. Instead of having disparate purposes, the tools varied in length or shape of handle. Examining them closer, she noticed a thin layer of dust covering one pair of sets, but not the other.

The implications hit her immediately. "Cap. I think there were two experimenters here, not one. The corpse had a partner." She thought of the photograph. "I think it might be his son."

"Is anyone else getting the creeps here?" DPS asked.

"Springfire, get out of there and head for the extraction point. We'll meet you there." Cap sent the ping to alert home base. "OpCon, this is Captain Kinetic. Target is breached and pacified. We've discovered two new locations, but have strong suspicions they're traps."

Trust for Cap sent Springfire running for the door, then through the jungle.

"Negative on extraction." Marks sounded tired. "I want you to check those two other sites first. I'll get the Navy team headed to Belém."

"Sir, we're not going to Belém. Omen is clear about that."

"Her ability is compromised."

Cap paused before answering. "I would rather trust her and have to come back next week than not trust her and get my team killed."

"That's not how this works, and you know it. I'm sending the order for the extraction team. Investigate the other two sites and meet them in Belém tomorrow night."

Springfire didn't need Cap to give her an order for her to know what to do. She pushed herself to her top speed, racing around trees and over water to reach Carapajó as soon as possible.

As she burst through the trees at the same point as the last extraction, she saw the boat crew untying their mooring ropes. The boat's engine hummed to life.

She raced up the dock and onto the boat. On the way, she clicked off her mic. As the craft pulled away from the dock, she stopped behind Captain Winters and pressed the barrel of her gun to the back of his neck.

"Turn around and wait for the team."

The other three men scrambled to raise their weapons.

"We just got orders—"

"I know. Our chain of command is ignoring our intel. There's no mission in Belém. The rest of the team will be at that dock in four hours, then we're going to extract and go home." She glanced at the next nearest soldier. "Do you really think you can get the drop on me? I'll fight you all and pilot this goddamned boat myself if you make me. We're not leaving my team behind."

If they didn't buy her bluff, she didn't know what else to do. She had no intention of harming any of them, and she didn't want them to shoot each other by accident.

They stood, guns pointed and tense, for a lot longer than Springfire found comfortable.

"Fine." Winters huffed and turned the boat around. "No one gets left behind."

His men lowered their weapons.

Springfire holstered her gun. She hugged herself to keep her hands from shaking. "Thank you."

"Remember that you thanked me when your CO chews your asses a new one."

# CHAPTER 9

## BEN

November 22, 2007
01:13

Ben didn't usually feel so conflicted when returning home. Marks wanted to see the whole team in the briefing room, an order Ben had elected to countermand. He'd done it off-mic so Marks could find out and yell about it without the rest of the team having to listen. This evening promised a lot of yelling.

Briefcase in hand, he trudged into the briefing room alone. Marks stood at the front of the room with his arms crossed. He watched Ben shut the door.

"So that's how it's going to be," Marks snapped.

"Yes, sir." Ben set the briefcase on the table in front of Marks and snapped into parade rest.

"Disobeying a direct order, hijacking an SWCC crew and their boat, and, apparently, convincing the rest of your team to disobey a different direct order. That's not a happy list, Captain."

"No, sir." He'd thought a lot about how to handle this situation during their travel time. None of this had happened before during his command. Once, when he first started, the officer in charge of his team  had led them against a direct order from OpCon. Ninja had sent everyone to their bunks on their return too, telling them she intended to let the CO get everything off his chest, then explain and defend the situation.

"I ought to write you up for a court-martial."

Ben said nothing. He stared at the whiteboard, wondering if he'd have to listen to his father shouting when he called to try to get Kay on an early flight home.

Marks shouted at him for five minutes about dereliction of duty, disappointment, and proper officer behavior. By the time he wound down, his voice sounded hoarse and he looked tired and spent. "Do you think the first Captain Tsukuda would be proud of you?"

The comparison came as no shock. Ben found it surprising Marks waited so long to make it.

"Yes, sir, I do. Because my grandfather knew to trust his precog and his gut. He also knew when to tell his CO that he had his head up his ass."

"Is that so?"

"Yes, sir."

Marks gave him a cold, hard stare. Ben ignored it. Silence built in the room until it felt oppressive.

"Report." Marks yanked out a chair and slumped into it.

Thankful the episode had gone according to his best case scenario, Ben opened the briefcase and spread out the papers and photographs. "We encountered a small number of supers in the Delta and Echo power range, and a squad of mercenaries. No prisoners."

After interrogation, he'd made the call to execute the two would-be Nazis. They'd gotten what they could from them, including their lack of remorse over taking willing part in experimentation on prisoners. Marks might have wanted prisoners but it wasn't his call. Ben could live with two more deaths on his hands.

"We have reason to believe Wilhelm Otto had a son who was his partner." He tapped the color photograph of the two men. "We don't know anything about him or what name he uses. The second facility appeared to be a base for housing their mercenaries, but it's unclear why they'd site such a facility so far away from the first, and why the vault would've had these materials and nothing else."

"Maybe it would be clear if you'd gone to Cametá or Belém," Marks growled.

"I doubt it, sir. Omen warned us against Belém, and these notes gave me enough suspicion to call off Cametá." He tapped the two handwritten notes. "I've studied them for several hours now, and I believe they were written to appear as German, and not as some kind of code. I think Otto's son wanted us to go to those two sites. And I think we were led to the second facility on purpose."

Marks looked through the photographs. "Nazis. The real deal."

Ben had believed his grandfather when he said the Nazis hadn't died out, they'd just adapted. He and his little sister had both learned German at their grandfather's knee, convinced a new Hitler would someday rise and use German out of respect for the original.

Stacking the photographs again, Marks slid everything back inside the briefcase. "Don't get Kay back. I'll have to send you back for those two other sites."

The idea of not spending Thanksgiving with Kay made Ben bristle. "With all due respect, sir, I believe that's a mistake. It was a waste of firepower to send us to the second site. Any team of deltas could've handled it. I can't imagine the other two, located inside a small town and a sizable city, would be any different."

After a long pause, Marks said, "I'll think about it. Go get some sleep."

Ben nodded and left with as much haste as he could muster. The team had elected not to hit the bar tonight, at least. He'd called it off on the concern that Marks would keep him for hours. Checking his watch, he saw it had only been half an hour. Still, he didn't think he had the energy to make it that far on foot. If he drove, he knew he'd fall asleep at the wheel.

The blinking red light atop the main gate's watchtower guided him home. He found the door unlocked, as he'd hoped. The light in the kitchen took him to Risa.

She'd changed out of her tac suit and into a short satin robe. The light pink contrasted with her dusky skin, and her braided hair stood out against it. "Did you get fired?" Her half-empty glass held her usual late-night snack of coconut milk, chocolate syrup, and protein powder.

"I'm sure he thought about it, but no." Ben slid his arms around her waist from behind.

"Are you hungry?"

"Yes, but not for food." He kissed her neck while she drank more from her glass.

The light turned off.

Ben wanted to see her. He waved a hand at the switch, too tired to flick it without the gesture. The switch clicked, but the light didn't come back on.

He raised his head and clicked the switch again. When nothing happened, he waved at the fridge to open the door. "Power's out," he grumbled.

Risa rubbed her hand down his thigh. "Are you afraid of the dark?" He heard the grin in her voice.

She had a point, and her touch persuaded him. He held her close and slipped his hand to her breast. "Never."

A thought about the oddity of a power outage on base wriggled in the back of his mind. He couldn't remember the power ever failing on base before. Even in the years when he'd lived here with his parents, they'd never lost electricity. The base had its own generators, upgraded over the years until they relied on local solar and wind with the most advanced storage tech available, and used all underground wiring.

Risa set her glass in the sink. "What's wrong?"

"For the power to go out, something would have to shut down the generator station."

"There could've been an equipment failure." Risa batted his hand. "In which case, we should go help. People could be in danger. Though I'd expect Vivian to call us for that. I'll go put on clothes anyway."

Ben sighed and let go. "If someone is responsible for this, I hate them."

Risa laughed as she headed to the bedroom.

Wishing he could just have sex and get some sleep, Ben pulled on his mask and replaced his gloves. He might as well wear the suit properly. Though the house had three flashlights, and he knew where to find them, he retrieved the one in his thigh pocket and clicked it on.

His phone wouldn't help if the whole base had lost power, because that included both cell towers in range. Vivian wouldn't call after all. Come to think of it, OpCon wouldn't have power either. He wondered if they had any teams on mission at the moment, and whether they'd face any unexpected jeopardy without a connection to base.

How had this happened? The more he thought about it, the less likely an accident seemed. He'd run into power station employees hundreds of times, and they all talked about the strict maintenance schedules and multiple backups to keep the station operational through major repairs.

"Ben, where's the fire extinguisher?" Risa sounded calm.

"In the kitchen. Why?"

"Your phone is smoking. I don't want the nightstand to catch fire."

He blinked and tried to process what she'd said. Too tired to understand, he hurried to the bedroom. The smell of burning plastic hit him at the doorway. Risa's flashlight shone on the small table where he'd left his phone before the mission. Black smoke surged from the device.

Waving his hand, he picked it up with his power and ran with it to the front door. He took it outside and dropped it on the driveway.

"What the fuck?" He noticed glowing in the window of

the house across the street. "Risa!"

She appeared by his side and frowned as she saw the other house. "What's going on?"

"I don't know, but we need to get people up and moving. Head for the barracks, then come back once you've got someone going. I'll work my way through the neighborhood." As she blurred into the distance, he ran across the street, picked up a rock from the neighbor's artistic gardening display and hurled it with his power. The rock slammed through their front door, destroying the knob.

The door drifted open. He ran inside and found a simmering fire centered on their extensive entertainment system. While waking the couple and helping them outside, pieces of information clicked in his head.

"Power outages don't fry electronics and start fires," he said to no one as he ran for the next house. "EMP pulses do." He didn't see any other fires lighting up neighborhood windows, at least. "Nukes generate EMP pulses." Area 51 had no nukes stored on site, and didn't lie anywhere near a major transportation line of any kind, so they had no possibility for an accidental detonation. Besides, nothing suggested a nuclear weapon had detonated close enough to cause the pulse.

The next house had someone coughing and hacking from smoke. He had no trouble convincing people to leave their homes and knock on other neighbors' doors to wake everyone. Within ten minutes, half his neighbors roamed the street, helping wake the rest of the development.

Risa appeared by his side as he knocked on another door. "Maverick, DPS, and Crash are organizing building evacuations. DPS is in a murderous rage over the massive amount of charred slag in his room."

Ben winced in sympathy. "I can imagine. Where's Omen? I thought you'd bring her."

"I don't know." Risa shook her head, in obvious distress. "She wasn't in her bed when I got there. Ben, there's something else."

"The school!" someone shouted.

Risa's eyes widened. "Jay," she whispered.

"Go! I'll be right behind you." He watched her go and ran back to the house. His car should work. Probably. Better to check it than to run across the base for no reason. Inside the house, he snagged his keys from their hook and smacked the garage door opener. It didn't work because it had no electricity.

He stomped the release for the door, hauled it open, and slid into his Firebird. The engine purred to life. Ben grinned and patted the dashboard. At least something worked. Once he got it out of the driveway, he had to dodge his neighbors until he reached the main road. There, he floored it and barrelled down the road to the Academy.

On the way, he saw a thick streak of lightning slam into the Academy's wall. Had it not traveled parallel to the ground, and had there been storm clouds overhead, he wouldn't have considered that strange. He slammed on the brakes before reaching the building. His car didn't need to get stuck in the middle of a fight.

"Maverick, I need—" He stopped himself. The entire team, including himself, had removed their mics and earbuds on the last leg of their journey home.

Ben jumped out of his car and ran for the building. They needed to get the kids to safety.

# CHAPTER 10

## OMEN / VIVIAN CROSS

November 22, 2007
01:47

As she stumbled to her room in the barracks, Vivian couldn't stop the visions from replaying in her head. She'd seen her friends ripped apart, blown up, riddled with bullets, and set on fire too many times to count. For the ride home, her memory had dredged up an old favorite from Ukraine that not even Kele would've walked away from. Knowing it hadn't happened because she'd prevented it didn't stop the memory.

Colonel Marks denying her unformed vision had started a spiral, and she couldn't stop it. No matter how long Risa kept an arm around Vivian's shoulders, she couldn't stop it.

One thing could stop it.

She fumbled with her keycard to get into her room. The single, bare bulb flickered to life, dangling from a wire long enough to hang herself if she ever needed it. Tour posters for Siouxsie and the Banshees, Nine Inch Nails, The Cure, and Depeche Mode covered the white walls of the single room apartment. If they let anyone paint anything, she would've made her walls black.

After shutting the door to keep her privacy intact, she dumped her backpack and ripped off her elbow pads. Her answering machine blinked with a new message. She slapped the button to let it play while she struggled to wriggle out of her tac suit as fast as possible. The longer it took, the longer until she found relief.

"Hey Vivi. It's Aaron." His light tenor made Vivian squirm. She hadn't liked their last conversation, but she focused on getting out of her clothes.

"I'm sorry about what I said. You know I'm not good with surprises. If you'd just eased into it or something. I guess. Anyway, I want to see you. I miss you. We can talk this over. Everything will be okay so long as you don't make me yell at you again, right? I just love you so much I can't stand it when you screw up. I can fix this. Let me take care of things. Call me when you get back."

She smacked the machine. It hit the floor and shut off. "I didn't screw up," she told the machine. "You did." Tears slipped down her cheeks. She didn't remember them starting. Her shirt came loose and she tossed it across the room, then she gave up on undressing herself and reached for the nightstand.

The drawer held blissful silence. Her practiced hands snagged a tiny bottle and a syringe, snapped in a fresh needle, and stuck it through the foil. Two missions in rapid succession meant she needed more than her usual dose of morphine to sleep tonight. She filled the syringe instead of stopping halfway.

She slid the needle into her arm in the crook of her elbow, then she depressed the plunger like the nurse had shown her, years ago. Though she could've stolen this stuff if she needed to, the med center handed it to her. They asked if she felt pain. She said yes. They handed her a fresh bottle and needle pack. She thanked them.

Problem solved.

Fuzziness blurred her vision. She removed the needle and set it aside before the full effects hit. No sense risking the main vial. That would make them ask real questions. A broken needle didn't matter, but needing a new syringe meant a visit with Doc. She didn't like visiting Doc when she didn't have a physical injury. He asked about things she didn't want to discuss.

As she closed her eyes to lie down, she felt a vision crawling through her head. Her sight blurred further and she saw amorphous blobs dancing with hazy lights. The curse of her lineage urged her to her feet. She shuffled out of her room and gained speed with every moment.

Nothing mattered except getting to where the power wanted her to go. Until she reached that spot, it wouldn't leave her alone. She loped out of the barracks, not sure which way she headed. The lights blurred, the signs blurred. Everything blurred. Without the unerring guidance of her power, she would've run in circles.

Panting for breath, she flinched at a distant boom. The lights disappeared. A building loomed ahead, its dark shape huge and hulking. She ran into the door with a thud and bounced to the ground. Obeying her power, she scrambled to her feet and left the door behind. It took her to the nearest window and made her thump her fist against it.

The window flipped open. She fell through and landed in a heap. Nothing hurt. Everything felt good. Cool marble on her bare skin gave her goosebumps, and she liked that.

"Who's there?" a man called out.

Vivian giggled at the unknown person. He wasn't Aaron. Other than that, she had no idea.

Someone crouched beside her, shining a flashlight over her body. "Ma'am? Are you…okay?"

She saw an explosion ripping their bodies apart. Still grinning, she rolled to her hands and knees, then tried to stand. Her body refused to obey her, instead dropping her on the floor again.

This guy needed to get them elsewhere. Now. "Take me to your room," she purred at him.

"I think maybe Medical is a better choice."

"Whatever floats your boat, sailor. Just hurry."

He helped her stand. Her legs didn't want to hold her. The guy scooped her up. She wrapped her arms around his neck. Another giggle slipped out of her mouth. He took her through a door.

An explosion rent the air and knocked them forward. Vivian lay on the floor, noticing a strange sensation in her arm. She raised it and discovered a thick shard of glass, at least two inches long, sticking out of her flesh. Blood oozed around it.

Her new friend coughed and rose to his hands and knees. "Jesus. What the hell?"

Vivian ignored him and crawled away, dragged by her power again. She stumbled through the building in a daze. Shouting and screaming came from every direction.

Warm hands grabbed her. "Vivian, what are you doing here?" Doc's warm voice made her squirm. She didn't want to have to explain anything to him. Not now, not ever.

He yanked the glass out of her arm and covered the bloody gash with his palm. Warmth flooded her.

"Doc! This way!"

The new voice sounded like Ben. Vivian didn't resist when Doc pulled her toward the voice. Ben would know what to do. He'd ask the right questions and she'd give him answers. They'd keep the team safe and finish the mission without going to Belém. Everyone had to stay away from Belém. Far, far away from it.

"Ben! We can't go to Belém! You have to tell Marks he's a fucking moron. We can't go there."

"What's she talking about?" Ben asked.

They reached Ben. Vivian clamped a hand around his arm. He seemed short. She looked down, but couldn't tell if she stood on a box. The ground swam, blurry and sharp at the same time.

"We have to get to the extraction point," she told him.

"I think she's drunk," Doc said.

"I'm not drunk!" She wondered why Doc had come to

Brazil, but didn't have time to worry about it. Maybe Marks had sent him to help them with Belém, because that asshole couldn't take no for an answer.

"In here!"

They followed Cap into a room filled with desks. Other people followed them. Cap raised his hand and used his power to shove all the desks to the walls.

"Nice tits," a man said in a Southern drawl.

"This is hardly the time, young man," Doc said.

"Guys," Cap said, "shut and barricade the door."

Vivian squinted, trying to see anything. "Where's Crash?" She saw a flash of lightning. "Everybody duck in three, two, one, down!" She threw herself to the floor and dragged Doc with her.

Light brighter than the sun flared. The windows exploded.

"You wanna see some light?" a boy screamed. "I'll show you some fucking light!"

"They're coming," Vivian said. She didn't know who or what would come through that hole, but she pointed for Cap so he knew.

"Cowboy! Block that space!"

"Cover your eyes!" the boy shouted.

Vivian saw a figure step into the hole where the windows had been and take hold of the edges. Crash had come to keep the bad guys from reaching them. She just heard Cap wrong. DPS stood behind Crash and stuck his hands through the gaps on either side. Brilliant, blazing fire, whiter and hotter than anything DPS had ever used before, exploded from his hands.

"The room two floors directly below us doesn't have windows," Vivian said, without knowing how she knew. That happened so often she didn't notice anymore. "It's safe for now, and it's big."

"Yes," Cap said, "the basement training room, good thinking. Phyllicia, contact Beth. Get her here, now."

The names confused Vivian, but she stuck close to Cap

anyway.

Someone outside cackled with a high, screechy voice.

A woman with blonde hair appeared in front of Cap and Vivian. Cap always knew everybody. Vivian had no idea what the other Novas could do, but Cap remembered their names, powers, and everything else.

"Beth, good," Cap said. "Work with Phyllicia to get as many people as you can into the basement training room. Start with Doc. Take care of any injured Beth brings, Doc!"

Cap always had good plans and ideas. He kept his cool no matter what. Vivian leaned against the wall, wishing she had her mic and earbud.

Fire blanked her sight as a vision sank its hooks into her and refused to let go. She knew nothing but the vision. Crash and Maverick sailed through the air together. Cap stood in a curtain of shimmering flames with his back to her. Springfire couldn't run. DPS fell to his knees and stared at his hands. Flames enveloped Crash, burning her faster than she could regenerate. Everyone wore strange black suits, tight on their bodies like diving gear.

Vivian gasped for breath as the vision withdrew. She hadn't had one that short-circuited all her senses in a while. Maybe the baby had caused all this. Covering her belly with one hand, she wondered if she'd killed everyone by making a mistake with Aaron.

In front of her, Crash punched someone. DPS held his head behind her. Springfire stood with Cap, her fingers at her temples. Cap held out his hands, concentrating on using his power.

She wanted to say something, but didn't know how to prevent any of what she'd just seen. Nothing showed cause and effect in the vision. Without that chain, she had nothing to offer.

Lightning crossed her sight.

"Everyone duck in three, two, one, now!" She dropped to the floor and covered her head.

The floor rocked beneath her feet. Light flashed. The

boy in the room screamed his defiance. Someone else screamed in pain in the distance.

Somewhere nearby, a woman shouted in Mandarin, "Get back! They're coming down the stairs!"

Vivian had no idea why they'd brought a boy to this fight. She giggled at the idea that he could save them all.

"Crash," Vivian shouted, "jump for the flier—"

"Are you fucking insane, lambchop?" that Southern man asked.

"Do it!" Vivian screamed. She didn't know why he cared, but she did know Crash could handle the flier as he swooped past. "In three, two, one, now!"

Crash hesitated, then she jumped through the hole. DPS sat beside the hole, hugging himself.

Vivian tugged on Cap's shirt. "Cap, get DPS to stop dancing with the fire. We need him to blast someone in about a minute."

Cap scanned the room. "Lightsaber, I need you on your feet. Cowboy's gonna be fine. We're all going to be fine. This is the kind of thing we're training for, right? If you choke now, how are you ever gonna get past that so you don't choke in the field?"

"I think I killed somebody," the boy whimpered.

"Fuck. Aunt Vivian, can you get us out of this room? We need an exit."

Vivian stared at Cap, wishing her ears would stop playing tricks on her. She felt like the future blended with the present. Would she someday work with Cap's son instead of Cap? How did that even work? Cap was only a few years older than her. She didn't want to keep doing this forever.

She turned to DPS and screamed at him. "Matias! Blast out the fucking hole! Do it now or we all die!"

The kid, tears streaming down his cheeks, screamed back at her in wordless agony while he turned and flung beams of pure white fire through the hole.

"Sweep the desks out through the hole, Cap. Let's get out of here."

# CHAPTER 11

## MAVERICK / CHARLENE ALDRIDGE

November 22, 2007
02:22

The whole base was one giant clusterfuck. Crash and DPS had left Maverick in charge of raising the alarm so they could try to find out what the fuck all the hooharaw at the Academy meant. Someone gave her a radio, and she worked as a spotter for the firefighting crew.

She had her back turned to the Academy when she thought she saw a flash of light. By the time she spun in the air, the light had faded and she saw nothing. The eerie, unnatural darkness reminded her of stolen moments in her childhood.

Little Charlene, cranky from molting, tried to sneak out and raise some hell. Momma didn't sleep much, and had caught her and made her sit on the screened porch in the dark. Their three-story home in Nofuckingwhere, South Carolina had a creek in the back with woodlands that stretched forever. Momma rocked her in a creaky old chair some long-dead ancestor had made by hand from trees he felled with his own axe. Or something like that.

She remembered the sky being so full of stars she couldn't imagine how it held so many. Dark and light at the same time. Momma told her stories about alligators and june bugs, about good times before her daddy fled, about running through fields in the sunshine and loving life.

And then they cried together about her little sister. Annabelle had survived long enough to love. Charlie had stared for a long time at the baby in the NICU with the beak and three-fingered hands. That part hadn't been the problem. Their little chickadee's organs had been all twisted up in her little body. She'd lasted longer than anyone thought, which had been both a blessing and a curse.

Another bright flash jolted Charlie from her memories. She caught sight of sideways lightning hitting the Academy building. That didn't make any sense, though. Whatshisname, some bravo Nova she'd slept with once, could shoot lightning like Matias could shoot fire, but neither man had reason to a blast the Academy in the middle of the night.

Unless this whole power outage thing had been a precursor for an attack. They hadn't seen anything to suggest an imminent assault on the base. Had they missed something? Vivian's news had surely thrown Charlie for a loop. Risa, though, hadn't seemed so shocked, and that woman could find needles in stacks of needles. If Risa hadn't discovered it, probably none of them could.

She raised the radio to her mouth. "Rescue Central, this is Maverick. I'm heading to the Academy. I think we might need rescue personnel over there soon, but I'm not sure what's going on. It looks like a combat, so approach with caution."

"Roger that, Maverick. Thanks for the help, and good hunting."

She tucked the radio in her pocket, thankful she'd taken a minute to change into her BDUs before running to help with the chaos. As she arced to approach the Academy, she saw another bolt of lightning hit the building.

Her birdlike eyes accepted the flash without blinding and she caught sight of Crash on the ground, trading blows with two women. White light in a thick beam, coming from inside the building, burned through a man's chest. A young man flung the broken body of an older man aside and kicked him, then turned and ran for the building. A bunch more people she couldn't identify scrapped against other people she couldn't identify. Among them, a handful of unmoving bodies littered the ground.

The light faded. Gunshots barked in the darkness. Charlie wished she had her gun. She had no idea how she'd choose targets, though. Was the young man an Academy kid or an attacker? She didn't know all the Novas on sight, let alone all the kids in training. Nobody had neon signs over their heads to identify them as friend or foe.

As she streaked past the mess, she noted a handful of people fighting on the roof. One fell. Maverick didn't know whether to save them or not. She swooped in, figuring she could find out before they splattered. Her arms closed around the body of a man who looked up, grinned, and pointed a gun under her chin.

She twisted in a spiral dive and threw him at the ground. While she recovered, another body fell off the roof. They hit the ground with a wet crunch before Maverick could reach them. The man she'd rescued sat up where he'd landed and fired his gun at her.

"Cap, I need backup!" Then she remembered she didn't have her mic or earbud, and neither did Cap. No one did.

Maverick flapped to gain altitude. She headed toward the building, hoping she could stop that part of the fight. Streaking toward it, she recognized Greg hiding behind the small block housing the stairwell.

Only danger could've brought her boyfriend to the roof at a time like this. His power had nothing to do with combat, and he had no fight training. The man could read books by touching them, and that was it. That meant the enemy had breached the Academy and he hadn't had anywhere else to go.

She landed beside him and her heart ached for how much fear she saw in his eyes. Wrapping her arms around him, she wanted to stay there and help him calm down. Neither of them could afford that.

"Hold on, sugar."

Her grip on him tight, she lifted him off the ground and ran for the edge of the building. The extra weight meant she needed more than a little jump to get altitude.

"Charlie," Greg whimpered.

She jumped off the building and pumped her wings to slow their descent. Her arc carried them away from the madness. Ben's old Firebird sat in the road far enough away to seem safe. That meant she could find Cap if she looked for him. He'd know what to do. He always did.

Touching the ground behind the car, she kissed Greg. "Stay out of sight."

"You can't go back into that." He clutched her arm.

She smirked. "Honey, this is my job. I do it all the time. I'll be fine. You just keep your pretty self behind this car, and you should be fine. I don't know what I'd do if you got hurt."

"Right." He let go and brushed her cheek. "Of course. I'll….I'll stay here. Be careful. Come back."

"I will, sugar. I always do." She pecked his cheek and leaped into the air. With that worry out of her mind, she gained altitude and soared over the battle, looking for ways to help.

Everywhere she looked, she saw signs of active powers. Small explosions poofed in and out of existence. Tentacles waved. Rocks and other debris shot through the air. Someone smashed through a wall of ice. Tiny things darted across the ground like schools of fish. Folks stronger and tougher than Crash pummeled each other.

A curtain of fire sprang out of the ground. Maverick knew Matias's flames anywhere. She headed for him, hoping he knew where to find Cap. The moment she landed beside him, Springfire appeared on his other side.

"Have you seen Ben?" Springfire asked, panting like a

wild thing and staring at the flames with her eyes wide.

"No," DPS said. He had that faraway, glazed look, like the fire had his attention more than the people around him.

"Me neither," Maverick said. "Breathe, honey. You're gonna pass out if you don't calm down."

Springfire laid her hands on her cheeks and took a deep breath. "I think the leader of all this mess is in the watchtower. We need Ben for a plan of attack."

"It's okay," Maverick said. "We got this. We're gonna be fine. Keep moving toward that tower, and we'll get there. I'm sure he's got his eyes on the prize."

"I'm just worried about Jay. I haven't seen him anywhere, and I have seen some of the kids on the field out here. They're fighting. They're not supposed to be fighting. They're just kids."

"Honey, you can't stop them from defending their home. You go on and scour that building from top to bottom, and you find your boy." Maverick smacked DPS in the back of the head.

DPS blinked and looked around, acting unaware he'd been hit. "Yeah." His fire faltered for a moment, letting them see the three people on the other side, trying to break through.

Springfire nodded and disappeared. Maverick squeezed DPS's shoulder and leaped into the air. DPS hadn't heard a word they said, which meant no one but Springfire and Maverick knew about the leader in the tower. Springfire had other things on her mind. She'd find Ben eventually. By then, the leader might move elsewhere, or have enough time to get more defenses set in their perch.

Maverick angled toward the watchtower. Someone had to get there and cut off the head of this assault. She circled it at a distance, hoping no one inside would notice her.

Like the rest of the base, the tower had no power, which meant no lights. She tightened her arc, moving closer and closer, trying see more detail in the darkness. Her eyes could see better than a normal human in darkness, but not as well as a true raptor.

Something hit her from above, landing a solid weight on her back. She spun, hoping to shake it off.

They squawked in surprise. Arms and legs clamped around her. "Buck all you like, little birdie bronco," the man said with a thick accent.

Maverick knew that accent. Those Brazilian mercenaries had used it.

She struggled against the man's arms, prying them open. Ducking her head, she rolled into a mid-air somersault. He flailed and let go. But he didn't fall. The man could fly, which explained how he took her by surprise in the first place.

On a mission, Omen would've warned her.

Cap was right. They'd gotten lazy.

Keeping him in front of her, Maverick surged at her attacker. They threw punches and kicks. He swung at her wing. She kneed him between the legs. He groaned and curled into a ball. She grabbed him by the shirt and threw him at the ground.

Free of distraction, she aimed for the tower. They expected her, and she didn't want to disappoint her hosts.

Sparks flew through the air toward her. She rolled to the side and avoided it. Twenty feet behind her, something exploded. The force of the burst knocked her forward and lower. Pumping her wings, she recovered in time to dodge a second flying explosive. The blast flung her at the tower.

She landed with her fist aimed at a man holding a rocket launcher. The launcher fired another explosive. Fire shot up the side of the tower. The third projectile exploded.

Intense heat seared Maverick's right side. Agony so complete it crossed over the line to numbness engulfed her. Flames billowed everywhere. The shooter screamed as his flesh caught.

Maverick stumbled and fell off the platform. She couldn't tell up from down and crashed into the ground. Bones crunched.

"Fuck!" DPS said, his voice close and distant at the same time. "Maverick! Fuck!"

She felt everything and nothing. Knives covered with acid sawed through her flesh in a bizarre pattern. Other parts stayed numb. Her right wing seemed empty, hollow. The left one hurt. She couldn't turn her head. Something warm slid across her cheek. Feet ran to her. Fire burned.

DPS crouched beside her and reached close without touching her. "Maverick, stay awake! Don't you die on me."

"I won't breathe on you," she mumbled. "I promise." The pain kept her still. She wanted to sit up and see, but couldn't.

"I didn't see you." DPS brushed hair out of her face. "I didn't see you there. It was dark and I just didn't see you." He straightened. "Springfire, Maverick needs Doc!"

"The bad guy is up there," Maverick said.

"We'll get him. Springfire found Cap and Crash. They're getting him. Fuck."

"Tell Greg…" She didn't know what to say. Thinking around the agony took too much effort.

"Keep your eyes open and you can tell him yourself."

"I lied to him. I said I'd come back."

"You will. I promise."

The ground rumbled. Glass and metal crashed nearby. Fire burned everywhere. Maverick couldn't keep her eyes open anymore.

# CHAPTER 12

## BEN

November 22, 2007
03:15

Ben needed backup. He hurried down a set of metal stairs to the Academy's second floor, having found resistance in the form of a pair of enemy supers on the third. By himself, he needed more than his power and his wits to take them. If he could find Crash, he could hold the whole damned building.

If he had his team, this wouldn't even be a problem.

So far, he hadn't run across any kids. Maybe they'd all jumped out of bed and run for…a shelter he didn't know existed? He'd helped build this fucking place. It didn't have rooms he didn't know about.

"Ben!"

He spun on his heel to see Colonel Marks, gun out and still in his uniform. Smears of soot and blood marred his otherwise pressed and polished appearance. Seeing him didn't bring any sense of relief.

"There are hostiles one floor up. I can't find any kids and my team is scattered. No comms."

"Great. Do they have disaster drills here?"

Something smashed into the ceiling from above, hard

enough to crack the plaster and knock dust loose. Ben tugged on Marks, urging him down the stairs.

"I think I remember Jay mentioning it once." If he had to design a disaster drill for kids, Ben thought he'd send everyone outside. If outside couldn't happen, then he'd choose someplace built to withstand damage.

They reached the first floor and the stairs kept going down.

Someplace built to withstand damage, like the basement training rooms. He remembered them pouring a mountain of reinforced concrete and laying miles of steel to contain kids expressing extreme strength and gross kinetic abilities. Shock padding with a covering conferring an impressive amount of resistance to fire, acid, lightning, and other kinds of damage had been layered over every interior surface.

"This way." Ben kept Marks moving down the stairs, wondering why he hadn't seen any kids headed in this direction. They had other stairwells, but some kids must've taken this one.

They reached the basement in the central intersection. Wide corridors lined with industrial tile and white paint ran in all four directions.

"Dad! This way!"

Ben ran toward his son's voice, not caring how the kid knew to shout. Marks followed on his heels. They turned a corner and saw Jay at the mouth of the largest training room. Jay's face lit with relief.

The building rocked. Springfire appeared beside Ben and slowed to run with him. "I found you! Ben, I think the person leading this is in the main gate watchtower. There's someone up there. We need a plan." She stopped in front of Jay and hugged him. "Thank God you're okay."

"I'm fine, Mom. Everyone is inside, and we're about to lock the door. Aunt Vivian said to wait for Dad."

Vivian had come here. Of course she had. With Vivian taking care of them, they'd be fine. Ben patted Jay on the shoulder. "Good work. Marks, stay with the kids. Keep them safe."

Marks raised his brow, but he nodded.

Ben considered that ordering around his CO didn't help with what had happened earlier. But he had an idea for assaulting the tower, and needed someone he trusted watching his son. He hoped Marks understood.

"We need Doc in the field," Springfire said. "There are some horrifying injuries."

"Doc! Front and center! Omen! Double-time!" Ben turned to Springfire. "Get him out there, then come back for me. We have to get past the attackers inside the building."

Springfire blurred into the training room, then blurred back out.

Putting his hands on Jay's shoulders, Ben saw his son as the man he'd one day become—strong, capable, and a leader who did the right thing. The kid had a lot to learn, but he'd already figured out how to prioritize.

"Son, I want you to go back into that room with Colonel Marks and lock the door."

The building rocked again.

Jay blinked at him. "What about you, Dad?"

"I'm doing my job. Listen to Marks. Do what he says. Stay safe." He hugged his son, not certain he'd ever get another chance to do it. Whatever happened next, Jay would survive it. Ben couldn't say the same for himself.

"You too."

"Cap!" Vivian stepped into sight wearing her tac suit pants and knee pads with a black bra and combat boots. She had a dazed, dopey expression on her face like she'd drank herself stupid drunk. "You should stay in here. It's nice." Her words slurred together.

After not touching her beer at the bar the other night, and revealing her pregnancy, she'd slammed down three or more in private? Ben didn't have time for this.

Marks gave him another look like they'd discuss this later.

"Never mind, Vivian. Jay, watch over her."

"She keeps calling me Ben," Jay muttered, "so yeah, she's kind of confused."

Ben shooed them into the training room. "Don't open this door until Vivian says it's safe." He watched his son nod. The building rocked again as the door slammed shut. The final clang sounded like a death sentence.

Shaking off that thought, Ben turned and jogged back the way he'd come. At the corner, he heard a crash and the squeal of twisting metal. He peeked around and saw a hulking brute of a man brushing debris off his broad shoulders. Dust filled the air. Instead of a doorway with a door for the stairwell, he saw a jagged hole in the wall.

The door to the training room should hold against him, even if he had twenty times the normal human's strength. Ben, on the other hand, wouldn't. He could manipulate a piece of debris, but without Omen's mark, he doubted he'd hit anything vital enough to hurt the man.

Springfire appeared beside him, her timing perfect. Without words, she stepped behind him, braced his head, and ran. He squeezed his eyes shut and snapped his mouth closed. When she stopped, he stumbled to one knee and opened his eyes.

Fire raged everywhere. The watchtower had fallen over. A man inside the booth struggled to escape through a broken window frame. Ben recognized the dome of flames to one side as DPS's handiwork. Kitty lay on the ground nearby, her body twisted and broken. More bodies of strangers littered the area.

He had to get a grip. Everyone needed him to take control and keep it. He pointed at the tower.

"Springfire, get that person, whoever they are. DPS! Stop the fire. Anyone else who can hear me, sound off!"

Springfire blurred. He trusted her to get that job done. No one else responded to him.

"Matias!" He screamed the name as loud as he could, knowing he had to punch through the fire to reach him.

The fire receded. DPS knelt beside a body with his head in his hands. Identifying the body took too long. One feathered wing, folded at an odd angle, lay splayed behind her. Charred feathers surrounded her. Blackened sticks sprouted from her back where the second wing should've been. Her BDU pants had melted into the flesh of her right leg.

Ben stood and rushed to Maverick's side.

"She's dead," DPS sputtered around sobs. "It's my fault."

Unwilling to believe that, Ben checked under Maverick's chin. She still breathed and she still had a weak pulse. "She's not dead, but she will be soon. Find Doc. He's out here someplace. He can save her."

DPS snapped to his feet and ran toward the building.

An explosion lit up the grounds near the Academy.

Springfire forced an old man to his knees near Ben. He wore a Nazi uniform. A bloody shard of glass stuck out of his chest, promising he wouldn't live much longer. Cuts and bruises marred his face and hands. Ben recognized him from the photographs anyway.

"Wilhelm Otto?"

The man grinned. He tried to laugh and coughed blood. "Für meinen Sohn," he said. He tried to raise his arm and instead crumpled to the ground.

Ben stared at Wilhelm, not interested in trying to save him. He didn't understand what had happened here. For his son? What son? Why attack the Academy for—

He remembered the picture at the end. A man and his son. The dead man in the lab had been Wilhelm's son, not his father.

He remembered the superpowered people they'd fought yesterday, and the hideous monsters at the first site. They'd succeeded with a super serum, enabling them to create all the people who'd attacked tonight.

He remembered that they'd gotten the intel about the Cairari site from an anonymous source. The encrypted data they'd found had led them to the second site. Addresses at the second site would've taken them to two more locations, which might've kept them in Brazil for two more days, or longer. Without Omen warning them away from Belém, they wouldn't have been at the base tonight.

They'd failed. In every way, they'd failed to put things together fast enough to prevent, or at least anticipate, this. His team's failure had put all those kids at risk, gotten people hurt and killed, and caused fires across the base. They'd crippled the entire battalion out of carelessness and stupidity.

Someone groaned. Ben turned and saw Springfire and DPS helping Doc reach Maverick. Doc looked like hell. His left side didn't move right and he couldn't sit up. Burn blisters decorated his flesh in random patches and mud or ash smeared what remained of his clothes. Despite that, he touched Maverick and groaned again.

Ben's order had brought Doc away from safety. When Risa had asked for Doc, he should've seen it as a request from his subordinate, not a plea from his wife. He knew better than to risk the medic.

Greg Boone found them. He knelt beside Maverick and wept over her, holding her unburnt hand. When he saw the old Nazi, he screamed at the body, kicked it, and shook it as if that would do any good. A book fell from the old man's jacket.

Ben turned away and stumbled toward the building. Doc couldn't heal Maverick's wing, only her bones and internal injuries.

The next few hours passed in a blur.

Cleanup would take weeks. Ben leaned against the wall of the Academy building in the orange glow of dawn, unable to look away from the blood-stained tarp covering Louisa Kilkenny's body. She'd fallen off the building in some kind of struggle. The impact had shattered too many bones in her body, and she'd bled to death within minutes.

Someone would collect her when they had a chance. He'd just finished helping police the wounded and dead, and trying to sort the enemies from their own people. They'd get their prisoners—a few, anyway. He wasn't going to shed any tears for prioritizing Academy staff. He did put a couple of the attackers out of their misery. Out of everyone's misery. After this, he could live with a few more field executions.

"Captain Tsukuda," Colonel Marks said. He sounded tired. Ben hadn't heard him approach. "I've just gotten off the phone with the Pentagon."

"And?"

"And they aren't happy with how this went down."

"Who the fuck would be?"

Marks sighed. "I tried to take responsibility."

Ben knew what came next. So much for his rank commission. If he worked his ass off, he could get it back. One fuckup didn't have to tank his whole career. "But they didn't let you."

"No. The President was briefed. He feels this falls on your shoulders. I think his Generals probably brought up the insubordination horseshit about Belém. The official report will take some time, but I've been ordered to remove you and your team from active duty, relieve you of your command, and advise you that things will be much better for all of you if you choose to retire now instead of waiting for disciplinary action."

Retire. They wanted him to retire. After countless successful missions, he'd expected to do this job a lot longer. In the face of such a gross failure, he couldn't find any arguments against firing him. The rest of the team, though, didn't deserve it.

He raised his hand in a salute. "I take full and final responsibility for this, sir. I'll begin the paperwork immediately." Letting his salute falter, he continued, "This isn't anyone else's fault. I can't let the rest of the team take the fall for this. I'll disappear from the world if that's what they want, but there has to be a way to let the rest of the team make their own decisions."

"Maverick is done. Omen is pregnant. Springfire is your wife. DPS almost killed Maverick." Marks sighed again.

"There's nothing I can do, Ben. My hands are tied."

He knew too many names to add to that list, of people who'd died or been injured beyond Doc's ability to heal, including Doc. "Crash, then. At least she should have the choice."

"I agree with you on her count, and told them as much. Her service record and lack of anything against her on those two missions should keep her in good stead. I'll mention it again when I have a chance. That's the best I can do. The Pentagon is looking to the future now."

Marks nodded to a group of kids with blankets draped over their shoulders. Several stared into space, their faces blank from the shock of what they'd been through or the horrors of what they'd seen.

Ben had done that to them. He nodded and groped for words to express his shame. "May Ichiro fulfill the role of Captain Kinetic better than his father."

Happy fucking Thanksgiving.

# CHAPTER 13

## BEN

November 17, 2017
06:00

The alarm buzzed, insistent and annoying as fuck. Ben tapped it, flipped the covers aside, and set his feet on the floor. Their dog, a shaggy mutt named Ell who slept at the foot of their bed, jumped for the door. Ben shambled to the master bathroom while Risa let Ell out. By the time he finished showering, the aroma of fresh-brewed coffee filled the house.

In the closet, his slacks hung below his suit jackets and shirts, arranged by color. Risa used a more arcane, less obvious method of clothing arrangement on her side. So long as his suits wound up in order, he didn't care.

He picked his usual Friday suit and tie. Dressing in the doorway, he used his power to make the bed. As he tied a Windsor knot, he flung a quarter at the bed. It bounced. Good.

Risa dressed for her day in black and pink spandex with a matching sweatshirt, her dark hair pulled into a ponytail. She planted a quick kiss on his lips when he reached the kitchen with his jacket over his arm. He licked chocolate and coconut from her breakfast off his mouth. The rice-based concoction had too much sugar for him, but he didn't mind a little taste.

"We should do something tonight," he said as he poured coffee into his plastic travel mug.

Ell crunched kibble in her bowl.

"Something like what?" She tucked a brown paper bag into his leather pack and zipped it shut.

"Whatever will get me out of whatever stupid social thing the guys at work want to do."

Risa laughed. He smiled at her. She kissed him on the cheek.

"Say you're going camping," she said with a coy bat of her eyes.

"In November?"

Grinning, she handed him his pack and his usual plain bagel with cream cheese. "I'll bring down a blanket. We'll 'camp' on the couch. Get naked. Watch movies. Eat popcorn. Maybe not in that order."

He chuckled. "I like that order the way it is. Don't let the teenagers run you ragged." The urge to take her in his arms and kiss her properly threatened to make him late for work.

"I'll make sure I'm up for a good workout tonight."

He patted her ass and stepped into his shoes, careful not to let the dog follow him into the garage. When he backed his silver box into the driveway, three other silver boxes slid out of their own garages. By the time he reached the street, another four had joined them.

Ben followed a car just like his to escape his Deer Park neighborhood. Every house and yard had the same tidy lawns, precise plantings, and dark trim. Without the numbers on the mailboxes he had no doubt he'd pick the wrong one and wonder why his garage door opener didn't work. Fucking HOA.

He remembered driving up this street for the first time and wanting to throw up. Kay had cried for two weeks. Risa...she'd gritted her teeth and done her best to make a home for them.

Traffic at its usual speed of ten to fifteen miles under the speed limit carried him along the roads to Interstate 71. As he finished his last bite of bagel, his phone rang through the car's handsfree system. He answered it without checking the caller ID.

"Hello?"

"Hi, Benjamin, it's Steve Hastert."

Ben scowled at the car in front of him. He could've glanced at the car's information screen and avoided this call. "What do you want?"

"Good morning to you too. It's time to schedule your annual inspection."

Their fucking government-appointed overseer checked on them once a year to make sure they hadn't done anything to call attention to themselves. As far as the American public knew, Captain Kinetic and his brilliant team had left public service with an impressive field record. No one knew about Ben's spectacular fuckup, Charlie's horrific injuries, or Vivian's pregnancy.

Everyone wanted things to stay that way, including Ben.

He took a deep breath to keep from snapping too much at Steve. Cogs in the bureaucracy didn't deserve his ire. He had no one else to direct it at, though. "We still live in Deer Park." Steve and his paperwork had forced them to relocate to their cookie-cutter, suburban hellhole outside Cincinnati, where they'd blend in and no one would notice them. Because its tiny Asian population concentrated on the other side of the city helped them blend so well.

"We haven't traveled anywhere but Guam and LA in ten years. Which you know, because we get detained by security every fucking time we fly." The longer he talked to Steve, the more surly he got, and he knew it. "I'm in my car, on my way to work at the job you got for me. Call Risa to schedule it."

"Fine. I'll see you soon." Steve hung up.

Ben glared at the traffic as it carried him to a place he hated even more than his house. At least his house had Risa. She didn't hate her job. Steve had gotten her a position at the high school, teaching gym class. Her work helped her miss Jay and Kay less.

Traffic ground to a standstill. Ben checked his phone for something to lift his mood and found a voicemail from a few days ago that he'd decided to save for posterity. He put it on speaker because the cars ahead of him moved again.

"Hi Dad." Jay's voice took a load off his shoulders. "I just wanted to tell you that I finally get why you don't like action movies. They're so full of shit. Characters are always so fucking stupid. I just wanted to tell you that. Tell Mom it's not looking good for Thanksgiving again, but I'm hoping I can get out to Guam for Christmas this year. And Phyllicia says hi. Talk to you later."

Nothing boosted his mood like hearing his son agree with him. Once he'd figured that out, he'd made a point to call his own father and agree with him about something at least once a month.

An hour after he left home, he slid his car into a space in the employee garage at the University of Cincinnati Medical Center. Once he reached the door, he looked back and had no idea which car belonged to him. Stupid silver boxes.

His Firebird sat in his father's garage. The car had been in pictures from that night at Area 51 that the Pentagon had released to the public. They'd carefully selected the shots taken by an on-base photographer that showed the least damage. No one needed to see anything more than necessary to approve funding for a new Academy site.

The base had been rebuilt without the Academy. Instead, they'd moved the kids to Cheyenne Mountain in Colorado. Twice, they'd allowed him and Risa to visit. The first time, they attended Jay's graduation. The second, they took Kay and helped her unpack for her first school year. Next June, they'd go for a third time, to watch Kay graduate.

Fluorescent lights buzzed in the insurance office at the hospital. He trudged to his cubicle. Co-workers greeted him. Ben forced himself to respond.

An uncomfortable plastic chair faced his computer at his desk. Binders full of regulations and procedures lined a shelf over his desk. Papers filled his inbox. Someone had emptied his outbox. His headset lay on the desk beside his phone. No photographs or other personal touches cluttered his workspace.

He sat and died inside. Again. Like he did every day, Monday through Friday. For the past ten years.

He'd resigned himself to this hell as a punishment he deserved.

Insurance paperwork filled his day. He transcribed data from patient forms to computer forms, made phone calls to verify information, and submitted claims. Steve couldn't have picked a more joyless or boring job if he'd tried.

For lunch, he retrieved the brown paper bag Risa had packed for him and ate his sandwich and fruit at his desk. His coworkers had long ago given up on asking him to eat with them. He knew, the moment he left the office, he'd have to struggle to not give the whole place two middle fingers and flee.

The hours trudged by like they always did.

"Hey, Ben," Dan from the next cubicle said.

Ben checked the clock on the wall—the official time in the office—to see it ticking past 3:30pm. Here came the invite.

"We're all going out for beers tonight. You want to come?"

He didn't hate any of his coworkers. They just reminded him of work. Bars reminded him of much better times with much better people, doing much better things. "My wife wants to go camping."

"You know, your wife is pretty demanding. She never lets you out to do stuff."

Without Risa by his side, Ben thought he might've shot himself after a few months of this torture. Maybe he would've lasted a year out of sheer stubbornness.

He shrugged. "I'm okay with her tying me up every weekend."

Dan stared at him for a beat. "Well, okay then." He disappeared behind the cubicle wall.

The last half hour of work dragged as much as the first had. For the five thousandth time, he considered calling someone else on the team. He just wanted to hear their voices, crack a few jokes, maybe share a beer and watch some soccer over a video conference. No contact, though. They'd all agreed to those terms. Fourteen years with Kele as his second and he couldn't even send her a fucking telegram anymore.

Ben finished everything he intended before the weekend and tidied his desk. The moment the wall clock reached 4pm, the entire office fled at once. He had to use the remote to find his car, then sit in the same terrible traffic as the morning commute.

He noticed Risa jogging with the dog as he turned down their street. Her ass, still tight and firm after all these years, distracted him enough that he had to focus to not swerve into a tree. If he did that, he'd have to force himself to pay money for another silver fucking box.

He pulled his car into the garage, slipped out of his shoes at the door, and left his bag on the hook above them. Using his power to undo the knot on his tie, he climbed the stairs and put away both it and his jacket. The idea of changing into sweats crossed his mind, but he heard the front door open and shut.

Risa told Ell he was a good boy. Ben needed to see her now. He hurried downstairs and found her in the kitchen, fetching a pitcher of her protein drink. Ell raised his head from his food bowl, yipped at Ben, then continued eating. Ben patted him on the back. Rescuing Ell from execution at a shelter had been the only good thing to come out of this damned place.

He slipped behind Risa and rested his hands on her hips while she poured a drink made from rice, mango, guava, and coconut into a glass. Getting between Risa and her food never turned out well.

"How was your day?' She asked as she raised the glass to her lips.

"Terrible." He kissed her neck and nibbled her ear. "Yours?"

She swallowed a gulp. "Same as always. Teenager drama."

Ben thought about bending her over the counter. No, the table. Better yet, the couch. Not until after she finished her drink, though. "What should we have for dinner?"

"Takeout."

"I like the way you think."

Risa grinned as she took another swig from her drink.

Ben's phone rang from his pocket. He fished it out and grimaced at the caller ID. Asshole Steve again.

For a moment, he considered throwing the phone across the room. Then he'd have to get a new phone, though, and Steve would just call Risa. Ben answered it and put the call on speaker. He set the phone on the counter so he could paw his wife.

"Now what? I told you to call Risa."

"We already scheduled that." For the first time, Steve sounded apologetic. The tone caught Ben off-guard. "This is about something else."

"Okay. What is it this time?"

"I…I hate making these calls." Steve sighed. "It's my unfortunate duty to inform you that Ichiro Jason Tsukuda… Jay was killed in action approximately two hours ago."

Everything stopped, including Ben's heart. Risa dropped her cup. Neither of them caught it. The cup sloshed thick, white liquid and hit the floor with a clunk. Ell yelped and whined. Solid plastic bounced and spilled Risa's drink everywhere.

Ben opened his mouth and some words fell out. "Are you sure?"

"Yes. I'm sorry. I don't have any details of the mission, just authorization to tell you it happened on one."

Risa gasped, trying to catch her breath.

Ben didn't know what to do. "Is Kyoko okay?" He didn't know why he asked. Of course she was fine. She wouldn't have been anywhere near the mission.

"She'll be informed shortly. They have people who handle things like this at the Academy. I really am sorry. He was a good man, and well-liked. This is a terrible blow to the Novas, losing an important, alpha-level Legacy. We'll postpone the inspection for a few weeks. In the meantime, someone will contact you as soon as the body is ready for transport. It shouldn't be more than a day or two."

Risa clung to his shirt, her eyes wide and unseeing, her breath ragged and uneven.

"Is the rest of his team okay?" The question made no sense. Ben had no operational authority, and no need to know anything about them. He didn't know why he asked.

"Another member of the team was also killed. Her family is next on my list. I don't know anything about injuries."

Jay's team had three women. Ben and Risa had met two of them. One had been Jay's best friend, the other a quiet sniper. He cringed as he asked a question he had no right to get answered. "It wasn't Phyllicia, was it?"

Steve paused. "It was. I've been directed to ask you not to contact her mother at this time."

"And there's no way this is a mistake," Risa said, her voice thin and breathy.

"I'm sorry. I wish it was. Call me when you're ready to tackle paperwork. Don't wait too long." Steve hung up.

# CHAPTER 14

## IARIESAH

November 17, 2017
19:20

For an hour, Risa cried in Ben's arms. He carried her to the couch and they sat together. Ell came and sat with them. When she ran out of tears, she stared at the mantle, where the boxed tank and Firebird models sat.

She remembered Jay as a little boy in the toy store, pointing to the box for the tank model and saying, "Daddy!" A nearby store employee had found it so cute.

"This is my fault," Ben said into the silence, his voice quiet and defeated. He'd shouldered the blame for everything since that night ten years ago. Sometimes, she appreciated that. Other times, like now, she wished he wouldn't.

"It's not," she whispered.

"I should've seen it." On his face, she saw how the old wound had ripped open. Never once had he cried about it, or done anything other than stare at walls.

The first summer after that night, she'd watched Ben and his father sitting together in the backyard of his parents' house in LA. Neither man had said a word, but they'd had an entire conversation anyway. Ben had walked away from his father exhausted and filled with even more shame than before.

"I failed everyone, especially Jay."

With her heart broken for her son, she had to hold her husband together. She touched his face and made him meet her gaze. "Ben, this isn't about the past. It's not about you. Someone killed our little boy."

He closed his eyes and shook his head. "This never would've happened—"

She laid a finger on his lips. "I lost him too. Kay lost her big brother. Phyllicia's mother lost her little girl. The rest of his team lost their friends."

Leaning forward, he touched his forehead to hers. "I have to know what happened."

"They won't tell us. You know that."

He kissed her and held her. She recognized his needy grasping for something to hold onto. He'd been this way after that night. He'd been this way after that worldless chat with his father. He'd been this way after Kay left for the Academy.

Ben needed to connect, to touch and feel, to love and be loved. If anything happened to her, she thought he might kill himself inside a month. Knowing that had made her take more care with herself.

On the couch, with the lights on and the dog lying on the floor, he made love to her. She convinced him to come upstairs to sleep in their bed.

In the middle of the night, she woke and had to feed herself. They'd skipped dinner, like morons. Her body wouldn't let her go that long without food. She vowed to make Ben eat in the morning and went back to bed.

She woke in bright sunshine to find Ben sitting up with his feet on the floor and his head in his hands. Ell sat with his head on Ben's knee.

"Answer, dammit," he grumbled.

"What?"

Ben turned and she saw he had his phone. "The Academy." He straightened. "Yes, hello. This is Benjamin Tsukuda, Kyoko's father. I'd like to speak— Yes, thank you. I'd like to—" He growled with frustration. "Shut up," he snapped. "I want to talk to my daughter. Put her on the fucking phone."

Risa couldn't decide whether to try to take the phone from him or not. Tears spilled down her cheeks because Jay would never see sunshine again. Kay would never plow into him again. He and Ben would never make another model together.

"What the fuck do you mean she's not available?" Ben shouted at the phone. "Her brother is dead and she can't talk to her father? No, I will not calm down! Put her on the fucking phone!"

Ell whined and slunk to the door.

Ben held the phone away from his face, shook it like he wanted to strangle it, and threw it at the wall with all the force he could muster. Before Risa could dart into its path to rescue it, he caught it with his power and deposited it on the nightstand.

Even in his worst moments, he still took care with his things.

Risa hugged herself. Ben took several deep breaths.

"They wouldn't let me talk to her. They said she couldn't come to the phone."

"Maybe I should try." Risa snatched a tissue from a box on her nightstand and wiped her nose.

"They said she'd call us later."

"Then we should wait."

"I don't want to wait. This isn't something I'm willing to wait for."

Risa imagined Kay sitting alone in her room, crying out her heart. If only she could be there for her daughter. She picked up her phone and called the Academy. As soon as the receptionist answered, she said, "I'd like to speak to Kyoko Tsukuda, please."

"I'm sorry, she's not available right now," the too-cheerful woman on the other end said. "May I take a message?"

She daubed under her nose with the tissue and willed herself to keep her grip. "If she can't come to the phone, then when can someone take her to the Denver airport? I'll get her tickets."

"Who is this?"

"Her mother, Iariesah Tsukuda."

"Ma'am, I'm very sorry for your loss, but this isn't something I can arrange. I'll have the right person call you as soon as possible to set that up."

"But I—" She stopped because the other woman hung up on her.

"These fuckers," Ben growled. He gathered her in his arms and let her cry again.

Risa thought about changing Jay's diapers, about his first steps, about his first taste of mashed rice. "Twenty-three," she sobbed. "He's only twenty-three."

"I know." He sighed and held her tight. "I need to let the dog out. I'll see if I can talk to anyone on base."

She nodded and let him go. For a few minutes, she sat with her hand over her mouth, trying to stop crying. Nothing would get done if she stayed in bed, though. Ell needed a walk, Risa needed a run, Ben needed food, the bathroom needed cleaning, the laundry needed washing, Ben's suits needed dry cleaning, the car needed an oil change.

The normality of all the items on her list gave her something to cling to. She slipped out of bed and pulled on spandex. Bathroom. Kitchen. Laundry. Jogging.

Ben sat on the couch with his phone while she soldiered through her day. On her way to the car with his dry cleaning, Risa overheard him speaking Japanese and knew he'd called his parents to tell them. Her grasp on the language gave her enough understanding to know he spoke with his mother.

A minute later, she sat in her SUV, a car bigger than she'd ever wanted, and stared at her phone. Her family needed to know too. Jay hadn't been to visit them since he graduated. First he had Ranger and Airborne training, then officer training. Then he'd gone into the field, and for some reason, they'd always put him on-call for Christmas. At least they'd seen him for two weeks last summer, in LA.

He'd sat in the backyard with his father and grandfather, drinking beer and enduring ribbing about finding a wife and having kids. He never did see Phyllicia as anything but his closest friend. Like Ben with Kele, or Matias with Charlie.

She tapped on her phone and made the call. Her mother answered. They cried together. Her parents had always expected to get the call about their daughter, not their grandson. The call lasted a long time, with them trading stories about Jay as a child and laughing.

When she hung up, feeling less awful for having shared with her mom, she took this week's suits to the dry cleaner and picked up last week's. Handling her usual Saturday shopping trips gave her more of an anchor to the present and sanity.

By the time she returned home, she felt ready to handle Ben's grief again. She away put the groceries, made him a meal, and shoved it under his nose. Comfort food—rice with chicken and vegetables—overcame his reluctance to eat. They ate together on the couch.

He'd mindlessly shoved four bites into his mouth when he said, "No one at the base will take my call."

Unwilling to remind him that he had no clout with anyone at Area 51, Risa sighed. "Steve said it might be a day or two before they call."

"It's been a day."

"But not two."

"Someone should've called us by now."

Arguing with Ben churned Risa's stomach. She set her fork in her bowl. "Someone did. His name is Steve."

He grumbled something under his breath and stuffed another bite in his mouth. "You need to eat."

"I'm fine."

"You're not fine." He raised his bowl to his mouth and shoveled in the rest of his meal.

She took a deep breath and reminded herself that she loved Ben and he needed to vent at someone. Her mother had listened to her, and now she'd listen to Ben. He'd held her, and now she'd hold him.

"You haven't worked out since Thursday."

He took his bowl and fork to the kitchen. "I'm still trying to get people on the phone."

"Go lift weights for a while. Maybe you'll think of another plan of attack. Exercise has always helped you think." She heard him run water in the sink, then open and close the dishwasher.

"You're right." He stood in the doorway and leaned against the frame with his arms crossed. "I just…want to do something."

"Exercising is doing something." She stood and carried her bowl to the kitchen. As she passed him, she kissed him on the cheek. "It's getting your heart pumping so you can think clearly."

Ben nodded and headed to the basement. Risa finished her food in the kitchen and loaded the dishwasher.

For the rest of the day, she forced herself to take on more and more mindless chores. The house had never been so clean. Sunday, she made Ben go for a walk with her and Ell. They saw a movie. At the end of the day, they sat on the couch, watching TV.

Risa flipped the channel when a program ended and they caught footage of soldiers removing two caskets from a plane. She saw her baby's name on the bottom of the screen and changed the channel before it could hit her.

Ben picked up the phone and dialed. "Hello, this is Ben Tsukuda." He sounded calmer than he'd been all day Saturday. "I'd like to talk to someone about claiming my son's body, please. Yes, I'll hold."

His words broke Risa's heart all over again. For a while, she'd convinced herself the phone call had never happened.

They hadn't seen Jay in a while, and hadn't expected to see him for at least another month, so nothing had really changed. Then they saw two caskets and Ben said the words out loud, and Risa had to cover her face.

"Thank you for speaking with me, sir. Yes, I understand it's a Sunday. I fail to see how that matters. Army doesn't take weekends off." Ben took a deep breath and let it out slowly. "What do you even need an autopsy for? Killed in action is killed in action. … That doesn't make any sense. … I should hope he's regarded as a hero. He died serving his country. Is there some question about that?"

Risa heard the tension in his voice. She laid her hand on his arm to help him let go of it.

"Fine, just tell me how long before we can claim him. … Then let us know. Please. We'd like to lay him to rest beside his grandfather as soon as possible. … Yes, sir. Thank you, sir."

Ben ended the call and hung his head. "They don't know when," he said.

She wrapped her arms around his shoulders and squeezed. It was all she could do.

# CHAPTER 15

## BEN

November 20, 2017
15:31

Monday morning, Ben tried to quit his job by phone. He didn't see the point anymore. His boss refused to accept anything more than a two-week leave of absence from her most reliable employee.

He sat on the couch with a framed photograph from last summer. Jay had been able to get two weeks of leave. Ben had been able to schedule his vacation for the same two weeks on short notice. They sat with Ben's father in lawn chairs, holding up beer bottles and smiling. Kay had taken the picture. In his phone, Ben had another picture, of Kay giving her brother a too-tight hug.

The base hadn't called back yet. Risa wanted to give them one more day before worrying. She thought they might've had trouble getting the required autopsy over the weekend. To Ben, this felt like stalling. He didn't know any reason they might stall, but he had that feeling in his gut.

His gut had once steered him wrong in a spectacular way, so he tried not to listen to it. Despite that, he opened the contacts on his phone and picked one.

Colonel Kevin Marks picked up on the second ring.

"Hi, Kevin. It's Ben." Though Ben and Risa had been told not to contact anyone who might connect them to the 11th Rangers, Ben had kept in touch with Marks. They talked once in a while. The last time had been March, when they'd chatted on Marks's birthday.

"Ben, damn. I saw the news. I'm sorry. Jay was a good man."

"Thanks. I'm hoping you can help me out with something."

"If I can, I will. You know that."

Thankful he'd made the call, Ben told him how he'd been treated over the phone. As he explained, he became more convinced he'd made the right choice in calling Kevin. "I don't know why, but I can't shake the feeling they're delaying. Would you check into it for us?"

"Of course. I may not be in the battalion anymore, but I still have my security clearance. I'll find out the holdup. I'm sure it's just a paperwork rigamarole."

"I hope so." Ben thanked him and hung up.

Risa returned from running with the dog. She'd also called into work, taking the week. As she pulled off Ell's leash, he barked his greeting, then he ran to Ben.

Ben pet the dog and tried to think of some other action he could take. Sitting and waiting when he had no clear end point bothered him too much. They still hadn't heard from Kay, which also bothered him. "Risa?"

She'd already disappeared into the kitchen for food. "Yes?"

"Do we have anyone in our address book who has a kid in Kay's class? I just had a thought that we could pass a message to her through them. Maybe she could get someone to drop information about Jay."

"I'll check."

Ben heard a drawer open and shut. Risa flipped through pages in a small book where they kept a hard copy of all their phone numbers in case of disaster. That EMP pulse incident had taught him a lot of lessons, some obvious and some not.

"Yes, there's one." She brought him the book. "It's for Kay's best friend's mom. That's the one she has the sleepover with every summer. Do you want me to call?"

"If you don't mind." Ben patted his lap. The dog jumped onto it. He half-listened to Risa on the phone.

"Hi, Priya, it's Risa Tsukuda, Kay's mom. Do you have a minute? … Thank you. I'm trying to get a hold of Kay, and the Academy isn't letting me talk to her. I was wondering if you'd heard from Alicia recently?" Her voice moved like she paced across the kitchen. "Would you mind calling her? I really need to talk to Kay about it. At the least, I want to make sure she knows she can talk to us about it, and if she doesn't want to, that she knows who else she can talk to about it. They were close, and I'm sure she's as upset as we are. … Thank you, Priya. I appreciate it."

She hung up the phone and came to sit with him, the cordless receiver still in her hand. "Priya said she'd call Alicia and at least find out how Kay is."

"She should've called by now."

"Maybe she's too upset."

Ben stopped petting the dog and let his hand rest on Ell's back. He draped his other arm around Risa's shoulders. "This seems so…"

"Unreal," Risa supplied. She leaned her head against him. "It doesn't feel like it really happened. I keep thinking he'll show up at the door to tell us it was all a big mix-up and he's fine."

"Yeah. That's exactly how it feels. Like they aren't releasing his body because there isn't one." Hope flickered inside him. Maybe they'd mixed up the tags, and some other family needed to mourn. He didn't wish this on anyone, but he didn't want it for himself either.

"We can't keep thinking this way," Risa whispered.

He brushed his thumb across her cheek and found it wet with tears. "I know." The models on the mantle caught his eye, as they often did. Twenty years ago on Christmas morning, he'd removed the wrapping paper from a box that rattled too much for him to guess at its contents. Risa's jagged handwriting on the tag had set his expectations low. What would a three-year-old pick for him?

Then he'd opened the box and stared at it. For Jay's benefit, he'd acted pleased. The boy had to spend so much time with Ben's parents during missions that he'd never wanted to ruin even a single moment.

Risa pointed to the model. "Do you remember building that with him?"

"I remember trying to weasel out of it."

"I had to promise you a blow job to get you to sit with your son and build a plastic model with him."

He grinned. "Which I never collected."

"Because you enjoyed it too much to care." She kissed him.

The phone rang. Risa answered the call immediately.

"Hello? … Hi, Priya." Risa looked at the wall instead of him. He watched her listen. Her brow furrowed and she lost all traces of amusement. "That seems strange, doesn't it?"

Ben opened his mouth. Risa touched a finger to his lips.

"Are you sure? If they're—" Her mouth snapped shut and he saw a quirk of frustration in the set of her jaw. "Thank you for calling me back. I'm sure you're right and it's nothing." She hung up and slumped against Ben. "They wouldn't let her talk to Alicia either. Something about finals. She doesn't want to press."

"Finals? Right before Thanksgiving? We've always had to schedule the Christmas trip to Guam to avoid interfering with finals, and we've never left earlier than the twelfth of December." He frowned at the phone in her hand. "It can't be a coincidence that both the Rangers and the Academy are giving us the runaround."

"It can, but it's not likely." Risa sat up. "I'm going to check with some other people we know."

Ben's phone rang with Marks's number. He answered

while Risa stood and returned to the kitchen.

"Ben," Marks said, "something strange is going on. I didn't expect to get details of anything, but I thought I'd at least be able to find out where in the process the body is. With my clearance, I should have access to that. What I found are files I don't have access to."

His shoulders slumping, Ben sighed. "I appreciate you taking the time to try, Kevin."

"This is horseshit, Ben. I want to know why these files are classified higher than my clearance, because that's not how these things work. I wrote too many of this kind of file myself, and I know how they should work. I'm going to call a few people and see what I can find out."

Ben rubbed his eyes. "You don't have to do that. I don't want you to get into trouble for me."

Marks huffed as if Ben had offended him. "You and your family have given more than your fair share to this country. I don't care about what happened ten years ago. You deserve better than this. I'll let you know what I find."

"Thanks, Kevin."

Risa brought the phone and address book to the couch and dialed on speakerphone. She touched a finger to his lips again, letting him know she wanted him to listen, not talk. He nodded.

The phone rang. A man picked up and answered.

"Hello, Jack, this is Risa Tsukuda. Springfire."

"Dayumn, you're a blast from the past." Ben recognized the Alabama twang of a charlie-level Nova they'd bumped into on base all the time. "I'm so sorry about your son. I saw the piece about him on the Teevee."

"Thank you. I'm calling because I thought I remembered you having a son at the Academy a year or two behind our daughter?"

"That's right. He's fifteen now. Real ball o' energy, that kid."

"Have you spoken to him recently? We've been trying to get in touch with Kay, and they're not facilitating."

Jack paused for a few seconds. "I don't keep too close track of him while he's there. When he wants to talk, he calls. We sometimes go all the way to Christmas without talking to him. I mean, you know they don't much care for us calling out there all the time. It's distracting and all that."

Ben wanted to call Jack some uncharitable things. He clenched his jaws to keep his mouth shut.

"Yes, of course. I was just wondering if anyone else can reach their child, in the hopes someone can pass a message along to Kay."

"Ma'am, I'm real sorry about Ichiro, but I don't want to cause trouble for my boy. I lost friends ten years ago, and I'm not inclined to let that touch him, not even the slightest whiff. I hope you find some peace." He hung up.

Ben stared at the phone. "What the fuck does that even mean?"

"It means he has anger issues." Risa flipped through the address book. She tried another number. The woman who answered had nothing to do with the Rangers or the Academy, and had gotten the number recently. The next number had been disconnected. Another reached a pizza parlor.

"That's all I've got." Risa sighed, the sound thick with defeat. "I haven't kept up with enough people."

"We were given orders not to." Ben tapped on his phone to check the internet for a few names he knew. Of them, only one gave him useful results. They linked to a newspaper report. He scanned the article and didn't know how to react to it.

"Angela Nuñez died in a car accident in Tampa. Three years ago. She was a delta on Kitty's team. The paper reported that the accident happened on an interstate in the middle of the night with no known witnesses, and by the time responders arrived on the scene, her car was on fire. At the time of this article, they hadn't determined the cause of the accident or fire, but they did find and clean up an oil patch on the road with tire marks leading to her car."

Risa shook her head. "That's terrible. But it doesn't help."

Agreeing with her, Ben nodded. That meant the only other people they knew how to contact were the old team. Until they had a concrete reason to suspect something more than a hiccup or oddity, he didn't dare violate the requirement to not contact them. They did know someone else in their same position, though.

"Maybe," Ben murmured, "we should call Tanisha."

"That poor woman." Risa shook her head. "I should've thought of that. Why didn't I think of that?"

He kissed her forehead. "Because you lost your little boy, and Steve told us not to."

Risa nodded and dialed the phone. Though Ben didn't want to hear or participate in this conversation, he stayed still, supporting his wife.

Tanisha answered the phone, her voice flat and lifeless.

"Hi, Tanisha. It's Risa. Jay's mom."

"Oh my goodness," Tanisha said. Her words warbled like she hovered on the verge of crying. "They told me not to call you."

"They told us the same thing." Risa's breathing grew more forced. She dragged her sleeve under her nose.

Ben kissed the top of her head.

Tanisha sniffled. "I don't think I should talk to you."

"Please, Tanisha. You know Jay and Phyllicia would've wanted us to help each other. They're so close. I remember the first time we met Phyllicia."

"I appreciate that our children are best friends." Tanisha cleared her throat, and Ben thought he heard the swipe of a tissue against the phone. "Were best friends, I mean. I have nothing but nice things to say for what a gentleman Jay was when he visited those times during the summer, and all her letters said he was that way at school too. But I don't think it's wise to defy a direct request from the military."

"Have they called yet to arrange for her release?" Risa

sounded so desperate and heartbroken. Ben wanted to move her to his lap, but he'd have to unseat the dog, and that would make too much noise.

"No. I'm sure it's just because of the weekend."

"It's Monday afternoon. They haven't called us either, and I just—" Risa stopped herself and buried her face in Ben's chest.

"I'm not saying I won't keep calling every morning and trying to get through, I'm just saying that I don't think there's cause for panic. Goodbye, Risa."

"Goodbye, Tanisha," Ben said. He hung up the phone. They had nothing left to do but wait.

# CHAPTER 16

## IARIESAH

November 23, 2017
14:17

Between the waiting and refused phone calls, Risa had had enough. She and Ben booked a flight to Colorado Springs, put the dog in a kennel, rented a car, and drove to the Academy on Thanksgiving morning. The scenery of trees and majestic mountains passed by as Ben navigated the twisting, turning road. At this point, Risa had difficulty thinking about anything besides seeing Kay.

They reached the gate in the early afternoon. Every other time they'd come, the way had been open, leaving the track for the gate empty. Today, a wide concrete wall blocked their path. The guard booth, a bunker with a thick window and no access from the outside, held a soldier in uniform.

With a few dozen feet to gain enough speed, Risa could run up that wall and down the other side. She remembered the freedom to run at any speed on base. For ten years, she'd kept herself to normal human speeds. Ten years.

Ben stopped the car at a speaker with a camera. He slid down the window.

Through the speaker, they heard the soldier's voice,

crisp and clear. "This is a restricted area. Present your credentials or turn around and leave."

"Army Captain Benjamin Tsukuda with my wife, here to visit my daughter, Kyoko Lily Tsukuda."

"I'm sorry, sir. The Academy is not currently accepting visitors."

Risa took Ben's hand to keep him from doing anything regrettable. He'd been so quiet and grim for the trip, she worried he'd explode at the worst possible moment.

He squeezed her hand. "I don't give a fuck, Corporal. We're not leaving without seeing her. Open the fucking gate or we'll open it for you."

Risa had no idea how he'd seen the soldier's rank insignia. She couldn't tell from the car. He could've been anything as far as she could tell.

They waited for several long seconds, with the soldier blinking at them through his window. "I'll, um, call up to the office for you, sir."

"You do that."

"Ben," Risa whispered.

"It's fine," Ben murmured.

"What if they still say no?"

He shrugged. "We break in. We've gotten into places more secure than this."

Staring at him, she realized he grieved a great deal more than he showed. Risa knew that already, of course, but hadn't thought about what it meant. Recklessness didn't suit him. "With the whole team. Not by ourselves."

Ben squeezed her hand and shut off the car's engine. "They'll let us in."

Bluffing didn't suit him either. Risa opened her mouth to tell him he needed to relax or settle down, but stopped herself. She wanted to see Kay as much as he did. Her own thoughts had trended toward how to get inside before he'd said a word.

They waited. She considered what she'd do if she had to run inside. Ben wouldn't be able to communicate with her, so she'd have to come up with her own approach. Without a gun, and out of practice with hand-to-hand combat, she'd have to rely on her speed to drag the soldier out of his booth and disable any other guards.

Ben could get out of the car and use the button or key to open the gate by looking through the window. With his power, he could put guns in their hands, and they'd storm the underground facility.

Risa hadn't fired a gun in a long time. When they left the Novas, she'd handed her service pistol to Ben, and he'd locked it up and kept it safe for her. He visited a shooting range once a month. She never touched another gun. To stay sane, she'd needed all the trappings of their former life locked out of sight. His uniform, their BDUs, their military portraits—everything stayed in the attic.

"You've been cleared to enter, Captain. Proceed to the main parking area and wait for your escort."

The gate slid open in slow motion.

"See?" Ben started the engine.

Dispelling her thoughts of assaulting the place, Risa watched while the gate revealed a giant tunnel into the mountain. She'd never liked this place. It felt cramped and confining, and didn't suit the task of training children. Once, Cheyenne Mountain had been the backup command center for the Pentagon. A few years before the attack on the Academy, they'd moved to a decentralized strategy, which had left this facility empty.

By the time they'd decided to relocate the Academy for the safety of the students, she and Ben hadn't had enough clout to object to the number of bathrooms, let alone the location.

Harsh overhead lights glared at them as they drove through the tunnel. They reached a parking area and left the rental car among a scattering of military vehicles and black SUVs. The main lot at Area 51 had often held similar vehicles.

Risa carried a paper shopping bag with a surprise for

Kay. It was a holiday, after all. She wanted to give Kay something to help her work through her grief, and had come up blank in her rush to find something. Then she'd stumbled across the perfect thing.

Huge metal doors barred entry deeper into the complex. They swung open as Ben and Risa approached. The person who stepped through surprised Risa. Despite the order not to, she'd tried to keep track of everyone on the team. Only one had dropped off the face of the Earth.

Charlie smiled as she walked toward them. She wore a blue service uniform with a handful of the medals she'd earned in the field, and her black Nova beret. They'd made her a Major. The non-standard glove on her right hand probably concealed her burn scars. One wing full of feathers puffed to the left. On her right side, a fuzzy sleeve covered what must have been the remains of her other wing.

Risa hugged her. "What are you doing here?"

"I'm the military liaison for the Academy." Charlie shook hands with Ben. Her South Carolina drawl sounded like home, in a way. "Have been for about nine years."

The unspoken comment weighed between them—Charlie had needed a year to recover. Risa bore the blame for that. Even if everyone blamed Matias, Risa had been the one who told them about the man in the tower. If she'd just kept her mouth shut until she'd found Ben, everything would've turned out better.

Ten years ago today. Thanksgiving. It had all happened by this time on that day.

She and Ben woke up that afternoon and had to pack. Steve had entered their lives. Before nightfall, Ben had signed a contract that let him keep his rank and pension but forced him to submit to relocation and obscurity. The alternative had been rank stripping, a court-martial, and a likely dishonorable discharge. He'd sacrificed to save his family's reputation.

Risa hadn't bothered asking if she had an alternative to her own contract and pension.

"I'm glad you've had a better job than me," Ben said.

Risa nodded her agreement. At least Charlie had stayed with the project, even if she couldn't do the work anymore. "Why didn't we see you at Jay's graduation or when we brought Kay?"

Charlie gestured for them to follow her inside. "Don't you remember how scarce the military personnel were when you did Jay's intake? The only thing that's changed is we're in a bunker instead of on a base. So I disappear for the few days when students show up for the new school year. For Jay's graduation, I think that was the year I had the flu. Real disappointed I couldn't see that one. Watched on video."

"I'm so sorry we missed you," Risa said. "No one told us you were working here."

"I'm not surprised." Charlie led them down the tunnel to the administration center.

Through the doors, the scenery transformed. Warm yellow light filled the new tunnel. Sky blue paint on the walls and ceiling gave way to green paint on the floor. Raised planters made of concrete housed real flowers, shrubs, and small trees. A light breeze drifted through the tunnel.

The designers had done their best to mimic the outdoors. They'd taken that approach throughout the facility.

"I'm sorry about Jay. I liked him." Charlie smiled at Ben. "He reminded me of you. Good head on his shoulders. Only asked the important questions, never useless ones."

"Thank you," Risa said. "Do you know why we haven't been able to contact Kay?"

Charlie rolled her eyes. "I'm real sorry about that. Anytime we have operational Novas here for any reason, we have to put the facility on lockdown. They've been here longer than anyone expected, and it's really fucked up holiday plans for everyone. But we have rules, and they're there for a reason."

They reached at the old Academy front doors, preserved from the original building. The tunnel continued to the right and left with a gentle arc and downward slope.

From previous visits, Risa and Ben knew where to find Kay's room and the graduation theater. They, like all the other parents, hadn't been allowed to tour the whole facility.

"I've called Kay to come down to the office."

"Mom! Dad!"

Risa turned to see their seventeen-year-old daughter. Kay showed her Islander heritage more than Jay ever had. Her nose had the same lines at Ben's, and her hair had never taken on Risa's waves. Otherwise, she looked like Risa and her family. Kay blurred and appeared next to them in an eyeblink, just like Risa could. Ben wrapped his arms around both of them.

"They wouldn't let me call, and then Alicia couldn't call her mom, and I don't even understand what happened to Jay, and none of it makes any sense, and I wanna go home." By the end, Kay sobbed. "Daddy, why did he die? It's not fair!"

"Come see me before you go," Charlie said. She opened the doors and disappeared inside.

Kay's tears made Risa cry. Ben held them both. Their stalwart protector stood as a barrier between them and the rest of the world. He edged them toward a planter, where they sat on the edge.

"We're all very lucky to have had Jay in our family for as long as we did," Ben said.

Risa knew how much it cost him to say that for Kay's benefit. Last night, he'd broken the punching bag in the basement after four days of venting his frustration and grief on it.

She offered Kay the bag she'd carried through airport security. "This is for you, Kay. I didn't have a lot of time to look, because we don't usually do presents for Thanksgiving, but I thought you'd get plenty of food here. And if you didn't, we can smuggle you out to a restaurant of some kind."

Kay sniffled and wiped her face as she took the bag. The box inside made her furrow her brow. She pulled out a model kit for an Abrams tank.

Ben made a strangled noise in the back of his throat. He hadn't known what Risa brought in the bag.

"Mom, this is…"

"I made sure to get glue and a knife."

"I need a walk," Ben said. He stood abruptly and strode away from them.

Kay watched him go, then she burst into tears again.

Risa held her and stroked her hair.

# CHAPTER 17

## BEN

November 23, 2017
15:23

No one stopped him. Ben wandered down the tunnel to clear his head, habit keeping track of his path in the back of his head. He turned a corner, then another. Within a few minutes, he emerged into a wide room aglow with simulated sunshine and filled with competing food aromas. Coffee overpowered everything. People filled plastic chairs around plastic tables. To one side, a long buffet counter offered an array of options.

Ben imagined that Kay spent a lot of time in the cafeteria. Jay wouldn't have.

He scanned the room, wondering if anyone would tell him to leave. Then he wondered if anyone here knew Jay. He'd graduated long enough ago that he doubted any of the students would remember him. The seniors might.

One person surprised him. Then he noticed three more he didn't expect. Charlie had mentioned the facility's lockdown happened because of the presence of Novas, but not these particular ones.

The four remaining members of Jay's team lounged in a corner. Three of them clustered together, and the fourth sat one seat away, huddled over a mug.

Ben crossed the room to reach them. He recognized the sandy blonde curls and square jaw of Cowboy from the original Allied Novas. A white girl with a low-cut top and a blonde braid hung on his left arm while a Latino man in jeans and a t-shirt sat on his right. The one sitting apart, he'd met and recognized as their sniper and scout. She wore a trenchcoat and a ball cap.

Cowboy noticed him approaching and nudged his two pals. All three of them watched him with near-scowls. Ben didn't quite know how they felt. He'd been to funerals for fellow Novas and friends, but had never lost a member of his own team to anything other than retirement.

"Hello. I imagine you know who I am."

"Sure. You're the guy who fucked up at the Academy so we all had to come to this shithole," Cowboy said. He drawled like a Texan. Ben thought he remembered the original Cowboy coming from Oklahoma.

Raising his brow, Ben crossed his arms. "I'm also a Captain, and Jay's father."

Cowboy shrugged. "I don't give a shit about a rank they only let you keep because you walked away."

The woman on his arm smirked. The Latino leaned away from the conversation. The other woman hunched her shoulders more.

"You could have some respect for your fallen teammates."

"I could, but you know what they say. The nut don't fall far from the tree."

Ben clenched his fists to hold his temper in check. He could shove the chair aside, throw coffee in their faces, or do any number of other things to retaliate for such gross insubordination. Except he had no authority here. Maybe Cowboy had a lot of anger to work through. Ben knew he had a fair amount of his own anger to sort.

The other woman stood and took her mug as she walked away. Ben knew a losing battle when he saw one, leading him to abandon Cowboy in favor of the woman. He caught up and walked beside her, wondering why she wore BDUs with combat boots inside the Academy.

"It's Mandy, right?"

"Scope."

If she wanted people to call her by her code name, he had no reason to object. "Scope, then. I've been trying to find out what happened to Jay. No one will talk to me."

Scope shook her head. "I don't know anything."

Ben doubted that. He did, however, understand a security clearance. Scope had one and Ben didn't, and they both knew that.

"Can you at least tell me why you're all here? The lockdown made it so my daughter couldn't come home to mourn with us."

Scope stopped and sighed. "I'm sorry. I liked Jay. He was a good guy." She turned to leave him behind again, but stopped after only one step. "They made us come here for evaluation. Standard procedure when Novas die on mission. There's some holdup or something. It should've been finished by Monday."

She grimaced. "No one is happy about it. We're supposed to go on two weeks of leave as soon as the evals are done. We could've all been off for Thanksgiving for once. I could be birdwatching in Nebraska right now. At least that would've been a silver lining for this shit sandwich."

"Thank you." He offered his hand to shake with her. "If you ever need anything, I don't know what I can do, but I'll do whatever I can."

After a moment of regarding his hand, Scope shook it. She had a good, firm grip. "I'll remember that. Thanks."

Ben let her go. He sighed and wanted to hit something. Scope knew what had happened. With a name like that, she had to. The rest of the team knew too.

Only DPS had seen what happened to Maverick. Ben and everyone else on the team knew what had happened anyway.

He returned the way he'd come to find Kay and Risa still sitting on the planter. Kay had set the model kit aside. Seeing it this time, he didn't feel the irrational surge of grief he had before.

Part of him wanted to take the model and build it. The other part wanted to destroy it. He'd already warred with himself over the original tank on the mantle. At once, he wanted to hide it, smash it, and carry it with him. Every time he saw it, he remembered the time they'd spent together.

Until they'd sat with it, he'd been less than enthusiastic about Christmas, about fatherhood, about everything. Holding his son on his lap to build that model had changed how he felt about so many things. Then they finished it. Jay had been so proud and pleased. He'd beamed at Daddy, filling Ben with a kind of pride he'd never experienced before.

Sure, he'd held Risa's hand when she gave birth. He'd cradled a tiny baby, knowing responsibility for his wife and son rested on his shoulders. That experience had impressed upon him the gravity of his situation. Not until he'd done something so stupid as build a model of a tank with Jay on his lap had he grasped the rest of it.

That stupid model kit reminded him of all his failings as a man, as a father, as a husband, as a son, as an officer, as a leader. It reminded him of how he kept his mouth shut at work to avoid drawing attention to himself. It reminded him of how much he missed Kele, Matias, Charlie, and Vivian.

Ben rubbed his face. He had to live with all that. For Kay's and Risa's sake, he soldiered forward. Losing his son didn't mean also losing his wife and daughter, and he meant to keep things that way.

Someone hugged him. He let his arms fall to find Kay with her arms wrapped around him. Risa slipped the model kit back into its paper bag and set it aside.

"I love you, Daddy."

He hugged the little girl he'd shown how to clean a carburetor and tweak a transmission. Jay had never shown an interest in those things. Someday, he'd get the Firebird out of storage and work on it with Kay again. They'd wear coveralls and get their hands greasy, then smear the grease all over his parents' walls. Nothing about it would make them think of Jay.

"I love you too."

Over Kay's head, he caught Risa's eye. She smiled at him. He saw the tension in her shoulders and around her eyes. He'd leaned on her too much over the past week. She needed more time leaning on him.

"Do you want to see my room?" Kay looked up with a sad smile, her eyes red and her cheeks blotchy.

He managed a weak smile. "I don't know. Do I? Will I be able to see the floor?"

"Dad," Kay groaned. "It was never that bad."

"I seem to recall one time when the toy chest exploded."

Kay punched him in the arm. "That was because the hinge broke and you made me empty it so you could replace it."

"I remember that differently." He held out a hand for Risa. She picked up her bag and joined them. "Never mind, though. Show us around. But not too much. I don't want you to get into trouble."

With Kay as their escort, they visited her room. She had a small bedroom to herself, cluttered with pictures and odd mementoes. Kay didn't want to stay long—she dropped off the bag with the model kit, then took them to the cafeteria so Risa could eat. There, they found her friends. Alicia had stayed with them a few times over the various summers, so they already knew the Native American girl. The other two girls, Eilis, a redhead, and Jiao, a Chinese-American, both seemed nice.

Ben noted that, despite Kay's choices in friends, most of the room seemed white. Novas had always been majority white, but the room seemed less diverse than he remembered. The women chattered about boys and other things while Ben tuned them out and took a good look at all the Novas-in-training.

The oldest kids had a more diverse collection of skin tones than the younger kids. He saw several kids with Asian heritage among the older teens. Plenty had Latinx blood. As ever, black Novas remained rare. Looking at the much younger kids, though, he saw only white skin.

Even more curious, he thought he heard kids at a nearby table speaking a language similar to German. Dutch or Swedish, perhaps. As far as he could remember, the Academy hadn't offered Kay the chance to learn any new languages. But then, she already spoke Japanese and German. Maybe they just didn't put it into her personalized course suggestions.

He saw Charlie heading toward them and thought they might have overstayed their welcome. Now that he'd relaxed some, he noticed how she seemed stiff and walked with a slight limp.

"Ben, Risa. I'm really sorry, but Administrator Boone is a little upset with me for letting you in. He's willing to chat with you before you leave, but it's time to go."

The name Boone stuck in Ben's head. He recognized it, but couldn't place it, so he said nothing.

Kay pouted. "Ma'am, can't they stay for dinner?"

"I'm sorry, Kay. Rules are rules. We stick to them for reasons."

Ben had never heard anything more absurd come from Charlie's mouth. He stood, though. The burns had affected her, he supposed, in ways beyond the physical.

"We'll see you for Christmas," Risa said. She kissed Kay on the cheek and hugged her. "It was so nice to see you again, Alicia, and to meet you two." She clasped each girl's hand.

After one more hug with Kay and one more kiss on the top of her head, Ben took Risa's hand and followed Charlie out of the cafeteria. Seeing Kay had lifted one weight from his shoulders, but done nothing about the other.

Triggered by nothing he'd noticed, Ben recalled how he knew the administrator's name. "Charlie, isn't Boone the name of the guy you were dating all those years ago?"

"Yes." Charlie nodded. "That's him. Greg took over as provisional headmaster after Louisa died." Her covered wing twitched. "He did such a good job during that transition period that they promoted him to the position permanently. We're married now. We don't go in the field, and neither of us reports to the other, so it doesn't matter."

Ben couldn't tell for sure, but he thought Charlie meant that as a dig against him and Risa. She'd become so hard to read. "Are you part of the recruiting team for the Academy?"

"Why? Do you know a child with a power?"

"No, just curious what you do here. The old Academy didn't have a military liaison."

Charlie shrugged. "The old Academy lived on a military base. This one doesn't. These kids are in a pipeline to join the military. My job is to oversee that. We face a new generation of threats. The world is nothing like when we worked in the field. Accordingly, neither is the job."

The answer said little, though Ben noted she'd mentioned the world, not the nation. In their day, more teams had worked inside the US borders than outside. "I've noticed there aren't many villain intercepts reported in the news."

"From what I've heard, it just doesn't happen much anymore. The prison in the Keys has been highly successful. No escapes in twelve years. It seems that's a pretty good deterrent."

Ben doubted people had stopped letting their powers drive them to criminal enterprises or insanity. In the absence of another explanation, though, he supposed it made sense. "What do all the teams do, then?"

She gave him a look like she knew he had more brains than he pretended. Charlie might have lost her sense of humor and playfulness, but she hadn't turned dumb.

"Mostly, they save lives. They're also assisting with research to help prevent disastrous mutations, like those monsters in Brazil." Her wing twitched again.

He knew Charlie also meant people like her little sister. She'd shared the story one night over a few too many beers with him and Kele.

Risa reached out and touched Charlie's arm. "He's not going to ask, but I am. Do you know anything about what happened to Jay? We're still waiting for...for the call to pick him up."

Ben squeezed her hand as they reached the doors for the administrative offices.

Charlie pushed open a door and shook her head. "I'm sorry. It's still under investigation, so there's no report yet. With the holiday, everything just seems to be taking longer than usual. I'm sure they'll release him soon. It might take until Monday or Tuesday at this point. But I'll check and make sure no one forgets about him."

"Thank you," Ben said.

The entry duplicated the marble and wood ambiance from the original Academy. In this version, the halls led to offices, and it had no stairs. Armchairs and short couches clustered around a coffee table on one side and a fireplace on the other.

Greg Boone stood in the center with a pleasant smile. "Hello," he said, sounding friendly and welcoming. He shook hands with Ben and Risa. "It's good to see you both." The smile dimmed.

"I'm sorry we crashed your gate," Risa said. "If it wasn't for Jay, we wouldn't have come."

"I understand," Boone said. "Would you like to sit? I imagine that, as long as you're here, you'd like to hear about Kyoko."

Interested in whatever Boone had to say, and hoping to weasel out whatever he could, Ben led Risa to the couch Boone suggested. They sat together, with Charlie and Boone in armchairs on the other side of the coffee table.

"We already know her grades and scores, of course," Ben said. "I was surprised to see her classified as a charlie this year, when Risa was a bravo. Their powers are so similar."

Charlie waved to dismiss the concern. "The system was extended a few years ago so there are now foxtrot and golf level Novas. You'd probably be a bravo in the new system, and Risa would probably be a charlie."

Ben raised his brow. "Are you saying you have kids more powerful than that?"

Boone shrugged. "There's more to the system now. That's all. Nuance. Clarification. What's important is it doesn't mean she's less capable. The Novas have uses for all levels, just like they always did."

His tone didn't invite further discussion. Ben wondered if they'd changed the prioritization of the classifications. In his day, they'd been most interested in versatility. If they'd shifted to classifying based upon something else, Kay's level made sense to him. Like Risa, she couldn't cause much damage, had situational stealth capability, and hadn't shown the tactical sense he and Jay had.

He hoped they hadn't decided to discount the value of keen observation and dogged determination.

"I know you can't tell us anything about the mission Jay was on," Risa said, "but I wonder if you could just tell us... Reassure us, I suppose? That the mission...that it meant something."

Charlie gave her a sad smile.

"It was a real mission, and the team accomplished their goals," Boone said before Charlie could speak. "Training exercises are conducted under controlled conditions, so they never result in deaths. That's the extent of what we know here. They don't tell us what's going on, they just use our facility to quarantine the survivors until they're fully debriefed."

The way Boone said that made Ben wonder how often

they lost Novas. A procedure like that made him suspect it happened a lot more often than the press knew. People cared when a well-known Legacy Nova died, but they had less interest in random Novas with no name recognition. In the old days, when he'd been in the loop, he knew they'd lost less than one per year, and those tended to happen to the delta and echo teams accidentally assigned intercepts above their capabilities.

Ben remembered every Nova funeral he'd ever attended, starting as a teen with his father and grandfather, and continuing during his fifteen years of service. Most had honored men and women who'd retired and died of old age, like Kenzo and Hurricane Betty. Eleven Novas were KIA in those twenty years. They'd had a protocol, but they'd treated every instance as a special, unusual event.

He glanced at Risa, who seemed upset again, and decided they should leave. They'd come to see Kay, who appeared happy, healthy, and in good hands. She still had until June before any of this applied to her.

"We appreciate your letting us in, and taking time out of your day for us." Ben stood and helped his wife do the same. He had a thought to ask about the vast sea of white kids, but suspected he'd hear some bland PR noise about how they'd only seen a fraction of the kids, or minority families had lower response rates, or some other excuse.

"It was good to see you," Charlie said.

"I'll be the boor here," Greg said, "and remind you that you're not supposed to have contact with former team members."

"We know," Risa said. She took a step to hug Charlie again.

Charlie glanced at Boone. They shared eye contact. She declined Risa's advance.

After an awkward moment, Risa looped her arm through Ben's.

They left the facility with Ben feeling Boone's eyes on his back.

# CHAPTER 18

## IARIESAH

November 24, 2017
09:15

Risa and Ben had little to say during the journey home. He seemed to need time to process again. Risa couldn't put her finger on how she felt about the visit. She replayed everything in her head through the drive to the airport, while waiting for their flight, on the flight itself, and during the drive home.

Exhausted by the traveling, she only climbed out of bed the next morning when her stomach growled. They shuffled through a normal weekend morning, keen to avoid anywhere related to shopping on Black Friday.

Ben ate oatmeal at the kitchen table while leafing through his favorite family photo album. Ell sat at his feet. He paused for a long time on the photograph of himself with his father, grandfather, and son, taken a few years before Kenzo passed. Jay had been eight at the time. Risa watched him from the other end of the table, wondering if he understood his own feelings.

Probably not.

She finished her protein drink and devoured a three-egg omelet stuffed with sausage, vegetables, and cheese. The

TV showed a football game between Hannover and Stuttgart. Risa didn't care about either team, but she liked the background noise. It helped her sort her thoughts.

"I don't like Greg Boone," she said. The sentiment had fluttered in her head while she tried to decide why. People didn't often bother her in such a short time. At this point, she still didn't know, she just needed to say it.

"He reminds me of insurance salesmen."

"I felt like…" She groped for a way to form the discomfort into words. "Like he doesn't care about any of the kids. Or maybe like he doesn't know anything about kids at all. If I asked him their number one concern, I don't think he'd know the answer."

"But he'd bluff by spewing something everybody knows teenagers worry about, like being popular or keeping up with homework."

Knowing he'd picked up on the same thing both relieved and worried Risa. If he hadn't noticed anything, she could've convinced herself that her guilt about Charlie colored her interaction with Greg. Instead, she worried about Kay in an environment where Greg had all the authority and power.

She frowned into her eggs. "And did you get the feeling like they've shifted focus for the Novas overall to international covert operations?"

"Yes." Ben shut the album. "I overheard kids speaking what sounded like Dutch. I think I also overheard kids speaking an Arab language of some sort. The sounds reminded me of missions in Afghanistan and the Middle East, at least."

"And I didn't like the way Charlie wouldn't give me a hug while he was watching. She gave me one when we first saw her. She always used to be good for a hug outside of missions."

Ben shrugged, though Risa knew he'd noticed. "I ran into the rest of Jay's team there. They're the Novas keeping the place on lockdown while waiting for some sort of evaluation. It bothers me they're doing evaluations at the Academy. In our day, they did that on base. I don't see the value of moving the process off base."

"Maybe it's a political thing." Risa stood and took her dishes to the sink. "Our generation was the first one not to have any Legacies openly active in politics. Maybe some of them have just been quiet about it."

"Maybe." Ben brought his dishes and rinsed everything to load the dishwasher. "Are you going for another run this morning?"

She kissed him on the cheek. "I wasn't planning on it. Did you want me to pace you?"

"No, but that doesn't sound like a bad idea. I haven't been running a while. Getting out into the fresh air with you might help."

He didn't have to say what it might help. Risa already knew how well a good run could clear her head. As Novas, they'd always spent a lot of time jogging, lifting weights, shooting, and fight training. Ben had avoided putting on a lot of weight when they retired by forcing himself to eat less. He'd lost his abs, though.

"I'll go easy on you." She took Ell's leash from its hook.

Ell bounced to his feet and darted to her side. He presented his neck so she could attach the collar and pat his head.

"Who's a good boy? Yes, you're a good boy."

Ben patted her ass on his way to the front closet.

"You're also a good boy," she called after him.

"Woof, woof," Ben said. He hadn't joked about anything since the call. Aside from the long stretches of blank silence, every day had been full of grim, direct, or non-verbal input from him.

Leading Ell to the front door, she smiled at Ben as they put on their shoes. "How about around Chamberlin and back? That's only about two miles."

He gave her a look that said she needed to scale back her expectations of him. "Do you have a one mile option?"

She laughed. "We could stop at the park for ten minutes before coming back?"

"Fine." He touched her cheek and flashed her a weak smile. "But if I can't go on, I expect you to run home and fetch the car for me."

"Maybe we should bring wheels we can strap to your shoes. Then Ell can pull you home." She kissed his hand. "Come on. You'll be fine. You use that damned treadmill all the time."

"To walk."

"Whiner."

"If you stay in front of me, I suppose I can be motivated by the view."

Risa lifted the back of her jacket to let him get a good eyeful of her ass, then hurried out the front door. Forcing herself slow, she pushed Ben to a moderate jog. By the time they reached the park, he had to stop to catch his breath. He collapsed on the bench of a picnic table.

"Maybe I should stick to the treadmill. It's easier than this."

His phone rang. While he answered it, Risa ran water from a fountain for Ell.

"Linda?" Ben frowned. "Is something wrong with Kevin?" He sat up and leaned against the table. "I'm so sorry, Linda. When did it happen?"

People named Linda associated with a Kevin narrowed the list of possible callers to one that Risa knew. Colonel Marks's wife had called Ben, something Risa had never known her to do except once for a surprise party for Kevin.

"I don't know what to say. I just talked to him a few days ago. Do you need anything?" He rested his head on his hand and stared at the table, his face blank.

Something had happened to the colonel. Risa recognized the same empty helplessness from a week earlier. First his son, now his close friend.

"Of course we'll be there. As soon as you have the details, let me know. Get some rest, Linda." He hung up. Ben dropped his phone like he considered it responsible for the news he heard through it. "Marks is dead. He crashed his car late last night, on his way home from the hospital to pick up an emergency refill for her blood pressure medication."

"Oh, no." Risa hugged him from behind. "She'll think it's her fault." Like Ben considered Charlie's wing his fault. "Is she at home?"

"No. They were visiting their daughter for the holiday. She thought she packed the meds, but couldn't find them in her bag. The funeral will be next week sometime. They have to transport the remains over state lines."

Ell barked at people walking nearby. Risa tugged on his leash to quiet him.

Ben snatched up his phone again and tapped on the screen.

Busy with the dog, Risa couldn't see what he did. She guessed he groped for details. The details made things make sense to him. If someone would just give him details about Jay, she knew he'd have an easier time accepting it.

"This is…" He frowned at his phone. "Risa? Do you remember that thing I read to you the other day? About Angela Nuñez?"

"Vaguely."

"According to police, the vehicle hit the side of the road and caught fire. The victim is believed to have been knocked unconscious by the initial impact, then killed by the fire. Though the crash itself had no witnesses, another driver reported seeing an oil slick on the road and tire treads leading from it, toward the victim's car."

Risa saw Ben's face and knew what he thought—two accidents in two different places, killing two people with something in common, and with details too similar for coincidence. "We shouldn't jump to conclusions."

"The conclusion is jumping out and slapping us in the face." Ben stood and resumed the run. He set a much harder, grueling pace for himself.

Risa struggled to avoid speeding too much while

keeping up with him. Ell couldn't maintain that speed for long, though, so she had to slow for the dog.

By the time she reached home, Ben had shed his shoes and sweater, and he paced across the living room while catching his breath. Risa made sure Ell had food and water, then she sat on the couch and waited for Ben to talk. When he decided to say something, it would come out in a long string, so she wanted to get comfortable.

He stopped after a few minutes, facing the fireplace and the models over the mantle. "I refuse to accept that those two deaths had nothing to do with each other. Someone killed both Angela and Kevin. Maybe they stole Linda's medication out of her suitcase, maybe they bugged his phone, whatever. Somehow, someone knew they could manipulate both into that same sort of situation, so they did it.

"The question is why. With Kevin, it seems clear he was investigating, and someone didn't like him snooping around. Instead of warning him off, or trying to get him to retire, they killed him. Probably, they knew him well enough to realize he wouldn't let go until he got the information. With Angela, I have no idea. I don't remember her well. We had some other disconnected numbers, though, so we have no idea what happened to them."

The implications left Risa chilled. Tapping Kevin's phone sounded like something from a spy story. It also meant… "Ben, if they tapped Kevin's phone, then they know you're the one who called him to ask for his help." She shivered because she didn't like a nameless, faceless enemy. Not when she didn't have a full team at her back.

"That's true." He stood with his back to her for a long time.

Risa imagined all kinds of horrible things happening because of those two phone calls. What if someone decided to delay those Nova evaluations just to put Kay out of reach? The idea sounded preposterous. Yet, she couldn't discount the possibility. What would these unknown people do if they found out she and Ben had visited and been granted access anyway?

"Risa, I think we need help."

She had no idea who could help them with something like this. They couldn't call on Charlie, because she swam in the thick of things. The police would laugh at them, and so would federal agencies. "What kind?"

"Vivian. Do you know where she went?"

"Of course I do. I send her Christmas cards every year." Risa frowned. "But we're not supposed to call her."

Ben turned to face her. "Fuck them. If they can tap a phone, we'll go visit her."

From the set of his shoulders and the grim line of his mouth, Risa knew she wouldn't win this argument. Besides, she missed Vivian. For the past decade, they'd traded one card per year. After more than a decade having each other's backs.

That night had been hard for so many reasons.

"You pack," she said, pulling out her phone. "I'll get the tickets."

# CHAPTER 19

## BEN

November 24, 2017
16:37

Ben stopped their second rental car in two days on the tree-lined driveway in front of a large colonial-style house in Wayland, Massachusetts. Decorative shutters framing half a dozen windows contrasted with the pale yellow siding of a sprawling, two-story home with a four-car garage. Brown grass surrounded the house, and a high, white picket fence disappeared into the distance on one side. The other side had no barriers other than trees.

"Are you sure this is the right address?"

Risa nodded. "She's lived her for seven years."

"It looks…"

"Pleasant? Idyllic? Charming?"

"Yes, all those things. Also, I'm jealous. If I got to come home to this every night, I'd hate Cincinnati a lot less." Ben opened the door and approached the house. He rang the doorbell.

Risa wrapped her arm around his. He felt her warmth through his winter coat. "You really hate Cincinnati that much?"

"Don't you? I can only think of one good thing there,

and that's you."

"Flattery will get you everywhere." She leaned against him.

The door opened before he could respond.

He stared at the person holding it and didn't know how to react. She had Vivian's eyes, but the rest of her mystified him. Her red hair hung to her chin, she wore no makeup, and her clothes…pink. Vivian wore a pink knitted cardigan over a soft pink shirt and floral leggings, with pink shoes.

Vivian's eyes widened in surprise, then she smiled with joy and leaped at Risa to hug her. "Oh my God! I had no idea you were coming! You should've called because the house is a complete mess, and I don't even know if we have a guest room in usable state right now."

She let go of Risa and hugged Ben. "Except you're not supposed to call, which you know, or come here, which you also know. Come in, though. I mean, now you're here, you might as well have coffee." Taking both their hands, She tugged them into the house. "Would you like coffee? We have dinner at six, so it's a little late for a snack."

"I'm starving," Risa said, "but I have my own bars."

Too stunned to react to the perkiest Vivian he'd ever experienced, Ben let the two women carry him inside and to a living room. He didn't see any sign of the mess Vivian had mentioned. Tasteful, fake floral arrangements in decorative vases topped wood tables of all shapes and sizes. Two floral-print armchairs faced a matching couch over a glass-topped coffee table holding a pair of coffee table books.

"Anna! Chloe! We have guests. They're safe."

Ben sat on the couch, wondering what she meant. He thought he knew Vivian. Apparently not. Risa sat beside him and didn't seem surprised or confused. What had she put in those Christmas cards, and why hadn't she shown him?

The best answer he could think of? Plausible deniability for Steve.

Vivian's smile faltered when she looked at Ben. "I'm so

sorry about Jay. It was on the news. I would've called, but, you know, we're not supposed to. He was a good kid."

At least, Ben thought as he nodded to accept her condolences, they didn't have to explain to anyone. He didn't have to say the words out loud.

"I hope the funeral was nice. He deserved a nice service."

"If it had happened yet, I would've brought pictures," Risa said. She sounded as bitter as Ben felt about it.

A woman stepped into the room through a doorway. She had shoulder-length brown hair hanging loose in waves, and wore jeans with a sweater matching Vivian's under a plain green apron. "Hi."

Behind her, a pre-teen girl poked her head into sight. Her straight red hair had a green bow holding it out of her face, and she wore a green dress with green tights.

"I know you," the girl said. She pointed at Ben. "You're Captain Kinetic, from the old picture on the wall. At school, they said you died in 2006."

Ben blinked at the girl. If he hadn't lost so much so recently, he would've chuckled. "That's my grandfather. We look a lot alike."

"Chloe, Anna, these are my friends Ben and Risa. They send us a nice card for Christmas every year. It's the one that always comes with a picture of their dog and twenty bucks for you, Pumpkin."

Risa stood and hugged the woman. "It's so nice to finally meet you in person, Anna." To Ben's surprise, Anna returned the hug as if they'd been lifelong friends.

"Oh! Cool." The girl marched to Ben and offered her hand to shake with grave solemnity. "Hello, Mr. Ben Mom's Friend. It's nice to meet you. I'm Chloe." She pronounced each word with crisp precision, marred only by her light Boston accent.

Ben shook her hand. Too much confusion swirled in his head to do anything other than take her seriously. "It's nice to meet you too, Chloe."

"Did you bring your dog?"

"No. Ell is in a kennel right now. Very nice people are taking care of him for us."

"Oh, that's a shame. He could've played with Buddy. Mom, are our guests staying for dinner tonight?"

"I don't know yet, Pumpkin." Vivian held out her arms and Chloe obliged by sitting on her mother's lap.

"You're welcome to stay if you like," Anna said. "We're having bread bowl clam chowder with a vegetable bake." She spoke with a thicker local accent, dropping her Rs and extending her vowels.

"That sounds wonderful." Risa brought Anna with her as she returned to the group, including Anna like family.

"It certainly sounds appropriate," Ben said. He had no idea what to make of any of this. Obviously, Vivian had been pregnant when he last saw her, so the fact she had a daughter shouldn't have surprised him. It still did. Everything about this surprised him more than he thought it should. And he didn't know what to think of Anna.

Anna sat in the other armchair. "What brings you here? I thought you weren't supposed to visit?"

Since Anna seemed to know enough, Ben sat forward to tell them everything. He glanced at Chloe and changed how he chose to approach the subject for her benefit. "Do you remember Colonel Marks?"

Vivian frowned and hugged her daughter tighter. "Of course. He's the one who gave us missions and yelled at you afterward."

"He was killed in a car accident yesterday."

"Okay. I'm going to stop you there." Vivian set Chloe on the floor and shared a look with Anna. "Pumpkin, this sounds like it's going to be boring grown-up talk."

"You know what, Chloe?" Anna asked as she stood and smoothed her apron. "We'll probably have a lot more fun working in the kitchen. We still have to cut up the vegetables."

Chloe curtseyed to Ben and Risa. "Excuse me, Mr. Ben

and Ms. Risa. We're going to check on dinner and make sure it's delicious." She skipped out of the room with Anna following.

"She's just like I pictured," Risa said.

"She's nothing like I pictured," Ben said.

Risa nudged his shoulder with a roll of her eyes. "Don't be a prat."

"What?"

Vivian giggled.

Ben had never before heard Vivian giggle like that. She sounded…happy. Carefree. At ease with herself. He squinted at her. "Are you sure you're Vivian? The one I know as Omen?"

Vivian's giggle turned into a guffaw. "Man, I was such an emo downer back then. After the Novas cut me loose, I spent some time with my family. They're annoying, but they helped me get on my feet so I could take care of Chloe. I mean, Aaron was a complete loser. My brother took one look at him and beat the shit out of him."

"You have a brother?" Ben kept squinting.

"Technically? Half-brother. Aaron stopped calling and I got over it." Vivian shrugged like it hadn't taken more effort than deciding what to order on a pizza. "And, of course, I had to get off morphine and have Chloe. Spent some time with my grandmother before she passed. She and Hurricane Betty were pen pals after the war, did you know that? I have all the letters. Grandma left them to me in her will. Maybe I'll let the Smithsonian have them at some point, but not yet. I don't think most people are ready to hear about her sham marriage, and Haywire's family would probably get upset."

Too much information bombarded Ben at once. He kept it all straight without a problem, but couldn't decide which thing to ask first. His mouth opened and something fell out. "Morphine?"

Vivian sighed and looked at the floor. Her hair fell forward to obscure her face. Ben had no idea how long it would take him to wrap his head around the copper color.

"Ben," Risa said, covering his hand with hers. "Maybe this isn't the time to go over everything Vivian's been through since we last saw her."

"No, of course not. I'm sorry, Vivian." Ben shook himself and set aside all the insanity she'd poured into his ears. "We need your help." He explained everything that had happened, starting with Jay's death and ending with the identical car crash reports. "I just can't shake the feeling something is going on at the Academy, and at Area 51. I'm worried about Kay and all those other kids, but I'm also concerned that they're keeping Jay's body for a reason."

"Ben. Risa." Vivian looked at her hands clasped in her lap. "Look, I know you came because of my power. And I'm happy to see you. Please stay for dinner, no matter what. But that's not me anymore. I don't really use it. Occasionally, I get warnings about mishaps at the roller skating rink or something at Anna's job, or that asshole Steve showing up. I'm pretty happy with it that way.

"Yes, I was addicted to morphine." Vivian leaned back with a grimace and gripped the arms of her chair. "They gave it to me when I told them I couldn't sleep because of visions. Every mission, I got to watch new movies about one or more of you guys dying in some spectacular, horrifying way. I did fine until we got home, because I could prevent those things from happening. Then I'd try to sleep, and they'd all come back like I needed to stop them from happening again. Over and over.

"Grandma told me she had the same problem, and so did my mom. Grandma got over it with Haywire's help because she was a tough old bird and they didn't do much after the war. Mom, on the other hand, was responsible for the Tet Offensive screw-up and killed herself."

Ben felt like he'd failed Vivian again. If only he'd seen how much pain she'd suffered all those years ago. Maybe that night would've been different. Maybe she would've seen it coming. He'd already known that fuckup was his fault, now he had extra proof.

Risa went to Vivian and hugged her. "I didn't know until that night," she murmured. "I saw the needle and the bottle when I came to get you. Then it was too late and we weren't supposed to talk anymore. That was terrible. Knowing and not being able to help."

Over Risa's shoulder, Vivian smiled. "I could tell from what you wrote in the cards. Later, I mean. Not that first one, but the later ones. Once I got clean. You were really great after I met Anna, especially. Neither of us has a lot of safe places to be open about our relationship."

"I'm glad it helped."

"Safe places?" Since he first saw Anna, Ben suspected he'd missed something.

Vivian and Risa parted, staying arm in arm. His wife gave him a look that suggested he should shut up. He knew that look too well to mistake it for anything else. Vivian, on the other hand, seemed amused by him.

"She's my girlfriend, Ben."

Risa squeezed Vivian and returned to Ben's side. She sat and leaned against him like a buffer between him and madness.

Ben didn't think he'd heard Vivian correctly. "What?"

"Anna and I are a couple." Vivian pitched her voice like she considered him a child or puppy who needed to understand a complex subject. "We can't get married, so it's not like you and Risa, but it's the same thing. If we were out about it, Anna would lose her job at the governor's office, so we have to pretend we're just roomies and she's like a sister who helps me take care of Chloe."

Now everything made sense. To a certain degree, anyway. Most people didn't talk about things like this, so Ben knew little on the subject. "So all those problems with Aaron were because you're a lesbian?"

Vivian snorted as she returned to her seat. "No. That was because he's an asshole. I could go into this and explain bisexuals if you really want, Ben."

"It's not a problem, just unexpected," Ben said and

tried to refocus on his purpose. They hadn't come to learn about Vivian's love life.

"I'm so glad you've found someone who makes you happy," Risa said. She squeezed Ben's arm. "That's the important thing."

"Yes, of course." Ben nodded. A sudden, distressing image popped into his head, of Vivian and Risa with their heads together at a bar in...he forgot where, but he remembered Germany playing China on the TV. Thank goodness for football. The hazy details of the game let him set aside the rest of the moment.

His phone rang as he opened his mouth to try to veer back on track. He pulled it out and frowned at the caller ID. If he didn't answer, Steve would just call Risa instead. Putting a finger to his lips, he answered the call on speakerphone.

"Hi Ben, it's Steve. Sorry to bother you. After your unannounced trip to Colorado, I've been asked to remind you that you're not supposed to have contact with your old teammates. I understand why you went there, and that whole situation was kind of a mess. Now that you've gone home, though, it's important that you stay there."

Something about the way Steve said that made Ben wonder if he had a man on their front porch, ringing the doorbell. "It seems a little unnecessary after all these years."

"You signed contracts, Ben. It'd be a shame if you violated federal law by doing something like flying to Boston."

Risa and Vivian both straightened.

Ben held up his hand to keep both women from speaking. "I understand."

"I know I said two weeks, but maybe we should schedule that inspection visit now."

"This isn't a good time." Ben knew how to handle this —keep things vague, set a date in the future, and get off the phone as soon as possible. "I'll call you on Monday."

"Sure. I'll talk to you then."

Ben hung up. "Someone knows we're here. They want

us to know they know, but not be sure about it." He looked to Vivian. "We didn't come here to cause trouble, and I don't want to force you to deal with your power. But we need your help. Something is going on. If that call doesn't prove it, I don't know what will. They have our daughter, Vivian. They took our son, they're watching us, and they want us isolated."

Vivian stood and hugged herself. She paced across the room, shaking her head. "I can't. I love you guys, I really do. And I want Kay to be safe. But I can't. The minute I use it, everything will crash on me."

Despite Risa tugging on his sleeve to make him stop, Ben stood and got in Vivian's way. He took her by the arms, trying to make her see him. If this shadowy, unknown "they" fronted by Steve only threatened him, he wouldn't press. With Risa and Kay under threat, he couldn't leave without doing everything in his power to keep them safe.

He gritted his teeth and did something terrible. "Vivian. What if it was your daughter?"

Vivian covered her face. "You asshole."

Ben agreed with her. He did it anyway. "I'm not asking you for me. I'm asking you for Risa and Kay. For Jay's memory. For his best friend, who died with him, and for her mother. For the other kids who've died in the field, facing situations we could've walked away from. Please, Vivian."

She sighed. "Fuck you."

Ben hugged her. No matter how much she'd changed, he could tell she'd just agreed to help.

# CHAPTER 20

## VIVIAN

November 24, 2017
17:17

Ben let go of Vivian. She sighed and dug in her cardigan pocket, finding nothing but a wadded tissue. Later, she'd drop a dollar into the swear jar. "I should probably meditate before trying. Like I said, I haven't used it on purpose in ages." She sat in her chair again.

Her phone rang, with the last caller ID she needed to see. Steve had already conducted his inspection last week. Whenever he called, she made a point to get it done as soon as possible. He made the household tense and cranky, especially Vivian. Everything about him reminded her of that horrible night, Aaron, needles, and pain. She wanted to leave all that behind, and his mandated inspections wouldn't let her.

"What?" she snapped at Steve.

"Hi Vivian, nice to talk to you too. I'm sure you saw the news about Ichiro Tsukuda. I can understand a desire to reach out to his parents, and I know you haven't done so, but I've been asked to remind you to not contact them, or anyone else from the team."

She stared at Ben and Risa without seeing either of

them. Calling now meant Steve knew. An urge to check for cameras and watchers roiled in her gut. Crazy people worried about being watched at home.

"Tell your handlers to stop wasting my time. And yours."

"I don't enjoy making these calls, Vivian. I also don't enjoy reminding you that living near your family is a risk we allowed you to take. So is having Anna live there. Oh, and I understand Chloe is under consideration for early enrollment at the Academy."

For once, his stupid casual threats shook Vivian. She knew they'd only let her live near her family because of Chloe. Steve hadn't been immune to the distress of a messed up pregnant woman with nowhere else to go. The time she'd spent with her grandmother in that New Hampshire commune had been the compromise for the first two years. Once she'd cleaned herself up, he'd let her stay with her father and stepmother, then buy a house near them.

For a beat, she said nothing. Then she shook herself and delivered the same response she always gave. "Whatever. Go away." With luck, he didn't read too much into the pause and didn't hear the tiny shake in her voice.

She hung up on him. "I've never thought of Steve as scary before. I think he just threatened to take Chloe away and possibly expose Anna so she loses her job."

Risa scooted closer and took her hand. "We won't let him."

Of everyone on the team, Risa had always understood her. She'd seen everything, even if she hadn't always been able to figure out everything. When Vivian had trouble with Aaron, Risa knew. When Vivian had trouble sleeping, Risa knew. When Vivian had trouble with anything, Risa knew. She just didn't know the details unless Vivian told her.

Vivian smiled at Risa and took comfort from her touch. She'd missed them so much. No matter how little she wanted to do that job again, she wished they could all live on the same street. She wouldn't trade the time with Grandma for anything, but later, she would've liked to see everyone on the weekends.

"Give me a few minutes here. Steve may not realize it, but he just made me want to do this more than before."

Begging in her mind for the old visions to stay away, she took a long, slow breath in and let it out through her nose. "What do you want me to focus on?"

"Kay," Ben said. "It's her future that matters right now."

"Kyoko Lily Tsukuda," Vivian murmured. She remembered Kay's birth. Risa's pregnancies had been so short the team had gone on hiatus for three months each time instead of taking missions without her. She also remembered holding Risa while she cried because she couldn't breastfeed. Her body refused to provide for her babies. Ben had never understood why that upset her so much.

But that had happened with Jay. By the time Kay was born, Risa knew to expect it. Vivian thought of the little girl who called her an aunt at parties and barbeques. The kid could pay attention to four things at once, and never wanted anyone to tell her how to do things. She loved her Daddy and his car.

The blank darkness inside her eyelids swirled, heralding a vision. She cringed and waited.

"Dinner's ready!"

Chloe's voice cut through the nothing in Vivian's head. She opened her eyes. The clock on the wall informed her she'd been trying to enter a trance for about forty-five minutes.

Standing, she frowned at Ben and Risa. "I'm not sure what happened. I got something, but not really." Not only did the blank vision confuse her, it also embarrassed her. The power of her bloodline, once so reliable, had failed her.

Risa frowned. "Maybe you're too out of practice?"

"I guess. Let's have dinner, then I'll give it another shot." She led Ben and Risa to the dining room, thick with the aroma of Anna's homemade chowder.

"Do you want to hear a story?" Chloe asked.

Risa nodded. "I'd love to."

"You can tell a story," Vivian said, "if you promise to eat."

Chloe raised her right hand. "I promise to eat my dinner." She smiled at Ben and Risa. "This is the story of when Buddy met our horses."

"You have horses?" Ben asked. He had a milder version of that stupid, poleaxed look on his face when she'd opened the door.

"Yes." Vivian pointed with her spoon at Chloe's bowl to make her daughter eat during the interruption. "Two of them. Because Anna wanted a pony, and sometimes you get what you want if you ask the right way."

Anna blushed.

Risa raised her brow, her mouth twitching with stifled amusement. "I guess you solved your problem with fast women."

Vivian laughed, which made Risa laugh. Chloe and Anna watched without understanding. Ben gave a fake, hollow chuckle like he always did when he missed the joke but wanted to participate or not seem rude.

She'd missed them. Having them here warmed a piece of her heart she'd forgotten existed. They didn't seem to blame her for that horrifying night, which made it harder for her to keep blaming herself.

If she hadn't been high, she might've seen it coming. If she had told Ben about the problems with her visions, he would've done something. If she hadn't been so unwilling to tell them about the baby, about the things Aaron did, about everything, they might've helped her through everything.

That night had meant losing the terrible visions and their echoes. She never would've met Anna if they hadn't forced her to retire.

That night had also meant Charlie losing her wing. A lot of people had died. Those lives didn't matter less than hers or Chloe's. The team had broken apart, and she knew how much the job of Captain Kinetic had meant to Ben.

If they'd still been on the job, maybe Jay would've survived his mission.

All her fault.

Vivian lowered her head and ate in silence while Chloe offered her version of Rescue Dog Meets Horses. Risa ate with speed. Ben drank a lot of water between bites. He seemed more interested in the vegetables with nothing but a bit of salt and butter than the flavorful chowder.

Anna took Chloe to handle chores, freeing Vivian to let Ben and Risa tell her more details about their attempts to get Jay's body and reach Kay. As they told her about meeting Maverick, Vivian thought she might throw up. Her sight clouded with a vision so intense that she needed a minute to let it settle.

She sipped her water and cursed the stupid gift. They didn't need vague, metaphorical predictions. They needed concrete, useful ones. The kind that saved lives.

"I think I need to come with you."

"What did you see?" Ben asked.

Vivian shook her head. "Birds. Grass. Dragons. Motorcycles. Barking dogs. White light. Flying wood and shingles. Dolphins. Nothing specific or useful. And before you ask, yes, I used to see Maverick as a bird, but not this kind. So it wasn't her."

The white light reminded her of that night. DPS had thrown white-hot fire then. Except it hadn't been DPS. She'd come to realize she'd shouted at a scared teenager to make him fight. She hadn't directed Cap that night, she'd directed Jay. Crash hadn't jumped through the hole in the wall, that Southern boy had.

At least she hadn't gotten any of them killed.

"I just have a feeling that if I don't come with you, I'm going to see all kinds of things and not be able to tell you. Because I think maybe it's not safe to use the phone?"

Ben set his phone on the table and glared at it. "I don't know. I doubt Marks did anything other than make a few phone calls, but who knows if it was the call itself that got him killed, or saying the wrong thing to the wrong person."

"Maybe I should shut off my phone?" Risa set hers beside Ben's. "Work is the only place I get calls from, other than you and Steve. I don't want to talk to Steve."

Ben nodded. "I don't want to talk to Steve either."

"No one does." Vivian smirked. "If Steve has a wife, she probably doesn't even want to talk to him."

Risa grinned. Ben chuckled.

"Would you like to stay for the night, then we can leave in the morning?"

They nodded. Vivian showed them to the largest of the guest rooms and made sure Risa knew how to get from there to the kitchen and back. She steeled herself to discuss the situation with Anna and Chloe, then found them Chloe's room.

Chloe sat in her desk chair, wearing her favorite princess pajamas. Anna sat on the princess-frosted bed behind her, braiding Chloe's hair. Buddy, their golden retriever, sat with her head in Chloe's lap while the girl brushed his coat.

Vivian wanted to isolate them and tell each the news in a different way. She didn't want to waste any time with either, though. Leaning against the door frame, she watched the most important things in her life and hated her power again.

"Hey," she said as Anna handed Chloe the brush to put away. "I need to spend some time with Ben and Risa for a few days."

Anna nodded. "That's fine. They'll be a nice buffer if anyone comes to visit."

"I can't wait to let them meet Buddy," Chloe said. She set both brushes on her desk.

Vivian grimaced. "Yeah, that's not actually what I meant. I'm going to leave with them. We're taking a road trip."

Chloe stared at her.

Anna pursed her lips and gave her a slower nod. She

bent and patted Buddy on the head. "C'mon, boy. Let's let Viv talk to Chloe alone."

As Anna and Buddy left the room, Vivian could see the tantrum building in Chloe's shoulders and neck. Her small hands balled into fists, and her eyes watered with on-demand tears.

Vivian sat on the bed with a sigh and waited for the inevitable.

Flopping across her lap, Chloe wheezed out a melodramatic groan. "Mooooooom, this is so unfaaaaaair. Why are you leaving meeeeee? It's vacaaaaaaation."

"Once upon a time." Vivian saw a bar with a soccer game on the TV and beer bottles on the table. Risa had a mug and empty shot glasses. Charlie laughed at Matias's joke. Kele sat with her feet up. Ben sat with his arm on the back of Risa's chair, smiling about a successful mission.

Chloe didn't need to know the reality of the situation. Telling her about Jay would only scare her. She decided to take as simplistic a tack as possible.

"There was a family of six brothers and sisters. They traveled a lot. Wherever they traveled, they helped people. Saved lives. Stopped bad guys. One night, the bad guys took them by surprise at home. They managed to stop the bad guys, but they were hurt. They were hurt so bad, they couldn't fight anymore. So they stopped and let other people step up to handle it. Except those other people didn't do as good a job. Even though the family didn't want to go fight the bad guys anymore, they realized they had to."

Chloe climbed onto her lap and hugged her. "I don't want you to go."

"I'm going to help Ben and Risa fight the bad guys. They're hurting people again, and we're the only ones who know how to stop it."

Vivian wished things could be so simple. They didn't even know who to chase or fight, or why. She only knew she needed to go and try. This time, she wouldn't fail them.

"If you knew someone was hurting a friend from

school, and you could stop them, wouldn't you want to do that?"

Chloe pouted. "That's not fair."

She hugged her daughter. Someday, Chloe would learn how harsh the world could get. That day needed to stay distant for as long as possible. "I'll come home as soon as I can. We'll go to Uncle Brian's and play hockey."

"Because everybody plays hockey," Chloe mumbled through her pout.

"Yep. I love you, Sweetie." She kissed Chloe's forehead and helped her climb into bed. "You're the best thing that ever happened to me. Even better than chocolate."

"Better than ice cream?"

"Better than ice cream."

"Better than cheesecake?"

Vivian smirked. "Don't go too far, kiddo."

Chloe kissed her cheek. "I love you too, Mom. Come home fast."

"As fast as I can."

# CHAPTER 21

## BEN

November 25, 2017
17:31

Watching Vivian and Anna exchange their farewells left Ben thinking about his attitudes toward gay people more than he'd ever thought about such things. They loved each other. If he ignored the fact of their genders, he could see it. Vivian and Anna reminded him of himself and Risa. He saw the same kind of affection and care in a one-minute goodbye between the two women as he saw between his sister and her husband, his parents, or Risa's parents.

He'd never thought about the subject. The drive to the airport, flight to San Francisco, and drive to Palo Alto passed with him thinking about it more than he wanted. The President hated gays with a violent, Bible-thumping passion, which meant they heard about it all the time. The gays apparently caused earthquakes, tornadoes, hurricanes, mudslides, the common cold, economic downturns, peanut allergies, moldy bread, everything.

None of that made any sense to him, of course. He'd just never thought about it. The subject had no effect on his life or family, so he had no interest in it. Knowing Vivian had to keep part of herself secret from the world bothered him. Maybe, he thought, he needed to take some interest in that. His grandfather had said, more than once, that he regretted not doing more to advance equality for groups other than Japanese-Americans.

They reached a condo complex with neat, manicured plantings and an underground parking garage. Ben parked in the only empty space he could find, which had a sign reserving it for potential new residents. Even the street outside had no empty spaces.

The door cracked open a few seconds after Ben rang the bell. Dramatic instrumental music greeted them, punctuated by the sound of explosions.

Ben remembered enough real explosions to recognize fake ones.

"Hi, can I—" The Indian woman who answered the door held it close to her body. She wore rumpled scrubs covered with multicolored smilie faces. Wisps of her dark hair floated around a messy, loose ponytail. Her brown eyes, lined with weariness, lit up when she saw Risa. "Risa! We had no idea you were coming!"

She and Risa hugged. Of course they did. Ben watched and traded a glance with Vivian, who shrugged.

"Matty, it's Risa and Ben!"

"What? Now? No wonder Risa won't join." Ben recognized Matias's voice.

A loud fan kicked on, and Matias opened the door wider. He grinned when he saw the three of them and stepped onto the front stoop to give all three of them hugs. Behind him, the woman shut the door.

"What are you doing here? Risa, we've been sending you joins for the past week." He seemed more worried than upset, though Ben had no idea what he meant.

"There's maybe a huge conspiracy to crack," Vivian said. She sounded casual, like she'd commented on the weather. "Why are we out here instead of in there? Is that okay to ask?"

"His sister," Risa said.

"Yeah, we have to give the fans a chance to start cranking and Gabi a few minutes to cover up, or else Dhanya and I spend the next five hours cleaning." He paused. Ben thought Matias saw his blank look, because he added, "She was in a fire I didn't cause when we were young. Permanent damage to her lungs and some areas of skin. Keeping the place dust-free is a pretty huge deal."

"Ah." Why the subject had never come up during their years on the team, Ben had no idea. It did explain where Matias went for all those off-duty weekends. The gold wedding band on Matias's finger explained Dhanya's identity.

"I'm so sorry we came without calling," Risa said. "We're concerned about someone bugging our phones."

Matias smirked. "They call it listening in now. Everything worth bugging is wireless, so everything is about finding the signal and tapping it. That takes a lot of expensive equipment, though, so it's mostly sophisticated operations and the government who're doing it. They still do physical listening devices in locations, though."

"And you know all that because…?" Ben had a fair idea of the answer, but he asked anyway.

His smirk becoming a grin, Matias snorted. "Like I wouldn't know that, Cap."

Dhanya opened the door behind them and handed everyone booties for their shoes. Fans whirred and pushed air against them as they stepped through a tiny alcove made of fingers of hanging plastic to reach the inside. When Matias closed the door, Ben's ears popped.

Computer equipment and screens dominated the front room. Three cushioned armchairs faced a bank of flat screen TVs hung across a corner with a wide, empty space between them. Tiny lights glowed and winked everywhere from a sea of black devices. Three keyboards sat on three wheeled TV trays with joysticks, game controllers, and trackball-style mice.

Ben expected to see cords snaking across the floor, but

they'd left none in sight.

On the other side of the room, a giant aquarium mounted to the ceiling and breakfast bar separated the living room from the kitchen. Brightly colored fish drifted around a living coral reef. Another plastic-guarded alcove led to a glass door for a balcony. Something about the setup bothered Ben, but he couldn't put his finger on it.

A woman in a gray hoodie and leggings, her hands covered with white cloth gloves, stood at the mouth of the hallway. She wore a white breathing mask. Her brown eyes matched Matias's.

"Hi," she said, her voice muffled by the mask.

"Dhanya, Gabriella, this is Ben, Risa, and Vivian. Otherwise known as Captain Kinetic, Springfire, and Omen."

"Ugh." Vivian grimaced. "That code name is so nineties emo goth. Everybody calls me Viv now."

"It's nice to meet all of you," Dhanya said. "We don't entertain, so there isn't really anywhere to sit."

With that statement, Ben realized the room had only three chairs—the armchairs for the computer setup. "It's fine."

Vivian shrugged and sat on the floor.

"Also," Gabi said, "we did see the news about Jay. It was impossible not to run across. I'm sorry. He sounded like a really good person."

"Yeah," Matias said. "I'm sorry about him. He was a good kid. Did they give him a nice send-off? I didn't see any pictures from the funeral."

"There hasn't been one yet. That's kind of why we're here." One more time, Ben related everything that had happened since the worst phone call of his life.

Two seconds after Vivian finished revealing the threats Steve had delivered to her, Matias's phone rang.

"Huh. Steve. How interesting." Matias answered it. "*¿Que paso, cabrón?*" He raised an eyebrow and made a talking puppet with his hand. "What the fuck, man? It's not enough you gotta come fuck up our lives for two days every year, now you're down for delivering threats? Fuck off, Steve, and go kiss a creeper." He hung up.

Dhanya huffed with a grimace. "That asshole is the reason we don't have chairs. He doesn't get to sit."

"Is he going to get suspicious because you just yelled at him?" Risa asked.

Matias barked a laugh. "No. He'd get suspicious if I didn't." He sobered. "But it's interesting that he called when he did, isn't it?"

"We should check into that." Gabi slipped around Ben to take a seat in the left armchair and pull the tray over her lap. The bank of screens took her attention.

Matias and Dhanya shared a glance. She nodded and headed down the hall. He smiled and jumped into the right armchair.

Ben considered sitting on the floor. "Is this likely to take a while?"

Gabi shrugged. "Maybe? Depends on what rabbit holes we find. For the moment, we're looking for the tracks you're leaving, then we're going to see if there's anything sniffing those tracks. This is all easy stuff. You just have to know what you're looking for and how to find it. Like…"

"Like searching for three crayons in a giant stack of hay," Matias said. "You have to go through a giant pile of hay for something you can see once you uncover it. The sniffers is more like the usual needles. There's a lot of bots that look like sniffers because they do the same thing for different reasons."

Sliding down the wall to sit on the floor next to Vivian, Ben shrugged. "I didn't understand any of that, except the crayons part."

Dhanya brought them pillows. "I don't understand half of what comes out of their mouths either. Can I get you anything to drink, or a snack? You must've flown here?"

Risa took a pillow and sat beside Ben. "I wouldn't mind a snack. We stopped for drive-through on the way here, but I never turn down food."

Ben draped his arm around Risa's shoulders and settled to wait. Maybe they shouldn't have come. Going to Vivian's house hadn't been a ploy to pry her out of her life. He'd only wanted to know what she could see, and to find out if she had any ideas for helping. Leaving Kay behind had made a sort of desperation churn in his gut.

With Vivian on one side and Risa on the other, he felt like they needed to get the team back together, aside from Maverick. She had too much at stake to dig into her employer or her boyfriend. They didn't need her to betray anyone.

That meant finding Kele. He didn't know what team she'd been transferred to, or have a way to reach anyone at Area 51. They could check the bar off base, he supposed. If Barry remembered them, he might say when she'd last been there.

Vivian growled in frustration. "I keep trying to get something on Kay, and I keep getting nothing."

Dhanya handed Risa a bowl smelling of spices Ben didn't know. "I don't know what a kay is, or what you're trying to do, but whenever I'm trying to treat a patient and a type of drug doesn't work, we try a different approach. Focus on different symptoms. That sort of thing."

Blinking at her, Vivian said, "You're brilliant."

"Okay," Matias said. "Guys, first, you need to stop taking commercial flights. Your names get automatically checked against the no-fly list, and there are so many ways to piggyback on that to find out who's traveling. The second thing you can't do is use your credit cards. That's too easy to track. Third, I'm going to need your phones. All of them. Turned off. I'll have to run out to a store to do it, but I can rig up a version of the mics and earbuds we used to use. For four sets—"

"Five," Ben said. "Expect we'll pick up Kele at some point."

A shadow crossed over Matias's face. "Shouldn't it be

six, then? So we have one for Charlie?"

Risa sighed. "I don't think we should plan to have her on the team again. And it's not just about her wing."

"She's not the enemy," Ben said, "but she's inside the system. They'll watch her more carefully and closely than they watch us. We need to let her keep plausible deniability. It's in everyone's best interest if we don't meet with her unless necessary."

Matias nodded and turned back to the screens. Ben thought he considered arguing for a moment, then dropped it. Text scrolled on three different panels, and websites or something similar filled the rest.

"Five sets of comms that will work over fair distances. I'll see what I can find. The next thing is that I found those articles in those papers, about Angela and Marks. Incidentally, Marks's funeral is next Thursday, at the Iowa Veteran's Cemetery in Adel, Iowa. But I also found two more, about car crashes that killed a delta and an echo. These articles have exactly the same details. All four."

"That doesn't happen." Ben stood and moved to stand behind Matias's chair. Where Matias pointed, Ben saw the articles. He'd arranged them all on a single screen. Like Matias had said, the details matched. The articles each had a different writer, but they reported all the same things.

"Wait. My spider found a fifth. But I don't know the name. Diane Carson."

Yet another blow landed on Ben's shoulders. Too many people had died for something he didn't understand yet. "Carson was on my father's team. Kele and I worked with her before she retired. Code name Ninja."

"I've got something else," Gabi said. "I wasn't expecting the Nova servers to be this easy to get into. I mean, we have a backdoor to the Pentagon for work, but—"

"We do not," Matias said. "We have a perfectly legal connection to a mining server someone was kind enough to set up inside the building. It is absolutely not our fault if the miner didn't think to lock down the network connection because he's using some of the power of the Pentagon's servers to make bank. And we, as patriots and upstanding citizens, would never think to abuse that for our own perfectly legal business purposes."

"No one else understands when you explain these things," Ben said. "You know that, right?"

Matias grinned. "I miss you telling me to shut up and get the job done."

Ben echoed his grin. "Shut up and get the job done."

"Yessir, Cap. Gabi?"

"I found some files. I don't have access to their whole server or anything, but I have a folder of documents that aren't encrypted."

One screen showed movement as several documents opened. Ben walked around the chairs to see the screen in better detail. He scanned the first document, surprised by the contents.

"This one is a memo from General Watts, who retired two years ago, to a colonel I think was a major ten years ago. She advised that Major Hayes should add a note to Kele's file to avoid contact at all costs. Did they cut her loose from the military? I thought for sure they'd just move her to another team after Marks made his recommendation." Ben checked with everyone else, not sure if any of them would know. His gaze fell on Risa.

Of course she knew.

Risa swallowed her mouthful of food. "Kele retired when we did. I don't hear much from her, but I know she has a motorcycle and a dog. If you want to find her, there's a bar in Sturgis, South Dakota, where we should be able to at least leave a message for her. She uses it as kind of a home base, especially around the holidays."

At Vivian's house, he'd been blindsided by her daughter, girlfriend, and horses. For Matias, he hadn't expected the wife and sister. When he saw Kele, he didn't want any damned surprises. "Is there anything else you'd like to share about her?"

Risa raised her brow. "If you ever looked through our Christmas cards, you'd know a lot more than you do."

"You could've told me we got cards from the team."

"I did. You said, and I quote, 'That's nice, dear.' After the third time, I stopped mentioning it."

Vivian giggled. "This is amazing. I've never seen you guys fight about anything before."

"We're not fighting," Ben grumbled. He turned his back on them and re-read the memo. That first year, he hadn't wanted to hear anything anything about the team. At Christmas, he'd still been raw and reeling. Once Kay left for the Academy, he'd wanted connections, but probably hadn't thought to ask about the team. They'd been told not to, after all.

He'd followed the fucking rules, dammit.

Risa and Vivian whispered to each other.

Ben ignored them. "Can you switch to the next document, please?" He checked the next document, another memo. "I think this folder might be all memos."

"I'll spread them out for you," Gabi said.

She arranged seven memos so they took up three and a half screens. Ben read one, moved to the next, and kept going. The picture they painted made his skin crawl.

"These four are from the first year after they retired us. Each one lists details of one of us. Place of employment, supervisor, address, associates, routine habits, monthly bills, savings, document tags for phone logs, major purchases, and store names where we routinely shop."

"That's not fucking creepy or anything," Matias said. "What the fuck do they need that much information for?"

"I knew they knew some of this stuff." After all, Steve had helped Ben and Risa find their house and jobs. He'd suggested the type of cars they get, and handed them a list of places to find necessities in their new neighborhood. They'd been told not to stand out, which meant they needed to know what normal people did.

"The breadth is jaw-dropping," Risa said. She stood

beside him. "Look, that's Greg Boone's name. What is this?"

Ben peered at the memo she indicated. "That one has a list of details coinciding with details of the car accidents. From the date, it followed the first accident."

"He might've noticed afterward and made a list," Matias said. "I'm going to go with him being fucking creepy like the rest of these assholes, though."

"Charlie married him." Risa frowned. "And he's the Academy Administrator. We didn't even realize that until we met him on Thursday. We didn't meet the headmaster. What was her name? She signs all the official correspondence we get. Why didn't we meet her?"

"Adelaide Miller. We probably didn't meet her because Charlie took us straight to Boone." Ben waved at the last two documents. "This one is a list of things that look like military project names—Spark Watch, Airwave Kraken, Spitfire Blindfold. Also with Boone's name on it, which is a little distressing. I don't see why he'd have any involvement with military projects that need vague code names."

"Maybe because of Charlie?" Risa shook her head. "She couldn't tell us what she really does as the liaison."

"Maybe. This last one is cryptic." Ben read it again, and then a third time, before he figured out the message between the lines. "It looks like a memo about supply chains that doesn't make any sense, but what I see is a note authorizing an insertion into someplace that retired general didn't want to admit she was authorizing an insertion into.

"We did a lot of covert missions," Ben said with a frown, "and each one had a specific, detailed authorization from Special Operations Command. I read them all to be clear on our orders. Those authorizations didn't come as vague memos. They came as classified documents indicating what we could and couldn't do, and where we could and couldn't go. They gave Marks the authority to request insertion and extraction teams, and detailed exactly what he could and couldn't negotiate with the locals for. This is..."

He read it again. "This is effectively a blank check. It

doesn't even define the mission area or timeframe. No one would have to issue authorizations for Nova missions after this. Ever."

The implications staggered him. Whoever ran the Novas could do anything they wanted. That didn't mean they would, but they could. Marks wouldn't have used it, and Ben didn't think his successor would have either. Its existence still made him squirm.

Matias cleared his throat. "I've been checking hits on that General Watts. She's dead. I'll give you three guesses how, and the first two don't count."

"Fuck," Ben said. "We need Kele."

"You gonna road trip to South Dakota?" Matias asked.

"Are you kidding, Matty?" Standing in the doorway to the kitchen, Dhanya planted her fists on her hips. "You're going with them."

Matias turned to face his wife. "I can't just—"

"Yes, you can just. Call work, tell them your sister needs you for a week or two. Then get your ass into the car and go with your friends."

Ben cleared his throat in the silence that followed. "In my experience, when your wife says to do something, you do it."

# CHAPTER 22

## KELE

November 26, 2017
21:13

At Kele's request, the bartender turned off the music and turned up the volume on a Flamengos vs Santos football game. She dropped enough money at Marty's place that he usually did what she asked. Her tab cleared every month with a bonus for him to make sure the place stayed open and had enough help. By now, she could've owned the bar if she wanted. She didn't want.

So long as he handed her a beer when she walked in, changed the channel to football, and didn't bitch about her dog, she didn't want a stake in the place. The welcome covered her needs.

She sat with her feet on her table, watching the game in progress. Kachina sat in the chair beside her, crunching kibble. The Australian shepherd had two Army camouflage bowls that Marty kept for her. He'd gone so far as to keep a bag of Kachina's preferred food at the bar.

The door opened, and she noticed Marty giving the newcomer a look. When she turned, she didn't know what to think of their visitor. She watched him survey the room, taking in the broken chairs, spilled beer, and unconscious bodies littering the floor.

Some idiot had started a bar fight. Kele had ended it. These things happened.

"Cap," she said, tipping her bottle in his direction. Seeing Ben brought a lot of things to mind.

She remembered meeting Ben for the first time. The rookie lieutenant had been so young. One Captain Kinetic retired, the next one took his place. The Legacies worked that way. At the time, Kele hadn't thought they'd gotten a good trade. Ninja, on the other hand, had seen potential and shaped Ben into the leader he eventually became.

"Kele." Ben picked his way through the incapacitated bikers to reach her. Something about the set of his shoulders or the lines around his mouth spoke to tension and despair. She'd known him too long not to see it. Even after ten years, she could still read him cold.

"Marty, get this man a beer. He looks like he needs one."

"Whatever's handy is fine," Ben said.

Kele smirked. "He's lying. He'll have one of mine."

Marty nodded and set a bottle of her imported Chilean microbrew on the bar for Ben. He took the bottle and sat across the table from her. For a long few minutes, they sat and watched the game. Kachina barked when Santos scored, showing her preference.

Kele watched Ben more than the game. He reminded her of his father when he started to see his retirement on the horizon. Life had worn him down. The years dragged in a way they hadn't a decade ago. She knew he had a shitty day job because Risa mentioned it in one of her cards.

Every year, Risa sent her a Christmas card with a fresh tube of tennis balls for Kachina. Kele sent back a picture of the dog in the sidecar of her motorcycle, happily displaying her new tennis ball.

Those first few had been tough to read. She imagined they'd been tougher to write. Risa probably had no idea how much she'd put between the lines of her short messages.

"You come all the way from Cincinnati to watch football and drink beer with me?"

"No. It's a nice perk, though. You drink better beer than I do."

"You're not chugging American crap these days, are you?"

He grinned. "No. German crap."

"German beer is overrated. Except that one we found in that shitty little village, brewed by those monks. That was a damned fine beer."

"Veitsrodt." Ben nodded, maybe remembering the bar they'd found with his father's old team after an intercept in the hills near Ramstein. They'd stolen a jeep and drove into the countryside, using Ben as a translator, just like they'd done with his father. The team had stopped when they found a place offering some pastry Ninja had wanted.

"Ninja is dead," Ben said.

"No shit? When did that happen?" Kele thought of how many teammates she'd lost through the years. One more kind of mattered, and it kind of didn't. She knew Diane had lived a good life. She would've hit her sixties or seventies by now.

"About six months ago." He ran his thumb over the pattern in the glass of his bottle. "Did you see the news about Jay?"

"No, but I can tell you the World Cup standings."

He didn't smile like she thought he would. That meant bad news. "KIA."

She shouldn't have a cracked a joke after the Ninja lead-in. "Fuck. I'm sorry, Ben."

"Someone killed him, Kele. And Diane, and Colonel Marks, and some other people. I can't prove it yet, but I'm getting there."

The idea of a mission crept through in Kele's blood. She caught a faint whiff of the sweet tang of copper and gunfire. Her muscles tensed, ready to spring into action. "Orders, Cap?"

She saw his back straighten. Army Captain Benjamin Tsukuda might have been forced into retirement. Captain Kinetic of the 11th Rangers, alpha-level Nova, still lived inside him. Ten years might have dulled the edges, but he still had plenty of fire inside.

"Has anyone from the Novas or the Pentagon contacted you about anything?"

"Nope. Haven't heard a peep or seen anybody." In deference to his posture, Kele sat up and leaned her arms on the table. "I don't carry a phone, though. If they wanted to contact me, they'd have to go through this bar or get lucky on the road."

Cap nodded. "I thought they were going to reassign you to another team."

"I wish." Kele flicked her gaze to the game. Both teams were Brazilian. She wanted to go back there and do the whole week over again. They should've found the second site on that first mission. Then they would've been in better shape, and Vivian would've seen the attack on the Academy coming. Kele had walked right past the stupid door. Her boot had probably stomped it.

She needed to think about something more productive. They couldn't go back in time and fix her fuckups. They couldn't go back in time to save Jay. They could move forward and give his parents some closure.

"Where was Jay killed?"

"On mission. That's all I know. No one will talk to us. At this point, they've got to be hiding something. It's been over a week and they haven't released the body yet."

He didn't have to say that he still harbored some hope they'd made a mistake. She heard it in his voice and saw it in his eyes. Until he saw his son lying in a coffin, it would eat him from the inside like cancer. On that day when they laid Jay to rest, Ben would crack.

Kele hoped Risa could handle it.

They needed a mission, and Ben didn't have one. He couldn't see past his grief to come up with one. Kele wanted back into the field so much, she'd follow him to Hell if he asked.

She opened her mouth and said what came to mind. "Do you want to stealth in and steal him?"

Ben frowned like he hadn't considered the possibility. "I don't know where he is."

"Then maybe we should figure that out. That's how we do this shit, Ben. We tug on a thread and see what it leads to. That's why we went to Brazil in the first place. Some anonymous asshole sent a tip and we went to check it out."

He drummed his fingers on the table. Unlike the raw, fresh wound left by his son, this one formed a scar he definitely needed to trace with his finger, a well-worn path he must've torn apart a thousand times and would tear apart a thousand more. "Do you ever wonder who that anonymous source was?"

She didn't. She never did. However the chain of events started, her concern always centered around the end. "Not really."

"I guess it doesn't matter, but I think it might've been the old man. Wilhelm Otto. I think he had something to say down in Brazil." Ben tapped the bottom of his half-empty bottle against the table. "I wish I knew what it was."

"The thing he had to say was fuck you, I'm making my own superpowered people so I can attack in the middle of the night on Thanksgiving." Kele shook her head. "There's no deeper meaning to search for, Cap. He was an asshole Nazi who didn't give a shit about other people. Saw them as animals." Her people knew a thing or two about that.

Ben watched his bottle as he kept tapping it on the table. "Or was he trying to save his son's life?"

Suddenly, Kele understood where this conversation needed to go. "Cap. Ben. You're nothing like that man, and you'll never be anything like that man. You never gave or followed shitty orders, and you always had my back."

He stopped tapping his bottle and drank the last of his beer. Whatever churned in his head, she knew he didn't agree with her. Of course there had been shitty orders he'd followed because he didn't know any better. There had been shitty orders he'd given as a rookie. Once he'd hit his stride, though, she'd been grateful he had the same code name as his father. More than a few times, she'd thought the elder Captain Tsukuda had rejoined the team.

"You're a lot like your dad." She thought he maybe needed to hear that. Some guys would take it as an insult, but not Ben.

"Thanks. But he retired on his own terms. I'm not that much like him."

"He fucked up sometimes, you know. Made a wrong choice. Failed at a mission objective. It happened."

"Did he ever get people killed? Because when I fucked up, I got people killed."

She wondered if he still had nightmares about that night like she did. "What happened that night wasn't your fault, Ben. It was a lot more my fault than yours."

"Nothing about that night was your fault. You did everything right."

"Like fuck I did." Kele snorted. "Have you been blaming yourself for the entirety of that clusterfuck all this time?"

He gave the wall his best grim stare, which answered the question well enough. "It was my responsibility."

"I'll grant that it was your job to take responsibility for the team's actions." She jabbed a finger at him. "But I won't let you keep thinking it was all your fault. You didn't create the too-lax security scheme for the base or the Academy. You didn't miss that secret tunnel any more than the rest of us did. We all missed stuff at those sites, and I'll bet the gals who did the data decryption did too. Questioning the intel that sent us to Brazil wasn't your responsibility, that belonged to everyone in the intel chain, plus Marks and Watts.

"You did listen to Omen and stand up to Marks, which got us home in time to be there that night. One hour later, and we wouldn't have been there. One hour. Did you see how many Novas fought that night? We were the only full team there. A handful of others came, and some of the kids defended themselves. Imagine that night without us there."

She watched the gears work in his head. He and his father both got the same distant gleam in their eyes when their brains worked on complex problems.

"They blamed us because they wanted to blame someone, and it all seemed connected. That doesn't mean we deserved it." She knew she should believe that, but it was hard. People like her, people like Ben, they'd been built to shoulder the blame. Fucking military used that against them. Fuck, she wanted to work for them again.

At least in the military, her life had some fucking meaning. Once upon a time, she did a job that saved lives. Sure, she took them. A lot of them. And maybe the meaning could get blurry, but she followed orders, did her job, and trusted that she was saving lives somewhere. It meant something.

He set his bottle on the table and stood. "I think I know where we need to go next. Risa has the address. She's in the car. You can come if you want."

Kele set her feet on the floor and patted Kachina on the head. Like she wouldn't go. Even if she wound up sitting on her ass like every other fucking day of every other fucking week, at least she'd sit on her ass with old friends for once. "C'mon, girl. We're going for a ride."

# CHAPTER 23

## IARIESAH

November 27, 2017
20:12

Risa stood with Ben as he rang a doorbell in a pleasant suburb of Chicago. Manicured lawns, tidy gardens, and sculpted shrubs surrounded stately homes with two or three floors. The street reminded Risa of a more upscale version of theirs in Cincinnati. Much as no other Asian or Islander heritage people lived near them, Risa suspected Phyllicia's mother might be the only black homeowner in the neighborhood.

Matias, Vivian, and Kele waited at the hotel they'd picked for tonight while she and Ben visited to find out if Tanisha would share Phyllicia's letters with them. He'd remembered her mentioning them when they talked on the phone.

Since neither she nor Ben had their phones, they didn't know if Steve or anyone else had called during the day, but she suspected not.

Tanisha answered the door in a fuzzy robe, sweatpants, and slippers. They'd met in person a few times before. She seemed older, more tired, and skinnier than a few years ago. Her dark, frizzy hair had turned a middling shade of gray, lending her the gravitas of an elder. Risa wondered if she looked like hell too.

"You're not supposed to be here." She frowned and started to shut the door.

Ben touched the door. Tanisha stopped trying close it.

Risa clutched her hands in front of her chest to beg. "Tanisha, wait. Please. Just give us a few minutes. We're on the same side. We want the same things. Our children were best friends. I can't speak for Phyllicia, but I know Jay would want us to help each other. He worried about you because you're alone."

After a long, tense pause, Tanisha nodded and sighed. "You're right. Come in. She'd want—" Opening the door for them, she dug a wadded tissue from her robe pocket and dabbed her eyes. "Come in."

Risa's shoes echoed on the hardwood floor. She stepped out of them beside the door and pulled her sweater closer. Nothing hung on the walls. In the front room, stacks of boxes huddled in the center. They followed Tanisha to the empty kitchen. Nothing sat on the granite countertops, nothing hung from the walls.

"Are you moving?" Risa asked.

"Without Philly's salary, I can't afford the mortgage. I'm downsizing so the bills can't take all our savings. It probably seems fast, but I can't… This house. She bought it for me when she got her commission. It's hers. I can't look at anything here without seeing my baby."

Risa hugged her. Tanisha's tears made her cry again. She thought of the argument she'd never have with Jay over whether he could make Phyllicia his best man at his wedding.

"I'm sorry I was short on the phone." Tanisha pulled away from Risa and wiped her nose. "I just don't want to talk about it. I don't want to think about it. It's like an open wound that keeps bleeding, and I don't even know if a funeral will help anymore."

"I know," Risa said. "I feel the same way."

Ben nodded. "Have you heard anything else from the Novas?"

"No. I called my congress people, though. One said he was proud to represent someone who made such a noble sacrifice for the country. I hung up on him instead of telling him to do terrible things to himself."

She shook her head and wiped her nose again. "I don't know what to do with Philly's things. She didn't leave much here, but every time she visited, she'd bring some stuff and leave it. For safekeeping, she said. And then all her letters home. It's just— I can't— I can't. I don't want to throw it out because I keep thinking, maybe someday, but I can't deal with it all right now."

Risa noticed Ben's head shifting. She glanced aside and met his gaze. He wanted her to ask. She agreed and tried not to lean too hard. The woman had been through enough already.

"Jay hardly ever wrote to us," Risa said. "He'd call once in a while."

"I still have a voicemail from him," Ben murmured.

"Philly wrote at least once a month, every month since she started at the Academy. Always telling me about the drama and the missions they did. She didn't get detailed or anything, but she knew I wanted to travel someday, so she'd tell me about the things they did off-duty without naming places. She and Jay, they were so good together. I asked her why they didn't date, and she said it'd be like dating her brother."

"That's about what he said." Ben nodded and managed a faint smile.

Risa covered Tanisha's hand with her own. She knew how she'd feel if Tanisha asked her for this, so she tread lightly. "If there's so much about Jay, I wonder if you'd let us look through some of them?"

"Oh my goodness." Tanisha gripped Risa's hand and shook her head. Her eyes watered. "Please take it all. Watch over it for me. I'm afraid I'll toss some of it in the middle of the night, then regret it later. Take my baby's legacy and keep it safe."

"We will," Ben said. He touched Tanisha's shoulder. "I promise. When you're ready, come visit us, and we'll all go through it together."

Risa nodded. "With wine. Lots of wine."

"Bless you both." Tanisha stood and battled her tears while showing them where to find all the letters and boxes.

The woman had no one to mourn with, no one to hold her. Risa held her and let her weep. Ben carried everything to the car, then waited there. He didn't try to hurry her, which she appreciated.

An hour later, Risa helped Tanisha up the stairs and to bed, then let herself out. Ben used his power to lock the deadbolt. He drove them back to the hotel. When they arrived at the cheap, crappy place, Matias and Kele helped carry the boxes inside while Risa splashed water on her face.

She hated how lucky she felt for having plenty of family. Tanisha had no one. Philly's father had never been in the picture, Tanisha's brother had died in prison without a family, and her parents had already passed.

Vivian touched her shoulder. "Do you want to go through those letters and things, or sit this out? I can see how it might be hard. Ben is stiff-upper-lipping all this, but I'm not buying it. He doesn't want to read any of it. If you don't, then don't."

"I do." Risa patted Vivian's hand and straightened. "I want to read it all. Every piece. Not all of it tonight, but I need to see him through someone else's lens. I need to know I did everything I could."

Vivian nodded. "Then hop to it, honey. I'm going out for food. Everyone else is next door."

Risa took a deep breath and joined the rest of the team as they sat on the two beds in the second small room. Ben stared at a box he hadn't yet opened. Kele and Matias had each opened a box already. Matias found a stuffed bear in lederhosen. Kele flipped through a notebook with handwritten notes.

She sat beside Ben and opened the box at his feet. He'd picked one with letters in opened envelopes. Tanisha had kept that one in a separate spot, so he knew what he'd find inside it. Ben chose this box for himself on purpose, then couldn't force himself to face it.

Thumbing through the envelopes, Risa discovered that Tanisha had arranged them in chronological order. She must have filed them in the box all along, because the top layer had the most recent letters. Risa read Philly's last letter, a single page of tidy handwriting. As she unfolded it, a picture fell to her lap.

Jay held the camera for a selfie of himself and Philly, both smiling. The pair stood in front of a church steeple, both wearing Army jackets. Risa recognized it. He'd texted her the same image. Seeing it in a larger format made her want to go through her phone, download all the pictures he'd ever sent, and print them all.

Handing the photo to Ben, she turned her attention to the letter. Philly avoided mentioning where they'd been or what they did, except for a few hints. Risa checked the picture again, looking at the shape of the steeple. Combined with the vague hints, she thought she knew where it had been taken.

Vivian walked in the door and handed out food. The smell of chicken, rice, and soy sauce threatened to derail all of Risa's thoughts. She opened her box and stuffed something into her mouth without looking. Her suspicions swirled while she chewed and swallowed.

"Do you remember when we were stationed at Ramstein for a few months? We took Jay with us, but Kay wasn't born yet."

Ben nodded, still looking at the picture. "They had that string of problems with locals. Took us a while to find them all. Three field executions, two put into prison. But I don't remember when it was."

"March, April, and May of '99," Matias said. "I

remember because Gabi had an attack, and I spent a day on the phone with her and her doctor. Cost me an arm and a leg to do that."

"What about it?" Kele said. "That was a long time ago."

"One day, after a mission," Risa said, "we hopped into a Jeep, and Ben drove us to a bar in the middle of nowhere. All the way there, you raved about some beer made by a group of monks or something. I didn't think it was that great, but you all liked it."

Ben squinted at the picture. "Veitsrodt. That's the church in Veitsrodt. What the hell were they doing in Germany? The German government threatened to reclaim Ramstein if the Novas didn't stop operating out of it in…oh-three, I think."

"After Kitty's team started a wildfire while off-duty," Vivian said. "I remember that because I was the one who called the fire in. We were in Afghanistan, and a vision about it woke me up."

"They might've renegotiated to have Novas there," Kele said.

Matias shrugged. "Does it matter? Shouldn't we be more interested in where they were for the final mission?"

"This…" Ben frowned and handed back the picture. "It makes it harder to believe the Novas aren't using the blank check Watts gave them."

"Good point," Vivian said. "By the way, I still haven't been able to get anything but that one unhelpful stack of metaphors. I've tried focusing on Kay, Boone, the Academy, even Charlie. Nothing. It's not just nothing, though. It's a lack of something. It's hard to explain, but I'm getting an empty vision, I guess. Like, there's something to see, but I'm blind for some reason."

Risa shook her head. She didn't know what to think or have any suggestions for Vivian. "If the Novas are using their blank check, who's calling the shots? Who's picking the missions, and what are the objectives? When we did this, it was all about national security and helping countries without their own supers. What's the goal now?"

She folded the picture into the letter and put it back in the box. "What did they have my baby doing?"

"Vivian, have you tried focusing on Jay?" Matias asked.

Vivian shook her head. "There's no future for a— For him. I can only get visions about living people."

Matias shrugged. "How about one of his teammates?"

"I don't know any of them." Vivian stopped, raised a finger, and said, "Actually, that's not true. Or, maybe it's not true. I don't know who was on his team, but if it was any of those kids in the room that night of the attack, then I can try to get something one of them."

"We've met the other kids a few times," Ben said. "I saw them at the Academy on Thanksgiving. He worked with Cowboy, a blonde girl, a Latino boy, and another girl called Scope. I don't know much about any of them. Jay never formally introduced us. Other than everyone knows Cowboy is from Oklahoma and has that stupid hat. I don't think his father served, though."

"I can try to get something on him. You never know." Vivian looked at her food. "After I eat."

Risa kept reading. She scanned another three letters while the others talked. "Guys, I don't think the team got along very well. Listen to this. 'I'm pretty sure Bobby and Meghan are dating, even though that's against the rules. Jay doesn't want to report it because it's not impacting the team, but I think he's biased because of his parents. I'd like to report it because getting either of them off the team would solve all these problems.'

"And here's another one. 'Once again, Jay and I are kicking it without the rest of the team. We're doing an insertion in two days, on a planned mission for once. I decided to ask about transferring to another team because of all the stuff going on, but they said if I transferred, it would just be me. They won't keep Jay and me together. So that's obviously not an option.' "

Risa shook her head and sighed. "This poor girl. I'm

not seeing mention of the problems or stuff she refers to, but maybe that was in earlier letters, or in phone calls."

"What the fuck?" Matias said. "If that's what she told her mom, the whole story must've been really shitty. Why didn't they split the team?"

"Why didn't Jay ever say anything?" Risa covered her face, wondering if he thought they would tell him to man up and soldier on.

"Because I wouldn't have," Ben murmured. "I would've done my job and not complained."

"And you would've covered for them at the same time," Kele said. "Making the team weaker. Which is why you were so good at your job. Because your team didn't need covering."

"Most of the team," Vivian said.

"You may have been fucked up," Matias said, "but you got the job done."

"And we love you," Risa said.

Kele held up a stuffed bear in a hula skirt. "I feel like we need beer and football for the turn this conversation just took."

Risa saw the bear and teetered on the razor edge between laughing and crying. Jay would hate to see her cry so much, she thought.

She burst into laughter. The rest of the room followed.

# CHAPTER 24

## MATIAS

November 28, 2017
00:31

Everyone went to bed except Matias. Still on Pacific time, and on a schedule that kept him up to midnight routinely, he didn't feel tired. Everyone else had gone to bed a half hour ago, though. Ben and Risa shared a room with Kele. Vivian slept on the other bed in the room with Matias.

The boxes had been repacked and stacked against the wall. He sat up with his laptop, typing to his sister and his wife. His VPN gave him an anonymous enough connection through the hotel's wifi, and they used encryption anyway for work. The team had been using cash since they left his place, which meant no obvious paper trail.

In the meantime, Gabi had been working on a deeper dive into the Pentagon's servers, and more webcrawlers. She sent him the names of three more former Novas who'd been killed in suspicious car accidents, and a long list of all the code names KIA or retired in the past ten years. Scanning the list, he saw every name he could remember.

Unless he had the wrong basic count, it looked like every single Nova who'd been active before the Academy opened had retired or died. The majority of the dates fell before 2012, with three teams remaining active for another two years.

Four years ago, the first Academy graduates had entered service.

The timing suggested someone had gone to a lot of trouble to force a turnover in Nova membership. For some reason. He remembered the fanfare about the Academy's first graduating class. At the time, he hadn't paid much attention to a group of kids rushing off to do the job he should've been doing.

He'd fucked up so hard that night. Charlie lost her wing because he lost his grip on the fire. Because he wanted to win. Because they'd never failed.

Ten years ago, his ego had almost killed his best friend, and he hadn't seen her since. He'd sat in that field long after paramedics had picked up Charlie and Doc. Not until Marks came and told him he needed to go home had he noticed the sun came up and someone carted away the bodies.

In arm's reach, one charred feather had stuck out of the ground. He remembered picking it up and shuffling back to the barracks.

The sprinklers had gone off inside because someone left their window open, so the building hadn't shielded their phone from the EMP pulse. The resulting smoke had set off the fire alarm about five minutes after Risa roused them and they all rushed for the Academy.

He still remembered the smell of fire retardant in his towel. Someone had suggested a shower to help him feel better about not-quite-murdering his teammate. Or maybe they thought it would scrub away the sight of her blackened wing and burned flesh.

Fried chicken hadn't been one of his preferred foods before, but he hadn't looked at it or smelled it without gagging since that night.

If only he hadn't heard Risa when she told them about that old guy in the watchtower. If only he'd ignored her and waited for Ben. If only he'd had more trouble with the assholes between him and the enemy leader.

Then Charlie would've been okay, and the team would've stayed together.

He never would've been around to fall for his wife, a tiny voice reminded him. Getting to know his sister's home nurse had been the best thing that ever happened to him.

Matias rubbed his face. "Stop thinking about it," he whispered.

Dhanya typed to him in Hindi. She switched to it when she knew he needed to focus, because it forced him to concentrate on the words and translate them in his head. He had no idea how she knew. The woman had her own specialized superpower of Understanding Matias From Anywhere.

The message made him smirk. *You're lagging.* She and Gabi must've noticed him not typing anything for too long.

He reassured them he was tired and asked if they had anything else.

Vivian sat up like a bolt of lightning, scaring the shit out of Matias. He fumbled to keep from dropping his laptop.

"Chinese." Vivian dropped to the bed again and slept on.

"Jesus fucking Christ!" Matias did *not* remember her ever doing that on any mission. He panted to catch his breath and had no idea what that outburst meant.

"Shut up," Vivian grumbled. "Tryna sleep."

"You're the one who shouted 'Chinese.' "

"Did not."

"Did you have a dream about something Chinese?"

Vivian sat up and rubbed her eyes. "No. I was dreaming about black horses in a museum."

Matias knew she had random dreams like anyone else, so he didn't press about it. "You must've said it for a reason."

"My dad made me learn Mandarin, but I haven't used it in a long time. I'm pretty rusty. I think the last time I heard anyone was…" She stood and shuffled to the bathroom.

Figuring she had to think about it, Matias returned to chatting with Gabi. She'd finished updating an app for work and wanted him to test it on his phone.

The toilet flushed and Vivian bolted out of the bathroom. "Okay. The last time I heard Mandarin was that night. There was a woman speaking Mandarin in the Academy, but she wasn't an attacker. She said something about the stairs up being blocked, I think? It sounded like she was herding someone to safety."

Matias stared at her. "Why would anyone speak Chinese at the Academy? All those kids spoke English. It was a requirement to get in. I remember the arguments about it boiled down to money, like they always do."

"She didn't sound like a kid."

They stared at each other.

Matias tapped a message to Gabi, asking her to check into the Chinese supers program. He had some vague memories about them having a few unusual psychic specialties, but they never went to China or ran across Chinese agents, so he never paid much attention to it. "I don't know what that means, but if you blurted it in your sleep, it's gotta mean something."

"Yeah. Something." Vivian sagged. "I need more sleep. It's past my bedtime."

"Night."

Five minutes later, Gabi dropped links into their chat. Matias checked them and found confirmation for his vague memory. Scanning the article made his brow climb with every paragraph. "Viv," he whispered. "Are you still awake?"

"Not really."

"One of the Chinese psychic specialties is fucking with other psychics."

"What?" She rolled to face him and propped herself up on one arm. "Say that again?"

"In the seventies, right before Vietnam ended, the Novas captured a Chinese supers team of three by hitting them with tranq darts. They learned that the Chinese had a limited number of power specialties, but their levels were off the charts. One was what they called a psychic nullifier. Her presence nullified or twisted their telepath's ability for anyone within a hundred yards. If the telepath was that close, she was just plain fucked. No effect on other kinds of abilities, which is why no one ever figured it out until they had prisoners."

Vivian stared at him. "Wait. You mean— But that means— My mom—"

The implications hit Matias. "Jesus. It means your mom didn't fuck up Tet. The Chinese had one of these supers close enough to affect her. They twisted her visions."

She covered her face. Matias saw her shoulders shake. He set aside his laptop and moved to her bed to hold onto her.

"It's okay, Viv. You weren't even born yet. This isn't your fault." More occurred to him. "And if there was a Chinese woman at the Academy that night, for whatever reason, then maybe she was a nullifier, and that's why you didn't see the attack coming."

"But my powers worked," she sobbed. "My power made me go there, and then it protected me and those kids. I mean, I thought it was you guys, but the power still protected them."

Matias shrugged. "Like I understand how your power works. Maybe you've got enough juice to overcome it when you're close or something. Or maybe the morphine fucked with her fucking with you. Or, hell, you were knocked up. Who knows? Whatever happened, you couldn't see it, and those fuckers in OpCon should've known why."

"My mom killed herself because of Tet."

"Yeah. I know." Matias rubbed her back. "I'm sorry."

"Why now?" She rubbed her nose on her sleeve. "Why make me sit up and shout now? Why not then?"

"I dunno." The question demanded an answer. Matias thought about it. If her power made her shout it now, that meant it made a difference now. "You said you keep getting blanks trying to use your power on Kay, Charlie, Boone, and anyone else at the Academy. So what if that Chinese lady never left? Or had a kid who's in the program now?"

Vivian stilled. "What if someone's going to attack the Academy again? Kay is there. Lots of kids are there."

"It's built into a mountain." Matias had seen the news reports. No cameras allowed in, and impressive security and lockdown procedures. He and Gabi had probed the location once, just to see what they'd find. Pros had set up the cybersecurity, and shielded the internal network from the external connections. The layout had impressed him and Gabi enough that they'd quit trying.

"I don't think anyone's going to get inside by attacking. Maybe someone who's there is in danger, though? Because they're planning on leaving soon?"

"Who would leave now? Don't they have two or three more weeks until the end of the semester?" She swiped her sleeve across her face again and snapped her fingers. "The rest of Jay's team. They're at the Academy for evaluations."

"So we need to check on them. I dunno about finding them, but everybody knows who Cowboy's family is." Matias hugged Vivian. "We'll tell the others in the morning, then I guess we get to go to Oklahoma while Ben and Risa head to Marks's funeral. For now, get some sleep."

Vivian nodded. "I just wish— Never mind. Good night. Again."

Matias had a fair idea of what Vivian wished for. He had wishes too. His didn't get solved or changed by the presence of a Chinese lady, though.

"Stop thinking about it," he murmured to himself.

Since that night, he hadn't used his fire. Not even a flicker. His skin stayed warm all the time because he didn't use that heat for anything. At this point, he didn't even know if he could make fire anymore.

He shouldn't have come. Everything he'd done so far, he could've done from home. They didn't need him. The biggest screwup on the team had nothing to offer but computer skills, and Gabi could program circles around him.

Dhanya sent him a picture. Sometimes they doctored pictures for Gabi, so she could pretend she'd visited faraway places. Matias usually picked locations of missions the team had completed, because he could tell her a story to go with each image.

This picture showed Dhanya and Gabi together at a cathedral in Salzburg. They'd plucked the background off the internet, because Matias had never been to Austria. France, Italy, Germany, and a bunch of other European countries, but not Austria. He typed his wife to let her know. She'd have to come up with a story on her own.

Germany. Jay's team had been in Germany. Why had Jay's team been in Germany, and had that been their final mission?

He checked for supers activity in Germany, wondering if their escapades had made any headlines. Nothing came up, so he asked Gabi to check German headlines for anything unexpected. She had a spider that could handle most languages.

When she said she'd get it rolling, he sent good night messages to her and his wife. He needed to get some sleep as much as Vivian. They had a long drive tomorrow.

# CHAPTER 25

## BEN

November 28, 2017
06:32

Matias wasted no time with technobabble as he explained everything to Ben over breakfast. He talked about Chinese nullifiers, reminding Ben about Jiao, Kay's Chinese-American friend, and visiting Cowboy's family. Then he returned Ben's phone with the web browser opened to a recent headline from a German newspaper based in Mannheim.

Ben stared at the screen, reading it five times before he could accept it. "They went to Germany to kill a politician. That's what you're saying."

"That's what it looks like. The date lines up, and we couldn't find anything else suspicious."

According to the article, the politician wanted to officially restart Germany's supers program. Popular opinion disagreed, though not by a wide margin. If the Vice President made any more idiotic comments suggesting the US would withdraw from NATO, Ben thought more Germans might agree.

"I can see a reason why someone might want this man dead." The idea left Ben wondering who had stepped into

General Watts's role of directing how to deploy the Novas. That person had used Jay and his team as pawns in some kind of international game. There had to be other instances. He couldn't believe they'd never done it before.

"Can you have Gabi check for other political assassinations of foreign leaders interested in resuming or stepping up their supers programs?"

"That's a pretty wide net, but I'll see what she can do." Mathias tapped on his phone. "Gabi and I set up an app that — You know, what? Never mind." He stacked everyone else's phones on the table. "Here's what you need to know. Don't call or text anyone you don't have to, and keep the GPS turned off. Let unnecessary calls go to voice mail, and don't reply to texts without a good reason. The fewer chances they have to bypass what Gabi and I did, the better."

Ben nodded and tucked his phone in his pocket. The others did the same.

"If we visit Cowboy's family today, we should have enough time to get to Marks's funeral on Thursday. I'm just not sure we should all go to Tulsa. Is there anything else you guys could do in a hotel in Iowa?"

"I could do plenty," Matias said. "But we'd have to rent another car."

Kele shrugged. "If you don't mind riding with Kachina in your lap, we can go. It's, what, a five hour ride from here?"

"If she doesn't mind and you have space for my stuff, I can live with that. Being in a single place will let me help Gabi more, and I'll have time to put together this radio stuff so we can have comms if we need them. I should be able to set them up so we can test them at the funeral."

Ben met Kele's gaze. She nodded. He, Vivian, and Risa would watch each other's backs, and Kele would keep an eye on Matias.

"Let's do it, then." Ben stood and dropped cash on the table to pay for their food. "We'll see you in Adel."

Risa sat in the backseat with Vivian, and they put their heads together over the remainder of Phyllicia's letters.

Settling in for a long, boring ride, Ben turned on the radio. He didn't want to think about anything except how to get to Tulsa and what he'd say when he got there.

Despite that, Ben's head filled with ideas about what he wanted to do to whoever had taken over the Novas. The missions Ben and the team had run always had a basic, foundational purpose of saving lives and making the world a safer place. Marks had never sent them to meddle in politics. They'd toppled a government or two in their time, but only after receiving intelligence about human rights abuses or gross international treaty violations.

Most of their foreign soil missions had cleaned up messes the local government couldn't handle for one reason or another. The number of countries with their own version of the Novas was small. Ten years ago, the Novas had become a sort of international police force. Covert missions had been few and far between.

He should've paid more attention to international news. Maybe he would've noticed the shift in purpose. Somehow. If he'd cared about anything beyond his shitty job, he might've saved his son.

Two hours later, Risa leaned forward and patted Ben's shoulder. "I'm not sure I like what I'm reading in these letters. It sounds like Cowboy formed a little posse with two other members of the team. He's sleeping with the other girl, and the Latino boy is his flunky."

Ben recalled meeting the rest of the team. "Aren't there two other girls? A blonde and Scope?"

"Phyllicia writes about Scope like he's a guy," Vivian said.

"But she's a girl." Ben did remember that Scope dressed like a boy, but the implications of a girl referring to another girl as a boy confused him.

Vivian shrugged. "Some people aren't what they seem to be. Like, you know, people who wear masks to hide their identity so they can shop at the grocery store without being recognized?"

Or, Ben thought, two women who pretended they shared a house as roommates instead of lovers. The idea of two women together distracted him for a few moments before Risa started talking again.

"Whatever Scope is or isn't, Phyllicia's letters seem to suggest the team was anything but one. There's a letter from a few years ago where she says Jay talked to their handlers about it, but they brushed it off as the group needing more team-building exercises. A few months later, she mentions that she and Jay decided to just suck it up and deal because no one wanted to hear about problems."

"I don't remember Jay ever bringing that up with me." Ben wondered if Jay ever would have talked about it with him. He knew Jay wanted to prove himself worth of Kenzo's code name. At his age, Ben hadn't considered asking his dad for advice about problems. But then, he'd had Kele by his side and his father's old team helping him grow up.

Jay never had the luxury of experienced Novas guiding him in the field. Of course, Ben never had the luxury of six years of training before joining the military.

"Ben, you were his hero." Risa kissed his cheek. "He wanted you to be proud of him."

Staring at the road, Ben knew he'd done the same thing. He'd taken his problems to Marks, Kele, or his mom, never his dad. When he talked to his dad, they laughed about the stupid shit he did long after the time for advice had passed.

Even now, he didn't ask his dad for help or advice. He'd spent far longer talking to his mother than his father about Jay's death. On those few occasions when he had an argument with Risa he couldn't figure out, he took it to his mother.

Ben couldn't look his father in the eye and admit he couldn't handle something or didn't know what to do. Jay, so it seemed, had felt the same.

"For this particular thing," Risa said, "he never came out and said there was a problem on the team. I wish I'd paid more attention when he asked about things skirting around the edges. We talked more than once about dealing with people who had different beliefs and understanding how to motivate people who had different ideas about risk versus reward, and things like that. I never thought he meant that his team wasn't working."

Vivian sighed. "These kids. It doesn't sound like they ever once had a beer together."

"Can you imagine trusting someone with your life but not being able to call them at least a friend?" Risa asked.

"We did that all the time. Pilots, insertion and extraction teams, boat captains."

"Bullshit, Ben." Risa swore so infrequently these days, he sometimes forgot she knew how. "You knew everyone who did any of that for us. You knew their names, their wives' names, how many kids they had, how long they'd served, and what they wanted out of their careers. Those are friends. Not close friends, but friends."

Rather than argue, Ben shrugged. If Jay's team had splintered into factions, everything about his encounter with them in the cafeteria made more sense. Cowboy wouldn't help them, but his parents needed to know that the Academy didn't do what they'd all intended for it to do.

They stopped for gas and food a few times on the way to the Mitchell ranch on the south side of Tulsa, somewhere between two tiny towns called Kiefer and Mounds. By the time Ben pulled into the driveway, he'd swapped driving with Risa and Vivian twice and the sun had set.

The area had no streetlights. In the car's headlights, the land seemed bleak and barren. One harsh light glowed on the front of a huge three-story house. Two empty rocking chairs on the wide front porch creaked in a chilly breeze.

As Ben took Risa's hand, the spitting image of the original Cowboy stepped through the front door. Tom Mitchell wore jeans, boots, and a belt buckle shaped like a cowboy hat. A revolver hung from his belt in a leather holster. The current Cowboy's father had lost some of the fitness he'd had when he'd worked for a security contractor. Ben remembered seeing him on the news when Congress called him to testify against his bosses for various kinds of corruption.

None of the men who'd used the Cowboy code name had ever worn masks. Ben thought that said a lot about the Mitchell men.

"What can I do for you, stranger?" His drawl dragged each word along as if he had to beat them into submission.

"I'm Ben Tsukuda. This is my wife Risa, and our friend Vivian Cross." Ben held out his hand to shake. "You might remember us better as Captain Kinetic, Springfire, and Omen."

"Huh." Tom shook Ben's hand, his fingers squeezing harder than Ben considered necessary. "How in heckfire did you find this place?"

Ben restrained himself from shaking out his hand. "My grandfather knew yours well enough to have traded Christmas cards. My father still had the address. We took a chance that you hadn't moved."

"Huh. I heard about your boy, of course. Damn shame, that. Seemed like a smart kid. Come on inside and I'll get the missus to rustle you up some coffee."

They followed Tom into a large, plush room full of couches, animal trophies, and pictures of the men who'd used the Cowboy name. Every picture had a famous person with one of the four men, or had been composed as a publicity thing.

"Tammy, we got guests!"

At Tom's gesture, Ben sat on a couch between Risa and Vivian. He noticed Vivian seemed clingy, like the decor intimidated her. Risa also seemed stiff and uncomfortable. For himself, Ben had never felt the need to display his medals, and saw such gross displays of prowess as a distasteful boast.

"What brings you folks down hereabouts?"

"No one will tell us anything about what happened to

Jay." Ben didn't see any point to letting Risa try to finesse anything from a man as subtle as a brick to the head. "And we're concerned about your son's safety because of some of the practices at the Academy."

"Huh."

A small, thin woman wearing a pretty floral print dress and a cheerful smile brought a wicker tray with three mugs full of steaming black liquid, a small pitcher of cream, and a sugar bowl with a spoon, all arranged with care.

"Welcome to our home," the woman said. The moment Risa thanked her for the coffee, the woman glanced at Tom, who flicked his hand to shoo her out of the room. She complied.

Ben cringed. He had no idea what Risa would do if he ever tried to shoo her out of anywhere, unless he meant it as a joke. Different families worked in different ways, he supposed.

"Bobby's here, of course," Tom said. "He's upset about the whole thing. Some kind of long, drawn out inquiry, which I see as a good thing. The two weeks of leave after that, not so much, but I'm sure losing two people off the team is something a body ought to reflect on for a bit. Besides, they gotta shuffle the teams now."

Two weeks of leave didn't sound like enough time to Ben. He had no idea how long it would've taken him and the team to recover from losing Charlie. Two weeks after that night, he didn't know if he could've taken another mission. Maybe it would've helped, or maybe they would've all fucked up and gotten each other killed.

Tom's gaze flicked to the doorway behind Ben and the two women. "Oh, there you are, boy."

Ben turned to see the younger Cowboy scowling at them.

"What're you doing here?"

"Settle down, boy. They're guests. There anything you can tell them about how Jay died?"

Bobby crossed his arms and shook his head. "It's all

classified. We're going out for a ride."

Tom waved him off. Bobby clomped deeper into the house.

"Kids," Tom said. He sounded like he thought of Bobby as a five-year old. "They aren't rightly old enough to appreciate that other people feel things, you know?"

Ben remembered learning about that as a child, so he had no idea what Tom meant. He decided to change the subject before either Risa or Vivian pressed him. "Have you paid much attention to the Academy's methods lately?"

"Methods? I'm not sure I follow."

Vivian stood and moved to inspect a photograph of Tom's father with President Kennedy.

"Looking back over some correspondence with Jay," Risa said, "we've noticed there are signs of disagreements among the members of the team that the Academy staff brushed off without addressing."

"Huh." Tom shrugged. He returned his gaze to Ben as if he didn't want to deal with Risa. "Well, I'm sure that probably had a lot to do with them losing their spotlight to a couple of newer teams coming up."

"We hadn't heard about that," Ben said.

"No? I guess maybe the boys were told not to talk about it. But, you know, Bobby's never been one for following the rules so much. He told me they put that team together because they only had two Legacies in their age group, then they packed alphas and bravos around them to make a sort of superstar team."

Ben's team had been the same, so he understood that idea well enough. "I hadn't realized they'd done that, but it makes sense. What about these newer teams?"

"I dunno much about that. Bobby just said there's some hotshot new kids come along lately. I guess he's hoping they slide a couple of them into the team to fill the empty spots. I don't mean any disrespect to your boy's memory by saying so. Just, life's gotta go on, you know?"

"Of course." Ben nodded to let Tom feel he hadn't said

anything hurtful. "But we harbor some concern that Academy practices may not have prepared these kids for a teamwork atmosphere. I recall—"

"Look." Tom waved to dismiss Ben, just like he'd dismissed his wife and son. "My father put a lot of money into that Academy when they first got the idea. I put in a fair amount when they had to rebuild because you folks let it get blown up. I trust the folks who're running it, and my boy is doing fine. I'm real sorry about your boy, but you know as well as I do that the job isn't all sunshine and autographs. He signed on with the military. You do that when you're willing to lay down your life for your country."

Risa squeezed his hand, which helped Ben bite back a sharp retort about Tom's lack of military service.

"Thank you for your time." Ben stood and tugged Risa to her feet. They'd learn nothing else of interest from Tom, and he wanted to hear what Vivian and Risa thought about what had and hadn't been said.

"I appreciate that you came a long way to see me." Tom walked them out. "I hope you have a safe journey home."

He shut the door as they stepped off the porch. Horses with riders approached the fence near the car, on the fringes of the porch light. Ben recognized Bobby with the blonde and the Latino from their team. Somehow, Ben suspected they weren't supposed to spend their leave time together. That he saw no sign of Scope didn't surprise him.

"I remember you," Bobby said. He pointed at Vivian. "You told me to jump out the fucking window. I did it because you were an adult and I trusted you."

Ben opened the car door for Vivian. "Ignore him," he muttered to her. "He's just a little prick."

"But you were drunk or some shit, weren't you? I didn't hit no fucking target enemy, and that fall didn't do me no fucking favors."

"Shut up," Ben snapped. He had a feeling Cowboy hadn't been blameless in Jay's death.

Risa stepped in the way, blocking Ben's view of

Cowboy. "We need to go," she told him in a harsh whisper. "Get in the car."

Stony-faced and silent, Vivian slid into the car and shut her door. Risa watched Ben, letting him see her impatience and annoyance.

Ben ducked into the car. As he shut the door, he heard the kids laughing at them. He started the car with his power because that forced him to use it for something besides attacking those three little fuckers.

# CHAPTER 26

## IARIESAH

November 30, 2017
12:15

The first volley of seven gunshots for Marks's twenty-one gun salute reminded Risa of too many other times and places. She leaned against Ben, her arm wrapped around his, and hated the reason they'd come.

Glancing aside, she saw Kele on one knee beside her dog, holding Kachina's ears against the noise. Kele murmured soothing noises to the dog, which Risa heard through their new earbuds. Matias had cooked up a miracle, creating a tiny, sleek little device that used bone vibrations, or something along those lines, to pick up and deliver their voices.

Through the dignified, rehearsed ceremony, Ben stood tall like a stalwart guardian. The way he stayed so still worried her. Since they'd strapped their service patches to their sleeves with a dark band, he hadn't spoken or done anything other than move from one place to another. He seemed hyperfocused on something no one else could see, as if he watched Marks's spirit leading them to the casket under the shelter, and nothing else.

Matias and Vivian stood together, quiet and solemn.

Risa knew Vivian had seen something at the Mitchell ranch, but hadn't heard anything about it yet. While Tom had kept Ben distracted with his bravado, Risa had noticed Vivian's shoulders tense the way they did with an unexpected vision.

Then they'd left and had nothing to say to each other. Despite Phyllicia's letters, Risa hadn't expected so much hostility from Jay's teammates or oblivious resistance from Cowboy's father.

Soldiers folded Marks's flag and handed it to his widow. The ceremony ended. As soon as they could, Ben and Risa approached Linda and hugged her. Risa wanted this closure for Jay. She needed it. If she had to lose her son, she needed to see him laid to rest.

The team clustered. Risa noticed white feathers on the edge of the crowd, coming closer. She pointed. Matias pulled up the hood of his jacket. He and Vivian blended with the crowd to return to the car. Kele took Kachina for a walk.

Ben took a deep breath, then brought Risa with him as he headed straight for Charlie. The crowd thinned until they saw who stood with her.

Steve.

He wore a stylish, dark suit appropriate for the occasion, making Risa feel underdressed. Ben had brought suits because he rarely wore anything else. Risa, on the other hand, had brought shirts, sweats, and yoga pants. At least everyone had thought to bring their service patches.

"I thought we might run into you here," Charlie said with a sad smile.

Risa hugged Charlie and noticed she had a new sheath for her dead wing. The smooth vinyl seemed to hold more bulk than before. On that night, Risa had seen her after Doc healed her. He'd grown a layer of skin over the bones and sinew, leaving her with no muscles or ways to grow feathers. It had seemed worse than amputation.

Maybe Charlie had to wrap it against the cold.

"Did you come to scold us?" Ben asked.

"For coming here? No."

Steve's mouth twitched. Risa thought he disagreed.

"I know you were friends." Charlie shook hands with Ben. "He was a good man, and it'd be cruel to ask you not to come here." Her smile faded. "But I do have to ask you to stop trying to pry information out of Jay's team. I get that you're upset. I really do. I can't imagine what it must be like to lose your son."

Ben opened his mouth. Risa took his arm. He stayed quiet.

"We haven't heard anything about his body yet, Charlie. You know we're not the kind of people who can just sit and wait."

"I get that," Charlie said. "I really do. But you have to trust us."

"Who's us?" Ben asked.

Risa wished he hadn't, but she wanted to know what Charlie meant too.

Charlie gave him a curious look. "The Novas. I may not work in the field anymore, but I'm still part of the team."

Though Ben didn't move, Risa could tell he took Charlie's words as a body blow.

Squeezing his arm again, Risa said, "It's hard to trust when we don't hear anything. We just want to know what happened to him and when we'll be able to have his funeral. He deserves to rest with his grandfather."

"I don't know what the holdup is at this point, but I'll make some calls for you. If that's what you need, you should go home and wait while I try to get it for you."

Risa didn't trust herself to speak. If she hadn't seen images of two caskets coming off a plane along with the media reports of Jay's death, she might've believed they needed longer. At this point, with both Jay and Phyllicia already on American soil, she didn't know what to think.

"Thank you," Ben said.

With luck, Charlie had forgotten how to read Ben. Otherwise, she'd know how little he meant that.

"Charlie?" Matias stood behind her. His face... Risa

wanted to hug him and tell him everything would be fine.

"Matty." Charlie turned around. "I didn't expect to see you here."

"Likewise. I, ah. You look…good."

"Sure. You look good too. Congrats on the marriage."

"Thanks." Matias rubbed his hand over his mouth.

"It's okay," Charlie said. "I won't breathe on you."

Mathias cracked a half-smile, but his eyes remained troubled as he gave her an awkward hug. "That Greg guy, he's, ah, he's treating you right?"

"Yeah. Worth giving up the flyboys for." She looked over her shoulder at Ben and Risa, her expression as clouded and conflicted as Matias's. "Go home." Charlie said. "All of you. We're taking care of him." She turned to go and tugged on Steve's arm.

He held up a hand. "Go ahead. I need a minute."

Charlie shrugged and left them with Steve.

Steve waited for a few beats, then he sighed and shook his head. "Ben. Risa. Matias. I get that Marks was important to all of you, and I know Vivian and Kele are here too. I have to say, though, you all really need to get back home. I don't want to pass on to my superiors that you're wandering around.

"They might decide that Kay isn't going to graduate this year after all. And I know how much of a hassle it would be to relocate Gabriella, but I don't make decisions like that. Really, any number of things could happen to any number of people, especially if someone notices you've been spending time with your old teammates."

He walked away.

Risa stared at his back. "He just threatened us."

"He just threatened all of us," Matias growled.

She looked at Ben and saw the defeat in the line of his jaw and the droop of his shoulders. Part of her wanted to shake him, to scream at him. They only needed a plan. With the right plan, they could get into the Academy and keep Kay safe. And Ben's parents. His sister. Her family. Risa's family. Vivian's daughter and girlfriend. Matias's sister and wife. Kele's dog.

They had no idea, she realized, to what depths these people would sink. Stopping Steve now might not even do anything. He worked for someone who had the resources of the Novas at their disposal. Someone like that could find out anything they wanted and do anything they wanted.

Like kill Marks and make it look like an accident.

"We have to go," Risa said. She tugged on Ben's arm.

Ben nodded.

"Tell me what he said," Kele said. "I only heard your sides."

"I'd like to wring that fucker's neck," Matias grumbled.

Risa felt the same, but she couldn't let Matias lose sight of what mattered. "Then they send a team after you and put you into the prison in the Keys. Gabi and Dhanya need you, Matty."

Ben told Kele and Vivian what Steve had said while they walked back to the car. "And now, we're going back to the hotel, Kele."

Matias slid into the back seat of the car and slammed the door.

"I'll meet you there," Kele said.

Risa suspected Kele knew someone else buried at the cemetery and wanted to visit their grave. "Of course," she said as she climbed into the car. "Take your time."

Ben started the engine and followed the procession to the front gate. He gripped the steering wheel hard enough to turn his knuckles pale.

"We should just take these fuckers down," Matias grumbled. "Look what they've done to Charlie. She's going around with Steve, thinking he's her pal and not shady as fuck. If I could just talk to her alone, then—"

"Then what?" Vivian said. "You two crack some jokes and everything is fine? You both pretend you didn't burn her wing off?"

"Fuck you," Matias snapped.

"Calm down," Risa said. "We all hate Steve."

Matias crossed his arms and stewed. Vivian covered her face.

"We have to go home," Ben said. He sounded as grave and dispirited as the morning after that night.

"You giving up, Cap?" Kele asked through the earbud.

Ben sighed. "I can't let us all risk our families and friends. Whoever pulls Steve's strings knows everything about all of us. We already know that. If we do what they want, they won't hurt anyone."

Risa had thought the exact same thing, but it broke her heart to hear Ben say it. "I can't lose Kay too. It would kill me to know we caused anything to happen to Chloe or Gabi, Dhanya, Anna, or anyone else we know."

"I don't have anyone but you guys," Kele said. Though she sounded casual, Risa heard the hard edge in her voice.

"What about that bartender who imports your beer for you?" Ben asked. "What would you do if they killed him?"

"I'd kill them back."

"And who are they? How do we find them, Kele? We don't even know who the fuck is making these puppets dance. Should we torture Charlie until she tells us everything she knows? Or maybe we should do all that to Steve, because he's not a real person. He's just some fucking puppet! Kele, I don't do that shit anymore, and neither do you. We're not soldiers. They retired us. We don't have a mission and we don't have any authority. We take a step down that road and we're criminals."

Hearing Ben admit that he'd tortured people for information cut Risa even deeper. She knew. They all knew. But he'd never said it out loud. So long as no one said anything, so long as the mission record never recorded anything, it didn't happen.

Ben carried so many scars, and he never let them show.

"We're going home," he said again, this time with a dark note of finality. "If it was just us that we're risking, it would be different."

"Understood." Kele said nothing else.

What she didn't say, Risa could tell Ben heard. His mouth became a thin, tense line, and the muscles in his jaw twitched.

Risa covered her face and cried. She didn't know how to pick up their lives and go on. Maybe when they lowered a casket into the ground and handed her a flag, something magical would happen to heal the deep, consuming ache in her heart.

"I miss my baby," she said, holding back as much of her sobbing as she could.

"That's why we're going home." Ben turned the car onto the freeway. "There's an airport in Des Moines. It's not that late. We should all be able to catch flights home."

Vivian sniffled from behind her hands. "I wish…"

"We all wish." Ben's voice lost the edge and grew softer. "But we're past the point when our wishes get granted."

Risa popped out her earbud and wept all the way to the airport.

# CHAPTER 27

## MATIAS

December 3, 2017
12:21

Dhanya handed Matias a bowl of curry. It held shrimp, rice, chickpeas, and lemongrass. The food smelled good. Picking through it with his fork stirred the scent of coconut and revealed cauliflower. He liked all these things.

Gabi devoured hers like she hadn't eaten in a week.

Dhanya brought her bowl to her chair and ate with more refined manners. She leaned toward him. "What's wrong?"

"Nothing." He speared a chunk of shrimp and lifted it. Though he needed to eat, he couldn't force himself to do it.

Once upon a time, he'd imagined seeing Charlie again. In that vision, they went to a bar, drank beer, and watched football. She ordered jalapeno poppers and breathed on him, on purpose. He stabbed himself with an epi pen. They called it even.

Reality had been much less friendly.

"That's four times since you got home," Dhanya said. "I didn't believe you the first time, and I still don't."

"I'm fine."

Gabi snorted and laughed. "You're about as fine as a dull razor." Her voice sounded off, but he couldn't think about it.

Matias kept seeing Charlie's strained smile. He'd taken too much from her to forgive and forget. How long had she struggled with finding a reason to keep living?

Dhanya took his bowl and set it aside, then sat on his lap. She cupped his chin and made him look at her. "Matty, you're hurting inside. What happened while you were out there?"

Closing his eyes, he tried to think of a way to explain it to her. "Too much."

His wife leaned forward and wrapped her arms around his neck. She kissed his cheek and settled against his chest. "I need you to talk to me. I can't read your mind."

Matias touched her dark hair and wished he could make Charlie's pain disappear. In the quiet, he noticed Gabi's breathing sounded wrong. She wheezed. He snapped his eyes open.

Gabi leaned her head back and grimaced. Blotches marred her face, darkening with every passing moment. "I can't breathe," she gasped.

"I'll go check the filters." Grateful for the interruption, Matias helped Dhanya to her feet so she could tend to Gabi. He stood and hurried to the closet where they kept replacements. Armed with a screwdriver, a key, and two fresh, plastic-wrapped air filters, he rushed to the balcony.

The padlock for the filter housing door lay on the ground below its latch. Matias stared at it for a long few moments before he crouched and picked it up. Someone had cut it. This kind of damage didn't happen by accident. He jumped to his feet and yanked open the housing door.

Instead of filters, he found dirty socks.

The scent hadn't survived the rest of the airflow system, but something had. He scooped out the socks and replaced the filters. For the next day or so, Gabi would have to wear her oxygen mask. Dhanya would have to help her bathe and treat her damaged skin.

As he closed the door again, Matias wondered who'd done this, and why. Teenage pranks didn't involve bolt cutters on someone's second floor balcony, especially when he hadn't interacted with any teenagers lately. The perpetrator couldn't have done it more than an hour ago, so they'd come and gone while Dhanya cooked. She would've said something if she saw or heard anything strange.

He looked at the cut padlock in his hand, feeling a chill creeping up his spine. The person who'd done this wanted him to know. They'd delivered a message.

Unless Gabi had made a new, specific kind of enemy without realizing it, he knew who to blame for this.

Steve's boss.

"I came home," he growled. He turned and gripped the railing. "I fucking came home!"

If he hadn't been here, Dhanya wouldn't have thought to check the filters until after she'd tended to Gabi. Whatever shit they put in those fucking socks would've spent a lot longer inside their house. Worse, without him, the asshole might not have stopped at fucking with the airflow. He might've forced his way inside.

Horrifying possibilities played in his head. He backed against the door, shaken by the implications of the cut lock in his hand. Was this a punishment for leaving? A warning against leaving again? What kind of sick fuck did shit like this, and how did they do it without making a fucking sound?

They wanted him scared. Too scared to leave. Too scared to think.

Fuck that.

His mind shifted into overdrive. He and Gabi hadn't found anything about other possible illegal Nova missions. Like they'd expected, they didn't have enough data to formulate reasonable searches. More importantly, Russia and China had their own supers programs, and North Korea remained challenging to investigate.

Germany, on the other hand, didn't have a supers program. Cap hadn't considered that important point.

Cap not thinking things through shook him in an entirely different way. He deserved some slack, though. Matias remembered how distracted Cap had been when he came back to work after each of the kids was born. Losing one… If he lost Dhanya or Gabi, Matias didn't think he'd function half as well as Cap. Almost killing Charlie had left him a wreck for over a year.

Dwelling on that accomplished nothing. It happened. He'd half-killed Charlie and taken her wing. He did that. His fuckup cost her a limb. Maybe he hadn't done enough to make up for it, but damned if he'd let that stop him from saving her from whatever she'd gotten tangled in.

Ducking inside, Matias dove for his chair. He had searches to run with new parameters. Once he got things going, he devoured his lunch and waited.

Water ran in the bathroom. He wouldn't see either woman again for at least an hour.

He watched three different progress bars.

What would he have done if he'd caught the person who fucked with the filters? His exercise routine didn't include anything combat-oriented anymore. He and Gabi did basic stuff designed for people who sat all the time. Dhanya kept him from eating so much he turned into a blob.

As a Nova, he'd always relied on his fire. His entire job had centered around the fact he could do that.

No one had used their powers much for those few, brief days while he tasted the freedom of doing the job again. He didn't think he could.

Matias had burned bodies before that night. He'd killed people with his fire. Once, he'd destroyed an entire village to save its people from a rampaging super in Bolivia.

Looking at his hands, he saw tools. Typing helped the team as much as fire ever had. He could still sit in his living room and assist them from afar.

Fire had protected his team so much better than

typing. Shimmering, gossamer curtains of rippling red, orange, and yellow filled his head. They whispered to him, their voices so soft he had to draw close to hear. The fire missed him. He missed the fire.

He saw Maverick's wing burning. Feathers shriveled and smoked. Her flesh curdled and blackened. She screamed, the sound of pure agony echoing forever. Burning meat overwhelmed his nose.

Pressure weighed on his shoulders. "Wake up, Matias. You're lost in the memory."

Matias sucked in a breath and blinked against the sight. He knelt on the floor of his living room. In his hands, he held one of Maverick's white feathers. That night, he'd picked it up and taken it with him. These days, he kept it in a drawer in the small table beside his chair.

Dhanya hugged him from behind, her ponytail brushing his cheek. Her body pressed against his, warming him and giving him something solid and tangible to hold. She brushed her thumb down the side of his face, making him notice the tears he'd shed.

"You're okay, *baalam*. You're fine."

He covered his face. "I killed her. Not her body, but what made her Maverick."

"I know. But you didn't do it on purpose. That matters."

"Not to her."

She kissed his hand. "I know you did some things as a Nova that you aren't proud of. That doesn't make you broken. It doesn't make you a bad person."

He shook his head. If he used the fire, he'd hurt someone else. "I can't."

She brushed her nose against his skin. "Yes, you can. I believe in you. Gabi believes in you. We trust you and we know you're the best there ever has been or ever will be at what you do."

Lowering his hands, he watched them and waited for the memory to hit him again. He wanted to call the fire, but he didn't want to hurt Dhanya. No, he didn't want to call the fire. He needed to call it.

"I can't protect you."

Dhanya kissed his cheek. "I don't need protection. I need my husband to love me. Nothing more and nothing less."

The front door exploded inward and harsh light flooded the condo.

Matias leaped to his feet without thinking and drew the heat from the air by instinct. Splinters and pieces of boards flew toward him. Fire roared out of Matias's hands, incinerating the pieces of the front door not stopped by the plastic sheeting.

He shoved Dhanya behind him and rushed the doorway. Flames roiled in the space before him. As he reached the gaping hole, he slammed into someone.

They tumbled down the stairs together.

Like he'd never stopped using it, the fire flickered around his body to cushion his fall.

At the base of the stairs, they hit concrete. Matias sprang to his feet. Flames danced around his body. His enemy groaned.

Before the guy could recover, Matias grabbed his black tactical suit and thumped his head against the ground. Fire rushed under the enemy's body and lifted him at Matias's command.

A kid.

He held a kid.

Dusky skin and dark hair marked him as a Latino, like Matias himself. The tactical suit looked too much like the ones he'd once worn for coincidence.

The Novas had sent a Latino kid to kill him, his wife, and his sister. He'd gone home like a good boy, and they still sent someone. What the fuck?

He hauled the kid to the complex's garbage dumpster. After knocking his head against the wall one more time for good measure, Matias ran home. The fire flickered and died around him.

Dhanya lay on the floor, holding her leg and panting. Blood stained her scrubs from the inside. Gabi knelt beside her, wearing her portable oxygen mask.

"It's not too bad," Dhanya said.

Matias dropped to her side and checked her thigh. A piece of wood stuck out of her muscle. "It doesn't look like it hit anything major."

Gasping for breath, Dhanya shook her head. "No, but it hurts like hell."

"Gabi, go pack some clothes for all of us. We have to leave. Hurry. Bring whatever you need. We'll have to drive a fair amount. And get some towels to wrap this."

"I guess I was wrong," Dhanya said. "We do need you to protect us."

Too angry about the Novas to handle anything other than the straightforward, Matias held her leg. "I'm going to take this out."

"It'll bleed a lot. If you're not careful, you'll leave splinters and it could get infected. I need a hospital."

"I can't risk them finding us at one. We need to get on the road and away from everything."

"Then pull it out and wrap it up, but I'll need to see a doctor soon."

Gabi threw towels at him.

To distract her from the pain, he kissed her. She squealed into his mouth while he yanked out the wood. With Gabi's help, he wrapped a towel around her leg and secured it in place.

"Did you see the results from your latest search?" Gabi asked.

"No." Matias found his earbud and stuffed it into his ear.

"I'll download it and read it on the road."

Matias nodded to Gabi and picked up Dhanya. "Is anyone still wearing their earbud?"

"Yes," Kele said.

"*Gracías a Dios*," Matias muttered. "Some punkass Nova kid just attacked my place. I need discreet medical assistance as soon as possible. Do you know anyone?"

"Doc lives in Vegas. Is that close enough?"

"Vegas is about nine hours," he told Dhanya as he carried her to the car. "Can we wait that long?"

"I think so." Dhanya nodded. "I'll just need lots of water and food. And some painkillers."

"Kele, meet us there?"

"I'm not far," Kele said. "I'll make sure Doc is available when you get there. Are you hurt?"

"No, my wife. And we can't stay here. She and Gabi both need someplace to stay for now. We should be there in the middle of the night. I'm not going to stop unless I have to."

"Keep the earbud in. Let me know if anything else happens. The range on these things is amazing."

Matias slid Dhanya into the back seat of his Tesla. "Yeah. They're piggybacked on a cell signal. I wasn't sure it would work as well as it does, but I'm a fucking genius, so I'm not surprised."

Kele laughed. "Take care of your ladies, Matty. I'll see you in the dark hours."

"Yeah. no more running from these fuckers." He hauled bags into the trunk, helped Gabi into the car, and drove.

# CHAPTER 28

## VIVIAN

December 3, 2017
15:31

Yoga went a long way toward soothing Vivian's ruffled nerves. Settling back into her routine for a few days helped too. Not enough, though. Failure shrouded her. The only vision she'd conjured on that whole crappy trip had shown her nothing. Standing in the Mitchell house, she'd experienced that same fire-fueled vision she'd seen that terrible night. Like before, it showed nothing of how to avoid anything.

Useless.

She'd contributed nothing to the trip with the team, except upsetting Chloe and Anna, and probably letting their stalkers find them easier. Way to go, precog.

Vivian shook her head and waited in Waltham traffic for a stoplight to change. She wanted a shower and some cheesecake. Chloe would approve. Anna would not.

The power reached out and took control of the wheel. Vivian let it take over. Several times over the years, the power had saved her from an accident. More than once, it had steered her around a traffic jam so she arrived in time to pick up Chloe from school, dance lessons, or field hockey.

She followed its direction into a parking garage. Signs marked it as closed for repairs. No other reason could ever empty a parking garage this close to Boston. Driving through the street level, she noticed another car turning into the garage.

Her power directed her to swerve around a corner as the pickup truck behind her roared in pursuit. The other vehicle slammed into the wall where Vivian's minivan had been a moment before. She floored the gas pedal and sped to the exit.

Though she thought she should leave, the power urged her to slam on the brakes and hop out of the car. She hurried back inside the garage to stand in the driving lane with a view of the truck.

Metal shrieked and squealed. The truck's driver side door flew away from the truck. It crashed into another wall.

Vivian gulped and watched a cowboy boot stick out of the truck's cab. The man attached to it surprised her. He didn't wear his signature hat, but she recognized Bobby anyway.

"You bitch, I liked that truck!" He hopped to the ground and didn't seem hurt. But then, everyone knew he could take a lot of punishment. Every man to bear the name Cowboy had the same power—superhuman strength with flesh that could resist bullets.

Back in the day, Vivian had relied her team to handle opponents. She had no team. If her power failed her now, she didn't think she could survive facing this on her own.

Time to fake confidence.

"Maybe you shouldn't have tried to hit my van with it." She rested a hand on her hip and checked her fingernails.

Cowboy smacked his fist against his palm and cracked his knuckles. "They let us pick which of you rejects to go after. I chose the fuckup who launched me out the window."

"If you'd jumped when I told you to, you would've hit one of the attackers." She shrugged and hoped he couldn't tell how much she quaked inside. "Not my fault you're a slow, piece of shit moron."

He charged her. She trusted her power. Her body stepped aside. He slammed into the wall. Concrete cracked. His impact left a dent. Dust rained on him.

Vivian hurried to the left, not sure what her power thought she could accomplish. She watched Cowboy shake dust out of his hair. He'd learned a lesson, because he stalked toward her without picking up speed.

She watched him. He threw a punch at her head. Her power helped her duck in time. His fist punched through the concrete behind her.

"What the fuck?" He delivered a one-two punch, hitting the wall behind her again.

Trying not to let him see her hands shaking, Vivian darted to the right. He chased her.

"Stand still, you bitch!"

"Didn't your daddy teach you any other swear words?"

"Don't you talk about my daddy," he snapped.

Vivian dropped into a crouch. Cowboy's fist sailed over her head. She resisted the urge to punch him in the balls. She'd only hurt herself. The power knew what to do.

All that time in the car she'd spent worrying about her power failing had been silly. It still worked. Some Chinese woman or girl blocked her at the Academy. Trying to see anything other than immediate danger had always been dicey anyway. That night, her power had steamrolled over the interference because of the need to protect those kids.

This kid. She'd saved this damned ungrateful bastard. When his ass was on the line, she'd been there. Maybe she'd thought he was Crash at the time, but she'd still saved him.

"Your daddy ever tell you that he tried serving in the Novas?" Vivian stood aside and watched Cowboy's fist hit the concrete so hard he exposed the rebar inside.

"He did not, you lying bitch."

She laughed at him. To her own ears, it sounded high-pitched and hysterical. "He so totally did. They rejected him. Said his temperament wasn't suited to the job. They didn't think he could work with a team."

Cowboy growled at her, no longer bothering with words. Rage painted his face with dark shadows too deep for concrete dust to obscure.

"You've got a little temper there, Champ."

She twisted out of his way. Her power danced her around the garage in a bizarre pattern. As the one following it, she had no idea what arcane symbol she plotted on the ground. Cowboy followed her, pursuing with the same relentless determination as Crash.

No. On second thought, he had nothing in common with Crash.

His fist made more and more holes. As she danced aside one more time, she noticed the cracks in the concrete stretching to meet. Her power carried her past one more punch, then she stuck out her leg and swept it in an arc.

Cowboy lifted his foot in perfect timing with Vivian's motion. She caught his ankle with her heel. He lost his balance and stumbled into the wall. The ground shuddered.

Vivian sprinted for her van. She didn't look back as the garage crumbled around Cowboy. Her van started and she floored the gas.

In her rearview mirror, she saw the garage fall.

"That's why you don't fuck with the precog," she snarled.

The nigh-invulnerable ass would probably climb out later. She hoped he'd at least knocked himself senseless. No, unconscious. He already had zero sense.

Wait, he'd said something about choosing his target. She pushed the button her steering wheel to activate voice commands. "Phone, call Tsukuda."

She listened to the phone dial Risa's cell while she wove through traffic on route 20. It rang. And rang. And rang. Risa's phone shunted her into voice mail.

Vivian didn't know what to think about that. She hadn't gotten Ben's number, so she didn't have another way to reach them. Why would she ever need Ben's number when she had Risa's? For the moment when Risa didn't answer her phone.

"Risa, I just got attacked by that piece of shit Cowboy kid. I'm fine. I'm also ready to say fuck the Novas and take this shit to their doorstep. Call me as soon as you can."

She ended that call and made another one. A woman answered Matias's phone on the third ring.

"Hi, this is Vivian. Can I talk to Matty?"

"He's driving right now. This is Gabrielle. I'll put you on speakerphone." The phone clicked.

"Viv, damn," Matias said. "I should've called right away. Some little shithead attacked our home, and Dhanya got hurt. We're on our way to see Doc. Are you okay?"

"I just dropped a fucking parking garage on Cowboy." Saying it out loud made Vivian giddy. "That dumbass did all the work. I just let him smash the place around himself. It was…crazy. Amazing. I haven't used my power like that in ages."

"Yeah, I know what you mean. Can you get out to Vegas? Kele gave me Doc's address."

"Not anytime soon."

"You dropped a parking garage on Cowboy and you can't figure out how to get across the country in twelve hours?"

Vivian burst into laughter. It sounded high-pitched and hysterical again. She hit her exit in Wayland and made an effort to calm down.

"Sorry. It was kind of scary, actually."

"I get that. As soon as you can, put your earbud in, and we'll get you to Doc's place. Have you talked to Ben or Risa?"

Vivian remembered leaving her earbud in her jewelry box. "Risa didn't answer her phone. Cowboy made it sound like we could all expect company. So that's a little… I don't know what to think."

"I'd get Anna and Chloe to stay someplace else for a few days. Someplace they'll be safe. Get your ass to Vegas, and we'll figure out what to do from there. I'll try to call

Ben."

"Yeah." Vivian shivered with a sudden chill. "That's a good idea. I'll get my earbud in as soon as I get home. Talk to you later."

Thank goodness she'd called Matias. She hung up and waffled over calling Anna. According to the clock, Anna wouldn't leave work for another half hour. No one at the Novas would be stupid enough to attack her at the governor's office. Would they? Anna rode the train to Kendal Green, then drove from there, which didn't give anyone much chance to cause a car accident. On the other hand, anyone could predict her commute.

She dialed the number. Anna's phone went to voicemail after one ring, which meant she'd declined the call. At least that meant Vivian had nothing to worry about for the moment.

"Call me when you can. I need to leave again, and I'm hoping you'll take Chloe to my brother's place for the weekend."

Fretting all the way home, she tried Risa's number again and still got no answer. If the asshole in charge sent one muscle-bound meathead to attack Vivian, what would they have sent for Ben and Risa? She hoped for the best.

As soon as she got home, she checked the internet for stories about deaths or destruction in Cincinnati and found nothing.

Maybe no one had noticed yet.

She found her earbud and stuck it in her ear. "Please tell me you've heard from Ben or Risa?"

"Negative," Kele said. "But I'm glad you're okay."

"Gabi is still trying. I'll let you know if Ben picks up."

Vivian rubbed her eyes, wishing she could get a vision to tell her they just shut off their phones for sex. On second thought, she didn't want that vision. Something else. "Should I head to Cincinnati?"

"It is on the way for you," Kele said. She sounded grim. "It couldn't hurt. The worst case scenario is we find out what happened to them."

"Don't say things like that," Vivian whined. "They're fine. Everything is fine. I'm sure they're completely fine."

"Vivian." Matias sighed. "None of us is there. We can't do anything about whatever is happening to them right now. Pack a bag and get moving. That's the best thing you can do."

"Right. Sorry. I'm just— After all these years—" Vivian smacked her hand on the wall. Unlike Cowboy, she had no effect on the surface. "I'm packing. I'll see you soon."

She stuffed clothes into a suitcase and prepared for the arduous task of welcoming Chloe home from school to tell her Mom needed to run out on her again. If she let herself, Chloe would enjoy a weekend with Brian and his family. They'd play hockey. A lot of hockey.

Everybody plays hockey.

# CHAPTER 29

## BEN

December 3, 2017
15:33

On Monday, tomorrow, Ben's leave time ended. Risa would have to go back to work too. They lay on the couch together with Ell, watching *Bend It Like Beckham* for the fiftieth time. Ben knew half the dialogue. The first few times they'd watched it, he'd appreciated the football scenes most. Once Kay became a teenager, he'd paid more attention to the rest.

Ell raised her head and whined at the door. Jess told her teammates that Indian girls don't play football. Ben patted Ell's head.

The dog jumped off the couch and barked.

Risa raised her head. "What's wrong with her?"

"I don't know. Maybe an encyclopedia salesman is coming."

She snorted. "They don't do that anymore."

"Jehovah's Witnesses, then."

Ell's whine turned to a growl.

Ben twisted to see her. He thought he saw a shape move past the front window. After everything that had happened, his brain kicked into high gear. Shadows plus dog equaled attack.

Without a word, he hauled Risa off the couch. They ran for the back door. Ell followed them.

As he shut the door, an oppressive, deafening crack of thunder boomed. Light so bright it hurt his eyes punched through the back wall of the house, a few feet from them.

Risa wrapped herself around Ben and sped him far enough from the explosion to avoid the debris. Ben used his power to pick up the garden hose in its reel, intending to use it as a weapon. Someone knew their identities and came to their house to attack them.

"Flank them," he said.

Risa blurred. Ben hurried around the house in the other direction. Ell followed him, quiet and holding her tail out straight.

At the corner, he peered around and saw a young blonde woman with two young men, both checking through the hole they'd made in the front of the house. They wore black tactical gear, similar to the suits Ben and Risa had worn too many times to count. He recognized the woman as Cowboy's arm candy, Bunny. The two boys he thought had been the ones speaking Dutch at the Academy.

If the Novas wanted them dead or scared, why send kids from the Academy? The boys looked old enough to graduate with Kay's class, or maybe in one more year. The Novas, though, had teams of adults. They could've sent an entire team, instead of one Nova with two untested kids.

Anyone familiar with Ben and Risa's operational records would've sent at least one full team, even if their purpose had been to scare them into submission instead of kill or capture. He doubted Nova Command had experienced so much turnover that no one remembered them and their capabilities. Even if they didn't have anyone like that left, he doubted they would err on the side of overconfidence.

Ben swung the metal hose reel in a wide arc to attack the closest boy. The kid grunted with the blow and pitched face-first into the front room. The girl squawked and flew backward to land on the front walk. Her head hit the brown grass.

The second boy raised his hands in Ben's direction. They glowed for a moment. Ben threw the reel at him. The boy panicked and tried to protect himself with his hands. Lightning blasted in every direction with no control. Tiny crackles of light arced to nearby plants and slithered across surfaces.

Risa appeared beside the first boy, picked him up by the back of his shirt, and dragged him inside.

The woman on the ground disappeared.

Ben raised the reel to clunk it into the lightning-caller's chest.

Instead of letting it hit him, the boy rolled to the side and scrambled to his feet. His hands glowed. Ben charged him. Ell leaped onto the kid's back, knocking him forward. More uncontrolled lightning sprayed everywhere. The dog yelped.

Ell barked in the kid's ear. The kid thrashed, throwing the dog aside. Ben jumped on the kid. They wrestled. Though Ben hadn't fought anyone in a long time, he overpowered the boy and knocked him unconscious with a few elbow jabs and a well-placed knee strike.

He raised his head in time to see Risa blur out of sight and Ell leap at the blonde. The dog smashed into the woman with an angry growl. They disappeared. The pair reappeared across the room. Risa appeared by their side and kicked the blonde's head. She delivered a follow-up punch, then dropped both her elbows onto the woman's back.

"What a good boy," Risa said. She hugged Ell and rubbed his side. "Such a good, strong, brave boy. Shit, Ben, he took a lightning hit."

Risa hadn't yet noticed the blood on her arm and side. Ben rushed to her to check her for injuries. Small shards of glass stuck out of her arm.

"Oh. Look at that," she said. "Your leg is bleeding too."

He noticed a dull ache in his left thigh and thick glass sticking out of his sweatpants. His phone. Pulling it out of his pocket didn't remove the glass from his leg. Smoke drifted from the smashed device.

Tossing the useless phone aside, he wondered how long it would take the person who'd sent these kids to notice their failure. "I think Ell might've saved our lives."

"He's a good boy." Risa ruffled the fur on Ell's head. "I'll get the first aid kit."

"See if you can find your phone. I doubt they only targeted us."

Risa blurred out of sight. Ben breathed and grimaced. He inspected Ell while waiting for her. Across one side, Ell had a blackened line of fur. Underneath that, Ben found a slice of skin with blackened, bloody burns. At least the wound had been cauterized.

"You're going to have an interesting scar, boy."

"My phone is slag." Risa dropped a melted lump of plastic onto the grass. "It was on the coffee table. That first bolt must've hit it." She handed him a white box full of medical supplies.

Ben nodded and retrieved packets of sterile gauze. "Make sure they're all tied up and out cold, then I'll bandage your arm."

While she tended to their attackers, Ben ripped his pants open and yanked out the glass. By the time she'd policed the bodies, he had thick wads of gauze taped to his leg.

Risa sat beside him so he could pry glass out of her arm and apply bandages. "Some contractor is going to see this and drool over how much he can charge us to fix the house."

He glanced at the gaping hole through the building. Debris covered the floor and furniture. The boxed tank and Firebird models still sat on the mantle, and he could see a few framed photographs on the floor. Had he ever cared about the house itself? No. This house meant a shitty job far away from his parents and sister. His wife made this place a home. Their cherished mementos made it a home.

"Fuck the house. Fuck Cincinnati. Fuck health insurance, data entry, that fucking car, and granite countertops. And fuck Steve and his fucking threats."

"Such a potty mouth." Risa kissed him.

Someone groaned. Ell growled.

"That girl is a teleporter." Ben sighed as he taped the last bandage in place. "As soon as she wakes up, she's going to go for reinforcements. We should leave. Preferably before the police or firefighters get here."

"I'll make sure she stays down for a while and pack food. You pack clothes and things. We'll take my car and figure out where to go once we're on the road?"

The smart, cool-headed woman in his arms made Ben wish they could stick around long enough to savor this small victory. "I love you."

"I love you too."

They helped each other to their feet. Ben hobbled to the bedroom upstairs. On the way, he used his power to pick up the models and photos. Also with his power, he made the contents of the room dance themselves into suitcases. Not having to use his hands meant he could sit and take the weight off his leg.

He reached for Risa's nightstand and opened the drawer, intending to fetch a box of photographs she kept there. Inside, he found their earbuds. With their phones both trashed, he had no other options in reach to contact anyone. Maybe Kele still wore hers.

He activated one and stuffed it into his ear. "Is anyone there?"

"*Gracías a Dios.*"

"Oh my God, I'm so glad you're okay."

"Welcome back to the party, Cap." Kele sounded a touch bitter.

"I'll take that to mean you were all attacked also." He snagged the box of photographs and added it to a suitcase.

"We're all headed toward Doc right now," Matias said. "Dhanya was hurt."

"Why there? He can't heal anymore." Ben clamped down the guilt. Doc's power, Charlie's wing, Louisa's life, so many other lives, all lost that night. They now knew it hadn't been all their fault, but that didn't change how responsible he felt.

"Yes, he can," Kele said. "It's been coming back. Gradually."

"I see." Not sure how to take Kele's knowledge or the fact itself, Ben focused on the immediate problems. "Risa and I both have minor injuries, so seeing him would also be helpful for us. Everything would be easier with a phone, so that's my first priority. Between lightning and assholes, both of ours were smashed."

"Which is why you didn't answer when I just tried to call five minutes ago," Vivian said.

"Yes. I don't know why they decided to go after us when we all split up and went home like Steve wanted, but we're done worrying about what they want or think. Everyone stay as far under the radar as you can and keep moving for now. We'll meet at Doc's as soon as possible. Let's not chatter too much on the way. When we get there, I want to go over everything we know, from start to finish, all at once, face to face."

"Sounds like a plan," Kele said.

Ben stood and zipped the suitcases shut. "I'm taking out my earbud now. We'll both wear them once we get on the road."

All three of them acknowledged him. Ben changed into fresh sweatpants, tucked both earbuds into his pocket, and hauled everything downstairs. The SUV already held Phyllicia's boxes, because they'd intended to take them to a storage unit this weekend. Risa added one more cooler of food to the back seat. Ben hefted the suitcases and added his box of photo albums.

For once, he appreciated the fact they had an SUV like

everyone else. As soon as possible, though, he wanted his Firebird. Every last vestige of this fucking city and its influence needed to get blasted into oblivion.

Risa helped Ell climbed into the back seat. Ben heard sirens in the distance. They got into the car, he backed out of the driveway, and he left the house for the last time.

Maybe later, when they'd dealt with this whole mess, he'd come back, sort through the wreckage, and save a few more things. Probably not. He already had everything that mattered inside the car.

"Fuck you, Cincinnati," he said. A weight lifted from his shoulders as he left the fucking neighborhood for the last time.

"I don't remember the last time I've heard you swear so much as you have in the past fifteen minutes."

He nodded. The sunshine seemed brighter, as if unseen clouds parted to lift a gray pall from the world. "You have to be alive to swear this much."

Risa ruffled the hair at the back of his neck. "And where is Alive Ben taking us?"

"Probably an airport." Ben tucked in his earbud. "Vivian, we need some bright ideas for getting to Vegas fast without putting our names on anything."

# CHAPTER 30

## IARIESAH

December 3, 2017
21:07

Ben and Risa met Vivian in Indianapolis. From there, Vivian and her power got them onto an undocumented flight with a crusty old man in an ancient biplane. Risa swore Ben spent the entire flight holding the thing together. They landed in Las Vegas as the sun set. Matias picked them up and brought them to Doc's tiny house in a tiny town between Vegas and Groom Lake.

Risa remembered seeing Doc that night, after she abandoned him. His injuries had been her fault. Ben may have given the order, but Risa had left him on the battlefield. She'd expected the spot to stay safe. She should've known better.

Ben sat at a small table in the kitchen with him. Risa, Vivian, Dhanya, and Gabi crowded the couch against the wall. Kele sat on a stool by his fireplace. Matias sat on the floor at Dhanya's feet, holding an oxygen tank for Gabi. Kachina and Ell both sat with Kele, having decided they liked each other.

Doc could walk with a cane, but one arm hung limp at his side. He took his hand off Ben's knee with sweat beading

261

on his forehead. Of course Ben made himself wait until after Risa had been healed.

"Hot damn, I haven't healed anyone in years." Doc leaned back and panted to catch his breath. "Three in one day."

Ben sat up straighter than he had in hours, and his shoulders relaxed. "We all appreciate your help. When did it start coming back?"

"Oh, about five years ago." Doc sipped hot tea from a mug. "I think the power was too busy holding my own parts together to worry about anyone else's. I suppose I'm glad I broke someone's fall, because he lived, and he was able to fight off the guy that would've otherwise finished me off. What a crazy night that was."

Risa covered her face and wanted to crawl into a hole. "I'm so sorry," she murmured.

"Wasn't your fault, Risa. It really wasn't. None of you are responsible for what happened that night. I can tell you all think you are, at least in some part, but I'm telling you there's only one person to blame, and his name was Wilhelm Otto. Blaming yourself for not seeing through his plots and schemes is stupid. You had handlers, data analysts, older officers, and other people reviewing everything, and none of them saw it until it was too late either."

Everything he said made sense, but Risa still couldn't look him in the eye.

"And, I'll add something else. Because I know how you soldiers are. Even if any of that was your fault, you've all more than paid for it. I signed up for that duty. It was voluntary. They gave me a long, drawn-out briefing on the risks, and it boiled down to saying that in the rear with the gear doesn't always mean safe. You can ask anyone who survived Tet, and they'll tell you the same."

Someone touched Risa's knee. She moved her hands aside to see Matias looking at her. He squeezed her leg and let go. Each of them had done the same thing that night. Trying to help the team without a plan had cost too much.

Far too much.

"Let's table this issue for now," Ben said. He shouldered the mantle of team leader in a palpable way. "We need to pool information. Here's what I know.

"Jay and Phyllicia were killed on a mission, and it appears to have been a successful assassination of a German politician advocating for a German supers program. The Novas still haven't released either body. There's evidence his team was dysfunctional, and their superiors knew and did nothing about it. A number of Novas we knew, and the general who oversaw the project, have been killed in car accidents over the past ten years, and several have the stink of forced retirement, as some agencies call it. When we asked Marks to check into Jay's mission, he was also killed.

"The Novas have a blank check for operations. Someone has been keeping close track of us and sharing that information with the Academy's administrator, Greg Boone, who is also Charlie's husband. She stayed in the military even though all of us were booted, and is now the military liaison for the Academy." Ben stopped and squinted at the wall for a moment.

"The attacks today. We need to talk about that. A team of three came for us. One was Cowboy's girlfriend, and the other two I recognized as students at the Academy. What about your attackers?"

"I didn't get attacked," Kele said. "But I decided to head here in the first place, so I've been on the road the whole time. They wouldn't have been able to find me."

"And they had a memo saying to leave you alone," Matias said. "One guy came for me. It was that Latino kid in Cowboy's posse."

Vivian sighed. "I guess I won the jackpot, because I got Cowboy himself. He's not too smart, so if there's some kind of conspiracy going on, he's not part of it. At best, he's a trained attack dog."

The way Vivian said that made wheels turn in Risa's head. "What if… I mean, they take them at twelve. That's an impressionable age. God, what are they teaching those kids? Did Jay never tell us about the team problems because they convinced him it was his fault if it didn't work? And what must they have taught them to make them think that mission in Germany was reasonable?"

"There was more than just Germany." Matias tapped Gabi's leg. "We ran some new searches, only this time we checked countries without supers programs. In the past few years, there have been politicians and scientists killed in over a dozen countries. All the politicians were advocating for some kind of local supers program, and all the scientists had the right backgrounds and specialties to head those kinds of program."

"They've been preventing competition," Ben said.

Risa shook her head. Her baby had been murdering people, for God and country, believing he did the right thing. She thought over their own missions and realized she knew exactly how the person directing the Novas had done it.

She shivered. "They're teaching these kids to obey authority and not question orders. To not think for themselves. To not think they deserve to see the intel for themselves."

The room fell silent. At every mission briefing they'd ever had, Ben had pushed and needled until he got as much information as possible. Even for scouting missions, he'd demanded more and more until they got as complete a picture of the situation as anyone could have.

"Which means," Ben said, "that they just accept the bullet point mission objectives and go do it. I taught Jay better than that." He paused and frowned. "Didn't I?"

"How could we possibly compete with all day, every day indoctrination?" Risa covered her face, ashamed of herself for never seeing the possibilities. Louisa had been such a good, kind person. They should've realized she wouldn't live forever. "We all thought the Academy was such a good idea. We all thought the sacrifices were worth it."

Ben tensed as if he meant to leap to his feet and do something. "We have to get Kay out of there. It's not too late for her."

Frantic need to see Kay and hold her close gripped Risa. She nodded and started to stand. "If we leave now, we can be there tomorrow."

"Whoa." Matias reached a hand in front of her and held up the other to stop Ben. "We can't storm the Academy."

"They won't let us in," Kele said. "As someone pointed out recently, we'd face criminal charges if we broke in. Supposing we did it anyway, we don't have enough intel on what we'd face in there."

"I can't get it until we're close." Vivian draped an arm around Risa's shoulders. "Even then, I still might not be able to. This isn't something we can do right now."

Risa wanted to cry again. Already sick of that feeling, she rubbed her eyes and huffed. "Then how do we get that intel?"

Ben tapped his fingers on the table. "We need someone who's been inside. Recently."

Doc cleared his throat, reminding Risa of his presence. "As I recall, teams have six people. I've only heard you talk about five so far."

"Scope," Ben said. "She talked to me a little, but not enough. I think she wanted to, but was afraid of being overheard."

Risa wondered if something else played a bigger part in Scope's reticence. "She's always struck me as shy, but comfortable with the military part of her role."

"Which means she should respond to my rank," Ben said.

Kele shook her head. "No, she won't. Sorry, Cap. Right or wrong, everyone knows you would've been stripped of your rank if you hadn't retired. Besides, you'll remind her of Jay."

"Then you should go." Ready to try anything if meant keeping Kay safe, Risa looked to Kele. "You're military.

You're well-known but not famous, you shouldn't remind her of anyone, and if she tries to kill you, you'll be fine." She couldn't think of a way to suggest Kele might better handle a woman who didn't seem to fit the "girl" mold without insulting both Kele and Ben.

"That's solid reasoning." Ben sounded pleased instead of affronted, which Risa took as a win. "When I met her, she said she'd rather be birdwatching in Nebraska."

"In her letters," Vivian said, "Phyllicia referred to Scope as a sniper and mentioned she liked camping. They went with her for leave once, and she wowed Phyllicia with her mad survival skills."

"She'll pick someplace where you can camp, then," Risa said. "Someplace where you can get lost in the wilderness for a week or two."

Matias held up his phone. "There are a few national parks in Nebraska, but this one specifically mentions birdwatching in the description—Samuel R. McKelvie National Park. If you can get me her phone number, license plate, or full name and date of birth, I can check if she's there. Otherwise, this is the best I can get."

Kele patted Kachina's head and stood. "I'll get moving now. I should be able to get there sometime tomorrow."

"Before you go," Doc said, "I'd like to make sure you all know this. Every six months or so, Charlie comes to visit. I don't know how you manage to miss her every time you stop by," Doc said to Kele, "but you do. I haven't told her my power is coming back because I don't want to be part of the Novas again. But she brings a kid in a lab coat with her. He draws my blood every time and they both talk about how they're trying to help kids with birth defects."

"Your blood?" Vivian asked. "Why would they take your blood for that?"

Doc shrugged. "They believe my power is useless now because it's keeping me alive and there's nothing left for anyone else. But I still have it, and they know that. I'm sure they wouldn't keep coming back for fresh samples otherwise.

Now," he held up a hand, stopping anyone from asking more questions. "There's something else. Charlie's wing isn't as dead as you think."

Risa blinked and stared at him. "What do you mean?"

"She hasn't pulled off the sheath and shown it to me, but I do shake hands with her every time she visits, and I can tell it's partially regrown. I can't be sure, because that's not something I'm familiar with, but I think she's got someone integrating electronic parts into it, like a high-grade prosthetic."

"So she may fly again someday." Matias smiled, small and hesitant. Risa imagined he found the idea bittersweet.

"It's possible. All that concerns me, though. That kind of research. The Nazis did that sort of thing."

"We did too," Kele said. "That's how I got my powers. I'd be dead without that project."

Doc held up both hands in surrender. "I'm just saying that it takes oversight and a good heart to keep something like that from turning dark. Everything you've said tonight leads me to believe this project lacks oversight, at the least."

"Charlie has a good heart," Matias said. "She wouldn't let anyone take it in the wrong direction. The whole thing is about her sister, after all. And if she's using the research to regrow her wing, that's great. It's part of her. One of her limbs. Like an arm. We have no reason to judge her for wanting it back."

Risa nodded, agreeing with Matias. "I feel like there's something a little less than stellar about her marriage, but that's no reason to get suspicious about Charlie." She wondered if Charlie didn't have kids as a conscious decision, or because she couldn't. The answer seemed like it might explain the way she'd deferred to Greg.

"I'm going." Kele patted her leg as she headed for the door.

Kachina licked Ell's muzzle, then followed Kele outside. Ell barked as the door closed.

Ben stood. "We should go find a hotel for the night."

"As soon as we've cleaned up our mess," Risa said. "And taken care of anything Ell needs. We also need to figure out where Gabi can stay, because I think she might stand out at a hotel."

"She can stay with me," Doc said. He smiled at Gabi. "Given some time, I might be able to help you."

Gabi nudged Matias's shoulder. Matias said, "Only if you'll let us do something about your shitty wifi."

Doc shrugged. "Do whatever you like, so long as it's not obvious. I like not being robbed because no one thinks I have anything worth taking."

Risa smirked and beckoned for Vivian to follow. "Ell won't let anyone rob you. We'll come back to pick you up when we have somewhere to go," she told Matias. In the meantime, she wanted a private hotel room with a hot tub, fluffy towels, and a big bed. If she couldn't save her little girl right now, she needed some pampering to take her mind off the situation.

# CHAPTER 31

## KELE

December 4, 2017
20:47

Kele parked her bike in a small lot and stared at the star-filled sky. The majesty of darkness had been part of her life since the beginning. Growing up in a tiny town on an Arizona rez, it'd been there all along. She remembered ducking outside while her father drank himself stupid, her big brother did Dad's share of the chores, and her mother took care of her little brothers. Half the time, she'd done nothing more risqué than lie in a field and stare at the stars.

On missions all over the world, she'd taken a moment to notice the night sky. She'd always had time. They'd always made her wait for something. Even in Brazil. Like football in a bar over beer, it gave her a way to center. Focus. Forget. Move on.

She took a deep breath of the crisp, clean air. Wood smoke drifted from a campfire nearby. The trees swallowed laughter. Dampness in the air promised rain tonight.

"I'm here," she murmured to anyone listening on the other end of the earbud. "Do we know any more about Scope than we did last night?"

"Did you sleep yet?" Matias asked.

"Yes." In the early parts of the morning, she'd stopped for an hour to nap and eat. Her regeneration let her soldier through long periods of time with minimal sleep, so long as she took in extra calories.

"Cool. Looking over news reports, it's clear that Scope hangs in the background, kinda like you always did. They always wanted to talk to Jay and Cowboy, the superstar, hotshot Legacies. She wore a mask on camera, and never gave any interviews. I found one exchange when they first stepped into the public eye and some reporter tried to get her to talk. The best he got out of her was a grunt."

"I can appreciate that." Kele refilled Kachina's water bowl while the dog relieved herself.

"Promo stills all show her wearing BDUs and the mask. Sometimes also a trenchcoat. There are a few with her in full ghillie suit sniper getup."

"Interesting. Do we know her powers?"

"All I can find from anything is various words that all mean it's vision-related, and she's referred to as the team's scout. Her Nova profile says she's Catholic, from an unnamed small town in Nebraska. In fairness, most Nova profiles don't say much."

Kele watched Kachina lap up her water, trying to decide if she should take the dog or leave her at the bike. "Is Ben available?"

"Eh, he's probably banging Risa. Viv said something about a bubble bath."

Risa and Ben needed each other. Even Kele could see that. She had no reason to begrudge them private time. Vivian had never been keen on roughing it, so Kele couldn't complain about that either.

Without access to Ben, she needed to think over the information herself. Matias could at least call bullshit on her or correct anything she got wrong, so she did it out loud. "As I recall, she told Ben about her idea of a fun trip on Thanksgiving. So she'd rather be birdwatching on

Thanksgiving, when most Catholics are going to be with family."

Kele hadn't seen her family for anything in a long time. And that family didn't have the same associations about Thanksgiving. Once she'd left the rez, she never went back. She could relate to someone who also avoided home.

"Since she's declared as Catholic but asks her friends to use male pronouns, I'm guessing she's lapsed. At the least."

"Sure," said Matias. "My mama was Catholic, so I get what's going on there. When she visits her family, they make her go to church on Sundays. When you go to church on Sundays, you wear your Sunday best. Girls wear dresses. And not just dresses, but nice dresses. The kind with lace or some shit. Even odds she had to go to Catholic school until the Academy, where the uniform is a skirt. Either way, she got the message that girls are supposed to be girly and her lack of girliness is a problem to fix."

Kele grimaced. "What a load of shit."

"Right. Anyway, all that says something about Scope, but I dunno where you're headed with it."

Had she just insulted Matias? Kele never asked anyone about their faith, and didn't enjoy hearing people try to proselytize her. So far as she could remember, she'd never seen him cross himself or heard him mention missing church.

She shook off the concern. Risa had skills for handling this sort of situation. Kele plowed onward. "I think she might be the type who knows how to live off the land and hide when she wants to. Because she's spent enough time on her own that she's learned those skills to survive. That means I'll have to hunt her, and she's nothing like easy prey. What kind of lure should I use?"

"Cheeseburgers?"

Kele chuckled. "Probably not. I think that would make her suspicious."

"She's looking for birds, so maybe if you can attract some of those, you'll find her nearby."

Kachina raced around the parking lot, getting her exercise after a long day in the sidecar.

"I wonder if she likes dogs." Kele decided to take Kachina with her on the chance she put Scope at ease.

"Can't say, but odds are good. From what I've seen, most folks into camping and that sort of thing are dog people, because dogs are good for that kind of stuff."

"Agreed. Let me know if you find anything else. I'll keep the earbud in." Kele checked a map of the park on her phone, getting a feel for the boundaries.

"Good hunting. I'll shut up now."

The thrill of a mission sang in Kele's blood. She packed enough food and gear for a few days, covered her bike, and plunged into the park with Kachina at a light jog.

In the dark, she couldn't find subtle clues. In the light, she might not see them either. After all, she hadn't seen that damned tunnel. Maybe she should've asked Risa to come with her. At least Risa had seen the second one.

Doc's words tumbled in her skull. Wilhelm Otto deserved all the blame for that night. Except her superiors had booted her. They must've had a reason. She knew they had a reason. Too slow, too many dead, too little benefit gained by her presence. After all her years of service, with a tiny number of botched missions, they'd decided she'd lost her edge.

She never did feel like she'd lost her edge, whatever that really meant. Would she know it? How did a person whose primary role involved relying on her power to not die in the face of overwhelming harm lose her edge?

That night, she'd waded through a sea of enemy supers, knocking them down and keeping them away from the building. Some got through. People died. She hadn't stopped them all. They'd retired her for it. She'd deserved that. Army brass didn't make that kind of mistake.

Doc had a point, though. Everyone had missed the incoming attack, not just their team. She'd told Ben the truth when he first came to see her—if they hadn't been there, that clusterfuck would've reached much worse proportions. Lots of kids might have died, including Jay. Instead, the old Novas crumbled and the kids rose to the occasion.

Kachina stopped and sniffed the ground. Kele hadn't given her a scent to track, so anything could've distracted the dog including squirrels, Matias's cheeseburgers, or another dog.

Kele sniffed the air and noticed how fresh it smelled. They'd passed the campground and its fires. Cars never came this deep into the park.

"Kele?" Vivian whispered into her ear.

"I'm here."

"Follow the dog."

Kele peered across the meadow that interested Kachina so much. "My dog, or some other dog?"

"I'm pretty sure it's your dog. When you reach the trees, go left for ten trunks, then dive in and follow your gut."

"Thanks." Kele patted Kachina's back. "Let's go, girl." She followed the dog down a grassy incline, over a tiny creek, and up a rolling hill.

They reached a treeline. Kachina stopped and scented the air again. Kele crouched beside her and thought about using her old, dulled stealth muscles. Once upon a time, she'd sucked at the creeping thing. Ben's father had been the one to teach her the why and how of sneaking. She, in turn, had taught Ben.

Did Scope need as much sleep as a normal person? Kele had never met anyone who could go without, but she'd known several who could short themselves at need like she could. This game got easier if Scope needed a full eight hours, especially if she chose to take some or all of them during the day.

"This way," she whispered. Kele counted ten trunks, then turned into the trees. Her gut said high ground with long sight lines.

Kachina barked. Kele shushed her and covered her nose long enough for the dog to understand. With a quiet little whine, Kachina followed her through the woods.

Kele took her time, stepping with care to avoid making noise. Brown pine and fir needles littered the ground with errant twigs and fallen branches. Several feet in, the trees crowded close enough to block the light. She had to make a choice.

If Scope slept tonight, she wouldn't hear small noises. If she didn't, she might see Kele coming and move.

Taking a chance, Kele kept going. Even if she found nothing, she'd get a sense of the area that might help her in the morning.

The pair walked through the woods. As she fell into the rhythm of stealth, Kele's body remembered how to do it. She moved with confidence, avoiding the deep shadows and leaping over deadfall. Chitters, cheeps, and chatter filled the air around her.

Her surroundings shifted to a mix of deciduous and evergreen. The first cluster of dead leaves took her by surprise, filling the air with a crispy crunch. Kachina jumped in the leaves and barked her happiness.

Kele stopped and watched the dog in thin moonlight. Though she considered shushing Kachina, her pure joy at flushing small animals and chomping floating leaves made Kele let her play for a minute.

"Excuse me?" The speaker had a soft, middling voice, neither deep nor high.

Peering in the direction she thought the voice came from, Kele saw only trees and shadows. "Yes?" Taking a cue from the speaker, she used a soft, low voice.

"Your dog is scaring the nightjars."

"Oh. Is that a kind of bird?"

"Yes. Nocturnal. If you head to your left, you'll leave their hunting ground."

Would anyone else ask politely in the middle of the night for someone to stop harassing birds? Kele doubted it. "Scope?"

Thick, deep silence shrouded Kele as if someone had

thrown a smothering blanket over her.

"What do you want?" Scope's voice took a dangerous edge.

"To talk. My code name is Crash, but the Novas didn't send me."

After a long pause, Scope asked, "The Crash? The regenerator? The one who worked with two different Captain Kinetics?"

People didn't usually gush at Kele about her identity. She crouched to pet Kachina, thinking she needed to appear less threatening. "Yes. That one."

"Oh. Wow. Um." A bulky shadow that Kele had mistaken for a rock stood and approached. "It's not every day you cross paths with a legend."

Scope offered a gloved hand. Kele shook it. Each used a firm, warm grip.

"I didn't know I was a legend."

Scope huffed a small laugh. "Half the Academy instructors think you're the best thing ever, and the other half are scared shitless of you. And then there's Jay, who calls you his aunt." She sighed. "Called. He called you his aunt. Anyway. There's a good place to sit not far from here. We can start a fire. It's pretty cold out here this time of year."

Kele nodded. "I'd like that." She stood and patted her leg. With Kachina by her side, she followed Scope.

Kachina made the most noise as they moved through the trees. Scope took them on a ten minute walk to a clearing with two fallen logs and a stone-ringed firepit. Stacked wood waited inside the pit, enough to fuel a small fire.

"I was planning on camping here tonight," Scope said as she retrieved a lighter from her coat pocket and started the kindling. "There's a cluster of cedar waxwing nests just over there, and I like to catch them early in the morning."

Kele dropped her pack and sat on a log. She found Kachina's bowls and filled them with food and water. "I take it you're familiar with this forest."

Flickering light revealed a slim, oval face with a sharp nose and lots of freckles. Wisps of brown hair escaped her Army beanie. "I grew up in a tiny hellhole just to the north."

"But you come back to it?"

Scope poked the kindling with a stick, then sat a few feet from Kele. "I know the area really well. It's more relaxing to come someplace where I don't have to worry about finding a campsite or fresh water. Besides, this is where I got my powers. Some kind of satellite fell here, and there was some experimental stuff inside. Maybe I shouldn't have stuck my head inside it, but I'd probably still be stuck in Valentine if I hadn't."

They sat and listened to the fire crackling. Kele wanted to ask about Jay and get this over with, but she had a feeling that wouldn't work. Instead, she needed to spend some time getting to know Scope. It already sounded like they had a lot in common, at least.

"I left home when I enlisted and have never been back. No reason to go." The conversation seemed like it had a lot of potential to get personal, so Kele popped out her earbud and stuck it in a pocket. Some things, her team knew. Other things, she preferred to keep to herself.

"I went back once after graduation. No idea why I thought anything would be different." Scope picked up a piece of wood and ran her thumb along the edge like she wanted to whittle it. "Mom had redecorated my room in pink and lacy shit, and filled the closet with dresses and skirts. I took one look at it and left."

Kele nodded. "When I was fourteen, my dad brought me to the bar where he met with his buddies every Friday night after work. He made me wear an old dress from my mom's closet. It hit me here." She marked a line a few inches above her knee. "I always wore pants. We didn't have much money, and I was sandwiched between one older and two younger brothers. Even if I'd wanted to wear dresses or skirts, which I didn't, my parents couldn't afford to get me clothes for myself.

"Anyway, short skirt plus bar plus depressed older men. Went about like you'd expect. Would have been worse if I hadn't broken someone's nose." And her father had taken the belt to her for doing it. Now, the story didn't inspire any particular feelings in Kele, other than disgust for her father. Even that was muted, since he couldn't still be alive. Not with the way he drank.

Scope crumbled bits of the wood with her fingers. "I… never had anything like that happen."

"Good. It shouldn't happen to anyone." Kele considered saying more, but stopped herself. Scope needed to talk about something, she could feel it like clouds about to burst with rain.

"I have a bunch of brothers too, but I'm the baby. Mom wanted a girl so bad, she just kept having kids until me. Everything in my life was pink, everyone acted like I was made of spun glass. Mom thinks there's something wrong with me that I never liked it. Always went for green instead."

Scope paused and watched the fire. "I guess there is something wrong with me because… I dunno. Do you ever feel like your body is…" Her hands moved like she needed to say some specific thing, but couldn't think of the right words or force them out of her mouth. "Like you have the wrong… I can't help it. I just…" She stopped and shook her head. "It's hard to explain."

Kele nodded, because she kind of understood, and committed herself to using the pronoun Scope wanted. "When my friends were younger, they were all about sex. You know Maverick? The lady with the one wing? Back in the day, she used to bang every fighter pilot she ran across. They'd all joke about it, tell stories, and all that. And I just never cared. Like something's missing inside me."

"Yeah. Like something's missing." Scope snapped the piece of wood in half. "Like we're broken." He handed half to Kele.

"Nah. Not broken." Kele held up the chunk of wood. "Different." She tossed it into the fire. "Just as useful, just as much value. I kind of think more people are like us than want to admit it. They slog through a miserable life, pretending to be something they're not because they're scared of how other people will react. I stopped giving a shit a long time ago. You lose people because of that, but they weren't worth it. The ones you gain are the ones who matter. Everyone else can go fuck themselves."

Scope regarded his chunk of wood for several beats before tossing it into the fire with Kele's. "I wish I could talk to my mom about this stuff. Or my dad. Or anyone, really. Jay and Phyllicia seemed like maybe, but I never did because I was afraid they'd take it to our handler."

Hearing that made Kele one part sad and one part angry. "I don't know what kind of horse's ass your handlers had their heads stuck inside. Your teammates are supposed to be the people you can trust with anything. I can't imagine not having that. If I need to talk to someone, I've got four people I know I can trust, anytime, day or night. My team worked. Yours, it sounds like, didn't. And that's fucked up. They should've shuffled the team a long time ago."

"We had two Legacies." Scope picked up a stick and scraped lines in the dirt. "They told Jay and Bobby they had to work together, or they'd be demoted and sidelined. Jay put in a lot of honest effort. Bobby…he's kind of…" He shook his head.

This felt like the moment to ask. Kele put a hand on his shoulder. "Scope, please tell me what happened on that mission."

Scope bent over and took his head in his hands. "It was a clusterfuck is what happened." For a moment, Kele thought Scope wouldn't tell her anything more. Then he opened his mouth again. "We were stationed in Germany for a few weeks. They wanted us in place when the intel came in.

"Brass decided to send a camera drone with us, to record the whole thing. I mean, it was supposed to be a standard terrorist takedown. I guess they thought it'd be simple, and good for showing higher-ups how useful we are.

Maybe there's been budget stuff. Whatever. Anyway.

"We roll into Mannheim near dusk, looking for the target. She's supposed to be at home, but she's not. Cap sends me up to a belltower because we need to scout. I find the target through a glass shopfront and tell the team over the mics. Cowboy says he's going over there. Cap tells him to hold off and wait. Cowboy tells him the lady is right there, and so is the camera. He wants to impress the brass so they'll stop fussing over these two new teams they've been excited about. Cap says something seems weird about this, and he's right. Something does seem weird about it. The mission is too easy, too pat. Like, why bother sending us when an ordinary sniper at my position could take her down?"

Scope sounded like the mission replayed in his head. Kele knew that feeling. When things went sideways, it took time to sort what happened from what she wanted to have happened, and to figure out the point where the shit started. Then came the guilt, piling on top of the wishes, drowning reality until nothing made sense anymore.

"They turn off their mics. Cowboy and Cap argue. Cowboy walks away. Lightsaber and Bunny go with him. Cap throws something at the wall with his power, I guess in frustration. I switch to watching Cowboy. He goes inside the store while Lightsaber and Bunny wait outside. I check on Cap and Interface, and find them moving toward the store.

"Cowboy crashes through the window. Everyone moves in. I've got my rifle, so I'm trying to figure out who I need to shoot. There's the target. I'm sighting her, and Cowboy fouls my shot. He grabs her and drags her down the street, attracting cops. Mics are still turned off. I know because I left mine on and I can't hear anything.

"I shift focus to see the whole team. Bunny is gone. Lightsaber is running up the street after Cowboy. Cap is trying to calm down the bodyguards. Interface is with him. They're surrounded with no way out."

Scope sat up and took a few deep breaths. "They weren't ordinary bodyguards. They were supers."

Kele stared at Scope, her mouth hanging open. The mission had gone much, much worse than she'd imagined. Compared to this, that night at the Academy didn't seem like such a colossal failure.

She touched Scope's shoulder again. "Did you see them die?"

"Yeah." Scope nodded, his gaze so distant that Kele knew he replayed the moments in his head. "I took down one. But Cap could only handle so many things at once, you know? And Interface... I think she tried to control them with her telepathy. She could do that. Most telepaths can't, but she could. Either it didn't work, or she picked the wrong target."

Not sure what Scope needed, Kele squeezed his shoulder and said nothing. Kachina moved to Scope and laid her head on the sniper's leg. Scope petted her.

They sat in silence for a long time.

Someone had video of what had happened in Germany. By now, they'd probably scrubbed it. She hoped they had, anyway. Ben needed to never see that. Even if the video didn't show the deaths, watching the team fracture like that would send him into a rage. She didn't look forward to telling him about it.

"There was nothing I could do. That's the worst part. I couldn't have stopped any of them from doing anything. They all had their mics turned off, so I couldn't tell them what I saw. Once we realized the target wasn't where they said, Cap said we were going to shift to scouting. Interface didn't link us because she wanted to conserve her power until we needed it, and we didn't need it. Mics were always enough for scouting."

"I understand." Kele did understand. She'd watched friends die before. "I'm listening, Scope. For as long as you want, you keep talking, and I'll keep listening." She settled on the log, ready for a long night of wallowing in someone else's horror.

# CHAPTER 32

## VIVIAN

December 3, 2017
13:27

The team sat in an otherwise empty dive bar on the south side of Denver. With no one else around to complain, the owner obliged them by turning off the music and turning on a football game. Vivian didn't care about either team, so she only paid a scant amount of attention.

Kele finished relating the horrifying story of the worst screw-up ever and sipped her beer. She'd left her dog behind with Scope, and seemed off-balance because of it. Ben looked like he could murder someone with his bare hands. Risa sat and stared at the table, chewing her sandwich mechanically. Matias kept his eyes on his food.

"That, of course, isn't everything. Once I got him to open up about the mission, we talked about all kinds of things. Most of it isn't relevant. What I found interesting is that their team was the go-to, top-shelf team, like ours was. About a year ago, these two new teams came up from training, and the brass started shifting favor to them. Both teams have a firestarter, a telepath, a soldier, a flier, and a gross telekinetic. They're doing five-man teams now. And when I say five-man, I mean it. Ten white boys."

Ben's beer bottle flew at the wall. It shattered, spraying beer and glass everywhere, and startling Vivian. He glared at the table. "What the fuck is going on there? Just what the actual fuck."

Vivian's vision misted with hazy shapes. A figure took shape. It leaned forward, detail filling in as a man loomed over the table. Wilhelm Otto smiled with malice at her, his shadow covering the table.

"Jesus," she said as she scooted out her chair, trying to get away from him.

Other voices blended in a cacophony of concern.

Otto leaned toward her, leering with menace, and drew a thin book out of his coat. He set the book on the table, then his shape darkened and expanded until he filled the room with shadow. Vivian stood and reached for the book. It melted into the table and became a rain of handwritten letters falling onto concrete. The letters soaked through. Tiny figures, crackling with lightning, streamed from the underside of the table.

The shadow lifted, and the figures exploded into fading sparks.

Vivian blinked and saw everyone watching her. "I had a vision." As if they couldn't tell. "It was Wilhelm Otto."

"But you only see the future," Risa said, "and he's dead."

"He had a book." Vivian rubbed her temple, feeling a headache building.

"He had a lot of books," Kele said. "Stacks of the things. We handed over what we took to OpCon. Brazilian authorities recovered the rest."

Ben growled under his breath. "Who gives a shit about a fucking book? We should just storm the fucking Academy."

Vivian looked down and saw dark water beneath her feet. Wind rushed past her ears, and cables near her head held a parachute. Stars filled the night sky overhead and she saw the shape of a small airplane streaking into the distance. She tugged on the parachute lines to aim for a bright beacon on an island.

They fell toward a concrete building with minimal lightning and only two cars in the small parking lot. Vivian braced for landing, then the vision lifted.

Matias stood behind her, holding her so she wouldn't fall. "Easy, chica."

"I don't know where that is," she murmured.

Everyone watched her again, though Risa did it with her hand over Ben's. Vivian shut her eyes and focused on Matias. That old vision of fire with Matias on his knees and Ben behind a shimmering curtain resurfaced, holding her in its steely grip.

The fire faded. Vivian gasped for breath. Matias held her on her feet. She needed to know what it meant. Visions didn't work that way, but she pushed it anyway. Diving in again, she focused on Risa.

Another parachute snapped open beneath Vivian's feet. She saw Risa hit the asphalt of the parking lot and release her parachute. She blurred, running at top speed, until she stood on the roof. She'd missed the target because they needed to breach the roof, not the front door. Following her sent Matias into a tree. A branch impaled him.

The vision released her. "Don't follow Risa," she said between gasps for air. Without waiting for herself to recover, she tried again, this time for Kele.

Kele stood in a tunnel, holding back a tide of indistinct shapes. Claws slashed her flesh, spraying blood everywhere, and it healed. Bullets slammed through her body, blowing holes through her back, and they healed. An explosion filled the air with red and orange, searing and flinging gobbets of flesh, and it blew Kele apart.

Once again, she lost the vision. Vivian growled in frustration and gave it one more shot. Ben would guide her right. He always did.

Ben landed on the roof of the concrete building, giving Vivian another look at the area. She saw a raised highway over the water, leading past the island without offering a exit for it. Lights glittered in the distance, on more islands.

"The Keys!" The vision released her, and she leaned against Matias, panting to catch her breath. "There's something we need to do or see in the Florida Keys."

Risa, Ben, and Kele glanced at each other.

Ben frowned. "That's where the supers prison is. What could we possibly learn there?"

"I don't know. Matias, can you look up a picture of that prison?" Vivian sat in her chair while Matias tapped on his phone. When he showed her a picture of that concrete building, she nodded. "That's where we need to go. It's important. I got three different urgings to go. We'll have to do a parachute drop, which sucks, but if that's what we have to do, then I guess we need to get ourselves a pilot and a plane we can jump out of."

"I don't—"

Risa covered Ben's mouth with her hand. "I know you're upset. I'm upset too. Charlie let that happen, which I don't understand."

"She couldn't have known," Matias said. "Just because she's a liaison doesn't mean she has a lot of contact with the kids. I'll bet most of her work is with the instructors."

Vivian grimaced at her beer. She didn't want it anymore. Seeing friends killed always dampened her appetite. Telling Kele—or anyone else—felt like it would make everything worse. Maybe Kele could recover from that? She didn't know. At least she could prevent what happened to Matias.

Clearing her throat, Risa held up a finger to shush Matias. "The point is, we're upset. That doesn't mean we should suddenly start ignoring Vivian. She's always right. Whatever is going on at that prison must be important. If you weren't so angry, you know you'd be thinking about how impossible it is that no one has escaped in twelve years. Twelve years, Ben. They used to get out once every few months, remember?"

"You know what I don't get?" Matias tapped on his

phone. "They never stopped putting people in there. The building is only so big. If no one ever escapes, and everyone gets a life sentence, where are they putting them? It can't have a basement. The island is too small."

Vivian leaned aside to see his phone. He showed her another picture of the prison, one that made the size more clear. At best, the building had twice the square footage of her house. She had a big house, but the structure couldn't fit more than two hundred cells, and that assumed they put nothing else inside it, like bathrooms and other facilities for the guards and warden.

In her vision, she'd only seen two cars in the parking lot. If they carpooled, the night crew consisted of, at most, eight guards? "Who's the warden?"

Matias tapped on his phone. "Not listed. Which is weird for a government facility. They've usually got a nice, friendly picture of the person in charge. This just says it's administered by the Pentagon, and they hold enemy combatant supers for all of NATO."

Risa nudged Ben with her shoulder. He sighed and rubbed his face. Vivian watched him stuff his anger into a box so he could think.

"I'll go make a call." Ben stood and pulled out his burner phone.

"Ben?" Risa took his hand as he turned to step outside. "Please don't destroy anything important or valuable."

He squeezed her hand and hurried for the door.

When the door shut behind him, Risa laid her head on the table. "I don't think I've ever seen him that angry."

Kele shrugged. "You know how he feels about military incompetence. Effectively, from his point of view, the Academy killed Jay, and he helped push for it in the first place. He helped build it. With his own hands and his power. He's the kind of man who takes the fall for anything under his watch, so he's seeing it as his own fault. In his head, he killed Jay."

Risa sighed. "Why do you understand that better than

me?"

"He's a lot like his dad."

Vivian rubbed her face, trying to push away the echo of her vision about Kele exploding. "Matias, when we jump, follow Ben, not Risa. You'll get hooked in a thermal if you follow Risa."

Matias nodded. "I can't believe we're going to do a jump insertion. After all these years, I'm not sure I remember how."

"It's like falling out of a plane," Kele said.

Tired, frayed by the rapid succession of visions, and unsure about the mission, Vivian giggled. "This is going to be horrible."

Risa grimaced. "It's already horrible. We just wanted to bring our son home to rest with his great-grandfather."

"Why hold onto the body this long?" Matias asked. "It seems…stupid? Unnecessary?"

Kele set down her empty beer bottle and waved for the bartender to bring her another. "Based upon the things Scope said and didn't say, I think there might've been evidence of something on his body. They've probably been waiting in the hopes it would mean you can't have an open casket, so you don't need a mortician to do anything, so you can't see anything. Someone there knows how good you two are at noticing things and drawing conclusions."

"That makes so much awful sense." Vivian focused on breathing, hoping to keep any further visions at bay. They'd served their purpose, and now her eyelids felt heavy. "Too bad for them they didn't realize acting like suspicious assholes would cause the same thing."

"I almost don't want to know whatever we're going to find at that prison," Risa said.

Matias nodded. "I have some ideas, and all of them are fucked up."

"It's important that we go, though." Vivian laid her head on the table. "Someone wake me when we have to jump off the plane. At night. We have to do it at night."

# CHAPTER 33

## BEN

December 6, 2017
14:51

Frosty December air thick with jet fuel and plastic pressed on Ben's new skydiving suit as he crossed the tarmac on the private side of Denver International Airport. He led his team to a King Air skydiving plane waiting under harsh sunshine. Carrying a backpack and parachute left him with one gloved hand free to hold Risa's.

He let go as they reached the pilot waiting beside the plane, and offered Captain Ramirez a crisp salute. Ramirez returned it with a broad smile. They shook hands and pulled each other into a one-armed hug.

"Good to see you, Cap."

"I'm glad you got your wings."

Ramirez grinned. He only looked a few years older than the last time they saw him. Ben didn't want to think about Brazil, though.

"It only took three years." Ramirez's smile dimmed. "I'm sorry for why we're all here, but I'm glad I can help."

Ben nodded. "We'll pay you back for the rental and fuel when we get back."

"Take your time." He offered Risa a hand to get inside

the plane. "My wife already finished all our Christmas shopping."

Though he wanted to catch up with Ramirez, Ben didn't want to delay their departure. He stepped into the plane and turned to offer Matias a hand. "I hadn't heard you got married. Congratulations. Any kids?"

"Second is on the way. We're hip deep in diapers and tiny clothing."

"That's great." Despite his own pain, Ben smiled as he helped Vivian inside. "I'm sure they'll both hate airplanes and want to join the Navy."

"Ouch." Ramirez chuckled as he followed Kele inside and secured the door. "You're a cruel, cruel man, Cap."

They laughed. Ramirez checked everyone's harnesses. He pointed out the ready light and the go light, then got to work.

Ben activated his earbud and made sure everyone else did the same. He sat beside Risa, facing the others across the plane, and waited as g-forces pushed him sideways, then leveled out. They had six hours, including a refueling stop, to the target, and not much to do in the meantime.

Matias pulled out a handheld video game. Risa retrieved a paperback book. Vivian popped gum into her mouth. Kele leaned her head to the side and fell asleep.

The sight of them doing what they always did churned his gut. He didn't know how he felt about it, he just knew he felt something deep.

Maverick was missing. That empty seat on Risa's other side stared at him. Without her to spot them on the descent, they had to work harder to find the target. He wondered if she missed doing this, or if she would've come had he asked.

At least this drop didn't need oxygen masks. Ramirez could drop them at a few thousand feet instead of twenty-seven thousand. No one cared about an American-registered plane piloted by an Air Force Captain on leave and full of American skydivers flying from American soil to drop into American waters.

He handed Risa a protein bar and leaned back to get some sleep. The past few days had been a whirlwind of driving and flying and rage and driving and flying. All of it had exhausted him. He needed time to deal with everything. He needed a twenty-one gun salute for his son.

Closing his eyes, he thought of the reason they did this. As a boy, after learning about the nine months that Japanese-Americans had spent in internment during World War II, he'd asked his grandfather why he joined the military, why he fought for people who hated what he looked like.

The original Captain Kinetic had sat Ben on his knee and pointed to the grainy, black and white photograph on the wall, of all the Allied supers. "Benjamin, we fought for humanity and decency. We fought for justice. I fought to show the people of my country that they can be better, they can do better. This nation is great and wonderful, and I'm proud to call it my home. I'm glad my great-grandparents came here. But never forget that it can always be better. It didn't start perfect, and it'll never be perfect. It's our job, all of us, to do our part and push it a little closer so things are better for our kids."

Kenzo Tsukuda had always turned a good phrase and given a good speech.

Ben fell asleep thinking about his last visit with his grandfather, when the old man had finally succumbed to the frailties of age. Bedridden and ready to breathe his last gasp, Kenzo had reminded him to be true to the principles of justice and honor.

He woke to Risa prodding his shoulder.

"The ready light came on a few minutes ago," she said while he rubbed his eyes. "Are you good to go?"

"I'm fine." He unbuckled his harness and double-checked his parachute.

Everyone else took his movement as a signal to get up. DPS set his game on the seat and strapped it down. Crash woke and stretched. Omen moved like a wooden doll, her nerves betraying her. Springfire stowed her book and let Ben check her parachute for her. Ben made sure everyone had their straps and buckles secure.

"We jump as a group, and chutes out on my signal. We'll open as soon as we're clear. Everyone stick close to me. If we miss the target, it means a lot more work, so let's not miss." He clipped onto a hook on the side and waited for everyone else to brace themselves, then he hauled open the door.

Outside, the stars above and lights below reminded him of a dozen or more other missions. His training took over. The moment the go light came on, they leaped in a clump. Ben saluted the plane, then gave the signal. They all pulled their chutes at once.

Few lights marked their target. It hulked in the darkness, easy to miss. Five red lights pulsed at the five corners of the pentagonal building, marking it for helicopters. Two lines of down-angled light flanked a path from the front door to the parking lot. Otherwise, it had nothing.

Ben had never seen such a poorly lit prison. Anyone could escape in that wide moat of darkness around the building. Yet, no one had. And it had no fencing or guard towers. Nothing overlooked the place. The structure also had no windows or sign of an outdoor area. He supposed that people who came here had all done horrible things, but he'd never realized the conditions. Every time he'd spared someone's life to send them to this place, he'd thought himself merciful.

He landed on the roof at a run and took control of his chute with his power. Springfire missed the roof by a foot. Everyone else hit in a circle around him. One by one, he took control of their chutes and repacked them.

"I'm okay," Springfire said through the earbuds. "I'll be up in a moment."

"DPS, Crash, find the way in. Omen, keep watch." Ben moved to the edge.

Springfire stood in the parking lot, a shadow on the

edge of the minimal lighting. A moment later, she stood beside him.

"I pulled left when I meant right."

Ben helped her remove her chute pack. The shape seemed wrong, so he checked inside it. "What did you do to this thing? It's…wadded."

She rolled her eyes. "You're the only person in the history of the world who folds parachutes on a mission. You know that, right? Everyone else is sensible and either let it go or waits until the mission is over."

"You're exaggerating."

"No," Crash said, "she's not. It's just you."

DPS nodded. "Agreed. Also, I found the hatch. It's not locked. No security at all. Not even a motion sensor.

"Crash, open it up and see what's inside," Ben said as he and Springfire crossed the roof to reach him. "If an alarm goes off and lights blare in our faces, we're going to blame DPS."

"I'm telling you, there's nothing. But only open it partway. I'll take a look inside."

Crash hefted the large, square hatch. No light shone from the inside.

"Don't let go." DPS stuck his head through the gap.

"Are you sure?" Crash asked. "Because you could use a haircut."

"I think that might be more extreme than my usual trim. The wife would probably get upset. It's clear down here. Opens into a janitor closet."

Mention of Matias's wife brought something to mind. Ben gestured for Crash to open the hatch all the way. "Hey, DPS? You don't have kids, right?"

DPS lowered himself into the closet and arranged a ladder for everyone else. "Affirmative." He flashed a thumbs-up.

Crash climbed down. Omen sat and dangled her feet off the edge. Springfire flipped herself inside.

"But you're married," Ben said. He stood beside Omen.

"Yep. Eight years in February."

"Why get married and not have kids?"

Springfire looked up at him like he'd offended her. "What kind of a question is that? In the middle of a mission? Why would you ask that?"

DPS crouched at the door. He chuckled. "It's okay. My mom used to ask that all the time. We just don't want kids, Cap. Hallway is clear."

"Let Springfire go first and scout the floor." Ben sat on the edge with Vivian. He watched DPS crack the door open and Springfire disappear through it. "But why don't you want kids?"

"Just don't feel the urge. Dhanya doesn't want them either."

Ben tried to wrap his head around that idea. "Really?"

"Really."

"Why is that so hard to understand?" Crash asked. "I don't want kids."

"You're not married."

"Cap, honestly," Springfire said. "Knock it off. Entire building is scouted. No cameras spotted. Two people, easy to avoid, working to the left of the door. I don't think they're guards. They might be supers, but they look like lab techs. As for the rest of this, you need to see it."

"Crash and Springfire, take down those two workers, but be gentle. We might want to talk to them." Ben climbed down the ladder and offered Omen a hand.

DPS opened the door for Crash. She slunk into the hallway.

"You really just don't want kids?"

Omen reached the floor. Ben waved the ladder aside.

DPS shrugged. "Neither of us have any interest in dealing with babies or small children. We've talked about fostering teenagers, but it's too hard with Gabi's issues."

"And it's not a medical thing?"

Springfire huffed. "Cap, will you knock it off? You're being incredibly rude. They don't want kids. Why is none of your business. Also, the two workers are down. Both on their knees. Crash is tying them up."

Ben opened the door without touching it and led DPS and Omen out of the closet. "I just want to understand."

DPS patted his shoulder with a grin. "Don't ever change, man. But also, don't ask Dhanya. She's a lot more touchy about it. People judge her for it a lot."

All thoughts of anything outside the mission evaporated as soon as they turned the corner. The lab they found reminded Ben of the Cairari site. Slabs, tubes, a bank of more advanced computer equipment, and medical instruments filled the room. Crash and Springfire stood over two kneeling people, one man and one woman, in lab coats.

Naked, unconscious people, each thin to the point of emaciation, lay on the slabs. Red tubes snaked from each body to unknown devices beside them. Wires stuck out of their flesh to connect to the slabs. Each slab had an LCD display Ben couldn't read from where he stood.

Along the far wall, more naked, unconscious people stood in lighted housings, held in place by clamps on their legs, shoulders, and torsos. Unlike those on the slabs, these people stood with their eyes open and retained normal body mass. One tube plunged into each person's body at their neck, holding light blue liquid.

"*Madre de Dios*," DPS whispered.

Ben squinted, sure he recognized two of the people in the wall housings. He crossed the room to get a better look. The man showed no sign of noticing him. His dark eyes didn't track Ben, and seemed fully dilated.

"I remember seeing this guy on the news. Taken down in Alabama, I think? By one of the teams."

"You're right," Omen said. "I remember that too. They said he blew up a church and killed some kids."

"DPS, I want to know everything there is to know about this place." Ben pointed at the computers.

"Yeah. Me too." DPS hurried to the workstation.

Ben tore his gaze from the disturbing sight and

focused on the two lab techs. He crossed the room to them and crouched beside the woman.

The woman flinched. Her eye darkened with a bruise, and blood crusted on her lip. "What do you want?"

Her fear tempered Ben's anger. He didn't want to become the thing he hated any more than he wanted to wind up in this place. "Information. Are these all supers captured by Nova teams?"

She nodded. "As far as I know, yes."

"Cap, there's a password," DPS muttered through the earbud. "I can crack it, but it'd be faster if you can just get them to tell you."

"How long have you worked here?" Ben asked the worker.

"Don't tell them anything," the man snapped. "No matter what."

Ben frowned at them. "I put people into this prison, and I'd like to know what happened to them."

The man raised his chin. "Who cares? They're bad guys. Whatever happens to them, they brought it on themselves."

"I just do my job," the woman murmured.

"Crash, would you give this man an attitude adjustment?" Ben hated himself for ordering that. He hated watching her drag the man by the hair, and he hated the guy's howling and screaming in fearful anticipation. Worse, he hated how the woman's eyes watered. He glanced at Springfire and asked her without words not to watch.

Springfire touched his shoulder as she left him with the woman.

"What's your name? Everybody calls me Cap."

"Gina. I'm Gina. Please don't hurt me." She flinched at the sound of her coworker screaming again.

"I'm not doing anything to him, Cap," Crash said. "He's just freaking out. I'm taking out my earbud for a minute, though. I'll see what I can get."

"Gina, I'm not going to hurt you." He kept his hands

close and avoided leaning toward her. Sometimes, threats and small violence worked best. Other times, treating a prisoner with decency worked a thousand times better. "I didn't come here to hurt anyone. I came here because I used to put people into this prison, and a little birdie told me that maybe what happened to them wasn't what I was told. Can you tell me what happened to them?"

"It's—" Gina gulped. "It's classified."

"I'm aware of that. If it wasn't, I could've discovered this without making the trip down here. How about if I tell you what it looks like, and you tell me if I'm right or wrong? Can you do that for me?"

She met his gaze and gulped again, then nodded.

"Thank you, Gina. It looks to me like you're doing experiments on captured supers. Is that right?"

Gina nodded. "I don't do any of that, though. We're just the night shift. We monitor and swap sample collection reservoirs. Day shift has all the scientists."

"Cap."

Ben twisted to see Omen and Springfire leaning over a subject on a slab.

Springfire pointed to something. "These people are alive and breathing, but they have open incisions that aren't bleeding."

"God, this is gross." Omen grimaced and poked the body with a steel instrument from a nearby tray. "There's some kind of weird insert in the incision, keeping it from healing. I can push this thing right through the inside membrane and pull it out again, and there's still no bleeding." She held up the tool with fresh blood on it so Ben could see it.

"DPS," Crash said, "the password is the word 'sierra' with an uppercase E."

"Thanks."

"This hacking stuff isn't so hard."

DPS snorted so loud that Ben heard it from across the room. "Sure. You can come back and handle the rest, then."

"I think I'll stick to intimidating weasels. Incidentally, I still haven't done more than scare the shit out of this guy. He's a whiny little fuck."

Ben nodded his satisfaction. "Crash, move him someplace secure. We'll leave him and Gina for the day shift to find. Gina, do you need a drink of water? You're going to be tied up until someone else gets here."

"Cap, you big softie," Crash said.

Gina shook her head. "They said we're protecting our country."

Ben thought of all the times he'd broken a bone, threatened someone with death, or performed a field execution. He'd done it to protect his country. Every single time, he'd believed he had no other options, and that his grandfather and father would've done the same thing in his place.

"That's what they always say." He sighed and used his power to assist as he stood and slung her over his shoulder. "And we always accept that. Because we want to."

# CHAPTER 34

## MATIAS

December 6, 2017
22:38

Once he got the password, DPS spent his time running a spider across the hard drive and reading files with his chosen keywords. After an hour of this, he checked on the rest of the team.

They stood in a cluster, not touching anything. All four had removed their earbuds to avoid distracting him while they talked about dealing with the prisoners. DPS wanted nothing to do with that conversation.

He turned back to the files. Memos and directives sent in electronic format painted a picture DPS didn't like. He wanted to delete everything and pretend he hadn't read any of it. The moment he opened his mouth, he'd have to accept a number of uncomfortable truths.

Back in the old days, they'd discovered things like this about people in foreign countries. When they did, they took evidence and cleaned up problems. Often, DPS had burned everything in their wake to avoid questions. Governments that involved shady shit like this got toppled, one way or another. Sometimes, Novas did that. Other times, regular military handled it.

Things, he thought, were simpler then.

"Suck it up, Matty," he grumbled to himself.

Time to try to make sense of all this. Waiting didn't change anything or make anything better.

"Guys? I'm ready to explain everything I found."

Cap raised a hand to acknowledge him. "Out of all the options," he said as they crowded around DPS, "I think the best thing to do is get some press down here."

"I've got to agree with that," Omen said. "It feels like the right thing to do."

Springfire nodded. "We'll have to make sure it doesn't fall off the news radar until someone starts a serious conversation about what to do with people like these. Maybe we should call some journalists now. So no one has time to clean up here."

DPS doubted the current political landscape allowed for nuanced discussions of serious topics. That problem belonged to tomorrow, though. "Let me do the briefing first. This facility conducts experiments into injectable serums designed to give powers to ordinary people. According to the latest progress report, they've isolated five powers. Fire generation, telepathy, the strength and durability package, flight, and gross telekinesis. Which should sound familiar."

"The two new teams," Crash said. "That's what each of them has."

"Yes. They're currently working on three additional powers—regeneration, healing, and lightning generation. They have plans for several other basic damage types, like ice and lasers, and they also want teleporters, speedsters, and sensory enhancement. This project provides its formulas directly to the Academy."

DPS turned away, unable to look at any of them while he told the next part of the story. "Charlie is the name on every single shipment of the serum. She receives and signs for it. I thought maybe she just signed for things without knowing what her husband ordered, but there are enough memos in here to say she had full knowledge of what she got.

"In particular, she sent several memos about the regeneration and healing serums. She's been testing the formulas on herself. Like Doc said, she's regrowing her wing. Which is fine." He held up a hand, expecting someone to want to interject. "Except that in some of those memos, she's asking why the other serums work so well but the healing ones don't."

"She looked us in the eye," Cap muttered.

Springfire shook her head. "We never talked about anything like this. It was all about Jay and Kay."

"There's a lot more," DPS said. "This isn't even the meat of it. Going back to those kids. I found documentation that all of them were picked up by Nova teams on raids in both the US and European countries. They were listed as victims of various kinds of terrorist plots. Greg Boone wrote a memo detailing exactly what he wanted the scientists here to do to those kids. He goes ahead and specifically states the terrorist thing is a cover and they're targeting homeless kids and European orphanages.

"After pickup, Nova teams deliver the kids here. There's a special note that only certain Nova teams do that, so I doubt Jay ever did. The kids get their first injection on arrival, and they stay for one week. If nothing bad happens, they get a second injection and third injection, each a week apart. After the third week, if the kids develop the correct power, they get a ride to the Academy and enroll.

"If they don't develop a power, they 'dispose' of the kids as unsuitable. If the kid develops the wrong power and it's useful, he gets a ride to the Academy. If it's not, or it goes wrong, he becomes a test subject." DPS waved to the room, indicating the slabs. "According to a memo from the head scientist guy here, the kids continue to need serum injections once a month for two years. Which is why Charlie takes those shipments."

"And here I thought it couldn't get any worse," Cap said.

DPS agreed. "I'm not done yet. They're not just targeting homeless kids and orphanages. They're targeting white kids. Even better, they're setting up the program to use the boys as soldiers and the girls as breeders. Now, Boone references a journal several times, and it got me thinking about that night." He wanted to stop. He wanted to crawl into a hole and hide. Instead, he sucked in a deep breath and faced it.

Maverick's pained groan echoed in his head. He saw the feather in his fingers. Blackened bones stuck out of her back. Glowing embers of burning flesh drifted in the noxious air.

Someone touched his shoulder. DPS shook his head. Springfire. Of course she saw it and did something.

"Otto dropped a book. Boone picked it up. I don't know if he took it, but he damned well knew it existed. That's a different book than the ones we found. Like a journal, right?" DPS pointed to the screen and arranged a collection of documents so anyone could step closer and skim them. "Boone's treasured journal apparently noted that white subjects are five times more likely to have a positive outcome with the serum."

"Otto was a Nazi," Crash said. "Of course that was part of his findings. How was Boone stupid enough not to realize that?"

Omen laid her palms on her cheeks. "Remember all those monsters?"

"All non-white," DPS said with a nod. He'd noticed it at the time. "I thought he used them because they were easy to get. I mean, it was Brazil. There are plenty of Latinos and natives at hand, and he could've lured them with all kinds of promises. But maybe it was more because he was a Nazi."

Omen nodded. "And he would've considered them expendable, so better used for earlier experiments."

"As he gets closer to a working serum, he switches to people he considers more valuable," Cap said. "Leading him to conclude that white people accept the serum better."

"Internal bias." Springfire sighed. "Either Boone didn't know Otto was a Nazi, or he has the same bias. Or both. He might not realize it."

"Sure. It looks like this project developed kind of by accident. Starting because he wanted to help Charlie with her wing, and also get some regularity to the Academy's enrollment." DPS pointed to the screen again. "Early memos to the head here are asking for information in a roundabout sort of way. He wants to know what's going on, how they're keeping prisoners from escaping, and everything else. Instead of explaining, the head scientist invites him to visit. He clearly did. Memos after that talk about production times, progress, and logistics for experimental subjects."

"Baby steps turned into a leap off a cliff." Cap leaned in, reading the pages. "Charlie was copied on some of these."

DPS nodded. "I don't think she came for Boone's first visit, but it looks like she came with him for a later one. And I don't understand any of that. This isn't the Charlie I knew. Yeah, she's Southern, but she was never— Racist. She never looked down on me for my skin color. She never let anything slip about anything like this, and I would never have imagined she'd go in for kidnapping kids."

"Except for her sister." Omen sat on the floor with her back to the screen. "She wanted so hard to never let anyone suffer like she and her mother did. And we have no idea what losing her wing did to her."

Springfire squeezed DPS's shoulder. "It's not your fault. None of this is your fault."

The words stabbed him through the heart. DPS hadn't considered the idea he bore some responsibility for this mess until Springfire said he didn't. For Charlie's wing, yes, he knew that. He'd burned her. She lost her wing because he didn't see her, because he didn't pay enough attention, because he didn't wait for Cap to make the call.

Charlie lost her fucking mind because she lost her fucking wing.

He leaned forward and cupped his face in his hands.

"*Perdóname Dios,*" he murmured.

Springfire hugged him from behind. "Regardless of how she felt about her wing, I doubt Charlie snapped one day and told Boone she wanted to turn white kids into supers without their consent. You didn't do this."

"I started it."

"No," Cap snapped. "No matter what happened that night, none of us caused this. Did we miss things? Yes. Did we fuck up? Yes. That doesn't make this our fault. No one pointed a gun at Boone's head and made him torture children to build a fucking army. Why the fuck are they even doing this?"

"Money." DPS showed them more documents. "Defense contracts. Boone wants to replace the whole military with supers. General Watts didn't like that idea. She wanted to stick with the existing paradigm and keep all the support personnel. I think he told her something about his kid pipeline."

"So he had her killed." Cap blew out a breath, expressing the same massive load of confusion, disgust, and despair at discovering all this that DPS felt. "I almost hate to ask, but is there anything else?"

"Yeah. Two things. One, I found documents tracing the lineage of every single Nova ever. He's even got information about my lineage that I didn't know. Apparently, my father was an unexpected success from an experiment by some Nazi scientist who wasn't Otto. The source of those experiments is listed as 'lost,' which maybe means Novas took down the site at some point. Charlie's lineage has a giant question mark, but there's a suspicion her grandfather was part of a line from a different Nazi experiment that produced random mutations in every generation."

DPS wanted to research his father at some point. For now, he clicked to an email about the last thing. This one blew his fucking mind. "Then there's this."

The stunned silence in the room seemed almost ridiculous. Almost.

DPS didn't like the current president and his policies, but he never thought the White House would get involved in shit this fucked up.

"He personally authorized this. With full knowledge of the activities." Cap waved to Omen. "I don't suppose you can find the physical letter referenced here?"

"I wish my power hadn't sent us here. I didn't want to know any of this." Omen stood and kept her back to the screen.

Feeling much the same, DPS rubbed his face. He wanted to go back three weeks and never learn about any of this. Blissful ignorance seemed so much better.

Springfire hugged Omen. "We had to come here. All of this needs to be exposed. If it stays in the dark, someone else will step in and continue it. Nothing will change."

As usual, Springfire was right. DPS sighed and tapped the keyboard. "I can notify a dozen or more journalists from here. We can get out before any of them show up. Where are we meeting Ramirez for the return flight?"

"Miami." Cap watched Springfire and Omen without interrupting. After another few moments of thought, he said, "We can get ourselves that far. Crash, take me to the prisoners. We're going to make sure they're easy to find and give them a message. Springfire, look for paper documents and leave things open and available. DPS, copy everything onto something portable and leave the system unlocked so anyone can come and read all this. Wait until we're about to leave before sending those messages. Omen, I need you to keep watch in case anyone shows up for a shift change."

The team moved, heading to handle their various assignments. DPS fished a flash drive out of a pocket and copied everything. He should've thought to do that himself. Thank goodness for Cap and his ability to think while processing this much shit.

# CHAPTER 35

## VIVIAN

December 7, 2017
05:38

Ben drove yet another rental car in the dark. This time, DPS had secured the vehicle online, using his internet magic to make the reservation anonymous. Crash had left her motorcycle at the nearest bar, so she took the front passenger seat and Springfire put her skinny butt between Omen and DPS in the back. Watching Springfire eat for an hour made Omen wonder how she kept her ass so damned small and tight. Blah blah metabolism and speed, but still— the woman could pack down so much food.

No one spoke. They all knew the plan and their goals. Omen had nothing to offer until her power overwhelmed the anti-psi. She felt so useless, but she came anyway. Her friends needed support, and she knew she could at least stand by their side.

DPS watched his phone. News about the prison hadn't broken yet. Once it did, Omen had no doubt Boone would expect them. Maybe he already did. Their attackers had all survived, after all. He'd probably prepped for an attack the moment his pets returned.

"Shit, there it is," DPS said. "National news just picked

it up from the local stations in Miami. Falling all over themselves to be first or have exclusive details. We're blown, Cap."

"Then it's a good thing we're almost there." Cap stopped the car.

Springfire climbed over Omen to reach the door. "I'll see you inside." She hopped out, shut the door, and disappeared.

Cap resumed their approach.

Every fiber of Omen's being wanted her to reach that facility as soon as possible. She didn't know what her power wanted her to do, except that she knew exactly what it wanted her to do.

They rounded the bend and saw the massive concrete barrier blocking passage inside. As the car closed the distance, the barrier slid open. Ben drove through and kept going. To the side, Omen saw Springfire tying up the man who must've been watching the gate. They entered the wide tunnel into the mountain.

The small parking area had no other cars. As soon as Ben stopped the car in a space, Omen scrambled to get out. Springfire appeared beside her.

"It's quiet," DPS said. He opened his mouth to say something else.

Omen held up a hand. "Don't even."

DPS grinned. "I'd say they're expecting us, Cap."

"Probably." Cap jogged toward the huge, metal doors barring further progress, gesturing for the rest of the team to join him.

Springfire blurred and reached the doors first. She inspected the wall on one side. "I have no idea how the doors are activated. It's a safe bet they have us on cameras, though."

"Looks like we need some force to get inside." Cap slowed to a walk. "We'll do a three-point entry. DPS, then Crash, with me backing up. Omen, you have the count."

Crash lifted her fists. "Oh, good. I haven't gone through fire for you guys in a while."

"Let's not joke about that," DPS said.

Omen stopped and pressed two fingers to her temple. She saw the entry as Ben described it, with a controlled explosion of fire followed by Crash hitting the center, assisted by Cap's power. "Springfire, get out of the way. Crash, go."

Crash sped to a sprint. Springfire blurred and reappeared at Omen's side.

Omen's power nudged. "DPS."

Fire billowed at the center of the doors, roaring with explosive force.

Another nudge. "Cap. Crash, dive."

Crash leaped into the fire. She hit the doors. Omen heard Crash grunt. The doors smashed open, and the fire flickered out of existence.

Her flesh still healing from the burns, Crash rolled to her feet. She landed with her fists up, ready to fight. Springfire dashed to her side. She brushed glowing embers off Crash's shoulder.

They faced an empty hallway with trees and shrubs in raised planters. Strips of lights across the ceiling offered only a dim glow, enough to see the path without tripping over anything.

"The lighting hasn't switched to daytime yet," Cap said. "Omen, which way should we go?"

Omen closed her eyes and let her feet carry her where the power wanted. She stopped after a short distance and found the team surrounding her, led by Crash. They stood in front of the wooden double doors from the old Academy. Considering how Boone used this place, the Nova symbol emblazoned on them seemed profane.

Her sight filled with ghostly images of people she didn't know, all running in one direction or another. She saw faint smears of fire and chairs flying through the air. As she opened her mouth to say she couldn't get anything concrete, the old vision hit.

Crash and Maverick sailed through the air together.

Cap stood in a curtain of shimmering flames with his back to her. Springfire couldn't run. DPS fell to his knees and stared at his hands. Flames enveloped Crash, burning her faster than she could regenerate.

The vision made even less sense than it had the first time.

Except… Everyone looked the same in the vision as they did now. Those suits she'd found strange ten years ago now covered all their bodies. Springfire and Crash both wore their hair the same way. DPS had the same amount of stubble on his chin.

Maybe the vision showed her this mission, but it still had no causal links. She didn't know what led to these outcomes, or if they wanted to prevent any of them. The information gave her no information.

"I don't know." She decided it made no difference, and trying to explain would take too long. "I think there's still too much interference. But it's… bad. We're outnumbered, badly. Be ready."

Cap nodded. "Then let's check inside the front office. Boone might be around."

Crash shoved open the front doors. Lights flickered on. It looked the same as the old Academy, aside from the lack of stairs. Omen stayed outside with Cap and DPS while Crash and Springfire surveyed the room.

Springfire flitted from door to door, pausing to listen at each. "I don't hear anything. It's early enough that everyone might not even be awake yet."

"They don't have just one gate guard," Cap said. "There's someone up and watching. Crash, back up Springfire and check through all the doors."

Omen saw ghosts of people approaching them. "Cap, we've got incoming. Lots of incoming."

Cap gestured to DPS and Omen. "Get inside."

The three of them stepped through the doors. Cap hauled them shut.

DPS checked his phone and frowned. "Security

should've come down on us by now, Cap. This is weird and it's bugging me. We knew they'd expect us to show eventually, but this is just making my trap senses tingle."

"This isn't what I expected either." Cap waved toward the doors. "I figured they'd set up at the outer doors and start a firefight there."

"Security is empty," Springfire reported. "The screens are turned off."

Cap frowned. "DPS, go check it out. Crash, I'm getting a bad feeling here. Come back to the main room."

Omen watched DPS hurry through a door. Her stomach churned with a sense of wrongness. Hoping to fix it, she shuffled deeper into the room, toward the administrator's open office door. She half-expected someone to burst out and start attacking, but Springfire had already checked for people inside.

Boone's office held a sturdy desk and bookshelves filled with books, with an American flag hanging in one corner. Dark rectangles on the walls suggested pictures had been removed at some point in the recent past. For all they knew, though, he might've been prepping to have the walls painted something other than blah beige.

As Omen stepped through the door, the queasiness faded enough to notice without disappearing. She approached the desk and noticed it had nothing of substance sitting out. Maybe Boone refused to leave anything sitting out or undone for the day. Hoping to find something of value, she opened the drawers.

Nothing, nothing, and nothing.

A man running a project of this size didn't leave his desk drawers empty. Omen checked the bookshelves, running her fingertips across the spines. At random, she picked a book. The pages had nothing printed on them. His books were fake.

"Cap, the feeds are re-routed elsewhere. I'm cutting the wires at the source so they lose the feed and can't get around a hack to re-establish visuals."

"Good plan, DPS."

Omen heard the front doors slam open.

"Cap's down!" Crash shouted.

"I'm fine," Cap growled. "Backup."

Needing to see, Omen ran for the door and peeked. Crash traded blows with two teenage boys who stood and took her punches. Cap lay on his side against a couch, struggling to his feet. Fire hung in a curtain, blocking the doorway. One of three coffee tables flew across the room to slam into one of the kids.

Springfire appeared in a doorway with DPS. She blurred again and he stumbled forward. Crash swept her foot and knocked down the distracted kid. Springfire reappeared next to Cap and helped him to his feet.

Cap held his head and shook it. "Someone's trying to hit me with telepathy."

A ghostly version of the fire curtain parted for Omen. "DPS! Ready to blast at the center of that fire on my mark." She surrendered to the power.

The curtain parted in the center.

"Now."

Fire blazed in a surging stream from DPS's outstretched hands through the hole in the curtain. Someone screamed. The hole shut. Omen heard shouting too unintelligible to understand through the fire.

Springfire dragged the kid on the floor into a wall at high speed, smashing him through it. She ducked through the hole, grabbed him by the shoulders, and disappeared.

DPS sent fire to Crash's remaining opponent, setting his combat boots alight. Crash's job got easier.

"Throw him through the fire and stop messing around," Cap said. He flung a second coffee table through the fire.

Omen saw the fire curtain's edges flicker with ghostly sparks. She had to concentrate to understand the warning. "Cap, they're pushing the fire inside."

Crash flung her opponent through the fire wall. He

screamed. Someone else squawked.

"Gimme a sec," DPS said. He jogged to the center of the room and faced the fire curtain.

"They're trying to chokepoint us into a dead end," Cap said. "We need to rush them and get to a better location with more space to maneuver."

Springfire appeared at his side. "The cafeteria has plenty of space. It's also on the way to Kay's room, so that's forward progress."

While Crash and Omen joined Cap, DPS filled the front quarter of the room with an inferno. Omen watched while he sculpted it to cover the same areas as the wall.

"Wait," she told DPS, not sure why. Nudges and urgings warred, pulling her in three different directions. The room filled with ghostly death. "Hit the walls and the floor," she gasped. "Now."

Everyone dove for a side office. They hit the floor around a desk. A man shouted with wordless strain. White filled the lobby. Heat poured into the small room, stealing Omen's breath and making her want a gallon of moisturizer.

"We're trapped," Crash said.

"Like they wanted," Cap grumbled. "Fuck that. DPS, counter-fire. Crash, check that wall."

Crash jumped to her feet and rammed her shoulder into the wall on the side facing the tunnels. She punched through plaster and drywall, making a hole to the next office.

DPS fed fire into the lobby. The white faded in favor of DPS's orangey-red.

Several voices shouted in shock and distress.

"Springfire, help Crash make us a path." Cap held out a hand and lifted the desk with a grimace. "DPS, give me a hole."

Omen saw his desk fly through the air and hit nothing, attracting attention to them. If he just waited a few more seconds... "Wait, Cap. One, two, three, and...go!"

DPS's fire billowed to form a hole. Through it, Omen

saw Cowboy and his Latino sidekick, Lightsaber, along with five other kids. The desk flew through and hit one kid in the face. DPS closed the hole and shoved his fire outward. He strained as he did so, though. "Can't keep this up much longer, Cap."

"Go, go, go!" Omen said. She and Cap hurried through the hole Crash had made. They found Crash throwing a teenage boy at two more teenage boys. Another two hit the floor under a high-speed hail of framed portraits flung by Springfire.

"DPS, get out of there!" Cap called. He held up a broken door to protect himself and Omen as they skirted around the fight to reach the front doors.

"Working on it." DPS, his body flickering with a shield of fire, leaped through the confused and distracted enemies to reach the team.

"Springfire, scout it. Crash, we're moving." Cap shoved Omen down the tunnel.

Omen ran as fast as her legs could carry her. She remembered sprinting taking less effort than this.

"Too many of them coming," Crash said. "I'll slow them down, you keep going."

Through the earbud, Omen heard Springfire say, "Charlie? What the hell are you doing?"

Her lungs burning, Omen slowed. She glanced back and saw Cap and DPS. Behind them, Crash had stopped and turned to face the oncoming rush of kids. Lightsaber stopped and blasted twin shafts of white light at Crash. Omen didn't see how Crash could survive it. The sight came too close to her vision. Her own vision blurred against the bright lights of fires and lasers, but she could still hear the voices. Crash would survive. Somehow. Omen had to believe that.

"Fighting for my country," Charlie said, her voice faint in the distance.

"Is that what you believe?" Springfire asked. "Treating human beings like lab rats is something you do for your country?"

"Run!" Crash bellowed.

"Springfire." Though he panted and probably needed a break, Cap kept DPS and Omen moving toward the cafeteria. "She's made her choice."

"We don't know that," Omen said. "We can't give up on her. She's not some random, cartoonish bad guy all of a sudden."

"Those things aren't people," Charlie said, her voice thick with disdain.

Omen couldn't believe Charlie could ever say something like that. "What happened to her?"

Cap ripped tiles off the walls and ceiling, littering their path with debris to slow any pursuit and drowning out Springfire and Charlie's voices.

They reached the wide doorway for the cafeteria. Charlie stood on a table, looking down at Springfire. She wore a black tac suit with a gun holstered on each hip.

DPS stepped into the empty space. "I burned off her wing," he murmured.

"Hello, Matias."

Tables fell over and scraped across the floor to block the doorway. Omen forced herself to step inside before Cap sealed the entrance. She didn't want to do this. She had to do this.

"The gang's all here." Charlie smirked. "Except Kele. I expect she's killing herself to hold off my teams and buy you all some time? Too bad it won't help." She yanked off a thick sleeve over her burned wing and snapped both open. Instead of barren sticks on the dead side, shiny chrome feathers hung from healthy tissues over the bone.

"Charlie," Springfire begged, "don't do this. Please. You're better than this."

"Better than what? Defending children from deranged ex-Novas who think they're above the law? Good thing we have a place for you in the Keys." Charlie leaped into the air.

Omen saw chaos erupting the moment before it

happened. "Cover!" She dove for the wall, knocking Cap off his feet with her.

Two boys smashed through Cap's table barrier, sending plastic and metal flying. Four more boys followed them through and raised assault rifles.

Gunfire echoed in the cavernous room.

# CHAPTER 36

## BEN

December 7, 2017
05:51

On the ground thanks to Omen, Ben dropped the remnants of his table barrier. Several more kids, enough to make three teams of five, stormed inside. If he remembered correctly, that meant three firestarters, three telepaths, three soldiers, three fliers, and three gross telekinetics.

They needed to prioritize. "Hit the guns first."

Ben scrambled to his feet and helped Omen do the same. Guns flew through the air, smacked aside by Springfire moving too fast to see. Flames followed her path. Kids screamed. Weapons clattered on the floor. Chairs chased Springfire, failing to catch her. More fire billowed, filling the room with heat, black smoke, and the stench of burning plastic. Someone screamed. Plenty of kids coughed.

"DPS, shielding." Ben tugged Omen toward the wall. He snagged tables and threw them at the kids, forcing them to defend themselves instead of attack. "Springfire, keep moving."

Hurrying to Ben's side, DPS held a wall of fire between them and the kids. Charlie disappeared in the haze, probably watching from the rafters. Ben chose to appreciate the fact she didn't take potshots at them. Maybe she still had a piece of her soul.

"Crash, report." He waited. She took too long. On any other mission, he thought he'd trust her to make it through the hellish nightmare she'd vowed to hold off. This time, the situation felt more final, less survivable. The odds stacked against them so high he thought they'd topple and crush the whole team.

"We have a small problem," Ben said. He didn't want to say this, but he had to. Walking away from Kele ten years ago had hurt, like losing an arm or an eye. Risa had kept him sane.

DPS snorted. His skin turned blue. "If by small you actually mean really big, then I agree with you."

Annoyed by the joke when he had something serious to say, Ben smacked his shoulder. His hand slid down a rime of ice. "Crash isn't responding. We have to assume she's dead." He saw Omen open her mouth to disagree. "Do you know for sure she's not dead?"

Omen stopped and covered her face. "No. I have no idea."

Springfire made a wounded puppy noise through the earbuds. He hated to hear that from her.

They didn't have time for this. He needed to get a grip and keep it.

"Mourn later. DPS can't keep up this fire forever. Neither can Springfire." He set a hand on Omen's shoulder. "Omen. Vivian. We need you. We can't do this without you."

"I second the part where DPS can't keep this up forever." DPS closed his eyes and lowered his head. Frost formed a circle on the floor around him. "We need a plan. She wouldn't want us to fall apart and get ourselves killed."

"Damned straight." Ben couldn't let this distract him any more than his team could. He needed to focus too.

"I'm running out of places to run," Springfire said. Her voice wavered like she hovered on the verge of tears.

"I'm trying!" Omen looked like she meant to say more, then she stiffened.

"Great timing," Ben grumbled. He picked up Omen and slung her over his shoulder. "DPS, we're moving to that wall. Springfire, divide them into groups."

"Cap," Springfire said, "if they set a trap for us, then they have Kay locked up. You know they do."

"Fuck. You're right." He should've thought of that. Maybe he should've slept on the plane. He'd tried, but he should've tried harder. "Omen, what can you give me about Kay?"

"Not a fucking thing. Wherever she is, Jiao is probably with her. DPS, Switch from shielding to a full-frontal blast in every direction. In three, two, one."

The fire fell. Ben saw Cowboy zero in on Omen and grin like he got his most demented birthday wish. DPS growled and shoved fire outward, flushing kids like quail.

Crash wouldn't have let that little fucker through. Ben scanned everyone diving for cover and ballparked the count at twenty-five. Without Crash and Maverick, they didn't stand a chance on open ground.

Springfire carried a chair through a line of kids, knocking two aside and separating them. Ben slammed tables into one side while DPS flung fire at Cowboy. Other kids blew fire in every direction, trying to hit Springfire with no success. More chairs and tables slid across the floor, also trying to intercept Springfire.

These kids had never practiced against a speedster. If they had, they'd know how to catch one. Whoever had made that decision should've known better. Ben scowled. They had Kay. She could've trained everyone over the years. He wanted to be glad they hadn't, but couldn't ignore one more example of incompetence.

"We need cover." Ben set down Omen.

"Out," Omen snapped. She grabbed his arm and tugged toward the wide doorway.

DPS stuck with them, tracing lines of fire to ward off

anyone who tried to approach. Not even Cowboy wanted to burn.

Ahead, Bunny and Lightsaber appeared in the doorway. They needed to get through without getting crispy. Ben patted DPS's arm, worried about losing him to the fire. "Flare!"

Intense, blinding orange light blasted the area. DPS traded heat and burning to simulate a flash grenade effect.

Ben and Omen ducked around disoriented kids and slipped out of the cafeteria. Bunny and Lightsaber disappeared. They popped next to Cowboy, who rubbed his eyes.

Omen laid a hand on DPS's back to stop him in the doorway. "There's a telepath coordinating. Take him out, you cut their marching orders."

"Which kid is that?" DPS asked.

"He's blond and tall," Omen said.

"You just described all of them except Bunny and Lightsaber."

Omen smirked. "Don't be ridiculous. Cowboy isn't tall. Or blonde."

"Gimme a better hint, Omen."

"He's in the back. Hand to his head," Omen said.

"Got him," Springfire said. "On it."

"Expect Charlie to engage soon," Omen said. She snapped her hand at Ben, waving for him to throw more stuff into the room.

Ben tore a concrete planter out of the hallway and launched it through the doorway, tree and all. He heard crunching and crashing, screaming and shouting. Gunfire erupted inside.

Someone had picked up a weapon and decided to use it.

Thinking over who he'd seen, Ben ticked off a list—Charlie, Cowboy, Bunny, Lightsaber, a bunch of kids, and…a notable missing person. "Does anyone see Boone?"

"Negative," DPS said. "No sign of him. Cap,

incoming!"

Omen groaned and gasped for breath. "Fuck, fuck, fuckity fuck fuck. I need a minute. Just don't get us dead." She popped out her earbud and held up her hands as if she needed the entire world to give her breathing room.

Wrapping his power around another planter, Ben wrenched it free and tossed it into the cafeteria. More crashing and more screaming followed. The gunfire stopped.

"Solid hit," DPS said.

Omen snagged Ben's jacket and wrenched him around to face her. "Okay. Cap. Listen. This is important."

"Springfire, keep moving. DPS, cover us. Omen, talk." Ben removed his earbud to give her his full attention.

"Kay and a bunch of other kids are locked up in the graduation theater. There's an explosive in there someplace, and it's enough to bring down that theater. The kids don't know it's there. They think they're hiding because of an attack, and that's the safe zone."

Ben paled. He couldn't lose his daughter too. If anything happened to Kay, he didn't know what he'd do. After losing Jay, losing Kay... But he suspected Omen had more to say. He hoped she had more to say. "What's the catch?"

"Boone is there. All the rest of this is to buy him time to get set up and ready to go so he can start over someplace else. If the rest of us leave here to deal with that, it becomes an even bigger disaster and everyone dies or worse. If you leave now, you can stop him and save those kids."

He let go and took a step. Omen held on. Her gaze bored into his.

"Cap. Ben. If you go, I don't think you're going to make it out. He's not that far from ready, and he has all the guards down there. They're expecting to have another ten minutes before we get there. You might surprise them. Maybe."

Choosing between himself and Kay took only a split-second. He touched her hand. "Then I have to hurry. Is he planning to blow the place when we get there?"

"Yes. After he uses the kids to get us to surrender."

"Of course he is." Ben scowled. He knew Boone could do it. He'd already proven how little he cared about human life.

She squeezed his arm. "You understand this is probably a suicide mission?"

"Vivian." He took a deep breath and remembered saying these words before. "What if it was your daughter?"

Omen's eyes widened, then they watered. "You asshole."

"Tell Risa I love her."

She hugged him. "Fuck you, you sonofabitch. Tell her your damned self." In tears, she let go and shoved him. "Get going. And hurry."

"Put your earbud back in and help them." He pointed to doorway and left her.

As he ran, Ben remembered Risa telling him when she got pregnant the first time. Panic had gripped him harder than any mission situation. A horrifyingly inept proposal had bumbled out of his mouth. Once they realized she'd only carry Jay for two months, they'd hopped into his Firebird for the world's least romantic wedding in Las Vegas.

Major Marks, at the time a year away from his promotion to Colonel, had yelled at him for five minutes straight about going AWOL for five hours and taking Risa with him. Then he'd produced a pair of cigars and they'd smoked the damned things outside OpCon while having a good laugh over the whole thing.

She'd been the best thing to ever happen to him, and he wanted to tell her that one more time. He wanted to kiss her one more time and hold her one more time. She'd hate him for taking that away from her. But she'd be alive, and so would Kay. That mattered more than anything he wanted.

He stopped at the first corner and checked in both directions. The earbud felt heavy in his hand. Risa deserved to hear from him one last time.

As he lifted the device, he noticed a lone figure

shambling toward him. The lights overhead brightened to daytime. Crash's arm popped into its socket. Her flesh rippled as it healed burns.

Relief washed over Ben. With Crash in that cafeteria, Springfire, DPS, and Omen would have all the backup they needed.

She grinned, a jagged gash across her cheek still hanging open. "Sorry I took so long, Cap. My earbud is fried or I would've called in as soon as those dumb fucks left me for dead."

Ben grinned and wanted to laugh. He should've known she'd survive somehow.

"Orders, sir?"

"I'm on Boone. The others are pinned down in the cafeteria. We're up against overwhelming odds. Small chance of success." The noise down the hall, of gunshots, explosions, and screaming, punctuated his statement.

"Sounds like a regular Thursday, sir." Crash grinned. "I'm on your six."

For a brief, shining moment, he considered agreeing. But Springfire needed help more than he did. If he lost her, he didn't think he could handle it. "No." Crash would need to coordinate with the team. He handed her his earbud. "The rest of the team needs you more. I'm good here. Omen has the call. Take down Maverick and Cowboy."

Crash's grin faded as she took the earbud. She hesitated for a moment, then nodded with finality. "Yes, sir. Watch yourself. You're not used to operating solo."

"Good hunting, Sergeant." He snapped a crisp salute. "And take care of my wife."

She returned the salute. "Yes, sir."

He watched her turn and run down the hall, pushing the earbud into her ear. Somehow, he thought she knew what he faced. The set of her jaw gave her away, along with a hardening of her eyes.

If Omen thought she could help him more than them, of course, she'd send Crash to rescue his sorry ass.

As much as he wanted to wait and see if Crash came back, he knew he'd already wasted too much time. He sprinted down the hall. When he reached the entrance to the graduation theater balcony, he tore the thick oak door off its hinges and used it as a shield.

The room looked the same as it had when Jay graduated, aside from the occupants. Stadium-style seats with plush red cushions covered a steep incline in a full circle, all facing a wide platform with a podium. Clear partitions separated one third of the seats—those facing the back of the podium—from the rest.

Kids filled that separate one third. The sea of young faces, in every skin tone imaginable, all turned to find the source of the noise. Boone had brought all the kids who didn't fit his ideal, or maybe all the kids he couldn't control as well as his created soldiers. A final solution for the Novas.

Guards in BDUs and helmets, with rifles hanging from straps across their bodies, jumped and scrambled to deal with him. He didn't stop.

"Kay! Run!" Still holding his door shield, he ripped up a seat cushion and flung it at the front two guards.

"Daddy?"

"It's a trap! Help Mom! Cafeteria!" He wrenched more cushions from the seats and flung them at the guards. "I love you!"

Chaos erupted among the kids. They jumped to their feet and streamed for the student exit. Panicked voices filled the theater.

Beyond the guards, Ben saw Boone inside the glass-walled sound and light control booth.

Boone stared at him, his eyes wide and panicked. The trap wasn't ready yet. Good. He couldn't blow up the kids as they escaped.

"Don't just stand there!" Boone screamed. "Shoot him! Shoot them all!"

Ben ripped up chairs and everything else he could to distract the men and protect the kids. Gunfire echoed. Metal clanged. Men grunted. Stuffing from bullet-riddled cushions drifted in the air. The old, familiar tang of a battlefield reminded Ben of different times in different places.

Harassed by cushions and seats, guards stumbled into each other. Bullets ripped through their rank and traced lines across the seats, toward the fleeing kids. They screamed and panicked.

Those kids had powers, Ben knew, but they'd never faced gunfire before. They hadn't completed their training. Scared and confused, told different things by different people, they didn't know what to do. He didn't blame them.

In the moment between three guards falling to friendly fire and the rest freaking over what had happened, Ben noticed Boone rushing out the back door of the booth. Either he'd finished his setup or he'd given it up as pointless.

Ben checked the kids and saw only a small pool of them still waiting for their chance to escape. If Boone blew the place the moment he got clear, those kids would die. If Ben protected them, he couldn't protect himself. Worse, Boone might not blow the place, which meant he'd sacrifice himself for nothing.

Something beeped. Ben had heard enough explosive devices announce their impending detonation to know what he faced. He made his choice. He threw chairs, bodies, anything into the pit to provide those last few kids a shred of protection when the place blew.

Gunshots echoed in the theater. As the first blossom of fire erupted from the podium, Ben ran for the door.

# CHAPTER 37

## SPRINGFIRE

December 7, 2017
06:04

They needed help. Or something. DPS used so much fire that light snow drifted around him. Kids lay on the floor with burned flesh and broken bones. Springfire's stomach growled. Exhaustion tainted every direction Omen gave. Gunfire echoed. Fire billowed. Thick, black smoke drifted through the room.

Somewhere, hidden by haze and confusion, Charlie waited. For what, Springfire had no idea. She wanted to believe they could save Charlie. She wanted to believe Charlie couldn't bring herself to attack her friends again, especially Matias.

Springfire didn't want to kill these kids. They didn't deserve it, and the whole team knew that. She threw tables and chairs, knocked weapons out of hands, and avoided hitting anyone at top speed. Likewise, DPS kept his fire defensive as much as he could, forming walls instead of throwing bursts at anyone.

"Crash reporting in. Omen, tell me where to go."

Hearing her voice made Springfire's eyes water with relief. Something caught her leg. Her body flew through the air at high speed. She hit a table and tumbled to the floor. The pain coursing through her felt diffuse, which meant no serious injuries. As she blinked to clear her vision, she saw Cowboy rushing her with a feral snarl.

"Springfire is down! Crash, hit Cowboy now! DPS, drop the wall and aim for those tables to your right. Make more smoke."

"That fucker is mine," Crash snarled.

Springfire scrambled to collect her wits and put her feet on the floor, knowing she couldn't survive even one punch from his fist.

As he reached her, she flinched to the side. Something dark streaked over her. Crash leaped over the table to slam into Cowboy and knock him on his ass. Springfire took the opening. She rolled to her feet and fled the spot.

Ahead, she saw a boy holding a hand to his forehead— the last telepath. Setting her sights on him, she slowed long enough to pick up a chair. She returned to top speed and aimed two feet to his left. The moment before she reached him, she gave the chair a tiny nudge and let go.

The chair hit him in the chest and threw him to the ground. She kept going. He cracked his head against the floor so hard that she heard it over everything else. Maybe he'd live. She wanted him to live.

A single gunshot rang out, close to Springfire. Pain lanced through her leg. This time, she managed to slow without hitting the floor. She sagged against an overturned table to check the damage. Blood surged from a bullet hole in the side of her calf.

Overhead, Maverick pointed her gun at Springfire without pulling the trigger again.

Springfire wanted to believe Charlie had gone for the wounding shot because she couldn't bring herself to kill them.

Bunny appeared next to Springfire, holding Lightsaber. He shoved his hand forward.

Reflex from years of combat training, dulled with time

yet still there, sent her arm slashing outward to block him. She ignored the ache in her leg and sped to the other side of the room. He sliced the floor behind her with his lasers. The heat chased her. She smelled burning rubber from her shoes.

"Springfire," Omen said, "keep moving. Hard left… now!"

Lasers and fire strafed along the line Springfire would've followed if she hadn't turned. Her leg hurt so much. She couldn't stop, couldn't go, and couldn't leave.

Across the room, Cowboy punched through Crash's thigh. Bunny dropped Lightsaber next to DPS. They threw synchronized punches, sending DPS staggering backward. Omen held up her fists like she'd win a boxing match against everything thrown at her by a telekinetic.

No one else would come to help. They had no hope of winning, let alone walking out.

For Ben's sake, though, she wouldn't give up. He'd rescue Kay and the two of them would escape.

If she had to die here, sacrificing herself for Kay and Ben, she'd give them as much time as she could. Biting back a cry of pain, feeling her body wanting to devour itself, she stood and ran one more time.

A blast of air hit the Bunny, Lightsaber, and three other kids near them. Kay followed, the girl zig-zagging through the ranks and kicking out knees. Springfire checked the doorway and spotted two dozen or more terrified students joining the battle. Kay's red-headed friend and the Chinese-American girl led the newcomers.

Her little girl came to save them. Springfire's heart swelled. She wanted to cry again. They could do this. Together.

Kay stopped in the doorway and pointed. "Mom! Look out!"

Springfire didn't look. She rolled aside, avoiding a blast of fire from another one of these damned kids. As she forced herself to her feet, she spotted the source. He ignored her to target someone else. Mistake. Keeping her speed down, she slammed into him. The boy slid across the floor and hit an overturned table in a crumpled heap.

"Brace!" Omen shouted.

Springfire flew to Kay's side, grabbed her, and pulled her down a moment before the ground rocked with a violent earthquake.

"Daddy," Kay whispered.

"Help Uncle Matty and Aunt Kele." Springfire had no idea why Kay worried about Ben. He could handle himself and knew his limits.

"Incoming," Omen said, "behind you!"

Springfire turned in time to see Boone hurry around the corner, holding an assault rifle. She ignored the pain in her leg long enough to make a dash. As the gun fired, she smashed into him. Momentum carried both into a wall. He squealed and dropped the gun. It clattered on the floor and slid out of reach.

"Fucking bitch!"

Her fists flew. She hit him again and again. His lip split. An eye swelled. Fingers broke as he tried to ward her off.

"You took Jay from us. And Charlie. And everything. I don't even know how much I hate you right now."

Boone whimpered.

Before he could say anything, she cracked his head against the floor.

"He's down." Omen's voice pierced through the fog. "Kids need help!"

Springfire whirled and scooped up Boone's assault rifle. She darted back to Omen's side. Kay and her friends fought a massive, messy battle with their classmates. DPS slumped against a wall, fire billowing from his hand to meet and resist a pair of white laser beams. Cowboy lay on the floor. Crash staggered through the battlefield, taking what hits she could for the kids.

Lightsaber's lasers pressed closer to DPS, winning the battle inch by inch. Springfire raised the rifle and braced it against her shoulder. An eon ago, she'd learned to use one of these things. Like blocking Lightsaber's strike, her body knew what to do. She aimed and fired. The lasers stopped. Blood stained a ragged hole in Lightsaber's shoulder.

They took her son. Jay had trusted his team. They'd abandoned him. She wanted to kill him.

She aimed at his head and fired again. The gun clicked. It didn't matter. DPS knew how to take advantage of a distraction. Flames surged. Lightsaber screamed in the center of a swirling bonfire and fell to his knees.

"DPS," Omen said, "Charlie is incoming."

Springfire tossed the useless gun aside and dashed inside. Her wounded leg, abused and ignored, buckled. She fell forward and slid to a stop beside DPS. Charlie's shadow passed over them.

His skin deathly blue and his breathing ragged, DPS raised his hands to blast her.

Charlie hovered above him, holding a gun pointed at him.

Neither pulled the trigger.

Hope swelled in Springfire's chest. Maybe they could still save Charlie.

"Do it now," Omen snapped.

DPS lowered his arms and sank to his knees. "I can't. It's Charlie."

Charlie bobbed her head in a shallow, firm nod and shot him. DPS's body jerked before he fell.

The world stopped. Springfire stared, unable to believe what she saw.

"Mom." Kay stopped beside her, holding back sobs. "Mom, what do we do?"

After everything they'd been through together, Springfire didn't understand how Charlie could shoot Matias like that, how Maverick could shoot DPS like that. She remembered the two of them joking, teasing, and watching each other's backs.

Their Charlie had died that night, all those years ago.

This…*thing* had forgotten everything she cared about. She'd become a monster.

Springfire couldn't think of her as Charlie anymore. Thinking of her as Maverick hurt less.

"We have to bring down Maverick." She took Kay's hand and squeezed it. DPS might have survived that bullet. For now, she turned her back on him. As long as she didn't look, he still lived. "Where's Cap?"

"Not here," Omen said.

Maverick stayed in the air and shot one of Kay's classmates. The boy dropped before the echo faded.

They had to stop her before she killed anyone else. Matias was down. Springfire had an injured leg and no gun. Crash couldn't jump that high.

Springfire only knew one other way to take down a flier. "Crash. Slingshot."

She turned to face her daughter. Kay's wide eyes seemed shocky, like she'd seen too many things in too short a time and didn't know what to think about any of them.

If they had all the time in the world, Springfire would've held Kay tight, promised the monsters couldn't hurt her, and walked her through what they needed to do as slow as possible. Instead, she squeezed Kay's hand again.

"Kay, listen to me. Your friend with the red hair, air control?"

Kay nodded, tears sliding down her cheeks. "Eilis. She tried to knock Mav down. Her power doesn't reach far enough. Not for a flier like Mav."

"Can she throw a person?"

"I think so."

"Get her ready." She explained what she needed and shoved her earbud into Kay's hand. They didn't have long. Kay could pass it on. "Trust Aunt Vivian."

Kay blurred into motion toward her friends, dropping two of the attackers along the way to make space. The two girls put their heads together, and Kay passed Eilis the earbud.

Springfire smiled through her pain, seeing echoes of Jay in his little sister. Ben would swell with pride when he heard about everything his daughter handled.

One critical component remained—Maverick. Springfire used the wall to pull herself up. She staggered and hopped out of cover. "Charlie! Stand down!"

The winged woman turned in mid-air, forgetting the kids and taking aim at Springfire.

They had no time for chairs, ropes, or preparation. Kay built up speed. Crash's neck probably broke with the sudden whiplash as Kay grabbed her at full tilt. At the very least, Springfire thought they'd wrenched her arm out of socket. Kay let go and stopped. Crash kept going.

Maverick smirked as she shot Springfire.

Wind gusted. Crash's flight shifted from forward to upward. She sailed through the air.

Springfire fell to the floor, clutching her shoulder. Omen might've warned her if she'd kept the earbud.

Crash collided mid-air with Maverick, her bloodied arms wrapping around and wrenching both wings.

"What are you doing?" Maverick shrieked. "We're going to crash!"

Springfire rolled onto her side, unable to watch. She could still get up. She could still move. She could still survive. Crawling across the floor, she reached for DPS.

Crash and Maverick hit a wall and punched through it. Blocks of concrete fell, and dust filled the air.

Kneeling beside DPS, Springfire hoped Kele survived the impact. She hated that she hoped Charlie didn't.

DPS lay on the floor, panting. "I'm not dead," he said as Springfire shoved his blood-stained shirt out of the way to see the wound. "Hurts like fuck, but I'll live. Probably." Bloody ice filled the hole in his belly.

Around them, the kids stopped fighting to stare at the fresh hole in the wall. Springfire saw Bunny crouch over Cowboy and disappear with him. That boy had a reckoning coming, and she didn't know if she wanted to see it happen.

Maybe. Other kids surrendered.

Kay appeared by Springfire's side and hugged her. They hit the floor together. "Mom. Daddy." She gasped and ripped off her sleeve to wad it against Springfire's shoulder. "Mommy, you're hurt." Tears streaked down her cheeks.

"I'll be fine." Risa patted Kay's hand. The bullet wounds hurt like hell, but she didn't think either would kill her unless she kept ignoring them. Neither bled too much, and no bones felt broken. The dizziness would pass.

She needed food. As she patted her pockets, hoping to find a forgotten protein bar, she peered through the smoky haze. "Matty, ask Vivian where Ben is."

"Mom, he came to rescue us." Kay sobbed. "There was a bomb, and the guards all tried to shoot him."

"Graduation theater," Matias said. "Omen says Crash is alive, but can't move yet. And she's buried. But she'll live until we dig her out." He stared at the hole in the wall they'd disappeared through. "Charlie is dead."

Risa stood with Kay's help. "Let's go find Daddy," she told Kay. "He must be hurt." With Kay's support under her good arm, she limped towards the graduation theater.

Chunks of rock and concrete blocked the door. Kay fell to her knees and dug through the debris with all her speed. Risa helped as much as she could. Breaking through took too long. Risa imagined Ben lying on the floor, hurt and needing help. After all this, they'd lie in bed together and take turns playing invalid.

Kay made a hole big enough to scramble through. More rock and concrete, dusted with shards of glass, littered the theater. On the upper walkway, Risa saw a combat boot sticking out of the dusty debris. Near the door, she noticed a dust-covered hand with a wedding ring. Her breath caught.

"Ben? Can you hear me?" She lurched across the rubble to the hand and touched it. The fingers stayed limp and unmoving. His flesh seemed cooler than she thought it should.

"Mom," Kay warbled.

Risa didn't believe it. She shoved aside rock, moving with slow, deliberate care to avoid hurting him. Tears blurred her vision as she uncovered his arm in his suit, and he still didn't react. He always got up after a fall. As long as she'd known him, he'd never once taken worse than a graze from a bullet.

She found his face and brushed away dust.

He didn't move. He didn't breathe. He didn't open his eyes and say something stupid.

Kay covered her face and sobbed. "Daddy," she whimpered.

"Ben, wake up." Risa's tears dripped from her chin to land on Ben's arm. "Benjamin Akio Tsukuda," she growled at him, "you wake up right now."

She remembered when they first met. The dashing young captain, a famous Legacy classified as an alpha, had introduced himself with a friendly smile. He'd tried so hard to welcome a nervous young woman who'd struggled so much through basic training. Matias and Vivian had joined his team that day too.

He'd taken the time to check on her that evening. They'd walked around the base, talking like regular people, not a superior and subordinate. She'd listened while, to her surprise, he'd trusted her enough to tell her about the challenges of living up to the code name he'd inherited.

She'd fallen for him within a day of meeting him.

Risa wept over his dead body. She pulled their daughter close, holding onto all she had left.

Part of her wanted to march back to Boone and shoot him between the eyes. That piece of shit didn't deserve to live after everything he'd taken from her.

The rest of her wanted him to live a long time. He deserved to spend the next forty years in a cage, knowing he'd never see Charlie again, knowing people would remember him as a monster.

Most of all, she wanted to go home. As soon as she figured out where to find it, she would.

# CHAPTER 38

## KELE

May 14, 2018
15:37

Kachina and Ell both braced their front paws on the railing of the ice rink with a third dog, Vivian's Buddy, while Kele batted a hockey puck to Matias. He fell on his ass for the fortieth time and knocked down Vivian's girlfriend. Kay and Risa both evaded the disaster with speed that sent them careening to the other end of the rink. Vivian had moved out of the way well in advance, and circled the goal her brother protected. Chloe and her cousins laughed.

Matias raised his hands in surrender. "I give up. Fire and ice were never meant to mix like this."

With the game on hold, Kele gave him a hand to get back to his feet and skate out of the way. He joined the dogs and watched while everyone else played.

Kele faced off against five kids between the ages of seven and fourteen. All of them played hockey at least once a week. Some practiced every day. She, Kay, Vivian, and Risa had no hope against them, but they'd faced worse odds and still lived to tell about it.

A pang of grief flickered in Kele's heart. She'd lost a lot

of good friends over the years. Ben hadn't been the first and wouldn't be the last, but his death remained the most fresh. She expected to feel something similar when Ben's father passed, but that old crank still had plenty of time left on his clock.

She slapped the puck toward Vivian's brother. He deflected it without trying. The kids swarmed the puck and carried it to the other end to face off against Brian's wife. Kele let them go.

"I think I'm done," she called out. "You guys go ahead!"

Risa skated to her side and looped her arm through Kele's. "Skating is more exhausting than jogging," she said with a huff.

"These people are way too into hockey." Kele helped Risa step off the ice and join Matias. "Proper sports have a ball. Grass."

Risa nodded. "Men wearing shorts."

Kele rolled her eyes.

"Red cards," Matias added.

Vivian hit the wall in front of them, scaring the dogs into barking at her. She shushed them. "You guys want to get a beer? No decent bar around here, but we have plenty at the house. There's a TV, too. We can watch football."

Kele attacked the laces of her borrowed skates. "Sounds good to me. Before you even suggest it," she pointed at Risa, "no one wants to race you there."

Risa chuckled and looked at Vivian as she attacked her skate laces. "Would you please thank your brother and his wife for hosting us today?"

"Pfft." Vivian waved her off. "Like they wouldn't be here anyway. They own the rink. I'll be out in a minute or so."

Kele set her skates aside and called Kachina to heel. The dog whined until Risa stood and brought Ell. Both dogs turned back to look at Buddy, then their owners, then Buddy, then their owners.

Risa patted Ell's head. "Buddy will come later. C'mon, boy. Let's get some food."

Both dogs perked their ears.

Matias snorted. "You said the magic word. I'm amazed your dog isn't round."

"He runs a lot more than you might think."

"With you and Kay for owners, I doubt it's more than we think," Kele said.

They left the building with two dogs in tow and walked up the street to Vivian's house. Vivian and Buddy caught up with them halfway there. The three dogs dashed for the house together. Vivian looped her arms through Matias's and Kele's. Risa hugged herself in the warm afternoon sunshine. At the house, Vivian set out food for all three dogs.

Matias found the TV remote and surfed until he found a game. America versus Germany, of course. Along the bottom, a news ticker reported that Robert Mitchell's court martial returned a conviction this morning. He'd been stripped of the Cowboy code name, rank, and benefits, and remanded to the new supers prison facility, where he could expect to spend the rest of his life.

Everyone had come to Vivian's place from DC after giving witness testimony for that hearing, and also to Congress for impeachment proceedings. Boone wouldn't have his trial until after that mess concluded.

Kele grabbed beer bottles from the fridge. She spent a long time staring at them before noticing a bin full of empties waiting for recycling. She set open beers on the round table, and put two empties in front of two empty chairs. Cap wouldn't have appreciated them pouring out perfectly good beer for him. Neither would the pre-Boone Maverick.

Vivian picked up her beer and clinked it against Matias's bottle "Did any of you hear what happened to Steve after he testified against Boone and his lackeys?"

Kele tried to remember hearing anything about it and

couldn't. "He just kind of disappeared."

"Yep." Vivian grinned. "I may or may not have 'accidentally' been in exactly the right place at the right time in DC to hear someone credible say he's been getting a lot of death threats, so the feds put him into the Witness Protection Program."

Matias barked a laugh. "Serves the fucker right."

Risa picked up her beer and held it without drinking. She ran her thumb over the bottle's raised design.

"That's a root beer," Kele told her. She hadn't dealt with Steve enough to care about his situation.

Nodding, Risa lifted the bottle to take a sip, then lowered it. Her gaze fell on the empty bottles. "We're going from here back to LA for Memorial Day. They have a really nice service every year for Kenzo. This year—" She covered her mouth. "This year, it'll be for all three of them."

Matias reached over and touched her back while she wiped her face. "I miss him too. I went ten years without someone telling me to shut up and do my job, then he did it once, and it was like he never stopped. And now I keep looking over my shoulder, expecting him to do it again."

Kele had a lot of stories about Cap. More than anyone else at the table. She picked one from their early years as a full team. "Do you remember that intercept in Alabama?"

Vivian crinkled her nose. "The one with that woman who called herself Freefall?"

"No, the one with that guy who could control horses. Rodeo, I think?" Kele grinned at the memory.

Matias echoed her grin. "Yeah, that Rodeo guy used a whole herd he stole like a shield."

"We brought a bunch of apples because I saw something," Vivian said. "I don't remember what I saw, but it made us bring apples."

"Cap picked up the apples and danced them in front of the horses. They all followed the floating apples," Kele said. "And then I beat the crap out of Rodeo."

Risa smiled with tears rolling down her cheeks. "I

remember when we came back from leave after Jay was born, and they sent us to assist the Mexican government with a little town with a bunch of teenagers with powers, all the same age."

Matias pointed with his bottle. "And it turned out they all had the same father, a luchador with powers who came through and charmed a bunch of young, unmarried women, got them all pregnant at once, and left. That was crazy. Cap tried to ask delicate questions, and he fucked it up all over the place. Man, did he suck at that."

"He really did." Risa covered her face. "I'm sorry. I don't mean to fall apart."

"It's okay," Vivian said. "We're all family here."

The door burst open and Kay appeared a few steps inside the house with a bright smile. She saw her mother and hurried to hug her from behind. "Oh, Mom. It's okay. We're okay. We're going to see Sobo and Sofu in about a week, and then we're going to the Aleutians. You can't cry in Alaska. I think it's against the law there."

"The Aleutian Islands?" Matias asked. "What's up there to see?"

"I dunno," Kay said with a shrug. "That's why we're going. Mom wants to see stuff, so we're seeing stuff. We already went to most all the countries on the west coast of Africa. Not as destitute and full of shacks as you think."

Kele smirked. She'd seen more than enough of Africa, good parts and bad. "Hardly anything looks like they show in movies and TV. Are you taking the car to Alaska?"

"Nah, we're going to leave it with Sofu. He got used to having it around all those years when Mom and Dad couldn't have it. Wants to drive it. Besides, can you imagine trying to maintain a Firebird in Alaska? We'd probably have to fill the trunk with spare parts and tools. Bad enough taking it cross-country five times. I never thought I'd use half that stuff Dad showed me about how to keep it going."

Risa kissed Kay's cheek. "I'm fine."

"Sure you are." Kay squeezed her.

Kele stood. She'd been waiting for the right moment for this, and figured she'd found it. "I've got something for you, Kay. It's on my bike." She beckoned for the girl to follow her outside. On second thought, Kay didn't qualify as a girl anymore—she'd grown into a woman.

Kay let go and followed Kele. They passed the three dogs, lying in a pile on the porch. Thank goodness Kachina had been spayed.

She rummaged through the luggage pod on the back rack until she found a bumper sticker. "I saw this a few weeks ago and thought of you." She handed Kay the sticker. It read *Proud Daughter of a Veteran* with the Army seal.

Kay ran her fingers over the dark words on a white background, then traced the seal. "Thank you. This is…" She clutched it to her chest and stood on her toes to hug Kele. "It's really great, Aunt Kele. I love it."

Letting go, Kay bounced to the Firebird, parked beside the bike. She used her sleeve to wipe dirt off the bumper chrome, then yanked off the backing strips. Holding it over the left side, she wiggled it for position. Kele saw her glance over her shoulder with an impish grin. Kay pressed the sticker to the chrome at an angle, on purpose.

She stepped back and admired her handiwork.

"That would've driven your dad crazy."

"Yeah. I know."

Kele chuckled. "There's a lot of him in you."

Kay sighed. "I miss him so much. And Jay too. Mom's having a lot harder time, though. I'm not sure what to do when we get back from Alaska. I mean, I want to stick around for Mom because I'm afraid she'll fall off the deep end, but, you know, I kind of want to have a life."

"She wouldn't want you to stay home for her. Neither would your Dad. Or Jay, for that matter." Kele laid a hand on Kay's shoulder. "Aren't you thinking about joining the Novas?"

"My friends are all waiting for me to make a choice. With the whole program in limbo and everyone getting psych rehab, no one is pressing any of us to do anything in particular. It's a thing we Tsukudas do, though, so I guess so. I just…" Kay twisted to see the house.

"I'll make you a deal. If you go in, I'll get myself back in and demand they put you on the same team as me."

Kay blinked at her. "Really?"

Nodding, Kele thought about her contact with the new colonel in charge of the Novas. She seemed like a decent person and a good officer, and she remembered Ben from before the forced retirement. Last January, the woman had asked Kele point-blank to return to active duty and left it as an open invitation. Kele had decided to wait until all the trials finished. So she could support the rest of the team.

"Really. Anyone tries to mess with you, they deal with me. Also, if you forget to call your mom, I'll let you know about it. Besides, you know Vivian will check up on her, and so will Matty. He's going to do some cybersecurity work for the Novas, so he'll watch over you too." She had a thought to check on Scope and ask him to rejoin with her. Maybe he would after he'd had some time to fade out of the public eye and do some birdwatching.

Kay giggled and hugged her again. "I'll let you know when we get back from Alaska? Because I'm not going to bail on Mom before that trip."

"Deal." Kele watched Kay bound to the house and disappear inside. She shut and locked her luggage pod. "Ben," she said as she returned to the house, "I promise I'll watch over your daughter like you would have. We'll all watch over Risa for you."

She headed inside to watch some football with her family. Ben would never forgive her for wasting good beer.

# OTHER BOOKS BY THE AUTHORS

Find all the books by Lee and Jeffrey, including amazing young adult titles, at clockworkdragon.net

## LEE FRENCH

### MAZE BESET
superheroes in denim
*Dragons In Pieces*
*Dragons In Chains*
*Dragons In Flight*

### DARKSIDE SEATTLE
cyberpunk stories
*Street Doc*
*Fixer*
*Mechanic*
*Hacker* (coming soon)

CLOCKWORKDRAGON.NET

# JEFFREY COOK

## DAWN OF STEAM
epistolary steampunk
*First Light*
*Gods of the Sun*
*Rising Suns*

## ANGEL'S GRACE
supernatural urban fantasy
*Airs & Graces*
*There But For the Grace*
*A Coup de Grace*

# WRITERPUNK PRESS
'punk adaptations of classic works
*Sound & Fury*
*Once More Unto the Breach*
*Merely This and Nothing More*
*What We've Unlearned*
*Hideous Progeny*

CLOCKWORKDRAGON.NET

# ABOUT THE AUTHORS

**Lee French** lives in Olympia, WA, with two kids, two bicycles, and too much stuff. She is an avid gamer and a member of the Myth-Weavers online RPG community. In addition to spending too much time there, she also trains in taekwando, keeps a nice flower garden with one dragon and absolutely no lawn gnomes, works an excessive number of book events, and tries in vain every year to grow vegetables that don't get devoured by neighborhood wildlife.

She is an active member of the Science Fiction and Fantasy Writers of America and the Northwest Independent Writers Association, as well as serving the Olympia region as a NaNoWriMo Municipal Liaison.

**Jeffrey Cook** lives in the wilds of Maple Valley, WA now, but has lived all over the U.S. (and a little bit of Canada). His mother insists he's wanted to be an author since he was six years old, but he didn't get his official start as a novelist until 2014. He now has 13 novels, many with frequent collaborator Katherine Perkins, and one non-fiction book with Lee French. He also heads up charity press Writerpunk Press, which currently has 5 anthologies out, benefitting PAWS Animal Rescue—a charity near and dear to Jeffrey, as the place he met 3 of his rescue dogs.

When not reading, researching, writing, or gaming, he is also a passionate football fan. (Go Hawks!)